Praise for Debbie Macomber's
bestselling novels from Ballantine Books

### The Best Is Yet to Come

"Macomber's latest is a wonderful inspirational read that has just enough romance as the characters heal their painful emotional wounds." —*Library Journal*

"This tale of redemption and kindness is a gift to Macomber's many readers and all who love tales of sweet and healing romance." —*Booklist*

### It's Better This Way

"Macomber has a firm grasp on issues that will resonate with readers of domestic fiction. Well-drawn characters and plotting—coupled with strong romantic subplots and striking coincidences—will keep readers rooting for forgiveness, hope and true love to conquer all."
—Kathleen Gerard,
blogger at *Reading Between the Lines*

"Macomber keeps her well-shaded, believable characters at the heart of this seamlessly plotted novel as she probes the nuances of familial relationships and the agelessness of romance. This deeply emotional tale proves it's never too late for love." —*Publishers Weekly* (starred review)

### A Walk Along the Beach

"Macomber scores another home run with this surprisingly heavy but uplifting contemporary romance between a café owner and a photographer. Eloquent prose . . . along with [a] charming supporting cast adds a welcome dose of light and hope. With this stirring romance, Macomber demonstrates her mastery of the genre."
—*Publishers Weekly* (starred review)

"Highly emotional . . . a hard-to-put-down page-turner, yet, throughout all the heartache, the strength and love of family shines through." —*New York Journal of Books*

### Window on the Bay

"This heartwarming story sweetly balances friendship and mother-child bonding with romantic love."
—*Kirkus Reviews*

"Macomber's work is as comforting as ever." —*Booklist*

### Cottage by the Sea

"Romantic, warm, and a breeze to read—one of Macomber's best." —*Kirkus Reviews*

"Macomber never disappoints. Tears and laughter abound in this story of loss and healing that will wrap you up and pull you in; readers will finish it in one sitting."
—*Library Journal* (starred review)

"Macomber's story of tragedy and triumph is emotionally engaging from the outset and ends with a satisfying conclusion. Readers will be most taken by the characters, particularly Annie, a heartwarming lead who bolsters the novel." —*Publishers Weekly*

*Last One Home*

"Fans of bestselling author Macomber will not be disappointed by this compelling stand-alone novel."
—*Library Journal*


## ROSE HARBOR


*Sweet Tomorrows*

"Macomber fans will leave the Rose Harbor Inn with warm memories of healing, hope, and enduring love."
—*Kirkus Reviews*

"Overflowing with the poignancy, sweetness, conflicts and romance for which Debbie Macomber is famous, *Sweet Tomorrows* captivates from beginning to end."
—*Bookreporter*

"Fans will enjoy this final installment of the Rose Harbor series as they see Jo Marie's story finally come to an end."
—*Library Journal*


*Silver Linings*

"Macomber's homespun storytelling style makes reading an easy venture. . . . She also tosses in some hidden twists and turns that will delight her many longtime fans."
—*Bookreporter*

"Reading Macomber's novels is like being with good friends, talking and sharing joys and sorrows."
—*New York Journal of Books*

*Love Letters*

"Macomber's mastery of women's fiction is evident in her latest. . . . [She] breathes life into each plotline, carefully intertwining her characters' stories to ensure that none of them overshadow the others. Yet it is her ability to capture different facets of emotion which will entrance fans and newcomers alike." —*Publishers Weekly*

"Romance and a little mystery abound in this third installment of Macomber's series set at Cedar Cove's Rose Harbor Inn. . . . Readers of Robyn Carr and Sherryl Woods will enjoy Macomber's latest, which will have them flipping pages until the end and eagerly anticipating the next installment." —*Library Journal* (starred review)

"Uplifting . . . a cliffhanger ending for Jo Marie begs for a swift resolution in the next book." —*Kirkus Reviews*

*Rose Harbor in Bloom*

"[Debbie Macomber] draws in threads of her earlier book in this series, *The Inn at Rose Harbor,* in what is likely to be just as comfortable a place for Macomber fans as for Jo Marie's guests at the inn." —*The Seattle Times*

"Macomber's legions of fans will embrace this cozy, heartwarming read." —*Booklist*

"Readers will find the emotionally impactful storylines and sweet, redemptive character arcs for which the author is famous. Classic Macomber, which will please fans and keep them coming back for more." —*Kirkus Reviews*

"The storybook scenery of lighthouses, cozy bed and breakfast inns dotting the coastline, and seagulls flying above takes readers on personal journeys of first love, lost love and recaptured love, [presenting] love in its purest and most personal forms." —*Bookreporter*

### The Inn at Rose Harbor

"Debbie Macomber's Cedar Cove romance novels have a warm, comfy feel to them. Perhaps that's why they've sold millions." —*USA Today*

"Debbie Macomber has written a charming, cathartic romance full of tasteful passion and good sense. Reading it is a lot like enjoying comfort food, as you know the book will end well and leave you feeling pleasant and content. The tone is warm and serene, and the characters are likeable yet realistic. . . . *The Inn at Rose Harbor* is a wonderful novel that will keep the reader's undivided attention."
—*Bookreporter*

"The prolific Macomber introduces a spin-off of sorts from her popular Cedar Cove series, still set in that fictional small town but centered on Jo Marie Rose, a youngish widow who buys and operates the bed and breakfast of the title. This clever premise allows Macomber to craft stories around the B&B's guests, Abby and Josh in this inaugural effort, while using Jo Marie and her ongoing recovery from the death of her husband Paul in Afghanistan as the series' anchor. . . . With her characteristic optimism, Macomber provides fresh starts for both." —*Booklist*

"Emotionally charged romance." —*Kirkus Reviews*

"There is a reason that legions of Macomber fans ask for more Blossom Street books. They fully engage her readers as her characters discover happiness, purpose, and meaning in life. . . . Macomber's feel-good novel, emphasizing interpersonal relationships and putting people above status and objects, is truly satisfying."
—*Booklist* (starred review)

"Macomber's writing and storytelling deliver what she's famous for—a smooth, satisfying tale with characters her fans will cheer for and an arc that is cozy, heartwarming and ends with the expected happily-ever-after."
—*Kirkus Reviews*

### CHRISTMAS NOVELS

#### *Jingle All the Way*

"[*Jingle All the Way*] will leave readers feeling merry and bright." —*Publishers Weekly*

"This delightful Christmas story can be enjoyed any time of the year." —*New York Journal of Books*

#### *A Mrs. Miracle Christmas*

"This sweet, inspirational story . . . had enough dramatic surprises to keep pages turning."
—*Library Journal* (starred review)

"Anyone who enjoys Christmas will appreciate this sparkling snow globe of a story." —*Publishers Weekly*

"*Twelve Days of Christmas* is a charming, heartwarming holiday tale. With poignant characters and an enchanting plot, Macomber again burrows into the fragility of human emotions to arrive at a delightful conclusion."
—*New York Journal of Books*

### Dashing Through the Snow

"This Christmas romance from Macomber is both sweet and sincere." —*Library Journal*

"There's just the right amount of holiday cheer. . . . This road-trip romance is full of high jinks and the kooky characters Macomber does so well." —*RT Book Reviews*

### Mr. Miracle

"[Macomber] writes about romance, family and friendship with a gentle, humorous touch." —*Tampa Bay Times*

"Macomber spins another sweet, warmhearted holiday tale that will be as comforting to her fans as hot chocolate on Christmas morning." —*Kirkus Reviews*

"This gentle, inspiring romance will be a sought-after read." —*Library Journal*

### Starry Night

"Contemporary romance queen Macomber (*Rose Harbor in Bloom*) hits the sweet spot with this tender tale of impractical love. . . . A delicious Christmas miracle well worth waiting for." —*Publishers Weekly* (starred review)

"[A] holiday confection . . . as much a part of the season for some readers as cookies and candy canes."
—*Kirkus Reviews*

*Angels at the Table*

"Rings in Christmas in tried-and-true Macomber style, with romance and a touch of heavenly magic."
—*Kirkus Reviews*

"[A] sweetly charming holiday romance."
—*Library Journal*

# DEBBIE MACOMBER

# All Roads
# Lead Home

*A Friend or Two*

and

*Reflections of Yesterday*

Ballantine Books
New York

2023 Ballantine Books Mass Market Edition

*A Friend or Two* copyright © 1985 by Debbie Macomber
*Reflections of Yesterday* copyright © 1986
by Debbie Macomber

Published in the United States by Ballantine Books,
an imprint of Random House, a division of
Penguin Random House LLC, New York.

BALLANTINE is a registered trademark and the colophon is
a trademark of Penguin Random House LLC.

*A Friend or Two* and *Reflections of Yesterday* originally
published separately in paperback in the United States
by Silhouette Books, New York, in 1985 and 1986.

ISBN 978-0-593-35982-2
Ebook ISBN 978-0-593-35983-9

Cover images: © PeopleImages/Getty Images (couple),
© Nomadsoul1/Getty Images (bench and park), © Jones M/
Shutterstock (flowers), © luck luckyfarm/Shutterstock (sky)

Printed in the United States of America

randomhousebooks.com

*Book design by Edwin Vazquez*

2 4 6 8 9 7 5 3 1

Ballantine Books mass market edition: July 2023

Summer 2023

Dear Friends,

The book you hold in your hands are two stories
I wrote early in my career. This was long before cell
phones and the Internet. I reread them recently and
realized that while they are devoid of modern
technology, a good story will always remain a good
story. I mean, does anyone question that no one in a
Charles Dickens book has access to Zoom?
(Not that I'm comparing myself to Dickens!)

I remember writing these books and the infusion
of joy I experienced each day as I sat in front of my
spanking new computer. Oh my, those were the days
when computer technology was in its infancy, and no
one had heard of Word or Outlook, and Apple was
something that grew on trees aplenty in my hometown
of Yakima, Washington.

Here's a fun fact for you: Titles have always been
tricky when it comes to publishing. Many of my titles
then and now were often rejected by my editors—
all for good reasons. A few years into my writing career
I found a valuable source of inspiration, and this will
surprise you—names of racehorses. I found a list of
registered names and several of my books share those
of highly celebrated winners. Word soon got around,
and my author friends often called asking for title
suggestions. Truth is, I don't remember if *A Friend or
Two* or *Reflections of Yesterday*, the original titles of
this combination volume, were racehorses, but I
strongly suspect they were.

It's an honor that you purchased this book based,

I suspect, on my name alone. I'm grateful for the faith my readers have placed in me. Now turn the page and return to a period not so long ago before we had text or emails and enjoy these fun stories.

As always, hearing from my readers is a bonus. Your letters and comments have guided my career from the very beginning. You can reach me through all the social media platforms. If you would rather write, here is my mailing address:

P.O. Box 1458, Port Orchard, WA 98366.

Blessings,

*Debbie Macomber*

*A Friend or Two*

# Prologue

—⁓—

"Miss Elizabeth?" The elderly butler's eyes widened, but he composed himself quickly. "This is a surprise. Welcome home."

"Thank you, Bently. It's good to *be* home." Elizabeth Wainwright felt comforted by his formality and British accent. She looked around the huge entry hall, with its elegant crystal chandelier and imported oriental rugs and sighed inwardly. Home. Would it offer her what she hadn't been able to find in Europe? Immediately doubts filled her.

"Would you see to my luggage?" she asked in a low, distracted tone. "And ask Helene to draw my bath?"

"Right away."

She looked around with a renewed sense of appreciation for everything this house represented. Wealth. Tradition. Family pride. With all this at her fingertips, how could she possibly be dissatisfied?

"Bently, do you know where Father is?"

"In the library, miss," he responded crisply.

Her smile faded as she started across the huge hall. She loved Bently. Nothing could ruffle him. She could recall the time . . . Loud voices drifted past the partially opened door, and she paused. Her father rarely raised his voice.

"I'm afraid I've failed her, Mother. Elizabeth is restless and unhappy."

Stunned, Elizabeth stood just outside the library door, listening.

"Give the girl time, Charles. She's suffered a great loss." Her grandmother's raspy voice sounded troubled, despite her words.

"She has no drive, no ambition, no purpose. Dear heavens, have you seen these bills from Paris?"

The sound of his fist against the desk shocked her.

"Elizabeth goes through money as if there's no tomorrow. I've pampered and indulged her since Mary died, and now I'm left to deal with it."

"But she's such a dear child."

"Dear, but hopelessly unhappy, I fear. The thing is"— her father's voice lowered and took on a slightly husky quality—"I don't know how to help her."

A twinge of guilt caused Elizabeth to lower her head fractionally. She'd thought she had concealed her unhappiness. And she couldn't argue with her father's earlier statement. Her spending *had* been extravagant the last few months.

"What can we do?" Again, it was her grandmother.

"I don't know, Mother."

Elizabeth had never heard such resignation from her

father. "I'll talk to her, but I don't know what good it will do. Perhaps if Mary had lived . . ." he continued soberly.

Elizabeth refused to listen to any more. Her father rarely spoke of her mother. Mary Elizabeth Wainwright's unexpected death two years before still had the power to inflict a deep sense of loss on them both. Elizabeth's brother had adjusted well, but he was older and constitutionally more able to cope with his grief.

Thoughtfully, she climbed the long, winding staircase to her rooms. A confrontation with her father was the last thing she wanted. How could she explain this lackadaisical attitude that had taken over her usually cheerful existence? And as for the benefits of wealth, she was well aware of the privileges and even the power that came with having money. But money wasn't everything; it didn't bring happiness or fulfillment. The best time she'd had in her life had been the summer she bummed her way across France, when she'd barely had two euros to rub together. Not only was she intelligent, she was gifted. She spoke fluent French, and enough Italian and German to make her last visits to Rome and Berlin worry-free. But what good was any of that to her now?

Sitting on her plush canopy bed, she forced her spine to straighten. She was a Wainwright. She was supposed to maintain her pride and independence at all times.

A gnawing ache churned her stomach. She didn't want to talk to her father. She didn't want to explain the fiasco in Paris and her extravagant expenses. All she wanted was peace and quiet. The germ of an idea began to form in her mind. Her bags were still packed. She could swear Bently to silence and slip out just as quietly as she'd slipped in. San Francisco sounded appealing. Her mother had spent a carefree summer there when she was about Elizabeth's age. With a renewed sense of purpose, she headed out of her bedroom door and down the back stairs.

# One

—⌇—

The ever-present odor of fresh fish and the tangy scent of saltwater followed Elizabeth as she sauntered down Fisherman's Wharf. The wharf wasn't far from where she was staying at the St. Francis, one of San Francisco's most prestigious hotels. A little breeze ruffled her golden-brown hair and added a shade of color to her otherwise pale features.

With the morning paper tucked under her arm, she strolled into a small French café. It had only taken three days for the restless boredom to make its way into her thoughts. How could she sit in one of the most beautiful cities in the world with the homey scent of freshly baked bread drifting from the restaurant kitchen and feel this listless?

A friendly waitress dressed in a crisp pink uniform with a starched white apron took her order for coffee and a croissant. She wasn't hungry, but she had noticed this morning that her clothes were beginning to hang on her and decided to make the effort to eat more.

Lackadaisically her eyes ran over the front page of the newspaper. Nothing had changed. The depressing stories of war and hate were the same on this day as they had been the week before and the month before that. Sighing, she folded the newspaper and waited for the waitress to bring her food.

"Are you looking for a job?" the young waitress asked eagerly as she delivered Elizabeth's order.

"I beg your pardon?"

"I saw you looking through the paper and thought you might be job-hunting. I wouldn't normally suggest something like this, but there's an opening here, if you'd like to apply. You could start right now."

Elizabeth's pale blue eyes widened incredulously. What was this girl talking about?

"I know it's not much, but a position here could tide you over until you find what you're really looking for. The other girl who normally works with me called in this morning and quit." She paused to forcefully release her breath. "Can you imagine? Without a minute's notice. Now I'm left to deal with the lunch crowd all by myself."

Elizabeth straightened in her chair. Why not? She didn't have anything better to do. "I don't know that I'd be much help. I've never been a waitress."

"It doesn't matter." The younger girl's relief was obvious. "I can guarantee that by the end of the day you'll discover everything you ever cared to know about waitressing and a few things you didn't." Her laugh was light and cheerful. "By the way, I'm Gilly. Short for Gillian."

"And I'm Elizabeth."

"Glad to meet you, Elizabeth. Boy, am I glad." The breezy laugh returned. "Come on back to the kitchen, and I'll introduce you to Evelyn. He's the owner and chef, and I'm *sure* he'll hire you." With determined, quick-paced steps, Gilly led the way across the room to the swinging double doors. She paused and turned around. "Don't be shocked if Evelyn kisses you or something. He's like that. I think it's because he's French."

"I won't be surprised," Elizabeth murmured and had trouble containing her smile. What would Gilly say if she knew that Elizabeth spoke the language fluently and had lived in Paris?

A variety of pleasant smells assaulted her as she entered the spotless kitchen. As a little girl, her favorite place in the huge, rambling house had been the kitchen. The old cook would often sneak her pieces of pie dough or a cookie. Her childhood had been happy and untroubled.

"Evelyn," Gilly said, attracting the attention of the chef who was garbed completely in white and working busily at the stove. "This is Elizabeth. She's going to take Deanne's place."

The ruddy-faced man with a thick mustache that was shaped like an open umbrella over a full mouth turned and stared blankly at Elizabeth.

Giving in to impulse, she took a step forward and extended her hand. In flawless French, she explained that she hadn't done any waitressing but would be pleased to help them out this afternoon.

Laughing, Evelyn broke into a wild speech in his native language while pumping her hand as if she were a long-lost relative.

Again in perfect French, she explained that no, she

wasn't from France or Quebec, but she had spent several years studying in his country.

An expression of astonishment widened Gilly's eyes. "You should have said you were from France."

"I'm not. I studied French in school." Elizabeth didn't explain that the school had been in Paris.

"You know, that's one thing I'm sorry for," Gilly said, thoughtfully pinching her bottom lip. "I wish I'd studied French. A lot of good Spanish does me here. But then"— she paused and chuckled—"I could always end up working in a Mexican restaurant."

Elizabeth laughed. Gilly was delightful. Amiable and full of enthusiasm, the younger girl was just the antidote for the long day that lay ahead.

Luckily, the two were close enough in size that Elizabeth could wear one of Gilly's extra uniforms.

After a minimum of instruction, Elizabeth was given a pad and pencil, and asked to wait on her first customers, an elderly couple who asked for coffee and croissants. Without incident, Elizabeth delivered their order.

"This isn't so bad," she murmured under her breath to Gilly, who was busy writing out the luncheon specials on the chalkboard that would be displayed on the sidewalk.

"I took one look at you and knew you'd do great," Gilly stated cheerfully.

"You took one look at me and saw an easy mark." A smile revealed deep grooved dimples in each of Elizabeth's cheeks.

"Does everyone call you Elizabeth?" Briefly, Gilly returned her attention to the chalkboard. "You look more like a Beth to me."

*Beth,* Elizabeth mused thoughtfully. No one had called her that since her school days, and then only her best friends. After all, she was a Wainwright. "Elizabeth" was the dignified name her family preferred.

"Call me anything you like," she said in a teasing tone. "No, on second thought, you better stick with Beth."

A half hour later Elizabeth was answering to a variety of names, among them "Miss" and "Waitress." Never had she imagined that such a simple job could be so demanding, or that there were so many things to remember. The easy acceptance given her by the customers was a pleasant surprise. Most of the café's luncheon crowd were regulars from office buildings close to the wharf. Several of them took the time to chat before ordering. A couple of men blatantly flirted with her, which did wonders for her sagging ego. A few asked about Deanne and weren't surprised when they learned that she'd quit.

The highlight of the afternoon came when she waited on a retired couple visiting from France. She spoke to them in their native language for so long that Gilly had to point out that there were several other customers who needed attention. Later Gilly was shocked to see that the couple had left a tip as large as the price of their meal.

"Tutor me in French, would you?" she joked, as she passed by carrying a glass coffeepot.

Elizabeth couldn't believe the time when she glanced at her gold wristwatch. Four o'clock. The day had sped past, and she felt exhilarated, better than she had in months. Tonight she wouldn't need a pill to help her sleep.

"You were terrific. Everyone was saying how great

you were," Gilly said, laying on the praise. "A couple of regulars said they hope you'll stay. And even if it was your first time waitressing, you were as good as Deanne ever was."

After all the orders she had mixed up, Elizabeth was surprised Gilly thought so. Of course, she had eaten in some of the world's best restaurants and knew what kind of service to expect. But giving it was something else entirely.

"Would you consider staying on for a while?" Gilly's tone held a mixture of hope and doubt. "I'm sure this isn't the kind of job you want. But the pay isn't bad, and the tips are good."

Elizabeth hesitated. "I . . . I don't know."

"It would only be until we could find someone to replace you," Gilly added quickly. "That shouldn't be long. A week or two. Three months at the most."

"Three months?" Elizabeth gasped.

"Well, to be honest, Evelyn saw you with the French couple and told me that he'd really like to hire you permanently. I suppose it's too much to ask, with your qualifications."

*What qualifications?* Elizabeth mused. Oh, sure, she knew all the finer points of etiquette, but aside from her fluency in several languages, she'd never had any formal job training.

"Just think about it, okay?" Gilly urged.

Elizabeth agreed with a soft smile.

"You'll be back tomorrow?" The doelike eyes implored, making it impossible to refuse.

Exhaling slowly, Elizabeth nodded. "Sure. Why not?"

*Why not indeed?* she mused later as she unlocked the

door to her suite at the St. Francis. Her feet hurt, and there was an ache in the small of her back, but otherwise she felt terrific.

The hot water filling the tub was steaming up the bathroom when she straightened, struck by a thought. There was no one she wanted to visit this summer, no place she wanted to go. There wasn't anything to stop her from working with Gilly. It would be fun. Well, maybe not fun, but . . . different, and she was definitely in the mood for different.

With the sound of the hot water still running behind her, she knotted the sash of her blue silk robe and eased her feet into matching slippers. Sitting atop the mattress, she reached for the phone. For the first time in months, she felt like talking to her father. He had a right to know where she was staying and what she was up to. Over the last year she'd given him enough to worry about.

Bently answered the phone. "Good evening, Miss Elizabeth," he said after she identified herself.

"Hello, Bently. Is my father home?"

"I'll get him for you."

Had she detected a note of worry in Bently's tone? He was always so formal that it was difficult to discern any emotion.

"Elizabeth, dear." Her father spoke crisply. "Just exactly where are you?" He didn't wait for her to answer. "Bently said that you were home, and then, before anyone knew what had happened, you were off again."

"I'm sorry, Dad," she said, though in fact she wasn't the least bit regretful. "I'm in San Francisco. I've got a job."

"A job," her father repeated in a low, shocked tone. "Doing what?"

She laughed, mentally picturing the perplexed look working its way across her father's face. With a liberal arts degree as vague and unimpressive as her grades, she knew he doubted that anyone would want to hire her. "I'm a waitress in a small French café called the Patisserie."

"A waitress!" Charles Wainwright exploded.

"Now don't go all indignant on me. I know this is a shock. But I'm enjoying it. Some of the customers speak French, and the chef is from Paris."

"Yes, but . . ." Elizabeth could feel her father's shock. "But if you wanted to work," he went on, "there are a hundred positions more suited to you."

"Honestly, Dad, I'd think you'd be happy that I'm out of your hair for the summer. Wish me well and kiss Grandmother for me."

"Elizabeth . . ."

"My bath's running. I've got to go."

A resigned note she recognized all too well entered his voice. "Take care of yourself, my dear."

"This is working out great," Gilly commented at the end of Elizabeth's first week. "I don't know what it is, but there's something about you that the customers like."

"It's because I can pronounce the name of Evelyn's pastries," Elizabeth returned in a teasing voice.

"That's not it," Gilly contradicted with a slight quirk of her head. Her short, bouncy curls bobbed with the action. "Though having you speak French does add a certain class to the place."

"My French may be good, but my feet are killing me." She faked a small, pain-filled sigh and rubbed the bottom of one expensive loafer over the top of the other.

"Your feet wouldn't hurt if you were wearing the right shoes."

Elizabeth glanced at her Guccis and groaned. Heavens, she'd spent more on these leather loafers than she made in a week at this restaurant. How could they possibly be the wrong kind of shoe?

"If you like, we can go shopping after work and I'll show you what you should be wearing."

Gilly's offer was a pleasant surprise. "Yes, I'd like that."

"It'll give me an excuse not to go home." Discontent coated Gilly's normally happy voice.

"What's the matter with home?"

One petite shoulder rose in a halfhearted shrug. "Nothing, I guess. It's just that I turned twenty last month, and I hate living with my parents."

"So get an apartment." Elizabeth suggested the obvious, wondering why Gilly hadn't thought of that herself.

Gilly's returning smile was stiff. "So speaks the voice of inexperience. I don't suppose you've gone looking for apartments lately. Have you seen how high rent is these days?"

Elizabeth had continued to live at the St. Francis. The hotel was convenient, and what meals she didn't eat at the Patisserie were promptly delivered to her room after a simple phone call.

"It isn't that I haven't tried," Gilly continued. "I

found a boarding house and stayed there until my mother found out about my neighbors."

"Your neighbors?"

"I admit they were a bit unusual," Gilly mumbled. "I never saw the girl in the room next to me, but every morning there were two empty yogurt cartons outside her door."

Elizabeth couldn't restrain her soft laugh. "Suspicious yogurt, huh?"

"That was nothing," Gilly continued, her own laugh blending with Elizabeth's. "The woman on the other side looked like a Russian weight lifter who had failed a hormone test. One look at her—or him, whichever the case may be—and my mother had me out of there so fast my head was spinning."

Elizabeth could sympathize with her friend. "I know what you mean. I moved away from home as soon as I could, too."

"And if I left, my younger sister could have her own room and . . ." Gilly paused, her hand gripping Elizabeth's forearm. "He's back."

"Who?" Elizabeth glanced up to see a tall, broad-shouldered man enter the café. The first thing that impressed her was his size. He was easily six-foot-four. Yet he carried himself with an unconscious grace that reminded her of a martial arts expert. He wasn't movie-star attractive. His jaw was too angular, too abrupt. His mouth was firm, and even from this distance she noticed that it was slightly compressed, as if something had displeased him.

"Him," Gilly whispered under her breath. "How long has it been since you've seen such an indisputable stud?"

"Obviously too long," Elizabeth responded, picking up a menu and water glass. "But then, isn't one stud just like another?" she asked blandly. Although not strikingly handsome, this man was compelling enough to attract women's attention.

"One stud is just like another?" Gilly repeated on a low, disbelieving breath. "Beth, this guy is Secretariat."

Elizabeth had difficulty hiding her smile as she moved across to the room to deliver the ice water and menu.

Secretariat turned and watched her approach. Dark sunglasses reflected her silvery image and disguised his eyes. The glasses rested on a nose that could kindly be described as aquiline. He removed the glasses and set them on the table.

Not until she was at his table did she realize how big he actually was. Massive shoulders suited his height. His muscular biceps strained against a short-sleeved shirt stretched taut across a broad chest. She imagined that someone of his build would have difficulty finding clothes that were anything except tight. It was unfortunate that apparently he couldn't afford to have his clothes custom-made.

"Good afternoon," she said as she handed him the menu and set the glass on the red-checked tablecloth. Her heart lodged near her throat as his fingers inno-cently brushed hers. There was something indefinable about him that was almost intimidating. Not that he frightened her; "intrigued" was more the word.

"Hello." His smile revealed even white teeth. He opened the menu and quickly scanned it. Without look-ing at her he said, "Don't worry, I don't bite."

"I didn't think you did," she returned, resenting his

absolutely incorrect belief that she was easily intimidated.

"I'll have coffee. Nothing more." A scowl made its way across his face.

She wrote down his order, thinking that he didn't look like the type to indulge in delicate French pastries.

As she returned to the counter, she could feel his gaze leveled between her shoulder blades. She was accustomed to the admiring glances of men. She had what her grandmother referred to as the Wainwright coloring, a warm blend of colors that often generated curious stares. Her eyes were the palest blue and her hair a lush shade of golden brown, worn loose so that it curled in natural waves at her shoulders.

"Did you notice the muscles on him?" she muttered under her breath to Gilly as she laid a spoon to the saucer. "I bet this guy wrestles crocodiles for a living."

Gilly pretended to be wiping down the long counter, her hand rubbing furiously as she stifled a giggle. "I think he's kinda cute."

"Yes, but you're so sweet you'd think boa constrictors were cuddly."

"He's different. I bet he's a real pussycat. Give me five minutes alone with him and I'll prove it."

"No way. He looks dangerous, like he would eat you for breakfast."

"You're teasing, aren't you?"

Elizabeth didn't answer as she delivered the coffee. Before she walked away, she noticed that he drank it quietly, cupping the mug with his massive hands as he stared out the window. A few minutes later, he stood and left a handful of change on the table, then turned to wink at Gilly.

"Goodbye." Gilly waved to him. "Come in again."

"I'd say you've got yourself an admirer," Elizabeth said, glancing from her friend to the retreating male figure.

"Not me," Gilly denied instantly. "He was watching you like a hawk. You're the one who interests him, not me."

"Then I give Tarzan to you," Elizabeth spoke somberly. "Men like him are a bit much for me." She had heard about egotistical males with bodies like his. They spent hours every day building up their muscles so they could stand in front of a mirror and admire themselves.

Just before closing time, Gilly stuck her head around the door into the kitchen, where Elizabeth was finishing refilling the condiments.

"I bet he works on the docks."

"Who?"

"Don't be obtuse."

"Oh, Tarzan. I suppose," Elizabeth murmured, not overly interested. "I don't think he'll be back."

"He will," Gilly asserted confidently. "And sooner rather than later. There was a look in his eyes. He's attracted to you, Beth. Even I noticed." The implication was that Elizabeth should have recognized it, too.

Gilly was right. The next afternoon he arrived at the same time. Elizabeth was carrying a tray of dirty dishes to the counter when she brushed against his solid male figure.

"Excuse me." The low, almost gravelly tone left no doubt as to who was speaking.

"My fault," she muttered under her breath, disliking the uncomfortable warmth that emanated from the spot where their bodies had touched. Easily six inches taller than she was, Tarzan loomed above her. Most women would have been awed by his closeness. But the sensations she was feeling were more troubling for the way they intrigued her than frightening. He wasn't wearing his reflective glasses today. The color of his eyes, along with his guarded look, was a surprise. Their amber shade resembled burnished gold marked by darker flecks, and he was staring at her as intently as any jungle beast. Again she had the impression that this man could be dangerous. Gilly might view him as a gentle giant, but she herself wasn't nearly as confident.

"What did I tell you?" Gilly whispered in a know-it-all voice.

"I guess you know your ape-men," Elizabeth returned flippantly.

For a second Gilly looked stunned at Elizabeth's cynicism. "How can you look at someone as gorgeous as this guy and call him an ape?" Righteously, she tucked the menu under her arm. "I'm taking his order today," she announced, and she strolled across the floor.

Watching her friend's movements, Elizabeth had to stifle a small laugh. Gilly's walk couldn't be more obvious; she was interested in him, and before the afternoon was over, Tarzan would know it.

"His name's Andrew Breed," Gilly cheerfully informed her as she scooted past Elizabeth on her return. "But he says most everyone calls him Breed." She moved behind the counter before Elizabeth could respond.

Elizabeth was too busy with her own customers to

notice much about either Gilly or Andrew Breed. Only once was she aware that he was studying her, his strong mouth quirked crookedly. His attention made her self-conscious. Once she thought he was going to ask her something, but if he was, the question went unasked. As he'd done the day before, he left the money for his coffee on the table and sauntered out of the café, this time before she was even aware he'd gone.

The remainder of the afternoon dragged miserably. The weather was uncharacteristically hot and humid, and she could feel tiny beads of perspiration on her upper lip. A long soak in the bath, a light meal, and the TV were sounding more appealing by the minute. She had spent most of her evenings looking for an apartment. The more she learned about Gilly's plight living at home, the more she wanted to help her friend. She had promised that if she found a place, they could move in together and share the rent, though Gilly need never know the actual figure.

Unfortunately, Elizabeth was quickly learning that Gilly hadn't underestimated the difficulty of finding a reasonably priced apartment in the city. She couldn't very well rent one for 2,000 a month and tell Gilly her share was 500. Her friend, although flighty, was smart enough to figure that out.

Gilly and Elizabeth worked together to close down the café that evening. Elizabeth's thoughts were preoccupied as Gilly chattered away excitedly about one thing or another. The girl's boundless enthusiasm affected everyone she met. She was amazing.

In the small break room behind the kitchen, Elizabeth sat, kicked off her shoes, and rubbed her aching feet.

Gilly hobbled around, one shoe on and the other off as she opened her purse and dug around for something in the bottom of the large bag. "What's the big hurry?" Elizabeth inquired.

"What's the hurry?" Gilly stammered. "Breed'll be out front any minute. We're going to dinner."

"Breed?" Her heart did a tiny flip-flop. "You mean to say you're going out to dinner with someone you hardly know?"

"What do you think I was telling you?"

Elizabeth straightened and slipped her feet back into the new practical pumps she'd purchased with Gilly's approval. "I guess I wasn't paying any attention."

"I guess not!" Gilly shook her head and did a quick glance in the small mirror. "Oh dear, I'll never make it on time." Her delicate oval face creased with concern. "Beth, do me a favor. Go out front and tell him I'm running a little late. I'll be there in a few minutes."

"Sure." Her response was clipped and short. She didn't want to date Breed herself, but she wasn't sure how she felt about Gilly seeing him. The thought was so ridiculous that she pinched her mouth closed, irritated with herself.

"You don't mind, do you?" Gilly jerked her head around to study Elizabeth.

"Of course not. It's the least I can do to smooth the course of true love."

"Not about that," Gilly said.

Elizabeth tipped her head to one side in confusion.

"I mean about me going out with Breed."

"Me mind?" Elizabeth asked, giving an indifferent shrug. "Why should I care one way or the other?"

Gilly arched both nicely curved brows. "Because it's really you he's interested in."

"You keep saying that," Elizabeth said, shaking her head in denial. "Either you've got some sixth sense or I'm completely dense."

Without hesitation, Gilly threw back her head, her tight curls bouncing. "You're dense."

Resolutely squaring her shoulders, Elizabeth headed for the front of the café. Evelyn followed her out to lock the door after her, just as Gilly stuck her head around the kitchen door. "He's coming!" she cried. "I can see him across the street." Her round, panic-stricken eyes pleaded with Elizabeth. "Keep him occupied, will you?"

"Don't worry." She smiled at Evelyn on the other side of the glass door as he turned the lock. He looked at her and playfully rolled his eyes.

When Elizabeth turned around, she was only a few inches from Breed. This man had the strangest effect on her. She wasn't sure how she felt about him. His appeal blossomed with every encounter. It hadn't taken her long to realize that her first impression of him as a muscle-bound egomaniac was completely wrong. He seemed almost unaware of the effect he had on women.

"Gilly will be ready in a minute. She's changing clothes now."

The tight corners of Breed's mouth edged upward. "No problem. I'm early."

She folded her arms around her slim waist. "She's looking forward to tonight." Realizing her body language was revealing her state of mind, she quickly dropped her hands to her sides.

"I make you uncomfortable, don't I?"

Color rose from her neck, brightening her cheeks. "It's not that. I . . . I don't think I've ever known anyone quite like you."

"As big, you mean?"

"No, not that."

His strong, angular chin tilted downward fractionally. "And I don't think I've ever known anyone as beautiful as you." The words were soft, husky.

She sensed immediately that he wished he could withdraw them. He hadn't intended to say that. She was sure of it.

"My size *is* intimidating," he stated flatly, taking a step in retreat. There was a strong suggestion of impatience in the way he moved, something she hadn't noted in the past. And right now he was angry with himself.

Ignoring his strong, male profile, she turned and looked up at the cloudless blue sky.

They both spoke at once.

"The weather . . ."

"How long . . ."

"You first." Breed smiled, and a pleasant warmth invaded her limbs.

"I was going to say that I was enjoying the weather this summer. After all that talk about the California smog and San Francisco's famous fog, I wasn't sure what to expect."

"You're not from California?" He looked surprised.

She didn't know why he should be; her light Boston accent wasn't difficult to decipher. "No, my roots are on the East Coast. Boston."

He nodded.

"Do you work on the wharf?" Conversation was easy

with him; something else she hadn't expected. "Gilly and I were trying to guess."

"I'm a longshoreman."

It was her turn to give a polite nod. "It must be hard work." What else would give him muscles like that?

Fresh as a dewy rosebud, Gilly floated out the door in a light-blue summer dress. "Sorry to keep you waiting, Breed."

His amber eyes crinkled at the corners with a warm smile. "It was worth it," he said as he moved to her side, taking her hand in his.

Wiping a bead of perspiration from her forehead, Elizabeth gave Breed and Gilly a feeble smile. "Have fun, you two."

"Would you like to join us?" Gilly said.

Elizabeth took a step backward. As crazy as it sounded, she was half tempted. "I can't tonight. I'm going to look at another apartment."

"Beth, it's hopeless," Gilly said, her voice emphatic.

Breed's eyes surveyed her with open interest. "You're looking for an apartment?"

"Are we ever!" Gilly proclaimed enthusiastically.

"Let me know what happens. I might be able to find something for you. My brother-in-law manages a building, and he told me he has a vacancy coming."

Gilly almost threw herself into his arms. "Really? Can we see it soon? Oh, Beth, what do you think?"

Elizabeth's smile wasn't nearly as enthusiastic. If Breed's brother-in-law showed them the apartment, he was sure to mention the rent, and Elizabeth knew Gilly couldn't afford much.

"Let me check out this ad tonight, and we can talk about it later."

A half hour later Elizabeth was soaking in a hot tub filled with light-scented bubble bath. With the back of her head resting against the polished enamel, she closed her eyes, regretting that she hadn't gone with Breed and Gilly.

# Two

"Oh, Beth!" Gilly exclaimed as she hurriedly stepped from room to room of the two-bedroom apartment in the marina district. "I can hardly believe how lucky you were to find this place. It's perfect."

Elizabeth was rather proud of it herself. The building was an older brick structure that had recently been renovated. She'd been fortunate to find it, even more fortunate to have convinced Gilly and Gilly's parents that the rent was cheaper for the first six months because there was still construction going on in the building. The perfection of the apartment made her deception easier. She could afford to pay three-quarters of the rent without Gilly ever being the wiser.

Polished wooden floors in the entryway led to a large carpeted living room that made liberal use of skylights.

"I still can't believe it," Gilly said as she turned slowly, her head tilted back to view the boundless blue sky through the polished glass ceiling. "I never dreamed you'd find something like this. Did you see that kitchen?"

She returned her attention to Elizabeth. "Even my mother doesn't have such new appliances." With a deep sense of awe, she stepped into the kitchen and ran her hand along the marble counter. "I can't believe how well everything is working out for us." Pausing to glance at her wristwatch, she shook her head. "I've got one last load to bring over. I shouldn't be more than an hour."

"Don't worry. I'll hold down the fort," Elizabeth returned absently.

There were several things she wanted to do herself, including grocery shopping. She could fill the cupboards and Gilly would have no way of knowing how much she'd spent. When they divided the bill, Gilly wouldn't realize that she was only paying a fraction of the total. Elizabeth was enjoying the small duplicity. With a growing sense of excitement, she changed her clothes and started to make out an errand list. The Wainwrights were known for their contributions to charity, but this wasn't charity. She felt as though she owed Gilly something. If it hadn't been for Gilly, she was convinced she would still be trapped in the sluggish indifference that had dominated her life these past months. Her mother would have liked Gilly. Elizabeth pulled herself up straight. She hadn't thought about her mother in weeks. Even so, the memory remained sharp, with the power to inflict deep emotional pain. Just then the doorbell chimed. She couldn't imagine who it could be. Her step quickened as she walked to the door and opened it.

"Hello, Breed." Her hand tightened on the glass doorknob.

He handed her a large bouquet of flowers. "Welcome to the neighborhood," he said with a boyish grin.

"You live around here?" Her voice caught in her throat as she accepted the flowers. "Come in, please. I'm not being much of a hostess." She stepped back to allow him to enter and closed the door with her foot. "Gilly isn't here, but you're welcome to come in and tour the place if you like."

A smile glinted from his eyes as he followed her into the kitchen. "I'd like."

Deftly, she arranged the flowers and set them in the middle of the round kitchen table before leading the way through the apartment, glossing over the details.

"You're renting this for how much?"

Her heart dropped to her stomach. Gilly had apparently said something to Breed about their rent. She gave a light, breezy laugh, or what she hoped sounded light and breezy, and repeated what she'd told Gilly.

"Funny, I didn't notice any construction." He stood at the picture window.

"Of course you didn't." She continued the deception while keeping her gaze lowered. "Even carpenters go home in the evening." She was rescued from any further explanation by Gilly, who breathlessly barged through the door carrying a large box.

"Let me help." Immediately Breed took it from her and helped her carry in the remaining boxes.

When they'd finished, Gilly strolled into the kitchen. "Breed offered to take us out to dinner. You'll come, won't you?"

Elizabeth's gaze flittered past her friend to Breed. She was uncomfortably aware of the unspoken questions he was sending her way.

"Not this time."

Gilly exhaled a heavy breath and pushed the curls away from her face in an exasperated movement. "But you will soon, right?" She glanced from Breed to Elizabeth.

"Another time," Elizabeth agreed, going back to her list.

"Promise?" Gilly prompted.

"Promise," Elizabeth returned, unsure why she felt the way she did. There was something about Breed that troubled her. Not his size, although he was right: that in itself *was* intimidating. His eyes often held a mischievous glint, as if he knew something she didn't. Not that he was laughing at her—far from it. There was understanding, compassion, and sometimes she thought she caught a glimmer of something close to sympathy. He was a complicated man, and she was afraid that if she investigated further, she would like him a lot more than she had a right to.

She should have realized that neither of them would go on accepting her refusal to join them. The following Saturday Gilly was adamant that Elizabeth go with them to the beach.

"You're coming!" she insisted, stuffing an extra beach towel in her bag.

"Gilly . . ." Elizabeth moaned.

"It's a gorgeous day. How can you even think about sitting at home when you can be lazing on the beach, soaking up the sun?"

"But I don't want to intrude."

"Intrude? Are you nuts? We want you to come."

Gilly had gone out with Breed twice in the last week. They'd asked Elizabeth along both times.

Elizabeth liked Breed. The intensity of her feelings both surprised and alarmed her. Each time Gilly and Breed went out they returned early, and then the three of them sat in the living room and talked while drinking coffee. At every meeting, Elizabeth grew more aware of him. Gilly had reacted naturally to the magnetic appeal of the man, but it had taken Elizabeth longer to recognize his potency.

He was a wonderful conversationalist. His experiences were broad and seemingly unlimited. Several times she had to bite her tongue to keep from revealing too much of herself and her background in response. In some ways she felt there wasn't anything she couldn't share with him.

She didn't know what to make of Gilly's relationship with him. They seemed to enjoy each other's company and had formed an easy friendship. But Gilly was the world's friend. After she and Breed had spent an evening together, Elizabeth would study her roommate closely. Gilly didn't appear to be falling in love, and Elizabeth found that conclusion comforting. Not that she was such an expert on love. There had been several times when she had wondered whether she was in love, but then she'd decided that if she had to wonder, she wasn't.

"Put on your swimsuit!" Gilly shouted from the kitchen now. "And hurry. Breed'll be here in ten minutes."

"You're sure you want me along?" Elizabeth continued to waver.

Gilly turned around and rolled her eyes theatrically. "Yes! You really do have a problem with the obvious, don't you?"

Elizabeth changed into her silky turquoise bikini. On

the beaches of the Riviera, the skimpy two-piece had been modest. Now, studying herself in the mirror, she felt naked and more than a little vulnerable.

Gilly gave a low wolf whistle. "Wow! That doesn't look like it came from Best Beach Bargains dot com."

"Is it okay? There's not much to it." Elizabeth's gaze was questioning.

"I know. It's gorgeous—*you're* gorgeous."

"I'm not sure I should wear it. . . . I've got a sundress that would serve just as well."

"Elizabeth," Gilly insisted, "wear the bikini." She bit into a carrot stick. "Honestly, sometimes I swear you're the most insecure person I've ever met." She took the carrot stick out of her mouth and held it in her fingers like a cigarette. "By the way, where *did* you get that suit? I've never seen anything like it."

Elizabeth hesitated, her mind whirling in a thousand directions. "A little place . . . I don't remember the name."

"Well, wherever it is you shop, they sure have beautiful clothes."

"Thank you," Elizabeth mumbled as she put on a white cover-up. Quickly she changed the subject. "You're looking great yourself."

Gilly lowered her gaze to her rose-colored one-piece with a deep-veed neckline and halter top. "This old rag?"

"You just got that last week."

"I know, but next to you, it might as well be a rag."

"Gilly, that's not true, and you know it."

"Yes, but look at you. You're perfect. There isn't anything I wouldn't sacrifice for long legs and a figure like yours."

Elizabeth was still laughing when Breed arrived. He

paused and gave Gilly an appreciative glance. "I should have suggested the beach sooner. You look fantastic."

She positively sparkled under his appraisal. "Wait until you see Elizabeth's suit. She's the one with the glorious body."

Breed didn't comment, but he exchanged a meaningful glance with Elizabeth that said more than words.

Admittedly, she wanted to impress him. Deep within herself she yearned for his eyes to reveal the approval he had given Gilly. To divert her mind from its disconcerting course, she tightened the sash of her cover-up and added suntan lotion to her beach bag.

"I'm ready if you are," she said to no one in particular. She continued to feel a little uneasy infringing on Gilly's time with Breed, but she was pleased to be spending the day in the sun. In past summers she had prided herself on a luxurious tan. Already it was the third week of June, and she looked as pale as eggwhite.

An hour later they had spread a blanket on a crowded beach at Santa Cruz, sharing the sand with a thousand other sun worshippers. Breed sat with his knees bent as Gilly smoothed lotion into his broad shoulders.

Mesmerized, Elizabeth couldn't tear her eyes away. Gilly's fingers blended the tanning lotion with the thin sheen of perspiration that slicked his muscular back. She rubbed him with slow, firm strokes until Elizabeth's mouth went dry. The bronze skin rippled with the massaging movements, his flesh supple under Gilly's manipulations. Lean and hard, Breed was excitingly, sensuously, all male.

Elizabeth's breath caught in her throat as Breed turned his head and she felt his gaze. His eyes roamed her face, pausing on the fullness of her lips. They were filled with silent messages meant only for her. They were messages she couldn't decipher, afraid of their meaning. Her cheeks suffused with hot color, and she dragged her eyes from his.

"You probably should put on some lotion, too, Elizabeth," he commented. The slight huskiness of his voice was the only evidence that he was as affected as she by their brief exchange.

"He's right," Gilly agreed. "When I've finished here, I'll do you."

Elizabeth was amused at the look of disappointment he cast her. He'd planned to do it himself, and Gilly had easily thwarted him.

After Gilly's quick application of lotion to her back, Elizabeth slathered her face, arms, and stomach, and lay down on her big beach blanket. A forearm over her eyes blocked out the piercing rays of the afternoon sun. Pretending to be asleep, she was only half listening as Breed and Gilly chatted about one thing or another.

"Hey, look!" Gilly cried excitedly. "They've started a game of volleyball. You two want to play?"

"Not me," Elizabeth mumbled.

"You go ahead," Breed insisted.

A spray of sand hit Elizabeth's side as Gilly took off running. Judging by her enthusiasm, no doubt she was good at the game.

"Mind if I share the blanket with you?" Breed asked softly.

"Of course not." Despite her words, her mind was screaming for him to join Gilly at volleyball.

He stretched out beside her, so close their thighs

touched. She tensed, her long nails biting into her palms. Her nerves had fired to life at the merest brush of his skin against hers. She attempted to scoot away, but granules of sand dug into her shoulder blade, and she realized she couldn't go any farther.

Never had she been more acutely aware of a man. Every sense was dominated by him. He smelled of spicy musk and fragrant tobacco. Did he smoke? She couldn't remember seeing him smoke. Either way, nothing had ever smelled more tantalizing.

Salty beads of perspiration dotted her upper lip, and she forced her mouth into a tight line. If he were to kiss her she would taste the salty flavor of his . . . She sat up abruptly, unable to endure any more of these twisted games her mind was playing.

"I think I'll take a swim," she announced breathlessly.

"Running away?" His gaze mocked her.

"Running?" she echoed innocently. "No way. I want to cool down."

"Good idea. I could use a cold water break myself." With an agility she was sure was unusual in a man his size, he got quickly to his feet.

As he brushed the sand from the backs of his legs, she ran toward the ocean. With her long hair flying behind her, she laughed as she heard him shout for her to wait. The water was only a few feet away, and they hit the pounding surf together.

The spray of cold water that splashed against her thighs took Elizabeth's breath away, and she stopped abruptly. Shouldn't the ocean off the California coast be warmer than this?

Breed dived into an oncoming wave and surfaced several feet away. He turned and waited for her to join him.

Following his lead, she swam to him, keeping her head above water as her smooth, even strokes cut into the swelling ocean.

"What's the matter?" he called. "Afraid to get your hair wet?"

"I don't want to look like Jack Sparrow."

He laughed, and she couldn't remember hearing a more exciting sound.

"You should laugh more often."

"Me?" A frown darkened his eyes. "You're the one who needs a few lessons on having fun." He placed a hand at her waist. "Let's take this wave together."

Without being given an option, she was thrust into the oncoming wall of water. As they went under the giant surge, she panicked, frantically lashing out with her arms and legs.

Breed pulled her to the surface. "Are you all right?"

"No," she managed to say, coughing and choking on her words. Saltwater stung her eyes. Her hair fell in wet tendrils over her face. "You did that on purpose," she accused him angrily.

"Of course I did," he countered. "It's supposed to be fun."

"Fun?" she spat. "Marie Antoinette's walk to the guillotine was more fun than that."

Breed sobered. "Come on. I'll take you back to the blanket."

"I don't want to go back." Another wave hit her, and her body rolled with it, her face going below the surface just as it crested. Again she came up coughing.

He joined her and helped her find her footing. "This is too much for you."

"It isn't," she sputtered. "If this is supposed to be fun, then I'll do it." With both hands she pushed the wet, stringy hair from her face. The feel of his body touching hers was doing crazy things to her equilibrium. The whole world began to sway. It might have been the effect of the ocean, but she doubted it.

"Will you teach me, Breed?" she requested in a husky whisper. She felt his body tense as the movement of the Pacific tide brought him close.

"Hold on," he commanded, just as another wave engulfed them.

She slipped her arms around his neck and held her breath. His arms surrounded her protectively, pressing her into the shelter of his body. Their feet kicked in unison, and they broke the surface together.

"How was that?" he asked.

Her eyes still closed, she nodded. "Better." Why was she kidding herself? This was heaven. Being held by Breed was the most perfect experience she could remember. That took her by surprise. She'd been held more intimately by others.

Slowly she opened her eyes. He pushed the hair from her face. "You're slippery," he murmured, pulling her more tightly into his embrace. His massive hands found their place at the small of her back.

"So are you. It must be the suntan lotion." Her breasts brushed his torso, and shivers of tingling desire raced through her. Such a complete physical response was as pleasant as it was unexpected.

"Watch out!" he called as they took the next wave.

With their bodies intertwined, they rode the swell together.

A crooked smile was slanting Breed's mouth as they surfaced. Again his fingers brushed the long strands of wet hair from her face. He tucked them behind her ear, exposing her neck.

Elizabeth could feel the pulse near her throat flutter wildly. He pressed his fingertips to it and raised his eyes to her. In their golden depths she read desire, regret, surprise. He seemed to be as unprepared for this physical attraction as she was.

His mouth gently explored the pounding pulse in her neck. Moaning softly, she rolled her head to one side. His lips teased her skin, sending unanticipated shivers of delight washing over her. When he stopped, his eyes again sought hers.

"You taste salty."

Words refused to form. It was all she could do to nod.

He had come with Gilly. She had no right to be in the ocean with him, wanting him to kiss her so badly that she could feel it in every pore of her body.

"We should go back." She heard the husky throb in her voice.

"Yes," he agreed.

But they didn't move.

His crooked grin returned. "Did you have fun?"

She nodded.

"I'm sorry about your hair."

"Are you trying to tell me I look like Jack Sparrow?"

"No. If you want the truth, I've never seen you look more beautiful."

Her skin chilled, then flushed with warmth. She

couldn't believe that his words had the power to affect her body temperature.

"You're being too kind," she murmured, the soft catch in her voice revealing the effect of his words.

They lingered in the water as if they both wanted to delay the return to reality for as long as possible. Then, together, they walked out of the surf, hand in hand.

When they reached their blanket, he retrieved their towels. "Here." He handed her the thickest one and buried his face in his own.

Sitting on the blanket, Elizabeth dug through her beach bag and came up with a comb. She was running it through her hair when Gilly came rushing up, a tall, blond man beside her.

"Breed and Elizabeth, this is Peter."

"Hi, Peter." Breed rose to his feet, standing several inches taller than the other man. The two of them shook hands. For a second Breed looked from Gilly to Peter, then back again. His brows pulled into a thick frown.

"Peter invited me to stay and play volleyball, then grab some dinner," Gilly explained enthusiastically. "He said he'd take me home later. You two don't mind, do you?"

Elizabeth's eyes widened with shock. Did Gilly honestly believe she should come to the beach with one man and leave with another?

"We don't mind," Breed answered for them both.

"You're sure?" Gilly seemed to want Elizabeth's approval.

"Go ahead," Elizabeth murmured, but her eyes refused to meet Gilly's.

"You guys looked like you were having fun in the water."

A gust of wind whipped Elizabeth's wet hair across her face. She pushed it aside. The action gave her vital moments to compose herself. Obviously Gilly had been watching her. Worse, it could be the reason her roommate had decided to stay there with Peter. She couldn't allow that to happen.

"We had a wonderful time." Breed answered for them both again.

"I'll see you tonight, then," Gilly said, walking backward as she spoke.

Frustrated, Elizabeth called out for Gilly to wait, but her friend ignored her, turned, and took off running. "We can't let her do that," she told Breed.

"What?" A speculative light entered his eyes.

"What's the matter with the two of you? Gilly's going off with a complete stranger. It isn't safe." She tugged the comb through her hair angrily. "Heaven knows what she's walking into. You didn't have to be so willing to agree to her crazy schemes. I'm not going to leave this beach without her." She knew she should say something about her fear that her own behavior with him had led to Gilly's decision, but her courage failed her.

"She's twenty and old enough to take care of herself." Despite his words, his low voice contained a note of vague concern.

"She's too trusting."

Ignoring her, he opened the cooler he'd brought and took out a bucket of chicken. "Want a piece?" he questioned, biting into a leg.

"Breed . . ." Elizabeth was quickly losing her patience. They were an hour from San Francisco, and he was literally handing Gilly over to a stranger.

"All right." He expelled his breath forcefully and closed the lid on the food. "Gilly knows Peter. I introduced them last week."

"What?" she gasped. None of this was making sense.

"The last time I went out with Gilly, we were really meeting Peter."

"I don't believe this."

"I didn't exactly need an expert to see that it was going to take weeks of coming to the Patisserie before you'd agree to go out with me."

"What's that got to do with anything?"

"Plenty." He didn't sound thrilled to be revealing his motivations. "I don't blame you. I know I can be a little intimidating at first."

She wanted to explain that it wasn't his size that intimidated her, but she didn't know how to account for her reticence. She couldn't very well explain that it was the way his eyes looked in a certain light or something equally vague. "So you dated Gilly instead?"

He nodded. "She knew that first night it was you I was interested in. We planned this today." The tone of his voice relayed his unwillingness to play the game.

No wonder Gilly had been so anxious for her to join them every time she'd gone out with Breed.

"But you looked surprised when Gilly brought Peter over." She recalled the partially concealed question his eyes had shot at Gilly and Peter.

"Those two should be nominated for the Academy Award. They were supposed to have been long-lost friends." His jaw tightened as he turned away from her to look out over the ocean. His profile was strong and masculine.

"You didn't have to tell me." His honesty was a measure of how much he cared.

"No, I didn't. But I felt you had the right to know." His arms circled his bent knees. "I hope Gilly realizes what a good friend you are."

Lightly, she traced her fingers over the corded muscles of his back. A smile danced at the edges of her mouth as she stretched out on the blanket. "No, I think you've got the facts wrong. It's me who needs to thank Gilly."

He turned just enough so that he could see her lying there, looking up at him.

"How could I have been so stupid?" She whispered the question, staring into the powerful face of this man whose heart was just as big as the rest of him.

He lay on his stomach beside her.

"Have you always been big?"

"Have you always had freckles on your nose?" he asked, turning the tables on her. His index finger brushed the tip of her nose.

Her hand flew to her face. "They're ugly. I've hated them all my life."

"You disguise them rather well."

"Of course I do. What woman wants orange dots glowing from her nose?"

"They're perfect."

"Breed," she said, raising herself up so that she rested her weight on her elbows, "how can you say that?"

"Maybe it's because I find you to be surprisingly delightful. You're refreshingly honest, hard-working, and breathtakingly beautiful."

She recalled all the flattery she'd received from men who had something to gain by paying attention to her. A large inheritance was coming to her someday. That was enough incentive to make her overwhelmingly attractive to any man.

But here she was on a crowded California beach with someone who didn't know her from Eve. And he sincerely found her beautiful. She cast her gaze downward, suddenly finding her deception distasteful. A lone tear found its way to the corner of her eye.

"Elizabeth, what's wrong?"

She didn't know how she could explain. "Nothing," she returned softly. "The wind must have blown sand in my eye." By tilting her chin upward toward the brilliant blue sky, she was able to quell any further emotion.

She lay down again, resuming her sun-soaking position. Breed rolled over, positioning himself so close she felt his skin brush hers.

"Comfortable?" he asked.

"Yes."

His large hand reached for hers, and they just lay there together, fingers entwined. They didn't speak, but the communication between them was stronger than words.

Finally she dozed.

"Elizabeth." A hand at her shoulder shook her lightly. "If you don't put something on, you'll get burned."

Struggling to a sitting position, she discovered Breed kneeling above her, holding out her cover-up. "You'd better wear this."

She put it on. "Is there any of that chicken left?"

"Are you hungry?"

"Starved. I was in such a rush this morning, I didn't eat breakfast."

Opening the cooler, Breed fixed her a plate of food that was enough to feed her for three meals.

She didn't say so, though. She just took a big bite of the chicken. Fabulous. But she couldn't decide if it was the meal or the man.

The sun had sunk into a pink sky when Breed pulled up to the curb outside her apartment.

"You'll come in for coffee, won't you?" Elizabeth spoke the words even though they both knew that coffee had nothing to do with why he was coming inside.

She continued with the pretense, filling the coffee-maker with water and turning it on. She turned to discover his smoldering amber eyes burning into her. Her heart skipped a beat, then accelerated wildly at the promise she read there.

Wordlessly, she walked into his arms. This was the first time he'd held her outside the water, and she was amazed at how perfectly their bodies fit together. The top of her head was tucked neatly under his chin.

Her smile was provocative as she slipped her arms around his neck and tilted her head back to look up at him.

His eyes were smiling back at her.

"What's so amusing?"

"The glow from your freckles is blinding me."

"If I wasn't so eager for you to kiss me, I'd make you pay for that remark."

Breed lowered his mouth to an inch above hers. "I have a feeling I'm going to pay anyway," he murmured as he tightly wrapped his arms around her.

Being so close to this vibrant man was enough to disturb her senses. She tried to ignore the myriad sensations his touch aroused in her. As silly and crazy as it seemed, she felt like Sleeping Beauty waiting for the kiss that would awaken her after a hundred years.

Tenderly his mouth brushed over her eyelid, causing her lashes to flutter shut. Next he kissed her nose. "I love those freckles," he whispered.

Lastly he kissed her mouth with a masterful possession that was everything she had dreamed a kiss could be. It was a kiss worth waiting a hundred years for. He was gentle yet possessive. Pliant yet hard. Responsive yet restrained.

"Oh, Breed," she whispered achingly.

"I know." He breathed against her temple. "I wasn't expecting this, either."

She closed her eyes and breathed in the mingled scent of spicy musk and saltwater. With her head pressed close to his heart, she could hear the uneven beat and knew he was as overwhelmed as she was at how right everything felt between them.

"I should go," he mumbled into her hair. He didn't need to add that he meant he should leave while he still had the power to pull himself out of her arms. "Can I see you tomorrow?"

Eagerly, she nodded.

He pulled away. "Walk me to the door."

She did as he requested. He kissed her again, but not with the intensity of the first time. Then, lightly, he ran one finger over her cheek. "Tomorrow," he whispered.

"Tomorrow," she repeated, closing the door after him.

# Three

———~~———

Elizabeth adjusted the strap of her pink linen summer dress as Gilly strolled down the hall and leaned against the doorjamb, studying her. "Hey, you look fantastic."

"Thanks." Elizabeth's smile was uneasy. Breed had been on her mind all day, dominating her thoughts, filling her consciousness. Yesterday at the beach could have been a fluke, the result of too much sun and the attention of an attractive man. Yet she couldn't remember a day she had enjoyed more. Certainly not in the last two years. Breed made her feel alive again. This morning she'd been cooking her breakfast and humming. She couldn't remember the last time she'd felt so content. When she was with him, she wanted to laugh and throw caution to the wind.

Continuing to date him was doing exactly that. She couldn't see herself staying in San Francisco past the summer. When it came time to return to Boston, her heart could be so entangled with Breed that leaving would be intolerable. No, she decided, she had to protect herself . . . *and* him. He didn't know who she was, and she could end up hurting him. She couldn't allow herself to fall in love with him. She had to guard herself against whatever potential there was to this relationship. She couldn't allow this attraction to develop into anything more than a light flirtation.

"I sure wish I knew where you got your clothes," Gilly continued to chatter. "They're fantastic."

Elizabeth ignored the comment. "Do you think I'll need the jacket?" The matching pink top was casually draped over her index finger as her gaze sought Gilly's.

Gilly gave a careless shrug, crossing her arms and legs as she gave Elizabeth a thorough inspection. "I think I'd probably take it. You can never be certain what the weather's going to do. Besides, Breed may keep you out into the early-morning hours."

"Not when I have to work tomorrow, he won't," Elizabeth returned confidently.

The doorbell chimed just as she finished rolling the lip gloss across the fullness of her bottom lip.

"I'll get it," Gilly called from the kitchen.

Placing her hands against the dresser to steady herself, Elizabeth inhaled, deeply and soothingly, and commanded her pounding heart to be still. The way she reacted to Breed, someone would think she was a sixteen-year-old who had just been asked out by the captain of the football team.

"It's Breed," Gilly said, sauntering into the room.

Elizabeth gave herself one final inspection in the dresser mirror. "I thought it must be." Folding her jacket over her forearm, she walked into the living room, where he was waiting.

"Hi," she said as casually as possible. He looked good. So good. His earthy sensuality was even more evident now than in the dreams her mind had conjured up the previous night. Suddenly she felt tongue-tied and frightened. She could so easily come to love this man.

"Beth didn't say where the two of you were going," Gilly said before biting into a crisp apple.

"I thought we'd take in the outdoor concert at the Sigmund Stern Grove. A cabaret sextet I'm familiar with is scheduled for this afternoon. That is"—he hesitated and caught Elizabeth's eye—"unless you have any objection."

"That sounds great." By some miracle she found her voice. The corded muscles of Breed's massive shoulders relaxed. If she hadn't known better she would have guessed that he was as nervous about this date as she was. He glanced at his watch. "If we plan to get a seat in the stands, then I suggest we leave now."

Gilly followed them to the door. "I won't wait up for you," she whispered, just loud enough for Elizabeth to hear.

"I won't be late," Elizabeth countered with a saccharine-sweet smile, discounting her friend's assumption that she wouldn't be home until the wee hours of the morning.

Breed opened the door to a late-model, mud-splattered, army-green military-style Jeep and glanced up at her quizzically. "I had to bring Hilda today. Do you mind?"

A Jeep! The urge to laugh was so strong that she had to hold her breath. She'd never ridden in one in her life. "Sure, it looks like fun."

His hand supported the underside of her elbow as she climbed inside the vehicle. A vague disturbance fluttered along her nerve-endings at his touch, as impersonal as it was. He'd placed a blanket over the seat to protect her dress. His thoughtfulness touched her heart. The problem was, almost everything about this man touched her heart.

Once she was seated inside the open Jeep, her eyes were level with his. She turned and smiled as some of the nervous tension flowed from her.

When his warm, possessive mouth claimed her lips, Elizabeth's senses were overwhelmed with a rush of pleasure. The kiss, although brief, was ardent, and left her weak and shaking. Abruptly, Breed stepped back, as though he had surprised himself as much as he did her.

Dazed, she blinked at him. "What was that for?" she asked breathlessly.

He walked around to the other side of the Jeep and climbed inside without effort. He gripped the steering wheel as he turned and grinned at her. "For being such a good sport. To be honest, I thought you'd object to Hilda."

"To a fine lady like Hilda?" she teased. A trace of color returned to her bloodless cheeks. "Never. Why do you call her Hilda?"

"I don't know." He lifted one shoulder in a half-shrug. "Her personality's a lot like a woman's. It seems when I least expect trouble, that's when she decides to break down." The mocking glint of laughter touched his amber eyes. "She's as temperamental as they come."

"Proud, too," Elizabeth commented, but her words were drowned out by the roar of the engine. Hilda coughed, sputtered, and then came to life with a vengeance.

"See what I mean?" he said as he shifted gears and pulled onto the street.

By the time they'd reached the park, her carefully styled hair was a mess. The wind had whipped it from its loose chignon and carelessly tossed it about her neck and face.

"You all right?" he asked with a mischievous look in his eye.

She opened her purse and took out a brush. "Just give me a minute to comb my hair and scrape the bugs from my teeth and I'll be fine."

The pleasant sound of his laughter caused the sensitive muscles of her flat stomach to tighten. "I think Hilda must like you," he said as he climbed out and slammed the door. "I know I do." The words were issued under his breath, as if he hadn't meant for her to hear them.

The park was crowded, the free concerts obviously a popular program of the Parks and Recreation Department. Already the stands looked full, and it didn't seem as if they would find seats together. Other couples had spread blankets on the lush green grass.

With a guiding hand at her elbow, he led her toward the far end of the stands. "I think we might find a seat for you over here."

"Breed." She stopped him and turned slightly. "Couldn't we take the blanket from Hilda and sit on the lawn?"

"You'd want to do that?" He looked shocked.

"Why not?"

His eyes surveyed her dress, lingering momentarily on

the jutting swell of her breasts. "But you might ruin your dress."

A flush of heat warmed her face at the bold look he was giving her. "Let me worry about that," she murmured, her voice only slightly affected.

"If you're sure." His eyes sought hers.

"Get the blanket, and I'll find us a place to sit."

A few minutes later they settled onto the grass and waited silently for the music to start. She had sat in the great musical halls of Europe and throughout the United States, but rarely had she anticipated a concert more. When the first melodious strains of a violin echoed through the air, she relaxed and closed her eyes.

The sextet proved to be as versatile as they were talented. The opening selection was a medley of classical numbers that she recognized and loved. Enthusiastic applause showed the audience's approval. Then the leader came to the front and introduced the next numbers, a variety of musical scores from classic films.

She shifted position, the hard ground causing her to fold her legs one way and then another.

"Here," Breed whispered, situating himself so that he was directly behind her, his legs to one side. "Use me for support." His hands ran down her bare arms as he eased her body against his. After a while she didn't know which score was louder, the one the musicians were playing or the one in her heart.

After the hour-long concert, Breed took her to a restaurant that he claimed served the best Mexican food this side of the Rio Grande.

"What did you think?" he asked as they sat across

from each other in the open-air restaurant, eating cheese enchiladas and refried beans.

A gentle breeze ruffled her sandy hair about her shoulders as she set her fork aside. "How do I feel about the concert or the food?"

"The concert." He pushed his plate aside, already finished, while she was only half done.

"It was great. The whole afternoon's been wonderful." She cupped a tall glass of iced tea. Breed would be taking her home soon, and already she was dreading it. This day had been more enjoyable than all of the last six months put together, and she didn't want it to end. Every minute they were together was better than the one before. It sounded silly, but she didn't know how else to describe her feelings. Deliberately she took a long sip of her drink and set her fork aside.

"Are you finished already?"

Her gaze skimmed her half-full plate, and she nodded, her appetite gone.

"I suppose we should think about getting you back to the apartment."

Her heart sang at the reluctance in his voice. For one perfect moment their gazes met and locked. She didn't want to go home, and he didn't want to take her.

"How about a walk along the beach?" he suggested with a hint of reluctance.

She wondered why he was wary. Afraid of what she made him feel? No matter. She herself demonstrated no such hesitation. "Yes, I'd like that."

Hilda delivered them safely to an ocean beach about fifteen minutes outside the city. Others apparently had the same idea; several couples were strolling the sand, their arms wrapped around each other's waists.

"Do you need to scrape the bugs from your teeth this time?" Breed asked as he shifted into Park and turned off the engine. A smile was lurking at the edges of his sensuous mouth.

"No," she replied softly. "I've discovered that the secret of riding in Hilda is simply to keep my mouth closed."

His answering smile only served to remind her of the strength and raw virility that were so much a part of him. Her gaze rested admiringly on the smoothly hewn angles of his face as he climbed out of the Jeep and came around to her side. She must have been crazy to ever have thought of him as an ape-man. The thought produced a grimace of anger at herself.

"Is something wrong?" He even seemed sensitive to her thoughts.

"It's nothing," she said, dismissing the question without meeting his gaze.

Again his touch was impersonal as he guided her down a semi-steep embankment. A small, swiftly flowing creek separated them from the main part of the beach.

She hesitated as she searched for the best place to cross.

"What's the matter?" he teased with a vaguely challenging lilt to his voice. "Are you afraid of getting your feet wet?"

"Of course not," she denied instantly. "Well, maybe a little," she amended with a sheepish smile. It wasn't the water as much as the uncertainty of how deep it was.

"Allow me," he said as he swept her into his arms. One arm supported her back and the other her knees. Her hands flew automatically to his neck.

"Breed," she said under her breath, "what are you doing?"

"What any gallant gentleman would do for a lady in distress. I'm escorting you to safety." His amber eyes were dancing with mischief. He took a few steps and teetered, causing her grip on his neck to tighten.

"Breed!" she cried. "I'm too heavy. Put me down."

His chiseled mouth quirked teasingly as he took a few more hurried steps and delivered her safely to the other side. When he set her down, she noticed that his pant legs were soaking wet.

"You *are* a gallant knight, aren't you." Her inflection made the question a statement of fact.

Something so brief that she thought she'd imagined it flickered in his expression. It came and went so quickly she couldn't decipher its meaning, if there was one.

The dry sand immediately filled her sandals, and after only a few steps she paused to take them off. He did the same, removing his shoes and socks, and setting them beside a large rock. She tossed hers to join his.

They didn't say anything for a long time as they strolled, their hands linked. He positioned himself so that he took the brunt of the strong breeze that came off the water.

Elizabeth had no idea how far they'd gone. The sky was a glorious shade of pink. The blinding rays of the sinking sun cast their golden shine over them as they continued to stroll. The sight of the lowering sun brought a breathless sigh of wonder from her lips as they paused to watch it sink beneath the horizon.

Watching the sun set had seemed like such a little thing, and not until this moment, with this man at her side, had she realized how gloriously wondrous it was.

"Would you like to rest for a while before we head back?" he suggested. She agreed with a nod, and he cleared her a space in the dry sand.

With her arms cradling her knees, she looked into a sky that wasn't yet dark. "How long will it be before the stars come out?"

"Not long," Breed answered in a low whisper, as if he were afraid words would diminish the wonder of the evening. Leaning back, he rested his weight on the palms of his hands as he looked toward the pounding waves of the ocean. "What made you decide to come to San Francisco?" he asked unexpectedly.

Elizabeth felt her long hair dance against the back of her neck in the breeze. "My mother. She spent time here the summer before she married my father, and she loved it." Her sideward glance encountered deep, questioning eyes. "Is something wrong?"

He was still. "Are you planning on getting married?"

She wasn't sure she was comfortable with this line of questioning. "Yes," she answered honestly.

He sat up, and she noticed that his mouth had twisted wryly. "I wish you'd said something before now." The steel edge of his voice couldn't be disguised.

"Well, doesn't everyone?"

"Doesn't everyone what?" His fragile control of his temper was clearly stretched taut.

Scooting closer to his side, she pressed her head

against his shoulder. "Doesn't everyone think about getting married someday?"

"So is there a Mr. Boston Baked Bean sitting at home waiting for you?"

"Mr. Boston Baked Bean?" She broke into delighted peals of laughter. "Honestly, Breed, there's no one."

"Good." He groaned as he turned and pressed her back against the sand. Her startled cry of protest was smothered by his plundering mouth. Immediately her arms circled his neck as his lips rocked over hers in an exchange of kisses that stirred her to the core of her soul.

Restlessly his hands roamed her spine as he half lifted her from the soft cushion of the sandy beach. She arched against him as he sensually attacked her lower lip, teasing her with biting kisses that promised ecstasy but didn't relieve the building need she felt for him.

"Breed," she moaned as her hands cupped his face, directing his hungry mouth to hers. Anything to satisfy this ache inside her. A deep groan slipped from his throat as she outlined his lips with the tip of her tongue.

Breed tightened his hold, and his mouth feasted on hers. He couldn't seem to give enough or take enough as he relaxed his grip and pressed her into the sand. Desire ran through her bloodstream, spreading a demanding fire as he explored the sensitive cord of her neck and paused at the scented hollow of her throat.

Her nails dug into his back as she shuddered with longing.

She felt the roughness of his calloused hand as he brushed the hair from her face. "I shouldn't have done that," he whispered. His voice was filled with regret. With a heavy sigh, he eased his weight from her. "Did I hurt you?" He helped her into a sitting position, but his hand remained on the curve of her shoulder, as if he couldn't let go.

"You wouldn't hurt me," she answered in a voice so weak she felt she had to repeat the point. "I'm not the least bit hurt." Lovingly, her finger traced the tight line of his jaw. "What's wrong? You look like you're sorry."

He nestled her into his embrace, holding her as he had at the concert, his arms wrapped around her from behind. His chin brushed against the crown of her head.

"Are you sorry?" She made it a question this time.

"No," he answered after a long time, his voice a whisper, and she wondered if he was telling the truth.

Without either of them being aware of it, darkness had descended around them. "The stars are out," she commented, disliking the finely strung tension their silence produced. "When I was younger I used to lean out my bedroom window and try to count the stars."

"I suppose that was a good excuse to stay up late," he said, his voice thick, rubbing his chin against her hair.

She smiled to herself but didn't comment.

His embrace slackened. "Do you want to go?"

"No." Her response was immediate. "Not yet," she added, her voice losing some of its intensity. She shifted position so that she lay back, her head supported by his lap as she gazed into the brilliant heavens. "It really is a gorgeous night."

"Gorgeous," he repeated, but she noted he was looking down on her when he spoke. "You certainly have a way of going to my head, woman."

"Do I?" She sprang to a sitting position. "Oh, Breed, do I really?"

He took her hand and placed it over his pounding heart. "That should answer you."

She let her hands slide over his chest and around his neck. Twisting, she turned and playfully kissed him.

"But the question remains, do I do the same thing to you?" he asked, his voice only slightly husky.

Elizabeth paused and shifted until she was kneeling at his side. Their eyes met in the gilded glow of the moon. "What does this tell you?" she said, more serious than she had been in her life. Taking his hand, she pressed it against her heart, holding it there as he inhaled a quivering breath.

"It tells me"—he hesitated as if gathering his resolve— "that it's time to go." He surged to his feet, then offered her a hand to help her up.

With a smile, she slipped her fingers into his.

The walk back to the Jeep seemed to take forever. Surely they hadn't gone this far.

"Isn't that Hilda?" she asked, pointing to the highway up ahead.

"Couldn't be." He squinted against the dark. "We haven't gone far enough yet."

"Far enough?" she repeated incredulously. "We couldn't possibly have wandered much farther than this." Their portion of the beach was deserted now, although she noted a few small fires in the distance, proof that there were others around. "Isn't that the rock where we left our shoes?" She pointed at the large boulder directly ahead of them.

"No." He was adamant. "We have at least another half mile to go."

*Another half mile?* Elizabeth's mind shouted. Already a chill had rushed over her bare arms, and the sand squishing between her toes was decidedly wet. The surf was coming in, driving them farther and farther up the beach.

"I'm sure you're wrong," she told him with more confidence than she was feeling. "That's got to be the rock." She was unable to banish the slight quiver from her voice.

Angrily, he stripped off his shirt and placed it around her bare shoulders. "You're freezing." He made it sound like an accusation. "For heaven's sake, why didn't you say something?"

"Because I knew you'd do something silly like take off your shirt and give it to me," she shot back testily. "That's the rock, I'm sure of it," she reiterated, hurrying ahead. The only light was from the half moon above, and when she knelt down and discovered a sock, she leapt triumphantly to her feet. "Ah, ha!" She dangled it in front of his nose. "What did I tell you!"

"That's not mine," he returned impatiently. "Good grief, Elizabeth, look at the size. That belongs to a child."

"This is the rock," she insisted. "It's got to be."

"Fine." His voice was decidedly amused. "If this is the rock, then our shoes would be here. Right?" He crossed his arms and stared at her with amused tolerance.

Boldly, she met his glare. "Someone could have taken them," she stated evenly, feeling suddenly righteous.

"Elizabeth." He paused and inhaled a calming breath. "Trust me. The rock and Hilda are about a half-mile up the beach. If you'll quit arguing with me and walk a little way, you'll see that I know what I'm talking about."

"No." She knotted her fists at her sides in angry resolve. "I'm tired and I'm cold, and I think you've entirely lost your sense of direction. If you feel this isn't the rock, then go ahead and go. I'll be waiting for you here."

"You're not staying alone."

"I'm not going with you."

His eyes became hard points of steel, then softened. "Come on, it's not far."

"No." She stamped her foot, and splashed grit and sand against her bare leg from an incoming wave.

"You're not staying."

"Breed, listen to reason," she pleaded.

A wave crashed against his leg and he shook his head grimly.

"All right," she suggested. "Let's make a wager. Are you game?"

"Why shouldn't I be? You're wrong." The mood lightened immediately. "What do you want to bet?"

"I'll march the unnecessary half-mile up the beach with you. But once you realize you're wrong, you have to carry me piggyback on the return trip. Agreed?"

"Just a minute here." A smile twitched at the corners of his mouth. "What do I get if I'm right?"

"A personal apology?" she suggested, confident she wouldn't need to make one.

His look was thoughtful. "Not good enough."

She slowly moistened her lips and gently swayed her hips. "Ten slow kisses in the moonlight."

He shook his head. "That's *too* good."

She laughed. "Are you always so hard to please?"

"No," he grumbled. "Come on, we can figure it out as we walk." He draped his arm over her shoulders, pulling her close. She wasn't sure if it was because he was as cold as she was now or if he simply wanted her near his side. She tucked her arm around his waist, enjoying the cool feel of his skin against her.

"It's a good thing you've got those freckles," he said seriously about five minutes later. "Without those lighting the way, we'd be lost for sure."

In spite of herself, she laughed. Breed had the ability to do that to her. If someone else had made a similar comment she would have been angry and hurt. But not when it was Breed.

Ten minutes later they spied another large boulder in the distance.

"What did I tell you?" He oozed confidence.

"Don't be so sure of yourself," she returned, only slightly unnerved.

"If my eyes serve me right, someone was kind enough to place our shoes on top so they wouldn't be swept out with the waves."

Her confidence cracked.

"Listen. If you ever get lost, promise me you'll stay in one place."

"I get the message," she grumbled.

"Promise me," he said more forcefully. "I swear, you'd argue with Saint Peter."

"Well, you're no saint," she shot back.

His grip tightened as his eyes looked into hers. "Don't remind me," he murmured just before claiming her lips in a hungry kiss that left her weak and breathless. "I think we'll go with those ten kisses after all," he mumbled against her hair. "You still owe me nine."

By the time they made it up to the highway and Hilda, then found an all-night restaurant and had coffee, it was well after one. And it was close to two when Elizabeth peeled back the covers to her bed.

When the alarm went off a few hours later, she was sure the time was wrong. Her eyes burned, and she felt as if she'd hardly slept.

Gilly was up and dressed by the time Elizabeth staggered into the kitchen and poured herself a cup of strong coffee.

"What time did you get in?" Gilly asked cheerfully.

"Two," Elizabeth mumbled almost inaudibly.

"I thought you were the one who insisted it was going to be an early night," Gilly said in a teasing, know-it-all voice.

"Do you have to be so happy in the morning?" Elizabeth grumbled, taking her first sip of coffee, nearly scalding her mouth.

"When are you seeing Breed again?"

He hadn't said anything the night before about another date. But they *would* be seeing each other again; Elizabeth had never been more sure of anything. A smile flitted across her face at the memory of their heated discussion about the rock. She could feel Gilly's gaze skimming over her.

"Obviously you're seeing him soon," the younger woman announced, heading toward her bedroom.

Breed came into the café later that afternoon at what she'd come to think of as his usual time.

He gave Elizabeth a warm smile and yawned. Almost immediately she yawned back and delivered a cup of coffee to his table.

"How do you feel?" he asked, his hand deliberately brushing hers.

"Tired. How about you?"

"Exhausted. I'm not used to these late nights and early mornings." He continued to hold her hand, his thumb stroking the inside of her wrist.

"And you think *I* am?" she teased.

His eyes widened for an instant. "Can I see you tonight?"

The idea of refusing never even occurred to her. "Depends." No need to let him feel overconfident. "What do you have in mind?" She batted her eyelashes at him wickedly.

"Collecting on what's due me. Eight, I believe, is the correct number."

# Four

—◊—

The moon silently smiled down from the starlit heavens, casting its glow over the sandy beach. Breed and Peter had gathered driftwood, and blue tongues of fire flickered out from between the small, dry logs.

Elizabeth sat in the sand beside the fire and leaned against Breed, reveling in his quiet strength. His arms were wrapped around her from behind, enclosing her in his embrace. His breathing was even and undisturbed in the peace of the night. Communicating with words wasn't necessary. They'd been talking all week, often into the early hours of the morning. Now, words seemed unnecessary.

"I love this beach," she murmured, thinking how easy it would be to close her eyes and fall asleep in Breed's arms. "Ever since the first night you brought me here, I've come to think of this beach as ours."

His hold tightened measurably as he rubbed his jaw over the top of her head, mussing her wind-tossed hair all the more. Gently he lowered his head and kissed the side of her neck. "I'd say we're being generous sharing it with the world, wouldn't you?"

She snuggled deeper into his arms. "More than generous," she agreed.

The sound of Gilly's laughter came drifting down the beach. She and Peter had taken off running, playing some kind of teasing game. Elizabeth enjoyed it when the four of them did things together, but she was grateful for this time alone with Breed by the fire.

"Where do they get their energy?" she asked, having difficulty restraining a wide yawn. "I don't know about you, but I can't take another week like this."

"I always mean to get you home earlier," he murmured, his voice faintly tinged with guilt.

They'd gone out every night, and she hadn't once gotten home before midnight. Each time they promised each other they would make it an early night, but they hadn't met that goal once. The earliest she had crawled into bed had been twelve-thirty. Even then, she'd often lain awake and stared at the ceiling, thinking how dangerously close she was to falling in love with Breed.

"I wish I knew more about the constellations," she whispered, disliking the meandering trail of her thoughts. Love confused her. She had never been sure what elusive qualities distinguished love from infatuation. And if she did convince herself she was in love with Breed, would she ever be certain that it wasn't gratitude for the renewed lease on life he had so unwittingly given her? Tonight, in his arms, she could lie back and stare at the stars blazing in the black velvet sky. Only weeks ago she would have stumbled in the dark, unable to look toward the light. He had fixed that for her.

A hundred times she had flirted with the idea of telling him who she was. Each time, she realized that the knowledge would ruin their relationship. As it was, she would be faced with leaving him, Gilly, and San Francisco soon enough.

She recognized that it was selfish to steal this brief happiness at the expense of others, but she couldn't help herself. It had been so long since she'd felt this good. Without even knowing it, Breed and Gilly had given her back the most precious gift of all: the ability to laugh and see beyond her grief. Being with them had lifted her from the mire of regret and self-pity. For that she would always be grateful.

"What's wrong?" Breed asked, tenderly brushing the hair from her temple.

His sensitivity to her moods astonished her. "What makes you ask?"

"You went tense on me for a moment."

She twisted so that she could lean back and study his ruggedly powerful face. His eyes were shadowed and unreadable, but she recognized the unrest in his look. Something was troubling him. She could sense it as strongly as she could feel the moisture of the ocean mist on her face. She'd recognized it in his eyes several times this past week. At first she'd thought it was her imagination. A yearning to understand him overcame her. "Things aren't always what they appear," she found herself saying. She hoped that he would trust her enough to tell her what was troubling him. But she wouldn't force his confidence.

Everything seemed to go still. Even the sound of the

waves pounding against the beach faded. "What makes you say that?"

She resumed her former position, disappointed and a little hurt. Still, if Breed had secrets, so did she, and she certainly wasn't about to blurt out hers, so in all fairness, she shouldn't expect him to.

"Nothing." Her low voice was filled with resignation.

Slowly, tantalizingly, he ran his hands down her arms. "I have to go out of town next week."

"Oh." The word trembled on her lips with undisguised disappointment.

"I'll be flying out Monday, but I should be back sometime Tuesday," he explained.

"I'll miss you."

He drew her back against the unrestrained strength of his torso. "I wouldn't go if it wasn't necessary. You're right, you know." He spoke so low that she had to strain to hear him. "Things aren't always what they appear."

Later, when Breed had dropped her off at the apartment and she had settled in bed, his enigmatic words echoed in her mind. She couldn't imagine what was troubling him. But whatever it was, she sensed he was planning to settle it while he was out of town. He'd been quiet tonight. At first she had attributed his lack of conversation to how tired they both were. But it was more than that. She didn't know why she was so sure of it, but she was.

When she had first met Breed, she'd seen him only as muscular and handsome, two qualities she had attributed to shallow and self-centered men. But he had proved her wrong. This man was deep and intense. So intense that she often wondered what accounted for the powerful attraction that had brought them together.

A shadowy figure appeared in the doorway. "Are you asleep?" Gilly whispered.

Elizabeth sat up, bunching the pillows behind her back. "Not yet." She gestured toward the end of her bed, inviting her roommate to join her.

Gilly took a long swallow from a glass of milk and walked into the moonlit room, then sat on the edge of the bed. "I don't know what's wrong. I couldn't sleep, either."

"Did you have a good time tonight?" Elizabeth felt compelled to whisper, although there was no one there to disturb.

"I enjoy being with Peter," Gilly confessed with an exaggerated sigh, "but only as a friend."

"Is that a problem?"

Gilly's laugh was light and airy. "Not really, since I'm sure he feels the same way. It makes me wonder if I'll ever fall in love."

Elizabeth bit into her lip to keep from laughing out loud. "Do you realize how funny you sound? First you're happy because you and Peter are happy being just friends. Then you're disappointed because you aren't in love."

Gilly's smile was highlighted by the filtered light of the moon passing through the open window. "Yes, I suppose it does sound a little outrageous. I guess what I'd really like is to have the kind of relationship you and Breed share."

"He's a special man." Elizabeth spoke wistfully. Breed had taught her valuable lessons this past week. Without her long walk in the valley she might not have recognized the thrill of the mountaintop. Breed and Gilly had taught her to laugh and love life again. Life was beautiful in San Francisco. No wonder her mother had loved this city.

"I've seen the way he looks at you," Gilly continued, "and my heart melts. I want a man to feel that way about me."

"But not Peter."

"At this point I'm not choosy. I want to know what it's like to be in love. Really in love, like you and Breed."

"In love? Me and Breed?" Elizabeth tossed back the words in astonished disbelief.

"Yes, you and Breed," Gilly returned indignantly.

"You've got it all wrong." Elizabeth's thoughts were waging a fierce battle with one another. Gilly had to be mistaken. Breed couldn't be in love with her. She could only end up hurting him. The minute he learned about her wealth and position, he would feel betrayed and angry. She couldn't allow that to happen. "We're attracted, but we're not in love," she returned adamantly, nodding once for emphasis.

The sound of Gilly's bemused laugh filled the room. "Honestly, how can anyone be so blind?"

"But Breed and I hardly know each other," Elizabeth argued. "What we feel at this point is infatuation, maybe, but no one falls in love in two weeks."

"Haven't you read *Romeo and Juliet*?" Gilly asked her accusingly. "People don't need a long courtship to know they're in love."

"Breed's a wonderful man, and I'd consider myself fortunate if he loved me." A thickening lump tightened her throat, making it impossible to talk for a moment.

"But it's too soon for either of us to know what we really feel. Much too soon," Elizabeth reiterated.

Gilly was uncharacteristically quiet for a long moment. "Maybe I'm way off," she murmured thoughtfully. "But I don't think so. I have the feeling that once you admit what's going on inside your heart and your head, you won't be able to deny it."

"Perhaps not," Elizabeth murmured, troubled by Gilly's words.

"Are you seeing him tomorrow?"

"Not until the afternoon. He decided that after all the sleep I lost this week, I should sleep late tomorrow."

"But you're awake because you're lying here thinking about him. Right?" Gilly asked softly.

"No." Elizabeth yawned loudly, raising her arms high above her head. She hoped her friend would take the not-so-subtle message.

"And not being able to sleep doesn't tell you anything?" Gilly pressed.

"It tells me that I'd have a much easier time if a certain know-it-all wasn't sitting on the end of my bed, bugging the heck out of me." As much as she wanted to deny her friend's assessment, Elizabeth had been impressed more than once with Gilly's insight into people and situations. At twenty, she was wise beyond her years.

"I can take a hint, unlike certain people I know," Gilly said, bounding to her feet. "You wait, Elizabeth Wainwright. When you realize you're in love with Breed, your head's going to spin for a week."

Turning onto her side, Elizabeth scooted down and pulled the covers up to her chin. "Don't count on it," she mumbled into the pillow, forcing her eyes closed.

Standing beside the foot of the bed, Gilly finished the rest of her milk. "I'll see you in the morning," she said as she headed toward the door.

"Gilly." Elizabeth stopped her. "Breed's not really in love with me, is he?"

Staring pointedly at the ceiling, Gilly slowly shook her head in undisguised disgust. "I swear the girl's blind," she said to the light fixture, then turned back to Elizabeth. "Yes, Breed's head over heels in love with you. Only a fool wouldn't have guessed. Good night, fool."

"Good night," Elizabeth murmured with a sinking feeling. She'd been naive to believe that she could nurture this relationship and not pay an emotional price. She had to do something soon, before it was too late. If it wasn't already.

"All right," Breed said, breathing heavily. He tightened his grip on Hilda's steering wheel. "Out with it."

Elizabeth's face paled as she glanced out the side of the Jeep. The afternoon had been a disaster from the start, and all because of her and her ridiculous mood. She had hoped to speak honestly with Breed. She wanted to tell him that she was frightened by what was happening between them. At first she'd thought to suggest that he start seeing someone else, but the thought of him holding another woman had made her stomach tighten painfully. The crazy part was that she'd never thought of herself as the jealous type.

"Are you pouting because I'm going away? Is that the reason for the silent treatment?"

"No," she denied in a choked whisper. "That's not

it." She kept her face averted, letting the wind whip her honey curls in every direction. She was so close to tears it was ludicrous.

When he pulled over to the curb and parked so he could face her, her heart sank to her knees. His gentle hand on her shoulder was nearly her undoing. She didn't want him to be gentle and concerned. If he were angry, it would be so much easier to explain her confused thoughts.

"Beth, what is it?"

Like Gilly, Breed had started calling her Beth. But it wasn't what he called her, it was the way he said it, the tender, almost loving way he let it roll from his lips. No name had ever sounded so beautiful.

Miserable, she placed her hand over his and turned around so that she could see his face. Of their own volition, her fingers rose to trace the angular lines of his proud jaw.

He emitted a low groan and took hold of her shoulders, putting some distance between them. "I have enough trouble keeping my hands off you without you doing that."

She dropped her hands, color rushing to her cheeks. "That's what's wrong," she said in a low voice she hardly recognized as her own. "I'm frightened, Breed."

"Of what?"

She swallowed back the uneasiness that filled her. "I'm worried that we're becoming too intense."

He dropped his hands and turned so that he was staring straight ahead. As if he needed something to do with his fingers, he gripped the steering wheel. She could tell that he was angry by the way his knuckles whitened. His look proved he didn't understand what she was saying.

"Things are getting too hot and heavy for you. Is that it?"

It wasn't, but she didn't know how else to explain her feelings. "Yes . . . yes they are."

"Then what you're saying is that you'd prefer it if we didn't see each other anymore?"

"No!" That thought was intolerable.

"The trouble with you is that you don't know what you want." The icy edge to his tone wrapped its way around her throat, choking off a reply.

He didn't appear to need one. Without hesitating, he turned the ignition key, and Hilda's engine roared to life. Jerking the gearshift, he pulled back onto the street.

"I feel we both need time to think." She practically had to shout to be heard above the noise of the traffic. Breed didn't answer. Before she could think of another way to explain herself, he had pulled up in front of her brick apartment building. He left the engine running.

"I agree," he said, his voice emotionless. "We've been seeing too much of each other."

"You've misunderstood everything I've said," she murmured miserably, wishing she had explained herself better.

"I don't think so," he replied, his jaw tightening. "I'll call you Tuesday, after I get back to town. That is, if you want to hear from me again."

"Of course I do." Frustration rocked her. "I'm sorry I said anything. I don't want you to go away angry."

He hesitated, and although he didn't say anything for several moments, she could feel the resentment fade. The air between them became less oppressive, lighter. "The thing is, you're right," he admitted tightly. "Both of us needed to be reminded of that. Take care of yourself while I'm away."

"I will," she whispered.

"I'll phone you Tuesday."

"Tuesday," she agreed, climbing out of the car. She stood on the sidewalk as he pulled away and merged with the flowing traffic.

A flick of her wrist turned the key that allowed her into the apartment. Gilly was sitting on the sofa, reading a romance novel and munching on a carrot. "How did everything go?" she asked.

"Fine," Elizabeth responded noncommittally. But she felt miserable. Her talk with Breed hadn't settled anything. Instead of clearing the air, it had only raised more questions. Now she was left with three days to sort through her thoughts and decide how she could continue to see him and not complicate their relationship by falling in love.

"If everything's so wonderful, why do you look like you're going to burst into tears?"

Elizabeth tried to smile, but the effort failed miserably. "Because I am."

"I take it you don't want to talk."

It was all Elizabeth could manage to shake her head.

Later that evening, as the sun was sinking low into a lavender sky, Gilly dressed for an evening out. Her cousin was getting married, and her parents expected her to attend the wedding although she never had cared for this particular cousin.

"Are you sure you won't come?" Gilly asked Elizabeth for the sixth time.

"I'm sure," Elizabeth responded from the kitchen table, making an exaggerated stroke along the side of her nail with a file. Fiddling with her fingernails had given the appearance she was busy and untroubled. But she doubted that her smoke screen had fooled Gilly. "I thought you'd conned Peter into going with you?"

"I regret that," Gilly said with frank honesty.

"Why?" Elizabeth glanced down at her collection of nail polish.

"Knowing my dad, he's probably going to make a big deal about my bringing Peter. This whole thing's going to end up embarrassing us both. I hate being forced to attend something just because it's family."

Elizabeth cast her a sympathetic look. She'd suffered through enough family obligations to empathize with her friend's feelings.

Gilly and Peter left soon afterward, and she finished her nails, wondering if Breed would notice when she saw him next. She watched television for a while, keeping her mind off him. But not for long.

She picked up the paperback Gilly had been reading, and quickly read the first couple of chapters, surprised at how much she was enjoying the book. The next thing she knew, Gilly was shaking her awake and telling her to climb into bed or she would get a crick in her neck.

It was the middle of the morning when she woke again. Feeling out of sorts and cranky, she read the morning paper and did the weekly grocery shopping. When

Gilly suggested a drive, she declined. Not until later did she realize that she'd been waiting for Breed to phone, even though he'd said he wouldn't, and was keenly disappointed when he didn't.

Monday evening, when her cell did ring she all but flew across the room in her eagerness to grab it from her purse. She desperately wanted it to be Breed. But it wasn't. Instead, she found herself talking to her disgruntled father.

"I haven't heard from you in a while. Are you okay?"

"Of course I am." Although disappointment coated her voice, she had to admit she was pleased to hear from her father. She was even more grateful that Gilly was taking a shower and wasn't likely to overhear the conversation. "I'm happy, Dad, for the first time since Mom died."

"I was thinking about this job of yours. Are you still working as a . . . waitress?" He said the word as though he found it distasteful.

"Yes, and I'm enjoying it."

"I've been talking to some friends of mine," he said in a tone that told her he was anxious about her. "If you feel you need to work, then we could get you on at the embassy. Your French is excellent."

"Dad," she interrupted, "I like it at the Patisserie. Don't worry about me."

"But as a common waitress?" The contemptuous disbelief was back in his voice again. "I want so much more for you, Princess." Her father hadn't called her that since she was thirteen. "When are you coming home? I think it might be a good idea if you were here."

"Dad," she said impatiently, "for the first time in

months I'm sleeping every night. I'm eager for each new morning. I'm happy, really happy. Don't ruin that."

She could hear her father's uncertainty, feel his indecision. "Have you met someone special?" he said.

The question was a loaded one, and she wasn't sure how to respond, especially in light of her discussion with Breed. "Yes and no."

"Meaning . . . ?" he pressed.

"I've made some friends. Good friends. What makes you ask?"

"No reason. I just don't want you to do something you'll regret later."

"Like what?" Indignation caused her voice to rise perceptibly.

"I don't know." He paused and exhaled forcefully. "Siggy's phoned for you several times."

Elizabeth released an inward groan. Siegfried Winston Chamberlain III was the most boring stuffed shirt she'd ever known. More than that, she had openly disliked him from the day a small, helpless bird had flown into a freshly washed window and broken its neck. The look in Siggy's eyes revealed that he'd enjoyed witnessing its death. From that time on she'd avoided him. But he had pursued her relentlessly from their teenage years, though she was certain he wasn't in love with her. She wasn't even sure he liked her. What she did recognize was the fact that a union between their two families would be financially expedient to the Chamberlains.

"Tell Siggy the same thing you told him when I was in Paris."

"Siggy loves you."

"Dad . . ." Elizabeth didn't want to lose her temper,

not on the phone, when it would be difficult to settle their differences. "I honestly don't think Siggy knows what love is. I've got to go. I'll phone you next week. Now, don't worry about me. Promise?"

"You'll phone next week? Promise?"

She successfully repressed a sharp reply. Her father had never shown such concern for her welfare. He was acting as though she was working undercover for the CIA.

Honestly, she mused irritably. Would she ever understand her father?

"You miss him, don't you?" Gilly asked her later that evening.

Elizabeth didn't even try to pretend. She knew Gilly was referring to Breed. She had confided in her friend, and was again grateful for Gilly's insight and understanding. He had been on her mind all weekend. Monday had dragged, and she was counting the hours until she heard from him again. "I do," she admitted readily. "I wish I'd never said anything."

Gilly nodded sympathetically.

But it was more than missing Breed, Elizabeth thought to herself. Much more. For three days it had been as though a vital part of her was missing. The realization frightened her. He had come to mean more to her in a few weeks than anyone she'd known. Gilly, too. As she'd explained to her father, she was making friends. Maybe the first real friends of her life. But Breed was more than a friend, and it had taken this separation to prove it.

Tuesday Elizabeth kept taking out her cell to see if she had missed his call.

"From the look of you, someone might think you're waiting to hear from someone," Gilly teased.

"Am I that obvious?"

"Is the sun bright? Do bees buzz?" Gilly sat on the chair opposite Elizabeth. "Why not call him? Women do that these days, you know."

Elizabeth hesitated long enough to consider the idea. "I don't know."

"Well, it isn't going to hurt anything. His pride's been bruised. Besides, anything's better than having you mope around the apartment another night."

"I do not mope."

Gilly tried unsuccessfully to disguise a smile. "If you say so."

Elizabeth waited until nine for Breed to phone. She could call him, but seeing him in person would be so much better. Maybe Gilly was right and, despite what he'd said about calling her, he was waiting for her to contact him. She wouldn't sleep tonight unless she made the effort to see him. It wouldn't do any good to try to fool herself otherwise.

"I think I'll go for a walk," she announced brightly, knowing she wasn't fooling her friend.

"Tonight's perfect for a stroll," Gilly murmured, not taking her attention from the television, but Elizabeth noticed the way the corners of her eyes crinkled as she struggled not to reveal her amusement. "I don't suppose you want me to wait up for you."

With a bemused smile, Elizabeth closed the door, not bothering to answer.

There were plenty of reasons that could explain why Breed hadn't called. Maybe his trip had been extended. He might not even be home. But as Gilly had pointedly stated, the evening *was* perfect for a stroll. The sun had set below a cloudless horizon and darkness had blanketed the city. The streets were alive with a variety of people. Elizabeth didn't notice much of what was going on around her. Her quick, purpose-filled strides took her the three blocks to Breed's apartment in a matter of a few short minutes. She had never been there, yet the address was burned into her memory.

For all her resolve, when she saw the light under his door, her heart sank. Breed was home and hadn't contacted her.

Her first light knock went unnoticed, so she pressed the buzzer long and hard.

"Beth!" Breed sounded shocked when he opened the door.

"So you made it back safely after all," she said, aware of the faintly accusatory note in her voice. He must have realized that she would be waiting for his call. "What time did you get back?" The minute the question slipped from her lips, she regretted having asked. Her coming was obvious enough.

"About six." He stepped back, silently and grudgingly issuing the invitation for her to come inside.

She was surprised at how bare the apartment looked. The living area displayed nothing that stamped the apartment with his personality. There were no pictures on the walls, or books and magazines lying around. The place seemed sterile, it was so clean. It looked as if he'd just moved in.

"I thought you said you would phone."

"I wasn't sure you wanted to hear from me."

Without waiting for an invitation, she sat on the sofa and crossed her long legs, hoping to give a casual impression.

He took a chair on the other side of the room and leaned forward, his elbows resting on his knees. There was a coiled alertness about him that he was attempting to disguise. But Elizabeth knew him too well. In the same way that he was sensitive to her, she was aware of him. He seemed to be waiting for her to speak.

"I missed you," she said softly, hoping her words would release the tension in the room. "More than I ever thought I would."

He straightened and looked uncomfortable. "Yes. Well, that's only natural. We've been seeing a lot of each other the last couple of weeks."

Her fingers were laced together so tightly that they began to ache. She unwound them and flexed her hands before standing and moving to the window on the far side of the room. "It's more than that," she announced with her back to him. Deliberately she turned, then leaned back with her hands resting on the windowsill. "Nothing seemed right without you. . . ."

Breed vaulted to his feet. "Beth, listen to me. We're tired. It's been a long day. I think we should both sleep on this." His look was an odd mixture of tenderness and impatience. "Come on, I'll drive you home."

"No." She knew a brush-off when she heard one. He didn't want her here; that much was obvious. He hadn't been himself from the moment she set foot in the door. "I walked here, I'll walk back."

"All right, I'll come with you." The tone of his voice told her he would brook no argument.

She lifted one shoulder in a half-shrug. "It's a free country."

He relaxed the minute he locked the door. There was something inside the apartment he hadn't wanted her to see, she realized. Not a woman hiding in his bedroom; she was sure of that. Amusement drifted across her face and awoke a slow smile.

"What's so funny?" he wanted to know.

"Nothing."

His hand gripped hers. "Come on, and I'll introduce you to BART."

She paused midstride, making him falter slightly. With her hands positioned challengingly on her hips, she glared defiantly at him. "Oh, no, you don't, Andrew Breed. If you don't want to see me again, then fine. But I won't have you introducing me to other men. I can find my own dates, thank you."

A crooked smile slashed his face as he turned toward her, his eyes hooded. "Bay Area Rapid Transit. BART is the subway."

"Oh." She felt ridiculous. The natural color of her cheeks was heightened with embarrassment.

"So you missed me," he said casually as they strolled along the busy sidewalk. "That's nice to know."

She greeted his words with silence. First he had shunned her, and now he was making fun of her. Other than a polite "good night" when they arrived at her building, she didn't have anything to say to him. The whole idea of going to him had been idiotic. Well, she'd learned her lesson.

"The thing is, I discovered I missed you, too."

Again she didn't respond.

"But missing someone is a strange thing," he continued. "There are varying degrees. Like after your mother died, I imagine . . ."

Elizabeth felt a chill rush over her skin that had nothing to do with the light breeze. "I never told you my mother was dead," she said stiffly.

# Five

—⁓—

"You don't mind, do you?" Gilly asked contritely. "I wouldn't have mentioned your mother to Breed if I'd known you objected."

"No, don't worry about it," Elizabeth said gently, shaking her head.

"Even though Breed and I went out several times before you started dating him, I knew from the beginning that he was really only interested in you. From the first date you were all he talked about."

Breed had explained to Elizabeth yesterday that Gilly had told him about her mother. Yet she'd doubted him. Everything about last night remained clouded in her mind. From the moment she'd entered his apartment, she had felt like an unwelcome intruder. None of his actions made sense, and her suspicions had begun to cross the line into outright paranoia.

"Peter and I are going to dinner and a movie," Gilly said, changing the subject.

"I have some shopping I want to do," Elizabeth returned absently.


Not until later that evening, when she was facing the store detective, did she remember that she couldn't phone Gilly, whose cell would be off in the theater, and have her come. A heaviness pressed against her heart, and she struggled to maintain her composure as the balding man led her toward the department store office.

She walked past the small crowd that had gathered near her and saw a tall, familiar figure on the far side of the floor in the men's department.

"Breed!" she called, thanking heaven that he had chosen this day to shop.

He turned at the sound of her voice, his brows lowering. "Beth, what is it?"

She bit into her bottom lip, more embarrassed than she could ever remember being. "Someone stole my purse. I haven't got any way to get home or a key to the apartment."


Elizabeth's face was buried in her hands when Breed delivered a steaming cup of coffee to the kitchen table where she sat. The manager had let her into the apartment, but she still had so much to deal with to straighten everything out that the feeling was overwhelming.

"Tell me again what happened," Breed said as he straddled a chair beside her.

She shook her head. Everything important was inside her purse. Her money, credit cards, identification. Everything. Gone in a matter of seconds. As crazy as it sounded, she felt as if she had been personally violated. She was both stunned and angry.

"I don't want to talk about it," she replied stiffly. What she wanted was for Breed to leave so she could be alone.

"Beth." He said her name so gently that she closed her eyes to the emotion he aroused in her. "Honey, I can't help unless I know what happened."

One tear broke past the thick dam of her lashes and flowed unrestrained down her pale face. Resolutely, she wiped it aside.

"I decided to do a little shopping after work. Peter had picked up Gilly, and they were going out, and I didn't want to go home to an empty house." Breed hadn't mentioned anything last night about getting together, and she didn't want to sit around in an empty apartment missing him.

"Go on," he encouraged. He continued to hold her hand, his thumb stroking the inside of her wrist in a soothing action that at any other time would have been sensuous and provocative.

"I'd only bought a couple of things and decided to stop in the restroom before taking BART home. I set my purse and the packages on the counter while I washed. I turned to dry my hands. When I turned back, my purse, the packages . . . everything was gone. I was so stunned, I didn't know what to do."

"You must have seen something."

"That's what Detective Beaman thought. But I didn't. I didn't even hear anything." She paused, reliving the short seconds. She could tell them nothing.

Even now, an hour later, sitting in her kitchen, a feeling of disbelief filled her. This couldn't really be happening. This was a bad dream, and when she woke, everything would be fine again. At least that was what she desperately wanted to believe.

"What did they take?"

"Breed, don't. Please. I can't talk about it anymore. I just want to take a bath and pretend this never happened." Later she would have to contact her father. It didn't take much of an imagination to know what his response was going to be. He would insist she leave San Francisco, and then they would argue. She let the unpleasant thoughts fade. She didn't want to think about it.

Breed released her wrist and stood. His hands were positioned on his lean hips, his expression grim and unyielding. "Beth," he insisted in a low, coaxing tone. "Think. There's something you're not remembering. Something small. Close your eyes and go over every minute of the time you were shopping."

She clenched her teeth to keep from yelling. "Do you think I haven't already?" she said with marked impatience. "Every detail of every minute has been playing back repeatedly in my mind."

He exhaled sharply, letting her know his patience was as limited as her own.

She stared pointedly at the bare surface of the table, which blurred as the welling tears collected in her eyes. She managed to restrain their fall, but she couldn't keep her chin from trembling. Tears were a sign of weakness, and the Wainwrights frowned on signs of weakness.

Breed sighed as he eliminated the distance between them and stood behind her. Gently he comforted her by massaging her shoulders and neck. The demanding pressure of his fingers half lifted her from the chair, forcing her to stand.

She held herself stiffly, angry. "This is your fault," she whispered in a faintly hysterical tone.

"Mine?" He turned her around. His amber eyes narrowed into thin slits.

She didn't need him to tell her how unreasonable she was being, but she couldn't help herself. Her tears blurred his expression as she lashed out at him bitterly. "Why were you so unwelcoming last night? Why didn't you want me at your apartment? Not to mention that you said you'd call and then you didn't." She inhaled shakily. "Don't bother to deny it. I'm not stupid. I know when I'm not wanted. And why . . . why didn't you come into the café today?" Her accusations were fired as quick as machine gun bullets.

He groaned as his hands cupped her face. Anger flashed across his features, then vanished. "There wasn't a single minute that you weren't on my mind." Self-derisive anger darkened his eyes.

"Then why . . . ?" Her heart fluttered uncertainly, excited and yet afraid.

Motionless, he held her, revealing none of his thoughts. "Because," he admitted as the smoldering light of desire burned in his eyes. His hand slid slowly along the back of her waist, bringing her infinitesimally closer.

When he fitted his mouth to hers, a small, happy sound escaped from her throat. His thick arms around her waist lifted her from the kitchen floor. Her softness was molded to his male length as he kissed her until her lips were swollen and trembling.

"I missed you so much," she admitted, wrapping her arms around his neck. "I was so afraid you didn't want to see me again."

"Not want to see you?" he repeated. His husky tone betrayed his frustration. "You confuse me. I don't know what kind of game you're playing."

Anxiously, she brushed the hair from his face and kissed him, her lips exploring the planes and contours of his angular features with short, teasing kisses. "I'm not playing any game," she whispered.

He loosened his grip so that her feet touched the floor once again. "No games?" Amusement was carved in the lines of his face. "I don't believe that."

Deliberately she directed his mouth to hers and kissed him long and slow, her lips moving sensuously over his.

He broke the contact and held her at arm's length as he took several deep breaths.

"What's wrong?" she whispered. She didn't want him to pull away from her. A chill seeped through her bloodstream as she tried to decipher his attitude. The messages he sent her were confused. He wanted to be with her, but he didn't. He liked coming to her apartment but didn't want her at his. His kisses affected her as much as they affected him, yet he pulled away whenever things became too intense.

The phone rang, and he dropped his hands and stared at it as if it were an intruder. "Do you want me to answer it?" he questioned.

She shook her head and answered it herself. "Hello." She couldn't disguise the soft tremble in her voice. "Yes, yes, this is Elizabeth Wainwright."

Breed brushed his fingers through his hair as he paced the room.

"Yes, yes," she repeated breathlessly. "I did lose my purse." Not until the conversation was half over did the words sink into her consciousness.

"Breed!" she cried excitedly as she replaced the receiver. "They've found my purse!"

"Who did?" He turned her in his arms, his tense features relaxing.

"The store. That was them on the phone. Apparently whoever took it was only after the cash. Someone turned it in to the office only a few minutes ago after finding it in the stairway."

"Your credit cards and identification?"

"There. All they took was the cash."

He hauled her into his arms and released a heavy sigh that revealed his relief. Her own happy sigh joined his. "They said I should come and pick it up. Let's go right away," she said, laughing. "I feel naked without my purse." Giddy with relief, she waltzed around the room until he captured her and swung her in the air as if she weighed no more than a doll.

"Feel better?"

"Oh, yes!" she exclaimed, kissing him lightly. "Can we go now?"

"I think we should." He laced his fingers through hers, then lifted their joined hands to his lips and kissed the back of her hand.

He locked the apartment with the spare key the manager had given her and tucked it into his pocket. Hand in hand, they walked outside.

She patted Hilda's seat cushion as she got in. "You

know what I thought last night?" she asked as Breed revved the engine.

He turned and smiled warmly at her. "I can't imagine." His finger lingered longer than necessary as it removed a long strand of silken hair that the wind had blown across her happy face.

"For one fleeting instant I was convinced you were hiding a woman in your bedroom." At the shocked look he gave her, she broke into delighted giggles.

"Beth." Thick lines marred his smooth brow. "Whatever made you suspect something like that?"

Pressing her head against his shoulder, she released a contented sigh. "I don't know." She *did* know, but she wanted to relish this moment. Yesterday's ghosts were buried. Today's happiness shone brightly before her. Her joy was complete. "Forward, Hilda. Take me to my purse."

Breed merged with the heavy flow of traffic. "I suppose you're going to insist on celebrating."

"Absolutely."

"Dinner?"

She sat up and placed her hand on his where it rested on the gearshift. She had to keep touching him to believe that all this was real. "Yes, I'm starved. I don't think I've eaten all day."

"Why not?" He gave her a questioning glance.

She poked his stomach. "You know why."

He reclaimed her hand, and again he kissed her fingers. She had the sensation he felt exactly as she did and couldn't keep his hands off her.

"What did Beaman say?"

"It wasn't Beaman. He said his name, but I can't remember it now."

"What did he say?" Breed glanced briefly in her direction.

"Just that I should come right away."

"That you should come right away." He drawled the words slowly. Then he dropped her hand and tightened his hold on the steering wheel as he glanced in the rearview mirror. The tires screeched as he made a U-turn in the middle of the street. The unexpected action caused Hilda to teeter for an instant.

"Breed!" Elizabeth screamed, holding on to the padded bar on the dash. "What is it? What's wrong?"

He didn't answer her as he weaved in and out of the traffic, blaring his horn impatiently. When they pulled up in front of her apartment again, he looked around and tensed.

She had no idea what had gotten into him. "Breed?" She tried a second time to talk to him. He sat alert and stiff. The look in his eyes was frightening. She had never seen anything more menacing.

"Call the police," he told her as he jumped from the Jeep.

"But, Breed—"

"Now. Hurry."

Confused, she jumped out, too. "What am I supposed to tell them?" she asked as she followed him onto the sidewalk and reached for his hand.

He pushed her arm away. "That wasn't the store that called," he explained impatiently. "It was whoever took your purse, and they're about to rob you blind."

"How do you know?" Nothing made sense anymore.

Breed was like a dangerous stranger. Rage contorted his features until she hardly recognized him.

He grabbed her shoulders, his fingers biting mercilessly into her flesh. "Look." He jerked his head toward a moving van parked in front of the building. "Do as I say and call 9-1-1," he ordered in a threatening voice. "And don't come into the apartment until after the police arrive. Now go."

"Breed . . ." Panic filled her as he walked toward the door. "Don't go in there!" she shouted frantically, running after him. He was so intent that he didn't hear her. His glance of surprise when she grabbed his arm was quickly replaced with an angry scowl. "Get out of here."

With fear dictating her actions, she ran across the street to the safety of a beauty salon. She was sure the women thought she was crazy when she pulled out her cell, dialed the emergency police number, and reported a robbery in progress, all the while staring out through the large front window.

Like a caged animal, she paced the sidewalk outside her apartment, waiting for the patrol car. She held both hands over her mouth as she looked up and down the street. Everything was taking so long. Each second was an hour, every minute a lifetime. Not until the first police vehicle pulled up did she realize how badly she was trembling.

"In there," she said, and gave them her apartment number. "My boyfriend went up to stop them."

Another police car arrived, and while one officer went into the building on the heels of the first two, the other stayed outside and questioned her. At first she stared at him blankly, her mind refusing to concentrate on her own responses. Her answers were clipped, one-word replies.

Fifteen minutes later, two men and a woman were led out of the building by the police. Breed followed, talking to an officer. He paused long enough to search out Elizabeth in the growing crowd and smile reassuringly.

Her answering smile was shaky, but she felt her heart regain its normal rhythm. Her eyes followed him as he spoke to one officer and then another. When he joined her a few minutes later, he slipped an arm around her waist with familiar ease. Her fears evaporated at his touch.

"Do you recognize any of them?" he asked her.

Lamely, she nodded. "The woman was in the elevator with me, but she didn't go into the restroom."

"But she got off on the same floor?"

She wasn't sure. "I don't remember, but she must have."

"It doesn't matter if you remember or not. There's enough evidence here to lock them up." His arm remained on her waist as he directed her inside.

"How'd you know?" Dazed and almost tongue-tied, she stared up at him. "What clued you in to what was going on?"

"To be honest, I don't know," he admitted. "Something didn't ring true. First, it wasn't Beaman who phoned, and then there was something about the way you were instructed to come right away. They were probably waiting within sight of the building and watched us leave."

"But how'd they know my address and phone number?" All her identification listed her Boston address.

Even her driver's license was from Massachusetts. There hadn't been any reason to obtain a California license, since she didn't have a car and was only planning on staying for the summer.

"Your name, address, and telephone number are printed on your checks."

She groaned. "Of course."

"We need to go to the police station and fill out a few forms. Are you up to that?"

"I'm fine. But I want to know about you. What happened in there?"

"Nothing much." It didn't sound like he wanted to talk about it. "I counted on the element of surprise."

"Yes, but there were three of them." She wasn't about to let the subject drop. "How did you defend yourself?"

His wide shoulders tensed as he hesitated before answering. "I've studied the martial arts."

"Breed!" she exclaimed. "Really? You should have said something." The longer she was with him, the more she realized how little she actually knew about him. She had actually avoided asking too many questions, afraid of revealing too much about herself. But she wouldn't shy away from them anymore.

Gilly and Peter returned to the apartment chatting happily.

Elizabeth glanced up and sighed. "Where were you when I needed you?" she teased her roommate.

"When did you need me?"

"Today. Someone took my purse."

"They did more than that," Breed repeated with a trace of anger.

"What happened?" Peter looked incredulous. "I think you better start at the beginning."

Slowly, shaking her head, Elizabeth sighed. "Let me explain."

An hour later Breed glanced pointedly at his wristwatch and held out his hand to Elizabeth. "Walk me to the door." The quiet firmness of his request and the tender look in his eyes sent her pulse racing.

"Sure," she said, eagerly moving around the sofa to his side.

He waited until they reached the entryway to turn her into his arms. Her back was supported by the panels of the door. His hands were on each side of her head as his gaze roamed slowly over her upturned face. For one heart-stopping second his eyes rested on her parted lips; his look was as potent as a physical touch.

"I want to see you tomorrow."

She released a heavy sigh. "Oh, thank goodness," she said, offering him a brilliant smile. "I was afraid I was going to be forced to ask *you* out."

His look grew dark and serious. "You'd do that?"

"Yes." She didn't trust herself to add an explanation.

He pulled his gaze from hers. "Would you like to go fishing?"

"You mean with poles and hooks and worms?"

"I've got a sailboat. We could leave tomorrow afternoon, once you're off work."

"Can I bring anything?"

"The worms," Breed teased.

"Try again, buddy. How about some sandwiches?"

She could have Evelyn make some up for her before she left the Patisserie tomorrow.

"Fine."

Breed's kiss was disappointingly short but immeasurably sweet. Long after he left, she felt his presence linger. Twice she turned and started to say something to him before realizing he'd left for the evening.

Elizabeth felt Gilly's curious stare as she came out of the bedroom the following afternoon.

"Where's Breed taking you, for heaven's sake? You look like you just finished plowing the back forty."

Self-consciously, Elizabeth looked down at her tennis shoes and the faded jeans that were rolled midway up her calf. The shirttails of her red-checkered blouse were tied loosely at her midriff.

"Fishing. I'm not overdressed, am I? I have my swimsuit on underneath."

"You look . . ." One side of Gilly's mouth quirked upward as she paused, her face furrowed in concentration. "Different," she concluded.

"I'll admit I don't usually dress like this, but—"

"It's not the clothes," Gilly interrupted. "There's a certain aura about you. A look in your eye."

Turning, Elizabeth found a mirror and examined herself closely. "You're crazy. I'm no different than I was last week—or last night, for that matter."

Gilly ignored her and paid excessive attention to the crossword puzzle she was doing.

"No quick reply?" Elizabeth asked teasingly. She was used to doing verbal battle with her roommate.

Gilly bit into the eraser at the end of the pencil. "Not me. I learned a long time ago that it's better not to argue with you." But she rolled her eyes when she thought Elizabeth wasn't looking.

Breed arrived just then, and Elizabeth didn't have the opportunity to banter further with Gilly. If there was something different about her, as her friend believed, then it was because she was happier, more complete.

Outside the building, Elizabeth scanned the curb for Hilda, but the Jeep wasn't parked within sight.

"Here." Breed held open the door to a silver sedan, the same car he'd driven before introducing her to Hilda.

"Where's Hilda?"

"Home." Breed's reply was abrupt.

"Good grief, how many cars have you got?"

The smile that lifted the corners of his mouth looked forced. "One too many," he answered cryptically.

She wanted to question him further, but he closed her door and walked around to the driver's side. He paused and glanced warily at the street before climbing inside the car.

"Are you planning on kidnapping me?" she teased.

For an instant his sword-sharp gaze pinned her against the seat. "What makes you ask something as crazy as that?" Impatience sounded in his crisp voice.

She had meant it as a joke, so she was surprised that he had taken her seriously. She arched one delicately shaped brow at his defensive tone and cocked her head. "What's gotten into you?"

"Nothing."

Releasing her breath slowly, she gazed out the side window, watching as the scenery whipped past. From the minute he had asked her on this outing, she had been looking forward to their time together. She didn't want anything to ruin it.

At the marina, his heavy steps sounded ominously as he led her along the long wooden dock toward his sailboat. But his mood altered once they were slicing through the water, the multicolored spinnaker bloated with wind. Content, she dragged her fingers in the darkish green waters of San Francisco Bay, delighting in the cool feel against her hand, while Breed sat behind her at the tiller.

"This is wonderful!" she shouted. But he couldn't hear her, because a gust of wind carried her voice forward. Laughing, she scooted closer, rose to her knees and spoke directly into his ear, smiling.

His returning smile revealed his own enjoyment. He relaxed against the gunnel, his long legs stretched out and crossed at the ankles. With one hand he managed the tiller as he motioned with the other for Elizabeth to sit at his side.

She did so willingly.

When he reached a spot that apparently met his specifications, he lowered the sails and dropped anchor.

Giving her nothing more than the basic instructions, he baited her hook and handed her a fishing pole.

"Now what?" She sat straight-backed and unsure as he readied his own pole and lowered the line into the deep waters on the opposite side of the boat.

"We wait for a hungry fish to come along and take a nibble."

"What if they're not hungry?"

"Are you always this much trouble?" he asked her,

chuckling at her indignant look. "Your freckles are flashing at me again."

Involuntarily she brushed at her nose, as though her fingers could rub the tan flecks away. She was about to make a feisty retort when she felt a slight tug on her line.

"Breed," she whispered frantically. "I . . . I think I've got one." The pole dipped dramatically, nearly catching her off guard. "What do I do?" she cried, looking back to him, her eyes unsure.

"Reel it in."

"I can't," she said, silently pleading with him to take the pole from her. She should have known better.

"Sure you can," he assured her calmly. To offer her moral support, he reeled in his own line and went over to her, encouraging her as she struggled to bring in the fish.

She couldn't believe how much of a battle one small fish could wage. "What have I caught?" she shouted in her excitement. "A whale?" Perspiration broke out across her forehead as she pulled back on the pole and reeled in the fish inch by inch.

When the line snapped and she staggered backward, Breed caught her at the shoulders. "You all right?"

"No, darn it, I wanted that fish. What happened?"

He looked unconcerned and shrugged. "Any number of things. Want to try again?"

"Of course," she replied indignantly. He seemed to think she was a quitter, and she would like nothing better than to prove him wrong.

With her line back in the bay, Elizabeth leaned against the side, lazily enjoying the sun and wind. "Have you ever stopped to think that after all the times we've gone out, we still hardly know anything about each other?" she asked.

Her statement was met with silence. "What's there to know?"

She was treading on dangerous ground, and she knew it. Her relationship with Breed had progressed to the point where she felt he had a right to know who she was. But fear and indecision prevented her from broaching the subject boldly. "There's lots I'd like to know about you."

"Like what?" There was the slightest pause before his mouth thinned. He didn't seem overly eager to reveal more of himself.

"Well, for one thing . . . your family." If she led into the subject, then maybe he would ask her about hers, and she could explain bits and pieces of her background until things added up in his mind, since telling him outright was bound to be fatal to their promising relationship.

"Not much to tell you there. I'm the oldest of four boys. My great-grandfather came to California from Germany in search of lumber. He died here and left the land to his son." He paused and glanced at her. "What about you?"

She pressed her lips tightly together. For all her desire for honesty and despite her earlier resolution, when it came time to reveal the truth about her family, she found she couldn't. The bright, healthy color the wind and the sun had given her cheeks was washed swiftly away, leaving her unnaturally pale.

"I've got one older brother, Charlie." She swallowed tightly. "I don't think you'd like him."

"Why not?"

She lifted one petite shoulder. "He's . . . well, he's something of a stuffed shirt."

"Lawyer type."

She nodded, wanting to change the subject. "How much longer before I lure another fish to my bait?"

"Patience," Breed said, his back to her.

Her eyes fluttered closed. Her heart was pounding so hard she was sure he would notice. Unwittingly, he had given good advice. She had to be patient. Someday soon, when the time was right, she would tell him everything.

# Six

———✦———

The stars were twinkling like diamond chips in an ebony sky. The water lapped lightly against the side of Breed's boat, which, sails lowered, rocked gently in the murky water of San Francisco Bay. Four pairs of eager eyes gazed into the night sky, anticipating the next rocket burst to explode into a thousand shooting stars and briefly light up the heavens.

"I love the Fourth of July," Elizabeth murmured. Breed sat beside her, his arm draped casually over her shoulder. Gilly and Peter sat on the other side of the boat, holding hands. They might not be in love, but as Gilly had explained, they were certainly good friends.

One burst after another brightened the sky. Breed had said something earlier that week about going to Candlestick Park to watch the fireworks, but once the four of them had piled into Breed's sedan, they discovered that the traffic heading for the park was horrendous. He'd suggested that they take his sailboat into the bay and observe the fireworks from there, instead, an idea that had been met with enthusiasm by the others.

For nearly a week Breed had taken Elizabeth out on his boat every night after work. Sometimes they fished, depending on how much time they had and what their plans were afterward. He had led her forward a couple of times to raise and lower the sails. She loved to sail as much as he did, and the time they shared on the water had become the high point of her day. They talked openly, argued over politics, discussed books. He challenged her ideas on conservation and pollution, forcing her to stop and think about things she had previously accepted because of what she'd been told by others. Gently, but firmly, he made her form her own opinions. And she loved him for it.

She hadn't told him that she loved him, of course. The emotion was new to her and frightened her a little. The love she'd experienced in the past for her family and friends had been a mixture of respect and admiration. The only person with whom she had ever shared such a close relationship had been her mother. Of course, she would have grieved if her father had been the one who had suffered the stroke and died. But her mother had been her soulmate.

The love she felt for Breed went beyond friendship. Her love was fiery and intense, and the physical desire was sometimes overwhelming. Yet the joy she felt in his arms exceeded desire. Yes, she wanted him. More than that, she wanted to give herself to him. He must have known that, but he never allowed their lovemaking to go beyond a certain point. She didn't know why he was holding himself back. Not that she minded; that aspect of their relationship was only a small part of her feelings. When they could speak openly and honestly about their feelings and their commitment to each other, then they could deal with the physical aspect of their relationship. Her love went so much deeper. In analyzing her feelings, she thought that they also met on a higher plane, a spiritual one. Perhaps because of that, he felt it was too soon to talk about certain things. In some ways, they didn't need to.

She often wanted to talk to Gilly about her feelings, but she wasn't sure her friend, who was so much younger, would understand. If her mother had been alive, Elizabeth could have spoken to her. But she wasn't, and Elizabeth was forced to keep the inexplicable intensity of this relationship buried deep within her heart.

The only thing that marred her happiness was the sensation that something was troubling Breed. She'd tried to question him once and run up against a granite wall. Lately he'd been brooding and thoughtful. Although he hadn't said anything, she was fairly certain he'd lost his job. His hours had been flexible in the past, but lately he'd been coming into the Patisserie at all hours. Some days he even came in the morning and then again in the afternoon. Another thing she'd noticed was that they rarely ate in restaurants anymore. All the things they did together were inexpensive. Every Sunday they returned to Sigmund Stern Grove for the free concert. They took long walks on the beach and sailed almost daily. His apparent financial problems created others, effectively killing her desire to tell him about her background. How could she talk about her family's money without sounding insensitive? She had no doubt that the information could ruin what they shared.

When she glanced up from her musings she noted that Peter's arm was around Gilly, who had her head pressed against his shoulder. The look in Gilly's eyes seemed troubled, although Elizabeth realized she could have misread it in the reflected moonlight.

"Gilly, are you feeling okay?" she felt obliged to ask.

Gilly straightened. "Of course. Why shouldn't I be?"

"You're so quiet."

"I think we should enjoy the novelty," Peter interjected. "Once ol' motormouth gets going, it's hard to shut her up."

"Motormouth?" Gilly returned indignantly, poking Peter in his ribs. Peter laughed and the joking resumed, but not before Elizabeth witnessed the pain in her friend's expression.

An hour later, she helped Breed stow the sails after docking. Gilly and Peter carried the picnic basket and blankets to the car.

"Something's bothering Gilly," Elizabeth murmured to Breed the minute their friends were out of hearing distance.

"I noticed that, too," he whispered conspiratorially. "I think she's falling in love with Peter."

"No." She shook her head decisively. "They're just good friends."

"It may have started out like that, but it's not that way anymore." He sounded completely confident. He hardly paused as he moved forward to store the sails.

Elizabeth followed him. "What makes you so sure Gilly's in love?"

A weary look stole across his features. "She has that look about her." From his tone, she could tell he didn't want to discuss the subject further.

"Apparently you've seen that look in a lot of women's eyes," she stated teasingly, though with a serious undertone.

"A few," he responded noncommittally.

The thought of him loving another woman produced a curious ache in her heart. She paused and straightened. *So this is jealousy,* she mused. This churning sensation in the pit of her stomach, this inexplicable pain in her chest. As crazy as it seemed, she was jealous of some nameless other woman.

Breed's hand at her elbow brought her back to the present. He took her hand as he stepped onto the dock. "Peter and Gilly are waiting."

The silence coming from the backseat of the car where Gilly and Peter were sitting was heavy and unnatural. A storm cloud seemed to have settled in the sedan, the air heavy with electricity. Breed captured Elizabeth's gaze and arched his brows in question.

She motioned weakly with her hand, telling him she had no more idea of what had happened between their friends than he did. Twice she attempted to start a conversation, but her words were met with uninterested grunts.

Breed pulled up and parked in front of the apartment she and Gilly shared. As he was helping Elizabeth, Gilly practically jumped from the car.

"Night, everyone," she said in a voice that was high-pitched and wobbly.

"Gilly, wait up. I want to talk to you." Peter bolted

after her, his eyes filled with frustration. He cast Breed and Elizabeth an apologetic look on his way past.

Breed glanced at Elizabeth and shrugged. "I'd say those two need some time alone."

"I agree."

"Do you want to go for a drive?" he suggested, tucking her hand under his folded arm as he led her back to the sedan.

"How about a walk instead? After sailing all evening, I could use some exercise."

He turned her in his arms. "We could. But I'd rather drive up to Coit Tower and show you the city lights. The view is fabulous."

Spending time alone with Breed was far more appealing than watching the city lights. "I'd like that," she admitted, getting back inside the car.

A long, winding drive through a dense neighborhood led to the observation tower situated high above the city. He parked, and as she stared out the windshield she realized that he hadn't exaggerated the view. She had seen some of the most beautiful landscapes in the world, but sitting with Breed overlooking San Francisco, she couldn't recall one more beautiful. Words couldn't describe the wonder of what lay before her.

"It's late," he murmured against her hair.

She acknowledged his words with a short nod, but she didn't want to leave and didn't suggest it.

"You have to work tomorrow." His voice was rough and soft, more of an aching whisper.

A smile touched her eyes. Breed couldn't decide if they should stay or go. Alone in the dark with nothing to distract them, the temptations were too great.

She tipped her head back. "Let me worry about tomorrow. I'll survive," she assured him. The night shaded his eyes, but she could feel the tension in him. His breathing was faintly irregular. "Why do you want to leave so much?" she asked in a throbbing whisper.

Her question went unanswered. A long moment of silence followed as he gazed down on her. Gently, he brushed the wispy strands of hair from her cheek, then curled his fingers into her hair. Elizabeth was shocked to realize he was trembling.

Slowly his head moved downward and paused an inch above her lips. "You know why we should leave," he growled.

All day she had yearned for him. Not for the first time, she noticed that he had been physically distant today, his touch casual, as though he was struggling to hold himself back. His restraint made her want him all the more.

"Beth." He whispered her name, and something snapped within him. His mouth plundered hers, and all her senses came to life. She rose slightly from the seat to press closer to him.

A tiny moan slipped from her as his lips found her neck and shot wave after wave of sensual delight through her. Her hands roamed his back, then moved forward and unfastened his shirt. Eagerly she let them glide down the smooth flat muscles of his broad chest.

He groaned and straightened, then buried his face in her neck and held her to him. "Beth . . ." he moaned. She could feel and see the conflict in his eyes.

He rubbed one hand across his face and eyes, but he

continued to hold her tightly to him with the other, as though he couldn't bear to release her yet.

His control was almost frightening. The marvel of it silenced her for several seconds.

With her arms linked behind his head, she pressed her forehead to his.

The tension eased from his muscles, and she could hear the uneven thud of his heart slowly return to normal. When his breathing was less ragged, she lightly pressed her lips to his.

"Don't do that," he said harshly, abruptly releasing her. The tension in him was barely suppressed.

She turned away and leaned her head against the back of the seat, staring straight ahead. When tears of anger and frustration filled her eyes, she blinked hurriedly to forestall their flow.

"There's only so much of this a man can take." He, too, stared straight ahead as he savagely rubbed his hand along the back of his neck. "You know as well as I do what's happening between us."

"I can't help it, Breed," she whispered achingly.

"Yes, you can," he returned grimly.

The aching desire to reach across the close confines of the car and touch him was unbearable. But she didn't dare. She couldn't look at him. "Is . . . is there something wrong with me?" she asked in a tortured whisper. "I mean, do my freckles turn you off . . . or something?" Out of the corner of her eye, she saw a muscle twitch in his lean jaw.

"That question isn't worthy of an answer." His eyes hardened as he turned the ignition key and revved the engine.

"Maybe we should stop seeing so much of each other." Her pride was hurt, but the ache extended deep into her heart.

"Maybe we should," he said at last.

Elizabeth closed her eyes against the onrush of emotional pain. One tear escaped and made a wet track down her pale face, followed by another and another.

When he pulled up in front of her apartment building, she didn't turn to him to say good night. She didn't want him to see her tears. That would only humiliate her further.

"Thanks for a lovely day," she whispered, barely able to find her voice; then she hurriedly opened the door and raced into the apartment foyer.

Breed didn't follow her, but he didn't leave either. His car was still parked outside when Elizabeth reached her apartment and, from deep within the living-room shadows, glanced out the window to watch him. The streetlight silhouetted a dejected figure of a man leaning over the steering wheel.

After a moment she realized that soft, whimpering cries were coming from the bedroom. Trapped in her own problems, she had forgotten Gilly's.

Wiping the moisture from her cheeks, she turned and headed down the hall to knock against her friend's open bedroom door.

"Gilly," she whispered, "what's wrong?"

Gilly sat up on her bed and blew noisily into a tissue. "Beth, I am so stupid."

"If you want to talk, I have all the time in the world to listen." She entered the darkened room and sat on the end of the bed. With all the problems she was having, she chastised herself for not recognizing what had been happening to her friend.

Gilly took another tissue and wiped her eyes dry. "Do you remember how I told you that Peter and I are just friends?"

"I remember."

"Well . . ." Gilly sniffled noisily, "something changed. I don't know when or why, but sometime last week I looked at Peter and I knew I loved him."

Elizabeth patted Gilly's hand. "That's no reason to cry. I'd think you'd be happy."

"I was, for two glorious days. I wanted to tell someone, but I didn't think it was fair to confide in you. I thought Peter should be the first one to know."

Her roommate *had* appeared exceptionally happy lately, Elizabeth recalled. Gilly had been particularly enthusiastic about the four of them spending the holiday together. She hadn't really thought much about it, though, because Gilly was always happy.

"Then I made the mistake of telling him," she continued. "You were helping Breed put the sails away, and Peter and I were carrying things to the car." She inhaled a quivering breath.

"What happened?" Elizabeth encouraged her roommate softly.

"I guess I should have waited for a more appropriate moment, but I was eager to talk to him. Everything about the day had been perfect, and we were alone for the first time. So, like an idiot, I turned to him and said, 'Peter, I don't know what's happened, but I love you.'"

"And?"

"First he looked shocked. Then embarrassed. He

stuttered something about this being a surprise and looked like he wanted to run away, but then you and Breed returned and we all piled into the car."

"What happened when Breed dropped the two of you off here?"

"Nothing. I wouldn't talk to him."

"Gilly!"

"You wouldn't have wanted to talk, either," she insisted, defending her actions. "I was humiliated enough without Peter apologizing to me because he didn't share my feelings."

"I'm sure he's going to want to talk to you." Elizabeth appealed to the more reasonable part of her friend's nature.

"He can forget it. How could I have been so stupid? If I was going to fall in love, why couldn't it be with someone like Breed?"

Elizabeth lowered her gaze to her hands. "There's only one Breed, and he's mine."

"Oh, before I forget . . ." Gilly sat up and looked around her, finally handing Elizabeth a piece of paper with a phone number written across the top. "Your brother phoned."

"My brother? From Boston?"

"No, he's here in San Francisco. He's staying at the Saint Francis. I told him I didn't know what time you'd be back, so he said to tell you that he'd expect you tomorrow night for dinner at seven-thirty at his hotel."

Ordering instead of asking. That sounded just like her brother.

"Did he say anything else?" It would be just like Charlie to say something to embarrass her.

Gilly shook her head. "Not really, except . . ."

"Yes?" Elizabeth stiffened.

"Well, your brother's not like you, is he?"

"How do you mean?" Elizabeth asked.

"I don't know, exactly. But after I hung up, I wondered if I should have curtsied or something."

After a single telephone conversation, the astute Gilly had her brother pegged. "He's like that," Elizabeth admitted.

"Well, anyway, I gave you the message."

"And I'll show up at the hotel and hope I use the right spoon or my dear brother will be outraged."

For the first time that evening, Gilly smiled.

The café hadn't been open for more than five minutes when Breed strolled in and sat at his regular table. Elizabeth caught sight of his broad shoulders the moment he entered. Even after all these weeks her heart stirred at the sight of him, and now it throbbed painfully. One part of her wanted to rush to him, but she resisted.

Carrying the coffeepot, she approached his table slowly. He turned over the ceramic mug for her.

"Morning," she said as unemotionally as possible.

"Morning," he echoed.

Her eyes refused to meet his, but she could feel his gaze concentrating on her. "Would you like a menu?"

"No, just coffee."

She filled his cup.

"We need to talk," he announced casually as his hands folded around the cup.

She blinked uncertainly. "I can't now," she replied nervously. "Mornings are our busiest time."

"I didn't mean now." The words were enunciated slowly, as if his control over his patience had been stretched to the limit. "Tonight would be better, when we're able to discuss things freely, don't you think?"

She shifted her weight from one foot to the other. "I can't," she murmured apologetically. "My brother's in town, and I'm meeting him for dinner."

His level gaze darted to her, his eyes disbelieving.

"It's true," she declared righteously. "We're meeting at the Saint Francis."

"I believe you."

Frustrated, she watched as a hard mask stole over his face. "Go have dinner with your brother, then."

"I wasn't waiting for your approval," Elizabeth remarked angrily.

His amber eyes blazed for a furious second. "I didn't think you were."

Indecision made her hesitate. She wanted to turn and give him a clear view of her back, yet at the same time she wanted to set things right between them. The harmony they'd shared so often over these past weeks was slowly disintegrating before her eyes.

"Would you care to join us?" The question slipped from her naturally, although her mind was screaming for him to refuse.

"Me?" He looked aghast. "You don't mean that."

"I wouldn't have asked you otherwise." What, she wondered, had she been thinking? The entire evening would be a disaster. She could just imagine Charlie's reaction to someone like Breed.

Breed appeared to give her invitation some consideration. "No," he said at last, and she couldn't prevent the low but controlled breath of relief. "Maybe another time."

"Do you want to meet later?" she asked, and her voice thinned to a quavering note. "Dinner shouldn't take long," she said, glancing down at her practical white shoes. "I want to talk to you, too."

"Not tonight." The lines bracketing his mouth deepened with his growing impatience. Although she'd asked him to join her and Charlie, she realized that he knew she didn't want him there. "I'll give you a call later in the week." He stood, and with determined strides left the café.

She watched him go and had the irrational urge to throw his untouched coffee after him. That arrogant male pride of his only fueled her anger.

That night Elizabeth dressed carefully in a raspberry-colored dress with a delicate white miniprint. A dress that would meet with Charlie's approval, she mused as she examined herself in the mirror. Not until it was time to go did she stop to consider why he was in town. The family had no business holdings on the West Coast. At least none that she knew about. She hoped he hadn't come to persuade her to return to Boston. She'd just about made up her mind to make San Francisco her permanent home. The city was lovely, and the thought of leaving Breed was intolerable. She wouldn't—couldn't— leave the man she loved.

The taxi delivered her to the entrance of the prestigious hotel at precisely seven-twenty. The extra minutes gave her the necessary time to compose herself. She was determined to make this a pleasant evening. A confrontation with her brother was the last thing she wanted.

"Lizzy."

She groaned inwardly. Only one person in the world called her that.

"Hello, Siggy." She forced herself to smile and extended her hand for him to shake. To her acute embarrassment, he pulled her into his arms and kissed her soundly. Her mouth was opened in surprise, and Siggy seemed to assume she was eager for his attention and deepened the kiss.

Without making a scene, Elizabeth was left to endure his despicable touch.

The sound of someone clearing his throat appeared to bring Siggy back to his senses. He broke the contact, and it was all Elizabeth could do not to rub the feel of his mouth from hers with the back of her hand. His touch made her skin crawl, and she glared angrily from him to her brother.

"There are better places for such an intimate greeting," Charlie said, slapping Siggy on the back. "I told you she'd be happy to see you."

Siggy ignored Charlie and said, "It's good to see you, Lizzy."

She was unable to restrain her involuntary grimace. "Don't call me Lizzy," she said between clenched teeth.

Charlie glanced at his slim gold watch. "Our table should be ready. Names are something I'll leave for you two to discuss later."

*Later.* She cringed at the thought. There wasn't going

to be a later with Siggy, though at least now she understood why Charlie had come to San Francisco. He wanted to foist Siggy on her. She hadn't thought about it at the time, but Charlie had mentioned Siggy at every opportunity lately. That was the reason she'd found herself avoiding her brother, who stood to benefit from any marriage between the two families. His selfishness made her want to cry.

By some miracle she was able to endure the meal. She spoke only when a question was directed to her and smiled politely at appropriate intervals. The knot in her throat extended all the way to her abdomen and felt like a rock in the pit of her stomach. The two men discussed her at length, commenting several times on how good she looked. Charlie insisted that she would make a radiant bride and declared that their father would be proud of her, knowing she had chosen so well. He made marriage between her and Siggy sound like a foregone conclusion. Questions buzzed around her head like irritating bees. In the past she'd had her differences with her father, but he wouldn't do this to her. She had to believe that. Yet her father *had* mentioned Siggy during their last few telephone conversations.

Resignedly, she accompanied her brother and Siggy to Charlie's suite for an after-dinner drink.

The small glass of liqueur helped chase the chill from her slender frame. Siggy sat on the plush sofa beside her and draped his arm possessively around her shoulders. She found his touch suffocating and pointedly removed his arm, then scooted to the other end of the sofa. Undaunted, he followed.

"I can see that you two have a lot to discuss," Charlie

said, exchanging knowing smiles with the younger man. Without another word, he excused himself and left Elizabeth alone to deal with Siggy. The moment the door clicked closed, Siggy was on her like a starving man after food.

Pinned against the corner of the couch, she jerked her head left and right in an effort to avoid his punishing kiss.

"Siggy!" she gasped, pushing him off her. "Stop it!"

Composing himself, Siggy sat upright and made a pretense of straightening his tie. "I'm sorry, Lizzy. It's just that I love you so much. I've wanted you for years, and now I know you feel the same way."

"What?" she exploded.

Siggy brushed a stray hair from her flushed cheek. "Charlie told me how you've had a crush on me for years. Why didn't you say something? You must have known how I feel about you. I've never made any secret of that."

A lump of outrage and shocked disbelief grew in her. Charlie had selfishly and maliciously lied to Siggy. Her own brother had sold her for thirty pieces of silver. She was nothing more to Charlie than the means of securing a financial coup that would link two wealthy families.

"Where is my brother?" Elizabeth managed finally. "I'd like to talk to him."

"He'll be back," Siggy said, as he stood, crossed the room and helped himself to another glass of brandy. "He wanted to give us some time alone. Want some, darling?" He held up the brandy and eyed her solicitously.

"No." Irritated, she shook her head. "So what would happen to the two companies if our families were linked?"

Smug and secure, Siggy silently toasted her. "A merger. It will be the financial feat of the year, Charlie says. My family will give him the exclusive distribution contract for our stores. Already we're planning to expand within a three-state area."

Momentarily shocked, Elizabeth felt tears form in her eyes. It was little wonder that Charlie was doing this. A lucrative—and exclusive—contract with Siggy's family's chain of department stores was something the Wainwrights had sought for years. But the price was far too high. Her happiness was not a bargaining chip.

Charlie returned a few minutes later, looking pleased and excited.

"If you'll excuse us a minute, Siggy," Elizabeth said bluntly, "I'd like to talk to my brother. Alone."

"Sure." Siggy glanced from brother to sister before setting his drink aside. "I'll be in the lounge when you're finished."

The second the door clicked closed, Elizabeth whirled on her brother. "How could you?" she demanded.

Charlie knotted his fists at his sides. "Listen, little sister, you're not going to ruin this for me. Not this time."

"Charlie, I'm your only sister. How could you ask me to marry a man I don't love? A man I don't even respect . . ."

His mouth tightened grimly. "For once in your life, stop thinking of yourself."

"Me?"

"Yes, you." He paced the floor in short, angry strides. "All right, I admit I went about this poorly, but marrying Siggy is what Mother would have wanted for you."

"That's not true." Her mother knew her feelings

about Siggy and would never have pressured her into something like this.

"What do you know?" He hurled the words at her furiously. "You only thought of yourself. You never knew what Mother was really thinking. It was your selfishness that killed her."

The blood drained from Elizabeth's face. She and her mother had spent the afternoon shopping, and when they got back her mother, who wasn't feeling well, had gone to lie down before dinner. Within an hour she was dead, the victim of a massive stroke. In the back of her mind, she had always carried the guilt that something she had done that day had caused her death.

"Charlie, please," she whispered frantically. "Don't say that. Please don't say that."

"But it's true!" he shouted. "I was with father when the doctor said that having you drag her from store to store was simply too much. It killed her. *You* killed her."

"Oh, dear God." She felt her knees buckle as she slumped onto the sofa.

"There's only one thing you can do now to make up for that, Elizabeth. Do what Mother would have wanted. Marry Siggy. It would have made her happy."

He was lying. In her soul, she knew he was lying. But her own flesh and blood, her only brother, whom she had loved and adored in her youth, had used the cruelest weapon in his arsenal against her. With hot tears scalding her cheeks, she stood, clenched her purse to her breast, and walked out the door.

She didn't stop walking until she found a taxi. Between breathless but controlled sobs, she gave the cabbie her address. Not until he pulled away from the curb did she realize how badly she was shaking.

"Are you all right, lady?" The cabbie looked at her anxiously in the rearview mirror.

She couldn't manage anything more than a nod.

When they arrived in front of her apartment, she handed him a twenty-dollar bill and didn't wait for the change. Though she had calmed down slightly on the ride home, she didn't want Gilly to see her, so she hurried in the door and headed for her bedroom.

"You're back soon." The sound of the television drifted from the living room.

"Yes," Elizabeth mumbled, keeping her head lowered, not wanting her friend to see her tears. She continued walking. "I think I'll take a bath and go to bed."

Gilly must have looked up for the first time. The sound of her surprised gasp was like an assault, and Elizabeth flinched. "Elizabeth! Good grief, what's wrong?"

"Nothing." Elizabeth looked at the wall. "I'm fine. I just need to be alone." She went into the bedroom and closed the door, leaning against it. Reaction set in, and she started to shake uncontrollably again. Fresh tears followed. Tears of anger. Tears of hate. Tears of pain and pride.

Softly Gilly knocked on the closed bedroom door, but Elizabeth ignored her. She didn't want to explain. She couldn't, not when she was crying like this. She fell into bed and curled up in a tight ball in an attempt to control the freezing cold that made her shake so violently.

When she inhaled between sobs, she heard Gilly talking to someone. Her friend's voice was slightly high-pitched and worried. She felt guilty that she was worrying

Gilly like this, but she couldn't help it. Later she would make up some excuse. But she couldn't now.

Five minutes later there was another knock on her door. Elizabeth ignored it.

"Beth," a male voice said softly. "Open up. It's me."

"Breed," she sobbed, throwing back the covers. "Oh, Breed." She opened the door and fell into his arms, weeping uncontrollably. Every part of her clung to him as he lifted her into his arms and carried her into the living room.

With an infinite gentleness he set her on the couch and brushed the hair from her face.

One look at her and he stiffened. "Who did this to you?"

# Seven

—m—

Elizabeth was crying so hard that she couldn't answer. Nor did she know how to explain. She didn't want to tell Breed and Gilly that the brother she loved had betrayed her in the worst possible way.

Breed said something to Gilly, but Elizabeth didn't hear. "Beth," he whispered, leading her to the couch and half lifting her onto his lap. "Tell me what's upset you."

Forcefully, she shook her head and inhaled deep breaths that became quivering sobs as she tried to regain control of herself. Crying like this was only making matters worse.

She knew the terrible, crippling pain of Charlie's betrayal was there in her eyes, and she couldn't do anything to conceal it. A nerve twitched in Breed's hard, lean jaw, his features tense, and pain showed clearly in his eyes. *Her* pain. She was suffering, and that caused him to hurt as well. She couldn't have loved anyone more than she loved him right at that moment. She didn't know what he thought had happened, and she couldn't utter a word to assure him.

"I'm fine. No one hurt me . . . not physically," she finally said in a trembling voice she barely recognized as her own. "Just hold me." She had trouble trying to control her breathing. Her body continued to shake with every inhalation.

"I'll never let you go," he promised as his lips moved against her hair. She felt some of the tension leave him, felt his relief that things weren't as bad as he'd thought.

Warm blankets were wrapped around her, so warm they must have recently been taken from the dryer. That must be what Breed had asked Gilly to do, Elizabeth realized.

He continued to talk to her in a low, soothing tone until her eyes drifted closed. Caught between sleep and reality, she could feel him gently free himself from her embrace and lay her on the sofa. A pillow cushioned her head, and warm blankets surrounded her. She didn't know how long he knelt beside her, smoothing her hair from her face, his touch so tender she felt secure and protected. Gradually a calmness filled her, and she knew she was on the brink of falling asleep. Breed left her side but she sensed that he hadn't gone far. He had told her he wouldn't leave, and she was comforted just by knowing he was in the same room.

"All I know," Elizabeth heard Gilly whisper, "was that she was meeting her brother for dinner. What could he have done to cause this?"

"You can bet I'm going to find out," Breed stated in a dry, hard voice that was frightening in its intensity.

"No." Elizabeth struggled to a sitting position. "Just drop the whole thing. It's my own affair."

Breed's eyes narrowed.

"Elizabeth," Gilly murmured, her eyes wide and worried, "I've never seen you like this."

"I'm fine, really." She brushed back her tear-dampened hair. "I'm just upset. I apologize for making a scene."

"You didn't make a scene," Gilly returned soothingly.

Breed brought her a damp cloth and, kneeling at her side, gently brushed it over her cheeks. It felt cool and soothing over her hot skin. His jaw was clenched and pale, as if he couldn't stand to have her hurt in any way, physically or emotionally.

Elizabeth stroked the side of his face, then pulled him to her, wrapping her arms around his neck. "Thank you."

"For what? I should have been there for you."

"You couldn't have known." It wasn't right that he should shoulder any blame for what had happened.

He took her hands and gently raised them to his mouth, then kissed her knuckles. "Beth . . ." His eyes implored hers. "I want you to trust me enough to tell me what happened tonight."

She lowered her gaze and shook her head. "It's done. I don't want to go over it."

The pressure on her fingers was punishing for a quick second. "I'll kill anyone who hurts you like this again."

"That's exactly why I won't talk about it."

The tension between them was so palpable that she could taste it. Their eyes clashed in a test of wills. Unnerved, she lowered hers first. "I need you here," she whispered in a soft plea. "It's over now. I want to forget it ever happened."

Gilly hovered close. "Do you feel like you could drink something? Tea? Coffee? Soda?"

The effort to smile was painful. "All I want is a hot bath and bed." Her muscles ached, and she discovered that when she stood, her legs wobbled unsteadily, so she leaned against Breed for a moment.

Gilly hurried ahead and filled the bathtub with steaming, scented water. Next she brought in fluffy, fresh towels.

"You want me to stay in the bathroom while you soak?" Breed asked, and a crooked smile slanted his mouth, because of course he knew the answer. The humor didn't quite touch his eyes, but Elizabeth appreciated the effort.

"No. If I need anyone, Gilly can help."

"Pity," he grumbled.

The hot water helped relieve the aching tension in her muscles. Even now her body was coiled and alert. The throbbing in her temples diminished, and the pain in her heart began to recede. As she rested against the back of the tub, she kept running over the details of the evening, but she forced the painful images to the back of her mind. She didn't feel strong enough emotionally to deal with things now. Maybe tomorrow.

Gilly stayed with her, more on Breed's insistence than because she felt Elizabeth needed her. Together they emerged from the steam-filled bathroom, Elizabeth wrapped in her thick robe. Breed led Elizabeth into her room. The sheets on her bed had been folded back, and her weak smile silently thanked him.

"You won't leave me?" Her eyes pleaded with him as he tucked her under the covers.

"No," he whispered. "I said I wouldn't." His kiss was so tender that fresh tears misted her eyes. "Go to sleep," he whispered encouragingly.

"You'll be here when I wake up?" She needed that reassurance.

"I'll be here."

The dark void was already pulling her into its welcoming arms. As she drifted into sleep, she could hear Breed's low voice quizzing Gilly.

The sound of someone obviously trying to be quiet and not succeeding woke Elizabeth. The room was dark, and she glanced at her clock radio to note that it was just after three. She sat up in bed and blinked. The memory of the events of the evening pressed heavily against her heart. Although she was confident Charlie would never have abandoned her to Siggy if her brother had known what Siggy was capable of doing, the sense of betrayal remained. To try to push her off on Siggy was deplorable enough. Slipping from between the sheets, she put on her silk housecoat and moved into the living room.

"Hello there," she whispered to Breed, keeping quiet so she wouldn't disrupt Gilly's sleep.

"Did I wake you?" He sat up and wiped a hand across his weary face. The sight of him trying to sleep on the couch was ludicrous. His feet dangled far over the end, and he looked all elbows and arms.

"You wake me? Never. I thought an elephant had escaped and was raging through the living room."

His smile was evident in the moonlight. "I got up to use the bathroom and walked into the lamp," he explained with a chagrined look.

"It was selfish of me to ask you to stay," she said, sitting down beside him.

"I would have stayed whether you asked me to or not." He reached for her hand and squeezed it gently. "How do you feel?"

She shrugged and lowered her gaze to her knees. "Like a fool. I don't usually overreact that way."

"I know," he murmured. "That's what concerned me most." He put his arm around her, and she rested her head against his shoulder. "Sometimes the emotional pain can be twice as bad as anything physical." She gave a long, drawn-out yawn. "When you love and trust someone and they hurt you, then the pain goes beyond anything physical." She began explaining the situation to Breed, though carefully tiptoeing around any discussion of her family's wealth. He'd asked her to trust him, and she did, at least with her feelings. It was important that he realize that.

He didn't comment, but she felt him stiffen slightly. When she leaned against his solid support, he pulled her close, holding her to his chest.

Soon the comfort of his arms lured her back to sleep. When she woke again, she discovered that they had both fallen asleep while sitting upright. His arm was still draped around her, and he rested his head against the back of the sofa. His breathing was deep and undisturbed.

Even from a sitting position, waking up in Breed's arms felt right. She pressed her face against the side of his neck and kissed him, enjoying the light taste of salt and musk.

"Are you pretending to be Sleeping Beauty kissing the handsome prince to wake him?" he asked, opening one eye to study her.

She barely allowed his sideways glance to touch her before straightening. "You've got that tale confused. It was the prince who kissed Sleeping Beauty awake."

"Would it hurt you if I did?" The teasing left his voice as he brought her closer within the protective circle of his arms.

Her eyes sought his. "You could never hurt me," she said in a whisper that sounded as solemn as a vow.

"I don't ever want to," he murmured as his lips claimed hers. The kiss was gentle and sweet. His mouth barely touched hers, enhancing the sensuality of the contact. His hands framed her face, and he treated her as if he were handling a rare and exotic orchid.

"You're looking much more chipper this morning," Gilly said, standing in the doorway of her bedroom. She raised her hands high above her head and yawned.

"I feel a whole lot better."

"I'm happy to hear that. I don't mind telling you that you had me worried."

"You?" Breed inhaled harshly. "I don't think I've ever come closer to wanting to kill a man. It's a good thing you didn't tell who did this last night, Beth. I wouldn't have been responsible for my actions."

Elizabeth lowered her gaze to the hands folded primly in her lap. "I think I already knew that."

"Take the day off," Gilly insisted as she sauntered into the kitchen and started the coffee.

"I can't do that," Elizabeth objected strenuously. "You need me."

"I'll make do," Gilly returned confidently. She opened the refrigerator, took out a pitcher of orange juice and poured herself a small glass. "But only for today."

Elizabeth returned to her bedroom to change clothes. When she studied herself in the mirror she saw no outward mark of what she'd been through, but the mirror couldn't reveal the inner agony of what Charlie had tried to do.

"I don't believe it," she grumbled as she walked into the living room. "Last night I wanted to die, and today I feel like the luckiest woman alive to have you two as my friends."

"We're the lucky ones," Gilly said sincerely.

"But I acted like such a fool. I can't imagine what you thought."

"You were shocked, upset," Breed insisted with a note of confidence. "Shock often exaggerates the messages transmitted to the brain."

"Such a know-it-all," Gilly complained, running a brush through her short, bouncy curls. She looked at Elizabeth with a mischievous gleam. "Why do you put up with him?"

Elizabeth shrugged and shook her head. "I don't know. But he's kinda cute."

"I amuse you, is that it?" Breed joined in the teasing banter.

"You're amusing, but not always correct," Elizabeth

remarked jokingly. "My brain wasn't confused by shock. But I'll admit, you had me going there for a minute."

He had the grace to look faintly embarrassed. "Well, it sounded good at the time."

Gilly paused on her way out the door. "Have a good day, you two. Call if you need anything. And"—she hesitated and lowered her gaze—"don't hold up dinner for me."

"Working late?" Elizabeth quizzed, experiencing a twinge of guilt that her friend would be stuck at the café alone.

Gilly shook her head. "Peter said he'd be coming by, and I don't want to be here when he does."

"Honestly, Gilly, you're acting like a child."

"Maybe." Gilly admitted. "But at least I've got my pride."

Breed murmured something about pride doing little to keep her warm at night, but luckily Gilly was too far away to hear him.

The door clicked, indicating Gilly had left for work.

"Are you hungry?" Breed asked as he walked across the living room, his hands buried deep inside his pants pockets.

She hadn't eaten much of her dinner the previous night, but even so, she discovered she didn't have much of an appetite. "Not really."

"What you need is something scintillating to tempt you."

Wickedly batting her eyelashes, she glanced at him and softly said, "My dear Mr. Breed, what exactly do you have in mind?"

He chose to ignore the comment.

"I think I'll go over to my place to shower and change. When I come back, I'll bring us breakfast."

Her mouth dropped in mute surprise. She couldn't believe he hadn't risen to her bait, and, selfishly, she didn't want him to leave her alone. Not now. "I'll come with you," she suggested eagerly. "And while you're in the shower, I'll cook us breakfast."

His expression revealed his lack of enthusiasm for her suggestion. "Not this time."

She bristled. "Why not?" The memory of her last visit to his apartment remained vivid. She hadn't been imagining things. He really didn't want her there. And yet she couldn't imagine why.

"You need to stay here and rest."

Her eyes widened in bewildered protest.

"I was thinking that while I'm gone you can get an extra hour's sleep."

Sleep? She was dressed and had downed a cup of strong coffee. He didn't honestly expect her to go back to bed, did he?

"I won't be long," he told her, and without a backward glance he hurried out the door.

"Don't worry about breakfast. I'll have something ready when you come back," she called after him. She didn't like this situation, but there wasn't much she could do. The impulse to speak her mind died on her lips. Now wasn't the time to confront Breed with petty suspicions about her cool welcome at his apartment.

With a cookbook resting on the kitchen counter, she skimmed over the recipe for blueberry muffins. For the moment, keeping busy was paramount. When she stopped to think, too many dark images crowded her

thoughts. For a time last night she had started to believe
Charlie's vindictive words, which fed on the fear that she
was somehow responsible for her mother's death, which
had haunted her ever since that awful day. When a tear
escaped, despite her determination not to cry, she wiped
it aside angrily and forced herself to concentrate on the
recipe. Rehashing the details of last night only upset her,
so she soundly rejected any more introspection on the
subject.

As promised, Breed returned less than an hour later.

A hand on each of her shoulders, he kissed her lightly
on the cheek. He looked wonderful, his hair still wet
from his shower.

"Hmm . . . something smells good."

"I baked some muffins," she said as she led the way
into the kitchen. Her culinary efforts were cooling on a
rack on top of the counter. "I don't know how they taste.
The cookbook said they were great to take camping."

"Are you thinking of taking me into the woods and
ravaging my body?" he joked as he lifted a muffin from
the cooling rack. It burned his fingers, and he gingerly
tossed it in the air several times until, laughing, she
handed him a plate.

"You might have told me they were still hot."

"And miss seeing you juggle? Never." Her mood had
lightened to match his. Sitting beside him at the circular
table, she peeled an orange and popped a section into her
mouth.

"How about a trip to our beach today?" he suggested,
and his mouth curved into a sensuous smile.

"Sure." Her glance caught sight of his massive hands.
A slight swelling in one of the knuckles captured her at-

tention. Had he been fighting? Showering wouldn't have taken him an hour. Immediately the thought flashed through her mind that he'd gone to see her brother. "Breed . . ." Her eyes sought his as she swallowed past the thickness lodged in her throat. "Give me your hand."

The teasing glitter didn't leave his eyes, and he didn't seem to notice the serious light in hers. "Is this a proposal of marriage?"

"Let me see your hand," she repeated.

He went completely still. "Why?"

"Because I need to know that you didn't do anything . . . dumb."

He smiled briefly and pushed his chair away from the table, then stood and walked to the other side of the room, folding his arms across his massive chest. Expelling an explosive breath, he replied, "I didn't, although the temptation was strong. While I live, no man will ever treat you that way again."

"I appreciate the chivalry," she said evenly, "but I wish you hadn't."

"I found it . . . necessary." The hard set of his features revealed the tight hold he was keeping on both his temper and his emotions.

Her composure cracked. "I'm not defending him. . . ."

"I should hope not." He shook his head grimly.

"But I don't want you involved," she said.

"I'm already involved."

She stood and, with her own arms folded around her narrow waist, paced the kitchen. The room was filled with Breed. His presence loomed in every corner. "Please understand, I don't want to argue with you."

His eyes narrowed as he moved into the other room

and sat on the arm of the sofa. "I've never met anyone like you, Beth. Those two deserve to have the stuffing kicked out of them."

"He's my brother!" she cried defensively. "He may not be a very nice guy, but he's the only one I've got."

He moved into the living room, his back to her. When he turned to face her again a moment later, his grim look had vanished. "Are we going to the beach or not?"

Numbly, she nodded.

"Good." With long strides he crossed the distance separating them. Then he took her by the shoulders and sweetly kissed her. "Let's hurry. It's isn't every day that I get you all to myself."

They rode in his silver sedan, and again she wondered why he no longer drove Hilda. Maybe the Jeep needed repairs and he couldn't afford to have them done until his finances improved. She wished there was some way she could take care of things like that for him without his knowing. Offering him money wasn't the answer, only a sure way of crushing his male ego. Even so, what was the use of having money if she couldn't spend it the way she wanted?

The surf rolled gently against their bare feet as they strolled along the smooth beach, their arms entwined.

"Tell my about your childhood," he asked curiously after a lengthy, companionable silence.

Under other circumstances she might have had the courage to reveal her wealth. But not today. She'd faced enough upheaval in the last twenty-four hours to warrant caution. Her mouth tightened with tension before she managed to speak.

"What's there to tell? I was born, grew up, went to

school, graduated, went to school some more, dropped out, and traveled a little."

"Nicely condensed, I'd say."

"Have you been to Europe?" she asked, to change the subject.

"No, but I spent six months in New Zealand a few years back." His response told her he knew exactly what she was doing.

"Did you enjoy it?" Relieved, she continued the game.

"I'd say it was the most beautiful country on earth, but I haven't done enough traveling to compare it with the rest of the world."

She recalled her own trip to the South Pacific. Her time in New Zealand had been short, but she'd shared his feelings about the island nation.

"My mother used to love to travel," she commented, mentally recalling the many trips they'd taken together.

"How long has she been gone?" he asked, his hand reaching for hers.

She swallowed with difficulty and forced her chin up in a defensive stance. "She died two years ago," she explained softly. "Even after all this time, I miss her."

He paused, and traced a finger over her jaw and down her neck. "I'm sorry, Beth. You must have loved her very much."

"I did," she whispered on a weak note.

"Did your family ever go camping?" The question came out of the blue and was obviously meant to change the mood.

"No." She had never slept in a tent in her life. Back-to-nature pursuits had never been among her father's interests.

"Would you like to sometime?"

"Us?"

"I was thinking of inviting Gilly along." Gently, his hand closed over hers. "And Peter," he added as an afterthought.

"Peter? You devious little devil."

"Of course, that will take some finagling," he admitted.

"Finagling or downright deception?"

"Deception," he immediately agreed.

"You shock me, Andrew Breed. I wouldn't have guessed that you had a sneaky bone in your body."

His gaze slid past her to the rolling waves that broke against the sand. "I suspect a lot of things about me would shock you," he murmured, and her thoughts echoed his.

"What really irritates me," Gilly continued her tirade as she hauled another box of cooking utensils out from the kitchen, "is the fact that I bare my heart to Peter and then he—he just disappears. It's been three days since I've heard from him. Count 'em, Beth, three long days."

"Well, you slammed the door in his face last time he came over, and you hang up on him whenever he calls."

"Well, he deserves it."

Hands on hips, Gilly surveyed the living-room floor. Half of the contents of their kitchen had been packed into cardboard boxes in anticipation of the weekend camping trip. "Is that everything?"

"Well, I certainly hope so." Elizabeth couldn't believe

that people actually went through all this work just for a couple of days of traipsing around the woods.

When Breed arrived he looked incredulously at the accumulated gear.

"Before you complain, I only packed what was on your list," Elizabeth said as she flashed him an eager smile. She was ready for this new adventure, although she was suffering a few qualms about not telling Gilly that Peter had been invited. In fact, he had left the night before and claimed a space for them in the Samuel P. Taylor State Park, north of the city.

"Well, maybe we packed a few things not on your meager list," Gilly amended. "You left off several things we might need."

"I don't know how Hilda's going to carry all this," Breed mumbled under his breath.

"Hilda," Elizabeth cried happily. "We're taking Hilda?" Before Breed could stop her, she rushed down the stairs to the outdated Jeep parked at the curb. Gingerly she climbed into the front seat and patted the dashboard. "It's good to see you again," she murmured affectionately.

"Will someone kindly tell me what's going on?" Gilly stood, one hand placed on her hip, staring curiously at her friend.

"It's a long story," Breed murmured, lifting the first box on board.

Admittedly it was a tight squeeze, but they managed to fit everything.

The radio blared, and they were all singing along as they traveled. When the news came on, they paused to listen. From her squashed position in the backseat, Gilly leaned forward. "Hey, Breed, I don't see any tent back here."

"There isn't one," he said with a smile, glancing at Elizabeth.

"I thought we were going camping?"

"We are," he confirmed.

"With no tent?"

Elizabeth didn't want to carry the deception any further. "Peter pitched the tent yesterday."

"Peter!" Gilly exploded. "You didn't say anything about Peter coming on this trip."

Elizabeth turned and faced her friend. "Are you mad?"

Gilly's gaze raked Elizabeth's worried face. Folding her arms, she resolutely stared out the window. "Why should I be mad? My best friend in the world has just turned traitor."

"If I'm your best friend, then you have to believe I wouldn't do anything to hurt you," Elizabeth returned with quiet logic.

"I'm not answering that."

"Because I'm right," Elizabeth argued irrefutably.

"Peter loves you," Breed inserted, matching Gilly's clipped tones. "And if it means kidnapping you so that he has the chance to explain himself, then I don't consider that much of a crime."

"I suppose you think that someday I'll thank you for this."

"I want to be maid of honor," Elizabeth said with a romantic sigh.

Gilly ignored her and sat in stony silence until Breed turned off the highway and entered the campgrounds. Peter had left word of his location at the ranger station, and within a matter of minutes they were at the campsite.

"I hope you realize that I don't appreciate this one bit," Gilly said through clenched teeth.

"I believe we got the picture." Breed's mouth curved in a humorous smile.

"Really, Gilly, it won't be so bad. All we want is for you to give the poor guy a chance."

Gilly ignored her friend and turned her attention to Breed. "Did you know Beth once called you Tarzan?" she informed him saucily.

"Tarzan?" Breed's large eyes rounded indignantly, and he turned to Elizabeth with a feigned look of outrage. "Beth, you didn't."

She forced herself to smile and nodded regretfully.

"In that case, will you be my Jane?"

"Love to," she returned happily, placing her hand in his.

Peter had the tent pitched and a small fire going when they arrived. Breed and Elizabeth climbed out of the front seat and stretched. Gilly remained inside, her arms folded as she stared defiantly ahead.

"Hi, Gilly," Peter said as he strolled up to the Jeep, his hands buried in his pockets.

Silence.

Peter continued, "I've always been one to lay my cards on the table, so you're going to listen to me. There's no place to run now."

More silence.

He went on, "You once told me that you loved me, but I'm beginning to have my doubts about that." He levered himself so that he was in the driver's seat and turned to face her. "I was so shocked at your announcement that I must have said and done the worst possible things." He hesitated slightly. "The thing was, I had no idea how you felt."

"Your reaction told me that." Gilly spoke for the first time, her words tight and low.

"You see, I'd realized earlier how much you'd come to mean to me. I'd been trying to work up enough nerve to tell you my feelings had changed."

"Don't you dare lie to me, Peter."

"I'm not," he returned harshly. "For too long I've had doors shut in my face, phones slammed in my ear. I've about had it, Gillian Haggith. I want you to marry me, and I want your answer right now."

Feeling like an intruder, Elizabeth leaned against the picnic table with Breed at her side. Fascinated, she watched as Gilly's mouth opened and closed incredulously. For the first time in recent history, her friend was utterly speechless.

"Maybe this will help you decide," Peter mumbled, withdrawing a small diamond ring from his jeans pocket.

"Oh, Peter!" Gilly cried, and she threw her arms around him as she burst into happy tears.

# Eight

—⚡—

"Shall we give the lovebirds some time alone?" Breed whispered in Elizabeth's ear.

Her nod was indulgent. "How about giving me a grand tour of the grounds."

"Love to."

"I'm especially interested in the modern technological advances."

His thoughtful gaze swept over her face. "Beth, we're in the woods. There are no technological wonders out here."

"I was thinking of things that go flush in the night."

"Ahh, those." The corners of his mouth twitched briefly upward. "Allow me to lead the way."

He set a comfortable pace as they wandered around the campgrounds, taking their time. The sky couldn't have been any bluer, and the air was filled with the scent of pine and evergreen. A creek bubbled cheerfully down its meandering course, and they paused for a few quiet moments of peaceful introspection. Elizabeth's thoughts drifted to her father. Their showcase home in Boston, with all its splendor, couldn't compare to the tranquil beauty of this forest. If he could see this place, she was confident, he would experience the serenity that had touched her in so brief a time.

Gilly had lunch cooking by the time Breed and Elizabeth returned. The two of them smiled conspiratorially, having agreed to pretend ignorance of the conversation they'd overheard earlier. With an efficiency Elizabeth hardly recognized in her friend, Gilly set out the paper plates, a pan of hot beans, freshly made potato salad, and grilled hot dogs with toasted buns.

"I'll do the dishes," Elizabeth joked as she filled her paper plate. Gilly sat beside Elizabeth at the picnic table.

"I'm sorry about what I said earlier," Gilly murmured as telltale color crept up her neck. "It was childish and immature of me to tell Breed that you once referred to him as Tarzan." She released her breath with a thin edge of exasperation. "Actually, it was probably the stupidest thing I've ever done in my entire life. How petty can I get?"

"You had a right to be angry." Even so, Elizabeth appreciated her friend's apology. "Not telling you that Peter was coming here was underhanded and conniving."

Breed lifted his index finger. "And my idea. I take credit."

Elizabeth's eyes captured his, and her gaze wavered slightly under his potent spell. "But if it had backfired, the blame would have been mine. I'm learning a lot about the workings of the male mind."

"Do you have to sit across the table from me, woman?" Peter complained as he settled next to Breed.

"I'll be sitting next to you for the rest of my life," Gilly returned with a happy note. "Besides, at this angle you can feast upon my unspoiled beauty."

The diamond ring on her finger sparkled almost as brightly as the happiness in her eyes. Things couldn't have worked out better. Elizabeth realized how miserable her friend had been the last few days and felt oddly guilty that she had been so involved in her own problems.

"Do you two have an announcement to make?" Breed asked as he stared pointedly at Gilly's left hand.

"Gilly and I are getting married," Peter informed them cheerfully.

"We haven't set a date yet," Gilly inserted. "Peter thought we should talk to my parents first. And my church has a counseling class for engaged couples. I thought we should take it. Plus, knowing my mother, she'll want a big wedding, which will take a while to plan. So the earliest we could set the date would be autumn. Maybe early November."

"I was hoping for a quiet wedding on the beach just before dawn with our parents and close friends. Preferably next month sometime," Peter said.

"Next month?" Gilly choked. "We can't do that. My mother would never forgive me."

"I thought it was me you were marrying, not your mother," grumbled Peter.

Setting the palms of her hands on the tabletop, Gilly half rose from her seat and glared jokingly at Peter. "Are you trying to pick a fight already?" she asked with a saucy grin.

"It's my wedding, too," Peter challenged. "I think, in the interest of fairness to your future husband, you should consider my ideas."

Gilly mumbled something under her breath, and reached for the potato salad.

Holding back a smile, Elizabeth glanced at Breed, who seemed to be enjoying the moment. She felt as if she could read his thoughts, and she agreed. Gilly and Peter fought much more now that they were in love.

They finished their meal, then got serious about setting up camp.

"I'll unload Hilda," Breed said as he stood.

"I'll help," Peter offered, pointing to Gilly. "The wedding will be next month, on the beach at sunrise."

"Thanks for the invitation, big shot. I hope I can make it."

"I'm doing the dishes," Elizabeth reminded them, and she hurriedly swallowed the last bite of her meal. Everyone was suddenly busy, and she didn't want to sit idle.

The paper plates were easily disposed of in a garbage container. She placed the potato salad and other leftovers in the cooler. The only items left were the plastic forks and a single saucepan.

With a dish towel draped around her neck, and the plasticware, liquid soap, and rag dumped inside the saucepan, she headed toward the creek she'd discovered with Breed.

"Hey, where are you going?" Gilly called out as Elizabeth left.

"To wash these." She held up the pan. "I'll be right back. Breed said something about taking a hike."

Gilly's smile was crooked. "Yes, but I think he was

referring to me and Peter. If we don't quit fighting, I have the feeling we may have to walk home."

Elizabeth located the stream without a problem and knelt on the soft earth beside the water, humming as she rubbed the rag along the inside of the aluminum pan. A flash of color caught her attention, and she glanced upward. A deer was poised in a meadow on the other side of the water. Mesmerized, she watched the wild creature with a powerful sense of awe and appreciation.

Slowly, she straightened, afraid her movements would frighten off the lovely animal. But the doe merely raised its regal head, and she stared into its beautiful dark eyes. The animal didn't appear to be frightened by her presence.

Wondering how close she could get, she crossed the burbling water, stepping carefully from one stone to another. When she reached the other side, the doe was gone. Disappointed, she walked to the spot where the animal had been standing and saw that it had gone farther into the forest, and now was barely visible. She decided to follow it, thinking she might be able to catch a glimpse of a fawn. She wished she'd thought to bring her camera. But she hadn't expected to see anything like this.

Keeping a safe distance, she followed the deer, rather proud of her ability to track it. She realized that the animal wasn't trying to escape or she wouldn't have had a chance of following it this far.

The lovely creature paused, and she took the opportunity to rest on a felled tree while keeping an eye on the deer. A glance at her watch told her that she'd been away from camp almost an hour. She didn't want to worry anyone, so even though the chase was fun, she felt forced to abandon it. With bittersweet regret, she stood and gave a waving salute to her beautiful friend.

An hour later, she owned up to the fact that she was lost. The taste of panic filled her mouth, and she took several deep breaths to calm herself.

"Help!" she screamed, as loudly as she could. Her voice echoed through the otherwise silent forest. "I'm here!" she cried out, a frantic edge to her words. Hurrying now, she half ran through the thick woods until she stumbled and caught herself against a bush. A thorny limb caught on the flesh of her upper arm and lightly gouged her skin.

Elizabeth yelped with pain and grabbed at her wound. When her fingers came away sticky with blood, a sickening sensation attacked her stomach.

"Calm down," she told herself out loud, thinking the sound of her own voice would have a soothing effect. It didn't, and she paused again to force herself to breathe evenly.

"Breed, oh, Breed," she whispered as she moved through the dense cover, holding her arm. "Please find me. Please, please find me."

Her legs felt weak, and her lungs burned with the effort to push on. Every step cost her more than the previous one.

She tried to force the terror from her mind and concentrate on happy thoughts. The memory of her mother's laughter took the edge of exertion from her steps. The long walks with Breed along the beach. She recalled their first argument and how she'd insisted that she could find the way back. Without him, she would have been lost then, too. His words from that night echoed in her tired mind. *If you ever get lost, promise me you'll stay in one place*. She stumbled to an abrupt halt and looked around her. Nothing was familiar. She could be going in the opposite direction from the campground for all she knew. She was dreadfully tired and growing weaker every minute, the level of her remaining endurance dropping with each step.

If she was going to stop, she decided, she would find a place where she could sit and rest. She found a patch of moss that grew beside a tree and lowered herself to a sitting position. Her breath was uneven and ragged, but she suspected it was more from fear than anything.

Someone would find her soon, she told herself. Soon. The word repeated in her mind a thousand times, offering hope.

Every minute seemed an hour and every hour a month as she sat and waited. When the sun began to set, she realized she would probably be spending the night in the woods. The thought couldn't frighten her any more than she was already. At least not until darkness settled over the forest.

Not once did she doze or even try to sleep, afraid she would miss a light or the sound of a voice. Tears filled her eyes at the darkest part of the night that preceded dawn and she realized she could die out here. At least, she was convinced, her mother was waiting for her on the other side of life.

Of course, she had regrets—lots of them. Things she had wanted to do in her lifetime. But her biggest regret was that she had never told Breed how much she loved him.

She stood up gratefully when the sun came over the

horizon, its golden rays bathing the earth with its warmth. She was so cold. For a time she had been convinced she would freeze. Her teeth had chattered, and she'd huddled into a tight ball, believing this night would be her last.

Her stomach growled, and her tongue had grown thick with the need for water. For a long time she debated whether she should strike out again and look for something to drink or stay where she was. Every muscle protested when she decided to search out water, and she quickly sat back down, amazed at how weak she had become.

She tried to call out, but her voice refused to cooperate, and even the attempt to shout took more energy than she could muster.

With her eyes closed, her back supported by the tree trunk, she strained her ears for the slightest sound. The day before, while walking with Breed, she had thought the woods were quiet and serene. Now she was astonished at the cacophony that surrounded her. The loud squawk of birds and the rustle of branches in the breeze filled the forest. And then there were the other noises she couldn't identify.

"Beth." Her name echoed from faraway, barely audible.

With a reserve of energy she hadn't known she possessed, Elizabeth leaped to her feet and screamed back. "Here . . . I'm here!" Certain they would never hear her, she ran frantically toward the sound of the voice, crying as she pushed branches out of her way. They would search in another area if she couldn't make herself heard.

She couldn't bear it if she had come so close to being found only to be left behind.

"Here!" she cried again and again, until her voice was hardly more than a whisper.

Breed saw her before she saw him. "Thank God," he said, and the sound of it reached her. She turned and saw the torment leave his face as he covered the distance between them with giant strides.

Fiercely, she was hauled into his arms as he buried his face in her neck. A shudder ran through him as she wrapped her arms around him and started to weep with relief. Huge tears of happiness rolled down her face, making wet tracks in the dust that had settled on her cheeks. She was so relieved that she didn't notice the other men with Breed until he released her.

Some of the previous agony returned to Breed's eyes as he ran his finger down the dried blood that had crusted on her upper arm.

A forest ranger handed her a canteen of water and told her to take small sips. Another man spoke into a walkie-talkie, advising the members of the search party that she had been found and was safe.

The trip back to camp was hazy in Elizabeth's memory. Questions came at her from every direction. She answered them as best she could and apologized profusely for all the trouble she had caused.

The only thing that stood out in her mind was how far she had wandered. It seemed hours before they reached the campground. Breed took over at that point, taking her in his arms and carrying her into the tent.

The next thing she knew, she was awake and darkness surrounded her. She sat up and glanced around. Gilly lay sleeping on one side of her, Breed on the other. Peter was beside Gilly.

Breed's eyes opened, and he sat up with her. "How do you feel?" he whispered.

"A whole lot better. Is there anything to eat? I'm starved."

He took her hand and helped her out of the sleeping bag. Sitting her at the picnic table, he rummaged around and returned with a plate heaped with food.

He took a seat across the table from her—to gaze upon her unspoiled beauty, he told her, laughing. A lantern that hung from a tree dimly lit the area surrounding the tent and table. His features were bloodless, so pale that she felt a surge of guilt at her thoughtlessness.

She set her fork aside. "Breed, I'm so sorry. Can you forgive me?"

He wiped a hand across his face and didn't answer immediately. "I've never been so happy to see freckles in my life."

"You look terrible."

He answered her with a weak smile. "You're a brave woman, Beth. A lot of people would have panicked."

"Don't think I didn't," she told him with a shaky laugh. "There were a few hours there last night when I was sure that I'd die in those woods." She glanced lovingly at him. "The craziest part of it was that I kept thinking of all the things I regret not having done in my life."

"I suppose that's only natural."

"Do you want to know what I regretted the most?"

"What?" he asked with a tired sigh, supporting his forehead with the palms of his hands, not looking at her.

"I kept thinking how sorry I was that I'd never told you how much I love you."

Slowly, Breed raised his gaze to hers. The look in his tired amber eyes became brilliant as he studied her.

"Well, say something," she pleaded, rubbing a hand across her forehead. "I probably would have told you long ago except that I was afraid the same thing would happen to me as happened to Gilly." She paused and inhaled a deep, wobbly breath. "I know you love me in your own way, but I—"

"In my own way?" Breed returned harshly. "I love you so much that if we hadn't found you in those woods I would have stayed out there until I died, looking for you." He got up from the picnic table and walked around to her. "You asked me if I can forgive you. The answer is yes. But I don't think my heart has recovered yet. We're bound to have one crazy married life together, I can tell you that. I don't think I can take many more of your adventures."

"Married life . . . ?" she repeated achingly.

Breed didn't answer her with words, only hauled her into his arms and held on to her as if he couldn't bear to let her go.

"If this is a dream, don't wake me," she said.

"My love is no fantasy. This is reality."

"Oh, Breed," she whispered as tears of happiness clouded her eyes. She slipped her arms around his neck and pressed her face into his strong, muscular chest.

"Are we going to argue like Peter and Gilly? Or can we have a quiet ceremony with family and a few friends?"

She brushed his lips with a feather-light kiss. "Anything you say."

"Aren't you agreeable!"

She curled tighter in his embrace. "Just promise to love me no matter what." She was thinking of what his reaction would be to her family's wealth and social position. He had a right to know, but telling him now would ruin the magic of the moment. As for not having said anything in the past, she was pleased that she hadn't. Breed loved her for herself. Money and all that it could buy hadn't influenced his feelings. Maybe she was anticipating trouble for no reason.

His smile broadened. The radiant light in his amber eyes kindled a soft glow of happiness in her. His fingers explored her neck and shoulders, holding her so close that for a moment it was impossible to breathe normally. When he moved to kiss her, she slid her hands over his muscular chest and linked them behind his neck. He allowed her only small gasps of air before a new shiver of excitement stole her breath completely.

Her parted lips were trembling and swollen from Breed's plundering kisses when he finally groaned, pulled himself away and sat up straight. "I think the sooner we arrange the wedding, the better." He sighed. "I'd prefer a tent built for two." He ran a hand over his eyes. "And this may be old-fashioned, but I'd like to be married when we start our family."

Elizabeth knew the music in her heart would never fade. Not with this man. He didn't sound old-fashioned to her but refreshingly wonderful.

"I'm so glad you want children." Her voice throbbed with the beat of her heart.

"A houseful, at least." His husky voice betrayed the

tight rein he held on his needs. "But for now I'd be content to start with a wedding ring."

"Soon," she promised.

"Tomorrow we'll go down and get the license."

"Tomorrow?" The immediacy frightened her. She wanted to get married, but she couldn't see the necessity of rushing into it quite *that* quickly.

"Maybe we should pack up and drive to Reno and get married immediately."

"No." Elizabeth didn't know why she felt so strongly about that. "I want to stand before God to make my vows, not the Last Chance Hitching Post."

She could see Breed's smile. "You're sure you want to marry me?" he said.

In response, she leaned over and teased him with her lips. "You'll never need to doubt my love," she said, and playfully nipped at his earlobe.

"Who would have believed you'd get lost in the woods?" Gilly commented late the next night as they unpacked the camping gear in the apartment kitchen.

"Who would have believed we'd both become engaged in one weekend?"

"Elizabeth, I can't tell you how frantic we all were," Gilly said tightly. "Breed was like a man possessed. When you didn't come back, he went to find you. When he didn't return, Peter and I went to look for you both."

Color heated Elizabeth's face. "I was so stupid." Her inexperience had ruined their trip. After a good night's sleep, they'd packed up and headed straight back to San Francisco.

"Don't be so hard on yourself. This was your first time camping. You didn't know."

"But I feel so terrible for being such an idiot."

Gilly straightened and brushed the hair off her forehead. "Thank God you're safe," she said, staring into the distance. "I don't know what would have happened to Breed if we hadn't found you. Beth, he was like a madman. I don't think there was anyone who didn't realize that Breed would have died in the attempt to find you."

Leaning against the counter, Elizabeth expelled a painful sigh. "On the bright side of things, getting lost has done a lot for Breed and me. I wonder how long it would have been otherwise before we admitted how we felt."

"It's taken too long as it is, I knew almost from the beginning that you two were meant for each other."

Elizabeth attempted to disguise a smile. "We don't all have your insight, I guess."

Gilly seemed unaware of the teasing glint in her roommate's eye. "Peter's coming to get me in a few minutes. We're going to go talk to my parents. Will you be safe all by yourself, or should I phone Breed?"

"He's coming over in a while. I'm cooking dinner."

Breed arrived five minutes after Gilly left with Peter. He kissed her lightly on the cheek. "How do you feel?"

"Hungry," she said with a warm smile. "Let's get this show on the road."

"I thought you were cooking me dinner."

"I am. But we left the food in Hilda, which means it's at your place. If I'm going to share my life with you, then the least you can do is introduce me to your kitchen."

That uneasy look came over his features again. "We could go out just as well."

"Breed," Elizabeth intoned dramatically, "how many times do we have to argue about this apartment of yours? It's so obvious you don't want me there."

His mouth tightened grimly. "Let's go. I don't want another argument."

"Well, that's encouraging."

The brisk walk took them about fifteen minutes. His apartment was exactly as she remembered it. No pictures or knickknacks that marked the place as his. That continued to confuse her, but she couldn't believe that he would hide anything from her.

There wasn't much to work with left from their trip, and his cupboards were bare, but she assumed this was because he ate most of his meals out.

"Spaghetti's my specialty," she told him as she tied a towel around her waist.

"That sounds good."

He hovered at her elbow as she sautéed the meat and stood at her side while she chopped the vegetables. He shadowed her every action, and when she couldn't tolerate his brand of "togetherness" another second, she turned and ushered him into the living room.

"Read the paper or something, will you? You're driving me crazy."

His eyes showed his indecision. He glanced back into the kitchen, then nodded as he reached for the newspaper.

Singing softly as she worked, Elizabeth mentally reviewed her cooking lessons from school. The sauce was simmering and the pasta was boiling. She decided to set the table. A few loose papers and mail littered the countertop. Humming cheerfully, she moved them to his desk on the far side of the kitchen. The top of the desk was cluttered with more papers. As she set down his mail, she noticed a legal-looking piece of paper. She continued to hum as idly she glanced at it and realized it was a gun permit. *Breed carried a gun.* A chill shot up her spine. The song died on her lips. Breed and firearms seemed as incongruous as mixing oil and water. She would ask him about it later.

"Anything I can do?" he volunteered, seeming to have relaxed now.

"Open the wine."

"Wine?"

"You mean you don't have any?" she asked as she stirred the pasta. "The flavors in my sauce will be incomplete without the complement of wine."

"I take it you want me to buy us a bottle."

"You got it."

"Okay, let's go." He stood and tucked in his shirttails.

"Me? I can't go now. I've got to drain the pasta and finish setting the table."

He hesitated.

"Honestly, Breed, there's a grocery just down the street. You don't need me to hold your hand."

He didn't look pleased about it, but he turned and walked out.

The minute the door was closed, Elizabeth returned to his desk. She knew she was snooping, but the gun permit puzzled her, and she wanted to look it over. The permit listed a different address, confirming her suspicions that he hadn't been in this apartment long. The paper felt like it was burning her fingers, and she set it aside, hating the way her curiosity had gotten in the way of her better judgment.

She could ask him, of course, but she felt uneasy about that. Where would he keep a lethal weapon in this bare place? She wondered about the kind of gun he carried. With her index finger she pulled out the top desk drawer. It wasn't in sight, but a notebook with her full name written across the top caught her gaze. Fascinated, she pulled it from the drawer and flipped it open. Page after page of meticulous notes detailed her comings and goings, her habits and her friends. *Breed had been following her since she arrived!* But whatever for? This was bizarre.

Coiled tightness gripped her throat as she pulled open another drawer. Hurt and anger and a thousand terrifying emotions she had never thought to experience with regard to Breed filled her senses. The drawer was filled with correspondence with her father. Andrew Breed had been hired by her family as her bodyguard.

# Nine

—⚊⚊—

Elizabeth backed away from the drawer. Her hand was pressed against her breast as the blood drained from her face. Her heart was pounding wildly in her ears, and for several seconds she was unable to breathe. So many inconsistencies about Breed fell into place. She was amazed that she could have been so blind, so utterly stupid. His cover had been perfect. Dating her had simplified his job immeasurably.

Her stomach rolled, and she knew she was going to be sick. She closed the drawer and staggered into the bathroom. It was there that Breed found her.

"Beth." His voice was filled with concern. "You look terrible."

She didn't meet his eyes. "I'm . . . I'm all right. I just need a moment."

He placed his arm across her back, and the touch, although light, seemed to burn through the material of her shirt, branding her. Leading her into the living room, he sat her down on the sofa and brought in a cool rag.

"I was afraid something like this might happen," he murmured solicitously. "You're probably having a delayed reaction to the trauma of this weekend."

She closed her eyes and nodded, still unable to look at him. "I want to go home." Somehow the words managed to slip past the stranglehold she felt around her throat.

Not until they were ready to leave did she glance out Breed's window and realize that, thanks to the city's hills, her apartment could be seen from his. No wonder he was able to document her whereabouts so accurately. Mr. Andrew Breed was a clever man, deceptive and more devious than she could have dreamed. And he excelled at his job. She didn't try to fool herself. She was a job to him and little or nothing more than that.

It was no small wonder he'd suggested they go to Reno and get married right away. He wanted the deed accomplished before they confronted her father. He knew what her family would say if she were to marry a bodyguard. Her emotions when her purse had been taken had been a small-scale version of what she felt now. A part of her inner self had been violated. But the pain went far deeper. Deep enough to sear her soul. She doubted that she would ever be the same again.

Concerned, Breed helped her on with her sweater and gripped her elbow. Several times during the short drive to her apartment he glanced her way, a worried look marring his handsome face. After he had unlocked her apartment and helped her into her room, she changed clothes, took a sleeping pill, and climbed into bed. But the pill didn't work. She lay awake with a lump the size of a grapefruit blocking her throat. Every swallow hurt. Crying might have helped, but no tears would come.

She didn't know how long she lay staring at the shadows on the ceiling. The front door clicked open, and she heard Breed whisper to Gilly. She was mildly surprised that he'd stayed, then grinned sarcastically. Of course he would; he'd been paid to babysit her. And knowing her father, the fee had been generous.

The front door clicked again, and she heard Gilly assure Breed that she would take care of Elizabeth. The words were almost ludicrous. These two people whom she'd come to love this summer had given her so much. But they had taken away even more. No, she thought. She didn't blame Gilly. She was grateful to have had her as a friend. Gilly might have been in on this scheme, but she doubted it.

Finally Elizabeth heard Gilly go into her bedroom. An hour later, convinced her friend would be asleep, she silently pushed back the covers and climbed out of bed. Dragging her suitcases from the closet, she quickly and quietly emptied her drawers and hangers. She only took what she had brought with her from Boston. Everything else she was leaving for her roommate.

The apartment key and a note to Gilly were left propped against a vase on the kitchen table. A sad smile touched Elizabeth's pale features as she set a second note, addressed to Breed, beside the first. She picked it up and read over the simple message again. It read: *The game's over. You lose.*

The taxi ride to the airport seemed to take hours. Elizabeth kept looking over her shoulder, afraid Breed was following. She didn't want to think of how many times this summer he had done exactly that. The thought made her more determined than ever to get away.

There wasn't a plane scheduled to leave for Boston until the next morning, so she took the red-eye to New York. Luckily, the wait was less than two hours. Her greatest fear was that Gilly would wake up and go to check on her. Finding her gone, she would be sure to contact Breed.

Restlessly, Elizabeth walked around the airport. She knew that she would never forget this city. The cable cars, the sounds and smells of Fisherman's Wharf, sailing, the beach . . . Her musings did a buzzing tailspin. No, thoughts of San Francisco would always be irrevocably tied to Breed. She wanted to hate him, but she couldn't. He'd given her happy memories, and she would struggle to keep those untainted by the mud of his deception.

The flight was uneventful. The first-class section had only one other traveler, a businessman who worked out of his briefcase the entire time.

Even though it was only 10:00 a.m. when her plane landed, New York was sweltering in an August heat wave. The limousine delivered her to the St. Moritz, a fashionable uptown hotel that was situated across the street from Central Park South.

Exhausted, she took a hot shower and fell asleep almost immediately afterward in the air-conditioned room.

When she awoke, it was nearly dinnertime. Although she hadn't eaten anything in twenty-four hours, she wasn't hungry.

A walk in Central Park lifted her from the well of overwhelming self-pity. She bought a pretzel and squirted thick yellow mustard over it. As she lazily strolled beside the pond, goldfish the size of trout came to the water's edge, anticipating a share of her meal. Not wanting to disappoint them, she broke off a piece of the doughy pretzel and tossed it into the huge pond.

A young bearded man, strumming a ballad on his guitar, sat on a green bench looking for handouts. She placed a five-dollar bill in the open guitar case.

"Thanks, lady," he sang, and returned her wave with a bob of his dark head.

Most of the park benches were occupied by a wide range of people from all walks of life. She had taken a two-day trip to the Big Apple the previous year and stayed at the St. Moritz, but she hadn't gone into Central Park. The thought hadn't entered her mind.

Today she strolled around the pond, hoping that the sights and sounds of the vibrant city would ease the heaviness in her heart. Unfamiliar settings filled with anonymous faces were no longer intimidating. San Francisco had done that for her.

An hour later she stepped into the cool hotel room and sighed. Reaching for the phone, she dialed Boston.

"Hello, Dad," she said when he picked up, her voice devoid of emotion.

"Elizabeth, where are you?" he demanded instantly.

"New York."

"Why in heaven's name did you run off like that?"

His question drew a faint smile. "I think you already know why," she answered softly, resignedly. "How often have you hired men to watch me in the past?"

"Did he tell you?" her father responded brusquely.

"No. I found out on my own."

"The fool," he issued harshly under his breath.

She disagreed. The only fool in this situation had been herself, for falling in love with Breed.

A strained silence stretched along the wires.

"How often, Dad?" she finally asked.

"Only a few," he answered after a long moment.

"But why?" she asked, exhaling forcefully. The pain of the knowledge was physical as well as mental. Her stomach ached, and she lowered herself into the upholstered wing chair in her suite and leaned forward to rest her elbows on her knees.

"That's a subject we shouldn't discuss over the phone. I want you at home."

"There are a lot of things *I* want, too," she returned in a shallow whisper.

"Elizabeth, please. Be reasonable."

"Give me a few days," she insisted. "I need time to think."

Her father began to argue. She closed her eyes and listened for a few moments. Then she whispered, "Goodbye, Dad," and hung up.

The next morning she checked out of the hotel, rented a car and headed north. Setting a leisurely pace, she stopped along the way to enjoy the beauty of the Atlantic Ocean. It took her three days to drive home.

She recognized that her father would consider her actions immature, but for her, this time alone with her thoughts had been vital. The long drive, the magnificent coastline, the solitude, gave her the necessary time to come to terms with her father's actions. Decisions were made. Although her father hadn't asked for it, she gave him her forgiveness. He had only been doing what he thought was best.

The thing that shocked her most had been her own stupidity. How could she have been so gullible? All the evidence of Breed's deceit had been there, but she had been blinded by her love. But no more. Never again. Loving someone only caused emotional pain. She had been naive and incredibly foolish.

She wouldn't allow her father to interfere in her life that way again. Once she got home, she would make arrangements to find a place of her own. Breaking away had been long overdue. This summer she'd proved to her father and herself that she was capable of holding a job. And that was what she decided to do: get a job. She spoke fluent French, and enough German and Italian to make her last visit to Europe trouble-free. Surely there was something she could do with those skills.

Not once during the drive home did she allow bitterness to tarnish her memories of Breed. Ultimately, the special relationship they'd shared led to heartache. But she was grateful to him for the precious gift that he'd so unwittingly given her.

One thing she couldn't accept was his calculated deception. Maybe forgiveness would come later, but right now the pain cut so deep that she knew it would take a long time, and maybe it would never come.

It was midafternoon when she pulled up in front of the huge family home.

The white-haired butler opened the door and gave her a stiff but genuine smile.

"Welcome home, Miss Elizabeth." His head dipped slightly as he spoke.

"Hello, Bently."

"Your father's been expecting you, miss. You're to go directly to the library."

Although he hadn't said as much, she knew he was warning her that her father wasn't pleased.

"I'll see to your luggage," he continued.

"Thank you, Bently."

Her elderly ally inclined his head in silent understanding.

Elizabeth stood in the great entry hall and looked around with new eyes. The house was magnificent, a showpiece, but it felt cold and unwelcoming. The heart of this home had died with her mother.

Knocking politely against the polished mahogany door that reached from the ceiling to the floor, Elizabeth waited with calm deliberation.

Charles Wainwright's reply was curt and impatient. "Come in."

"Hello, Father," she said as she walked through the door.

"Elizabeth." He raised himself out of his chair. Relief relaxed the tightness in his weathered brow and he gave her a brief, perfunctory hug. "Now, what's all this nonsense of needing time away?"

She was saved from having to reply by the arrival of Helene. The maid seemed to appear noiselessly, carrying a silver tray with a coffeepot and two delicate china cups.

Both Elizabeth and her father waited to resume their conversation until Helene had left the room.

"I have a few unanswered questions of my own," she said as she stood and dutifully filled the first cup. She handed it to her father. Charles Wainwright's hair was completely white now, she noted as he accepted the steaming cup from her hand. Once, a long time past, her father's hair had been the same sandy shade as her own. The famous Wainwright blond good looks. Charlie was dark like her mother. But other than her coloring, Elizabeth felt as if she had nothing in common with this man. He wasn't affectionate. She couldn't ever recall him bouncing her on his knee or telling her stories when she was a child. The only time she recalled seeing deep emotion from him had been after her mother's funeral.

Her reverie was interrupted by coffee that dripped from the spout of the silver service and scalded her fingertips. She managed to set the pot aside before giving an involuntary gasp of surprise. Tears filled her eyes, but not from physical pain.

"Elizabeth." Charles Wainwright leapt to his feet. "You've burned yourself." He turned aside. "Helene!" he shouted. Elizabeth couldn't remember hearing that much emotion in his voice for a long time. "Bring the first-aid kit."

"I'm fine," she struggled to reassure him between sudden sobs. She hadn't wept when she learned of Breed's deceit. Nor had she revealed her grief at her mother's funeral. After all, she was a Wainwright, and tears were a sign of weakness. Now she was home, with possibly the only person alive who loved her for herself, and they sat like polite acquaintances, sharing coffee and shielding their hearts. A dam within her burst, and she began to sob uncontrollably.

She could see by the concerned look on his face that her father didn't know how to react. He raised and lowered his hands, impotently unsure of himself. Finally he circled his arms around her and patted her gently on the back as if he were afraid she was a fragile porcelain doll that would break.

"Princess," he whispered, "what is it?"

Helene burst in the door, and Charles dismissed her with a wave of his hand.

"Who's hurt you?"

Between a fresh wave of sobs, she shook her head.

Her father handed her his starched and pressed linen handkerchief, and she held it to her eyes.

"My dear," he said, smoothing her back. "You have the look of a woman in love."

"No." She pulled free of his loose embrace and violently shook her head. "I can't love him after what he's done," she choked out between sobs.

"And what did he do?"

She sniffled. "Nothing. I . . . can't talk about it. Not now," she whispered in painful denial. "I apologize for acting like an idiot. I'll go upstairs and lie down for an hour or so, and I'll be fine."

"Princess, are you sure you won't tell me?"

Fresh tears squeezed through her damp lashes. "Not now." She turned toward the great hall. "Dad," she said with her back to him, "I'll probably be leaving for Europe within the week."

Her father was silent for a moment. "Running away won't solve anything." His haunting voice, gentle with wisdom, followed her as she left the library.


One suitcase was packed and another half-filled. She'd realized after one night that she couldn't remain in this house. Once the tears had come, the aching loneliness in her heart had throbbed with its intensity. Her father was right when he told her running away wouldn't heal the void. But escaping came naturally; she had been doing it for so long. Last night she hadn't gone down to dinner, and she'd been shocked when her father brought her a tray later in the evening. She had pretended to be asleep. She regretted that now, and decided to go downstairs and say goodbye to him.

Tucking her passport in her purse, she examined the contents of her suitcases one last time before securing the locks and leaving them outside her door. The reservations for her flight had been made earlier that morning, and plenty of time remained before she needed to leave for the airport. But already she was restless. Forcing a smile on her pale features, she descended the stairs.

She was only halfway down the staircase when she heard Bently engaged in a heated argument with someone at the front door. The other voice was achingly familiar. Breed.

That he was angry and impatient was apparent as his raised voice echoed through the hall. She took another step, and then her father appeared in the foyer.

"That'll be all, Bently," her father said with calm authority. "I'll see Mr. Breed."

She restrained a gasp and drew closer to the banister. Clearly neither man was aware of her presence.

Breed stepped into the house. His deeply tanned features were set in hard lines as he approached her father.

"I appreciate the fact that you're seeing me." His voice was laced with heavy sarcasm. "But I can assure you that I was prepared to wait as long as it took."

"After four days of pounding down my door, I can

believe that's a fair assumption," her father retorted stiffly. "But now that you have my attention, what is it you want?"

"Elizabeth," Breed said without hesitation. "Where is she?"

"Your job of protecting my daughter was terminated when she left San Francisco. I believe you've received your check."

She watched, fascinated and shocked, as Breed took an envelope from his pocket and ripped it in two. "I don't want a dime of this money. I told you that before, and I'm telling you again."

"You earned it."

*Every damn penny,* Elizabeth wanted to shout at him.

"I kept my word, Wainwright," Breed explained forcefully. "I didn't tell Beth a thing. But I hated every minute of this assignment, and you knew it."

"Why? I thought this type of work was your specialty. You came highly recommended," her father said quietly.

Breed rubbed a hand across his eyes, and she knew the torment she saw in his features was mirrored in her own. When he lowered his hand, he must have caught a glimpse of her from out of the corner of his eye. He hesitated and turned toward her.

"Beth." He said her name softly, as though he was afraid she would disappear again. He moved to the foot of the stairs. The tightness eased from his face as he stared up at her.

"Mr. Wainwright," Breed said, and the anger was gone from his voice as he glanced briefly at her father, "I love your daughter."

"No," Elizabeth said in agitation. "You don't know

the meaning of the word. I was nothing more than a lucrative business proposition."

Breed pulled another envelope from his shirt and handed it to her father. His eyes left her only briefly. "While we're on the subject of money . . ."

Her gaze wavered under the blazing force of his.

"This paper proves that I'm not a poor man. I own a thousand acres of prime California timberland. The land has been in my family for a hundred years," Breed stated evenly, then turned toward her father. "I have no need of the Wainwright money. From the first day I met your daughter, it's stood between us like a brick wall."

He turned back to the stairs, and his look grew gentle. "I love you, Beth Wainwright. I've loved you from the moment we went swimming and I saw you for the wonderful woman you are."

Her heart was crying out for her to run to Breed. But the feelings of betrayal and hurt kept her rooted to the stairs. Her hand curved around the polished banister until she was sure her fingernails would dent the wood.

At her silence, he returned his attention to her father. "Mr. Wainwright, I'm asking for your permission to marry your daughter—"

"I won't marry you," she interrupted in angry protest. "You lied to me. All those weeks you—"

"You weren't exactly honest with me," he returned levelly. "And there was ample opportunity for you to explain everything. You have no right to be mad at me." He paused, and the hardness left his chiseled features. "I'll say it again. I love you, Beth. I want you to share my life."

Indecision played across her face, and her gaze met

her father's. Breed's eyes followed hers, and a proud look stole over them.

"I'm asking for your permission, Wainwright," Breed said coolly. "But I'll be honest. I plan to marry your daughter with or without it."

A hint of mirth brightened her father's face. "That's a brash statement, young man."

"Daddy!" Elizabeth called, knowing what her father would say to someone like Breed. Her heart and her pride waged a desperate battle.

Charles Wainwright ignored his daughter. "As it is, I realize that Elizabeth loves you. I may be a crusty old man, but I'm not too blind to see that you'll make her happy. You have my permission, Andrew Breed. Fill this house with grandchildren and bring some laughter into its halls again."

Breed appeared as stunned as Elizabeth.

"Go on." Charles Wainwright flicked his wrist in the direction of his daughter. "And don't take no for an answer."

"I have no intention of doing so," Breed said as he climbed the stairs two at a time.

Elizabeth felt the crazy desire to turn and run, but she stayed where she was, her body motionless with indecision. She bit into her trembling bottom lip as her pride surrendered the first battle.

"Your money will go into a trust fund for our children, Beth," Breed began with a frown. "I don't want a penny of what's yours. There's only one thing I'm after."

"What's that?" she asked in a quiet murmur, battling with the potency of his nearness.

He slid his hands around her waist and pulled her into the circle of his arms. "A wife."

Her breath came in small flutters as he lowered his mouth and paused a scant inch above hers. Their breath merged. She swayed against him, her hands moving over his chest. The entire time her pride urged her to break free and walk away. But her heart held her steadfast.

"Don't fight me so hard," he whispered, claiming her lips in a kiss so tender that she melted against him.

"Together we'll build a lumber kingdom," he whispered into her hair.

"I don't know," she faltered. "I need time to think. I'm confused." She wanted him so much. It was her pride speaking, not her heart.

"Elizabeth," her father called from the hall. "I think it's only fair to tell you that your Andrew came to me a few weeks back and asked to be relieved of this case. Naturally, I declined and demanded that he maintain his anonymity."

Her eyes met Breed's. "Your business trip?"

He nodded and placed his hands on her shoulders. "Is it really so difficult to decide?" he asked in a husky whisper.

She stared at the familiar features and saw the pain carved in them. "No, not at all."

For a breathless moment they looked at each other.

Then Elizabeth's pride surrendered to her heart as she pressed her mouth to his.

*Reflections of Yesterday*

# Prologue

—⁓—

An iridescent moon lit up the sky above Groves Point, South Carolina. Simon Canfield sat in his Mercedes, opening one aluminum can after another until he'd downed the six-pack. Beer cooled the burning ache in the pit of his stomach. Beer helped him remember. For three hundred and sixty-four days of the year he successfully curtailed thoughts of Angie. Only on June 7 did he pull out the memories, roll them around in his tortured mind, and relive again the golden days of his abandoned youth.

After ten years it astonished him that the memory of Angie's passionate young body under his held such power. Closing his eyes produced a flood of images and a sensation of almost painful pleasure. He hated her, and in the same breath realized that he'd go to his grave never having loved another woman the way he'd loved Angie. Only thoughts of her were capable of reducing him to this pensive melancholy. Rarely did he indulge himself the way he had tonight.

Normally, Simon Canfield lived his life as a respected

citizen, vice president of the local bank, the man who made decisions that set the course of an entire community.

Tonight he drank beer instead of whiskey. Tonight he wore jeans instead of a pin-striped suit. Tonight he yearned for a time long past, and the young man who had loved with a passion he never hoped to recapture.

Simon's grip compressed around the hard steering wheel. The pleasure of those youthful days had been swept away by the pain that had followed in the backwash of her deception.

A turn of the key fired the car engine to life. Simon drove carefully, his convertible cruising through the dark streets unnoticed. His first stop was outside the Catholic church, Saint Elizabeth's. His figure hadn't darkened the doorway in ten years. Fleetingly he wondered if the priests kept the church doors locked these days.

Without conscious direction, he headed through town, ignoring the changing message of the time and temperature flashing from the sign above the bank. In the still, silent streets he drove over the railroad tracks until he was parked outside of Angie's old house. The white paint had peeled and the flowerbeds were sadly neglected, the once-well-groomed lawn forsaken. A string of toys and a tricycle on the sidewalk assured him the house wasn't empty. Somehow, Simon doubted that the halls rang with music as they once had.

A surge of anger rose within him until the taste of bitterness erupted in his mouth. He'd wanted children even then. They'd talked about what they would do if Angie were to have a baby. Ironically, their last conversation had been over the possibility of her being pregnant.

He could picture her as clearly today as he had ten years before: Her long brown hair had been pulled away from her face and tied back with a red chiffon scarf, her brown eyes as round as a deer's, mirroring her troubled heart. She'd looked so unhappy, but she had quietly assured him that there wasn't any need to worry, she wasn't pregnant. Oh, he wished she had been.

Now there would be no children for him. He was twenty-seven, and with one disastrous marriage in his wake, he wasn't about to try again. He'd like to blame Angie for that fiasco. But he was the one foolish enough to marry a woman he didn't love, and he had paid dearly for the mistake. He wouldn't marry again.

The ache grew within him until his chest hurt with the intensity of it. Dear sweet heaven, he'd loved Angie.

Simon drove around for what seemed like hours, not surprised that his unplanned route led to the backwoods. His parents had owned these twenty acres. Simon had purchased the land after his divorce from Carol was final. He'd built the house a year later. But it wasn't the welcoming of his home he sought now. Instead, Simon drove down the long driveway that stretched from the road to the back of his house. The harsh slam of his car door echoed through the quiet night. Enough was enough. The axe was stored in the garage, and with an impatience he couldn't understand, Simon fetched it, then carried it deep into the twenty acres to the small clearing. He hadn't come here in years, and the memories this land evoked were bittersweet. But Simon had neither the patience nor the desire to explore its significance.

He located the large pecan tree with some difficulty.

The only light was the silken shine of a distant moon, slowly creeping toward the horizon.

On the first swing, the axe met the tree's bark with an unrestrained violence. The second and third that followed were born of anger and frustration. Blow followed blow, and he paused only once, to remove his shirt. Uncaring, he tossed it aside and resumed his task until his muscles quivered with the effort and his shoulders heaved with exertion.

The huge tree began to fall, and a panting Simon stood back. His lungs hurt as he sucked in huge gulps of air. His naked torso glistened with perspiration in the glow of the moonlight.

"It's over," he mumbled, chest heaving, as the mighty pecan slammed against the earth.

# One

—⁓—

The day was as flawless as only Groves Point could be in the summer. The golden sun shone brightly from a sky as clear as the Caribbean Sea. Angie Robinson stood outside the hotel. Her fingers toyed nervously with the room key in her pocket as she glanced down Main Street.

Nothing was different, but everything had changed. A traffic signal had been added in front of Garland Pharmacy, and the JCPenney store had installed a colorful awning to shade the display windows. The beauty shop was in the same location, but the neon sign flashed a new name—Cindy's.

Drawing in a deep breath to calm herself, Angie walked toward the bakery at the end of the block. A quick survey inside revealed that the small Formica tables and the ever-full, help-yourself coffeepot were still there. But Angie didn't recognize the middle-aged woman behind the counter. The clerk caught her eye through the large front window and smiled. Angie's smile in return felt stiff and unnatural.

She crossed the street and was halfway down the second block before she noticed that the bank had put up a sign that alternately flashed the temperature and the time of day. For a full minute she stood in a daze, watching, as if it could tell her what would happen once she walked inside the double glass doors.

Angie had expected to feel a surging wave of anger, but none came. Only a blank, desolate feeling. A hollow emptiness that was incapable of echoing in the dark emotion that had dictated her life these past twelve years.

She took a step in retreat, swiveled, and walked away. *Not yet,* she thought. She'd been in town only a few minutes. A confrontation so soon would be unwise.

Crossing the street at the light, Angie's quick-paced steps led her to the beauty salon. Cindy would tell her everything she needed to know. Cindy had been her friend. Her best friend. She'd loved working with hair and talked one day of opening her own salon. This must be Cindy's salon.

"Can I help you?" A blue-eyed blonde at the reception desk glanced curiously at Angie. The girl transferred a wad of gum from one side of her mouth to the other as she waited for Angie's response.

"Is Cindy available?" she asked, trying to keep her voice even.

"Sure, she's in the back room. If you'll wait a minute, I'll get her."

"Thank you."

The girl slid off the stool and headed for the back of the salon. Empty chairs and a stack of magazines invited Angie to sit down, but for now she preferred to stand.

The bead curtain that covered a rear doorway made a

jingling sound as a tall brunette appeared. Two steps into the room she paused in mid-stride. "Oh my heavens, Angie." A rumbling laugh followed. "Good grief, girl, where have you been all these years?" Before another moment passed, Angie was hauled into open arms and hugged as if she were a lost child returned to a worried mother. "I don't believe it." A hand gripping each shoulder pushed Angie back. "Let me look at you. You haven't changed at all."

A smile lit up Angie's soft brown eyes. Cindy was one person she could always count on to welcome her. "Neither have you."

The musical sound of Cindy's laughter followed. "When did you get into town?"

"Just a few minutes ago." Angie felt breathless and a little giddy. Her friend looked wonderful. Cindy had been the tallest and thinnest girl in class; now she possessed the womanly curves that rounded out her height.

"Can you stay?"

"I'm only here for a couple days."

"Angie, Angie," Cindy murmured, and released a long, slow sigh, "it's good to see you."

Her friend's unabashed enthusiasm for life had always been infectious. Angie had often thought that if someone could tap into Cindy's knack for seeing the bright side to everything, the world would be a much happier place. "Tell me about everyone. I'm dying to know what's been going on in Groves Point."

"Filling you in on the last . . . twelve years . . . Has it really been that long?" Cindy shook her head in slow amazement. "Mimi, I'll be at King Cole's. Call me if something disastrous comes up."

Mimi smiled. "Don't worry, I'll hold down the fort."

King Cole's was one of three restaurants in town. The food had always been moderately good and relatively cheap. Angie's father used to take her there for dinner once a month on payday. She'd never told him that she would have preferred hamburgers at the A&W on the outskirts of town.

"Bernice," Cindy cried out, as they slid into the vinyl booth. "Bring us a pair of javas."

"You got it." The slim waitress in the pink uniform brought out two cups of coffee.

"You remember Bernie, don't you?" Cindy prompted. "She was a couple of classes behind us."

For the life of her, Angie didn't, but she pretended to, smiling up at the waitress, who looked as blank as Angie. "Good to see you again, Bernice."

"You, too." She set the beige mugs on the Formica tabletop. "You want cream with this?"

"No, thanks."

With a slow gait, Bernice returned behind the counter.

"We tried to get hold of you for the ten-year reunion," Cindy said with a hint of frustration. "But no one knew where you were."

"Charleston."

"Really? Bob and I were there just this summer."

"You married Bob." That deduction wasn't one of her most brilliant. Cindy and Bob had dated exclusively their senior year.

"Going on eleven years now. We've got two boys. B.J.'s ten and Matt's eight."

"Wonderful." Angie couldn't have meant that more.

Her childhood friend deserved a life filled with happiness.

"Bob was in the service for a time and I went to beauty school in Fayetteville and lived with my aunt." Her finger made lazy circles around the rim of the mug as she spoke. "What about you? The last thing I remember is that you were working as a clerk at the pharmacy."

Angie stared into the dark depths of the coffee cup. "Dad and I moved the February after graduation." Neither mentioned that she had left Groves Point without a word or a forwarding address. Not in twelve years had she contacted anyone.

"Remember Shirley Radcliff?"

Angie wasn't likely to forget her. Simon's mother had been furious when he'd asked Angie to the junior-senior prom instead of Shirley.

"What ever became of Shirley?" The muscles of her stomach knotted. If Mrs. Canfield had gotten her way, Shirley would have married Simon.

"She married a guy in real estate. From what I understand, they're living the good life in Savannah. No kids, mind you. It would ruin their lifestyle."

A smile tugged at the corners of Angie's mouth. No, Shirley wouldn't be the type to appreciate children.

"Gary Carlson's a lawyer in Charlotte. He's married and has a daughter. And Sharon Gleason's a flight attendant."

"I don't believe it." Angie couldn't control a soft laugh. Sharon had always been extremely shy.

"What about you, Angie? Are you married? Do you have children?"

For an instant, one crazy instant, she hesitated. "No

to both." Averting her gaze, fearing what her eyes would reveal, Angie asked, "What about Simon? Whatever happened to him?"

"You two were really thick for a while, weren't you?" She didn't wait for Angie to reply. "He married a girl from college. I can't recall her name offhand . . . Carol, I think. It didn't last long—two, three years. Simon's kept to himself since."

"Is he at the bank?" The question was unnecessary, Angie already knew without having to ask, but she had to do something to disguise the pain. So he had married. She'd known it, in her heart she'd always known it. Angie had assumed that after all these years what Simon did couldn't hurt her anymore. But she was wrong.

"His daddy's the president and Simon's the vice president. But these days I think Simon runs most everything. He's gotten to be a real stuffed shirt, if you know what I mean."

Angie did. Simon had become the mirror image of his father in spite of his best intentions.

Cindy downed the last of her coffee. "Listen, I've got to get back to the shop. Mrs. Harris, my two-o'clock appointment, is due any minute. Can you come to dinner tonight? I'll see if I can get a few of the ol' gang together."

"That'd be great. But don't go to any trouble."

"Are you kidding, I haven't got time. Come around six-thirty. We're in the old Silverman place across the street from the park."

"Sure, I remember it. I'll see you tonight."

Cindy pulled some change from her pocket. "Coffee's on me."

"Thanks."

Angie left King Cole's with a sense of exhilaration. After everything that had happened in the past twelve years, she had thought she'd hate Groves Point. But it wasn't in her. The best times of her life had happened in this small community. As much as she'd wanted to blot out the past, it was impossible. Glenn had tried to explain that to her, but she hadn't understood. Now she did. He had been right to tell her she had to confront the past before looking to the future. She'd known that, too, but the past was so painful that it had seemed simpler to ignore the hurt and go on with her life.

The urge to talk to Glenn directed her back to the hotel. Her room was clean but generic. A double bed, a nightstand, a dresser, and chairs made up the room's furnishings. The one window looked over Main Street, and from where she stood, Angie could see the sign above the bank. An indescribable pain flashed through her. Angie reached for her phone.

"Glenn Lambert."

The warm familiarity of his voice chased the chill from her blood. "Angie Robinson here."

"Angie," he said softly. "How was the trip?"

"Uneventful."

"And Groves Point?"

She smiled gently. "The same. I looked up an old friend who clued me in on what's been happening. The class brain's a lawyer and the shyest girl at Groves Point High is a flight attendant."

"I thought you were the class brain," he said with a chuckle.

"Gary and I shared the honors."

A short silence followed. "I miss you, babe."

Angie always felt uncomfortable when he called her that, but she'd never told Glenn. "I miss you, too."

"I wish I could believe that." A trace of impatience tinged his voice, but he disguised it behind a cheerful invitation. "When you come home I'm going to cook you the thickest steak in Charleston."

"I'll look forward to that."

"Good. Have you finished . . . your business yet?"

Glenn didn't know exactly what it was she had to do in Groves Point, and Angie had never explained. That lack of trust had hurt Glenn, and she felt a twinge of guilt. Glenn was the best thing to happen in her life in twelve years. "I've only been in town an hour." But it had to be today. The banks were closed on weekends.

"Will you call me tomorrow?"

"If you want."

"I want you for the rest of my life, Angie. I love you."

"I love you, too," she echoed softly. "I'll talk to you tomorrow." Gently, she ended the call.

Talking to Glenn reinforced her determination to be done with the purpose of her visit. A quick check in the mirror assured her that she was now a composed, mature woman. Simon Canfield Senior would be incapable of destroying her as he had so long ago.

Not once on the walk to the bank did Angie hesitate. Her heart leaped to her throat as she pushed the glass door that opened into the interior. That, too, hadn't changed. Marble pillars, marble floors, marble hearts.

The woman gave no indication that she recognized her, but Angie remembered Mrs. Wilson, who had been with Groves Point Citizens Federal for years, working as Simon's father's assistant.

"I'd like to see Mr. Canfield," she announced in a crisp voice.

Mrs. Wilson's lined face revealed nothing. "Do you have an appointment?"

"No, but I'm confident he'll see me." She wasn't the least bit sure, but Mrs. Wilson didn't know that. "Tell him Angie Robinson is here."

Again Mrs. Wilson's features remained stoic. "If you'll wait a moment." She left Angie standing on the other side of the counter as she walked the length of the bank and tapped against a frosted glass door. She returned a minute later, her face a bright red hue. "Mr. Canfield suggests . . ." she started, then swallowed with difficulty. "He would prefer not to see you, Ms. Robinson."

*How dare he!* Angie fumed inwardly, but she gave a gracious smile to Mrs. Wilson. "Thank you for your trouble."

The older woman gave her a sympathetic look. "Nice seeing you again, Angie."

"Thank you."

Her heels made clicking sounds against the marble floor as she turned and walked toward the exit. How dare he humiliate her like this! He had no right. None. With one hand against the metal bar on the glass door, Angie forcefully expelled her breath. She wasn't scum he could walk over. She wouldn't let him.

With an energy born of anger and pride, she pivoted sharply and walked the length of the bank lobby, her chin tilted at a proud angle. She wasn't a member of the country club, nor had she been a member of the upper class, but she was going to have her say to Simon Canfield Senior whether he wanted to hear her or not.

Not bothering to knock, Angie let herself into the office. "Excuse me for interrupting . . ." She stopped and swallowed back the shock. It wasn't Simon's father who rose from the large oak desk to confront her, but Simon. Time had altered his dark good looks. The gray eyes that had once warmed her with his love were now as grim as the storm-tossed North Sea. Tiny lines fanned from them, but Angie was convinced he hadn't gotten them from smiling. He was so cold that in his gray flannel suit he resembled a stone castle whose defenses were impenetrable. Cold and cruel. The edge of his hard mouth twisted upward.

"Hello, Angie."

"Simon." The oxygen returned to her lungs in a deep breath.

Neither spoke again. The chill in the room was palpable, Angie mused, and a smile briefly touched her eyes. It hadn't always been that way with them. Years ago, the temperature had been searing and they couldn't stay out of each other's arms.

"Something amuses you?"

"No." If anything, the thought should produce tears. But Angie hadn't cried in years. Simon had taught her that. She lowered her gaze to the desktop. Crisp, neat, orderly.

"You wanted to see me?" he began, in starched tones.

"I wanted to see your father."

"He isn't well. I've assumed most of his duties."

They were speaking like polite strangers . . . No,

Angie amended the thought. They were facing each other like bitter adversaries.

"I'm sorry to hear about your father."

"Are you?" He cocked a mocking brow.

"Yes, of course." She felt flustered and uneasy.

"I'd have thought you hated him. But then, it must be difficult to dislike someone who has been so generous with you in the past."

Simon's biting comment was a vivid reminder of the reason for her being in Groves Point. The color flowed from her face, leaving her sickly pale. "Taking that money has always bothered me," Angie confessed in a weak voice that she barely recognized as her own.

The pencil Simon was holding snapped in two. "I'll just bet it did. Ten thousand dollars, Angie? I'm surprised you didn't want more."

"Want more?" she repeated, her heart constricting painfully. "No." Slowly, she shook her head from side to side. She wouldn't bother to explain that it'd nearly killed her to accept that.

Her fingers fumbled at the snap of her purse and were visibly shaking as she withdrew the narrow, white envelope. "I'm returning every penny, plus ten percent compounded interest. Tell your father that I . . ." She hesitated. "No. Don't tell him anything."

"I don't want your money." Simon glared accusingly at the envelope on the edge of his desk.

"It was never mine," Angie said, her voice laced with sadness. "I took it for Clay."

"My, my, aren't you the noble, self-sacrificing daughter?"

The words hurt more than if he'd reached out and

slapped her. Involuntarily, Angie flinched. "It bought you your freedom," she managed awkwardly. "I would have thought you'd treasure your marriage more. You paid enough for it."

It looked for a moment as if Simon wanted to physically lash out at her. His fists knotted at his sides, the knuckles whitening.

"I didn't mean that," she whispered, despising their need to hurt each other. "I know you won't believe this, but I wish you well, Simon."

He didn't answer her; instead his troubled gaze narrowed on the envelope.

"If you don't want the money," she murmured, her gaze following his, "then give it to charity."

"Maybe I will," he said, and his lip curved up in cynical amusement. "I believe that was my father's original intent."

To her dismay, Angie sucked in a hurt gasp. Slowly the ache in her breast eased so that she could speak. "Oh Simon, you've changed. What's made you so bitter?"

His short laugh was mirthless. "Not what, but who. Leave, Angie, before I do something we'll both regret."

With an inborn dignity and grace, Angie turned and placed her hand on the doorknob. But something deep within her wouldn't allow her to walk out the door.

"Go ahead," he shouted.

"I can't," she murmured, turning back. "It's taken me twelve years to come back to this town. Twelve years, Simon." Her voice was raised and wobbled as she fought to control the emotion. "I refuse to have you talk to me as though I did some horrible deed. If anyone should apologize, it's you and your family."

"Me?" Simon nearly choked. "You're the one who sold out, so don't play Joan of Arc now and try to place the blame on someone else."

"I did it for you," she cried.

His harsh laugh was filled with contempt. "Only a moment ago you did it for Clay, or so you said."

Angie swallowed back the painful lump that tightened within her throat. Sadly she shook her head. "I'm sorry, Simon, sorry for what happened and sorry for what you've become. But I won't accept—"

"Our love had a price tag—ten thousand dollars," he shouted. "It was *you* who took that money and left. So don't try to ease your conscience now." Leaning forward, he rested the palms of his hands on the edge of the desk. "Now I suggest that you leave."

"Goodbye, Simon."

He didn't answer, but turned and faced the window that looked out onto the parking lot.

The door made a clicking sound as she let herself out. Several pairs of eyes followed her progress across the marble floor. Undoubtedly her sharp exchange with Simon had been heard by half the people in the bank. A rush of color invaded her pale face, but she managed to keep her unflinching gaze directed straight ahead as she returned to the hotel.

The key to the hotel room wouldn't fit into the lock as Angie struggled to steady her hand. She felt as if her legs were made of rubber. By the time she'd manipulated the lock, she was trembling and weak.

A soft sob erupted from her throat as she set her purse on the dresser. Angie's hand gripped the back of the chair as another cry threatened. Tears blurred her eyes so that the view from the third-story window swam in and out of her vision.

At first she struggled to hold back the emotion, disliking the weakness of tears. Her fingers wiped the moisture from her cheek as she began to pace the room, staring at the ceiling. Soon every breath became a heart-wrenching cry for all the pain of a love long past. She fell across the bed and buried her face in the pillow, crying out a lifetime of agony. She cried for the mother she had never known. And the weak father whom she loved. She cried for the empty promises of her father's dreams, and the Canfield money that had given him the chance to fulfill them. And she cried for a town divided by railroad tracks that made one half unacceptable to the other and had doomed a love from the start.

Fresh tears filled her eyes. Glenn loved her enough to force her to settle the past. He loved her enough to want her for his wife.

Twisting around, Angie stared out the window at the blue sky. She wept for Glenn, the man she wasn't sure she could marry.

And for Simon, the man she had.

# Two

—⌇—

The gleaming white envelope remained on the corner of Simon's desk as he rolled back his chair and stood. For Angie to come to Groves Point had taken courage. To confront him and return that money had cost her a lot of pride. One thing Simon remembered vividly about Angie was that she might not have had two pennies to rub together, but when it came to pride, she had been the richest lady in town.

When he'd told her to leave, she'd turned for the door and hesitated. Her back had stiffened with resolve as she refused. In that minute it was as if twelve years had been wiped out and she was seventeen again. She'd been so beautiful, and she was just as beautiful today. Naturally, several things about her were different. No longer did her silky brown hair reach her waist. Now it was shoulder length and professionally styled so that it curled around her lovely oval face.

Her graceful curves revealed a woman's body, svelte and elegant beneath a crisp linen business suit. There had been a time when Angie hated to wear anything but washed-out jeans and faded T-shirts.

Angie had been his first love and he had been hers. Together they had discovered the physical delights of their bodies. With excruciating patience, they had held off as long as they could, because it had been so important to Angie that they be married first.

Discipline might well have been their greatest teacher. In restraining their physical desires, they had learned the delicate uses of kissing and the exquisite pleasure of exploring fingers. Their hearts beat as one and they were convinced their love could overtake convention, prejudice, and everything else that loomed in their path.

Only it hadn't. Angie had prostituted herself. Simon had loved her so much he would have willingly given his life for her. And now he wanted to hate her with the same intensity and discovered he couldn't.

The bank was empty when Simon left his office. The envelope remained on his desk. He would do as Angie suggested and give it to charity. Money meant little to him. He'd had it all his life and had never been happy. The only real contentment he'd ever known had been those few months with Angie. Now it seemed that she, too, had discovered money's limitations.

The Mercedes was parked in the side lot, and Simon was on Main Street before Angie drifted into his thoughts again. He wondered where she was staying and if she had come to town alone. She had used her maiden name, but he hadn't thought to look for a diamond on her ring finger. If she hadn't married, it would be a shock. One glance at the woman she had become revealed a rare jewel. Angie was a prize most men wouldn't ignore.

Engrossed in his thoughts, Simon automatically took a left turn off Main onto Oak Street on his way to the country club. Tonight he needed a long workout. A flash of color captured his attention and he glanced across the green lawn of the city park. Cindy and Bob Shannon were in the front yard, firing up a grill. Dressed in blue shorts and a faded T-shirt was Angie. She sat on the Shannons' porch with a beer bottle in her hand, chatting with her friends as if she hadn't been away for more than a week. Charlie Young, their high school class's football hero and the new owner of the town hardware store, came out the screen door and plopped down beside her. He said something to Angie, who threw back her head and laughed. The musical sound of her mirth drifted through the park to Simon, assaulting him from all sides.

The muscles of his abdomen tensed. Angie was where she belonged. She was with her friends.


The Mercedes caught Angie's eye as it peeled down the narrow street. Simon. It had to be. She didn't know of anyone else in town who could afford such an expensive car. The ten thousand she'd brought was petty cash to a man like Simon. Returning it was a matter of pride. She hadn't touched a dime of it. Clay had spent it chasing dreams. Her father had insisted that the Canfields owed her that money. As far as Angie was concerned, the Canfields owed her nothing.

"You have to remember we're rubbing elbows with the upper echelon," Bob teased, twisting off the cap of a beer bottle. "Ol' Charlie is now a member of the Groves Point Country Club."

"Charlie!" Cindy gave a small squeal of delight. "That's really something."

Angie thought it revealing that a club would decide Charlie unacceptable one day and welcome him the next.

"I knew there was a reason I bought that hardware store."

With the agility of a man well acquainted with the art of grilling, Bob flipped over the hamburgers as if he were handling hotcakes. "And tell us mere serfs, Your Worship, what's it like to mingle with the Canfields and the Radcliffs of our fair city?"

Casually Charlie shrugged one shoulder. "Why not find out yourselves? There's a dinner tomorrow night and I'd like the three of you to come as my guests."

Cindy tossed her husband a speculative glance. "Oh Bob, could we? I've always wanted to know what the inside of the country club looks like."

Uneasy now, Bob cleared his throat. "I suppose this means I'll have to wear a suit and tie."

"Honey, you've got the blue one we bought on sale before Easter," Cindy argued. The burst of excited happiness added a pinkish hue to her face. "Of course I'll need to have something new," she said, and shared a conspiratorial smile with her friend.

Admirably, Angie refrained from laughing. From the sound of them, they were all seventeen again and discussing prom night.

"What about you, Angie? Can you come?" Charlie was regarding her with an eager expression. From the minute Charlie had arrived he'd made it plain that he liked what he saw. His divorce was final, and he looked as if he was ready to try his hand at love again. In an effort to steer clear of his interest, Angie had taken pains to mention Glenn.

"Like Cindy, I'm afraid I haven't a thing to wear," Angie explained, and lifted her palm in a gesture of defeat.

"We'll both go shopping!" Cindy exclaimed with enthusiasm. "I know the perfect shop in Fairmont."

"Fairmont!" Bob choked. "Just don't go using any credit cards."

Slowly shaking her head, Cindy tossed her husband a playful look. "Robert, Robert, Robert. I've always said if the shoe fits, charge it."

Angie woke with the first light of dawn. Sunlight splashed through the open draperies and spilled over the bed and walls. Sitting up, she rubbed the sleep from her face and stood. Her watch announced that it was barely six, hardly a decent hour to be up and about on a Saturday. Cindy wasn't expecting her until ten. With four hours to kill, Angie dressed in old jeans and an Atlanta Braves T-shirt.

A truck stop on the outskirts of town was the only place open where she could get a cup of coffee. She'd hoped to avoid that area of town because the Canfields' twenty-acre property was in that direction.

As Angie climbed inside her small car, she realized coffee was only an excuse. Yes, she'd pull over at the truck stop, but her destination was the small clearing on the Canfield property. Something inside her needed to return there. The thought was a sad reflection of her emotional state. Twelve years had passed, and she hadn't been able to forget the love she'd shared with Simon in that small clearing in the woods. The physical aspect of their relationship still had the power to inflict a rush of regret and sorrow. They'd been wrong to sneak into the church that night. Wrong to have gone against convention and the wishes of his parents. A few words whispered over her mother's Bible had never been legally binding. But Angie had felt married even if Simon hadn't.

The years had changed the land, and Angie nearly missed the turnoff from the highway. A long, sprawling house had been built, and the paved road led to the back and a three-car garage.

Hesitating, Angie decided to ignore the house and go on. The morning was young, and it wasn't likely that she'd wake anyone. The road went deep into the property, and she could steal in and out without anyone knowing she'd ever come.

Leaving the car, Angie took care to close the door silently, not wanting the slightest sound to betray her presence. With her hands stuffed deep within her jeans pockets, she climbed over a fallen tree and ventured into the dense forest. A gentle breeze chased a chill up her arm, but the cold wasn't from the wind. Her breathing had become shallow and uneven, and for a moment she wasn't sure she could go on. Only once had she felt this unnerved, and that had been as a child, when she'd visited her mother's grave.

There were similarities. In this clearing she was returning to a time long past and a love long dead. But from the way her nerves were reacting, nothing about this time and place had been forgotten. Every tree, every limb, was lovingly familiar.

To someone who didn't know these woods, the clearing would come as a surprise. The climb up the hill was steep, and just when she felt the need to pause and rest, the quiet meadow came into view. Even now, the simple beauty of this small lea caused her to stop and breathe in the morning mist. The uncomplicated elegance had been untouched by time. As she walked down the hill to the center, Angie felt like a child coming home after a long absence. The urge to hold out her arms and envelop this feeling was overwhelming. She wanted to swing around and sing, and laugh . . . and cry.

It had been here that Simon had held her in his arms and assured her that heaven and earth would pass away, but his love wouldn't. It had been here that they'd talked of the children to come and the huge house he'd planned to build her.

She'd laughed when he'd taken a stick and drawn out the plans in the fertile ground. They'd have lots of bedrooms and a large kitchen with plenty of cupboard space. He'd build it himself, he claimed. And remembering the skill he had with wood, Angie didn't doubt him.

Then that night in June, he had brought her to their imaginary home, lifted her in his arms, and carried her over the threshold. Drunk with happiness, she'd looped her arms around his neck and kissed his face until he demanded she stop.

"Just where are you taking me?" Angie had murmured, playfully nibbling on his earlobe with her teeth.

"To the master bedroom, where else, Mrs. Canfield?"

Angie tossed back her head and laughed. "Oh Simon, I do love you. I'll make you the best wife in all of South Carolina."

"I'm holding you to that," he said, and kissed her until she was weak with longing. His tenderness had brought tears to her eyes as he unbuttoned her blouse and slowly slipped it from her shoulders. Her long hair fell forward as she bowed her head. Tears filled her dusky, dark eyes.

"Angie, what's wrong?"

"Nothing," she whispered. "I love you so much. It's just . . ."

"What?" Gently, he had brushed the hair from her face and kissed the corner of her eyes, stopping the flow of tears. "Angie, I'd do anything in the world for you."

"I'm being silly to cry over a piece of paper. I don't need it. Not when I have you. But, Simon, do you think we'll forget our anniversary?"

"I'll never forget anything about you, or this night," he vowed. Straightening, he had taken the knife from his pocket and crossed the meadow to a huge pecan tree. It stood regal and proud, the tallest tree on the edge of the clearing. With painstaking effort he'd engraved the date and their names in the bark. The tree would stand for all time as their witness.

A distant sound of a barking dog shook Angie from her reverie. The tree. That was what was missing, gone. Sadness overwhelmed her when she located the stump. From the look of it, the tree had been crudely chopped down years ago. Simon had done this, cutting her out of his world as ruthlessly as the axe had severed the life of the mighty pecan. It shouldn't hurt this much, she told herself. But it did. The pain dug as deep as the day Simon's mother had come to her with the money.

Her legs felt as though they would no longer hold her

upright, and she slumped down, sitting on the stump as the strength drained from her. Gone was the outrage, vanishing as quickly as it came. Her tears were those of sorrow for what they had lost. There was no more fight left in her. Simon had appointed himself judge and divorced her with an axe. If their marriage had been a document instead of bark, she at least would have had the advice of counsel. Without conscience he had cast their love aside as though it had no meaning.

A dog barked again and the sound was noticeably closer. Brushing the hair from her forehead, Angie straightened. A black Labrador raced into the clearing, barking, his tail and ears alert.

A sad smile touched Angie's eyes. "Oh Blake, is it really you?" Simon had trained the dog from a pup.

The angry dog ignored her, intent only in voicing his discovery.

"Blake, don't you remember me?" Crouched as she was, Angie held out her hand for him to smell. Blake had once been her friend as well.

"That isn't Blake."

Simon's gruff voice from behind startled Angie. She sprang to her feet, her eyes wide and fearful as they fell on the rifle in his hands.

"This is Prince, Blake's son." He lowered the gun at his side so that the muzzle was angled toward the ground.

Prince continued to voice his displeasure, but one sharp word from Simon silenced him.

"What happened to Blake?"

"He died," Simon answered starkly.

"I'm sorry . . . I know how much you . . ."

"You're trespassing."

The sun was high enough now so that it invaded the clearing, its brightness peeking through the limbs and bathing the earth with a gentle glow.

"Am I?" she asked, in a voice so soft it could barely be heard. "Once it was my home."

"Don't try to make this place something it wasn't." A withdrawn look marked his features. His calm declaration chilled her more than angry words. "There was only one room here and that was the bedroom."

"Oh Simon," she pleaded. "Don't ruin that, too."

"Too?" His intense gray eyes narrowed and a bitter laugh escaped his throat. "If anything was ruined, it was your doing, Angie."

Their gazes clashed for a long moment, and Angie swallowed back an angry retort.

"Look at us, treating each other this way." She tucked the tips of her fingers into her jeans pockets and looked past him into the clearing. There had always been a special magic to this place, a calming reassurance she hadn't found elsewhere, even in church. Here, the love they shared had sheltered and protected them from the influence of the outside world. "At one time we were best friends, and . . . and a lot more. There wasn't anything we couldn't share."

Simon tensed. "That was a long time ago." Again bitterness coated his words.

"I've hurt you, and, oh, dear Simon, I'm deeply sorry for that. But you need to realize that I was hurt, too. It nearly killed me to leave you and Groves Point."

"Did the money help soothe the pain?"

Stinging tears welled in her eyes, but she blinked them away, turning her hurt, questing gaze to him. She'd come to Groves Point to make peace with Simon, but he seemed intent on lashing out at her with a storehouse of twelve years' resentment.

The curve of his mouth quirked in a derisive frown. "Tears, Angie? Believe me, I'm too old and too wise for that female trick."

Her heart wanted to cry in anguish, but no sound came. Proudly, she lifted her trembling chin. "It's taken me so long to come back. This place has haunted me all these years. But I never thought to find you so cold and bitter." The hard lump in her throat caused her to swallow before continuing. "I'm sorry for you, Simon. Sorry for what you've become, but I can't accept the blame." Her gaze swept the meadow, and again she was soothed by its peacefulness.

Turning away from him, she started down the steep slope toward her car. She felt Simon's presence looming above her. Proud, bitter, hurtful . . . hurting. A part of her yearned to ease that pain, but she doubted that anything she could do would touch Simon now.

Once inside the car Angie risked a look into the trees, but Simon and his dog were gone. Her hands gripped the steering wheel until the grooves made deep indentations into her palms. This wasn't the way she'd wanted things to be. Deep in her heart she'd expected to find Simon married . . . and happy.

The sudden need to escape was almost overwhelming. Glenn was right; she had needed to come back to Groves Point, but it wasn't working out as either of them had anticipated.

The turn of the car key produced a dull, grinding sound. Angie tried again. There shouldn't be anything wrong, she thought. She'd driven there without a problem. Again she tried the ignition, but only a sickly coughing sound returned.

"Oh great." She slammed her fist against the steering wheel and groaned. She didn't know a thing about the internal workings of a motor. Pulling back the hood release, she climbed out of the car. The hood was open and she inserted a finger to release it fully. A full three minutes later, her finger hurt and she had yet to loosen the hood latch.

"What's the problem?" Simon's gaze impaled her, grim displeasure thinning his mouth.

"My car won't start." She felt like an idiot, standing there massaging her finger.

"Why not?"

"Go ahead, car, tell me why you won't start." She turned and mockingly questioned the Ford. "How am I supposed to know? Believe me, Simon, I want out of here just as much as you want me gone."

A brittle smile cracked his mouth. "I sincerely doubt that. Here, let me take a look." He handed the rifle to Angie. "Hold this."

Doing her best to disguise her uneasiness, Angie accepted the gun.

"It isn't loaded," he said with his back to her, as he released the latch and lifted the hood. "Has this car been giving you problems?"

"No. I drove from Charleston without a hitch."

"Charleston," he repeated.

"I live there now."

The hesitation was barely noticeable. "It's a beautiful city."

Angie was holding her breath. This brief exchange was the first civil one she'd had with Simon. His dog was eyeing her again, his sleek ebony head tilted at a curious angle. Crouching down, Angie held out her hand to him a second time.

"I remember your daddy," she told him softly.

The long, black tail began to move as his cold nose smelled her fingers.

"How long have you had Prince?" Angie asked, more to carry the conversation than any desire to know the dog's age.

"Must be five, six years now." Simon's voice was muffled, his upper body folded over the side of the car. "I'm going to need a couple of tools."

"Can I get them for you?" Angie's voice was faintly high in her eagerness to help. "Believe me, car problems were the last thing I expected." She gave a small, tight laugh. "Truth be told, I was hoping to make a grand exit."

A hint of a smile came and went. "My tools are in the garage."

The house had to be a good quarter-mile down the gravel road.

Simon's gaze followed Angie's. "You can wait here if you prefer."

"I'd like to come with you." It felt so good to talk to Simon again without more than a decade of bitterness positioned between them like a brick wall. There was so much she wanted to say, and just as much she had hoped to ask. Tomorrow she'd be gone.

His gray eyes brushed over her speculatively. "If you like."

Fingertips tucked in her pockets once again, Angie matched his stride as they walked toward the house. Covertly, she studied him. The sprinkling of gray hairs at his temples gave him a distinguished look. His hair was shorter now than she recalled. But little about Simon was the way she remembered.

Her mind searched for something to say and came back empty. They were strangers. But intimate strangers. She doubted that others in this world knew Simon as well as she had at seventeen. He lived behind a stone mask now, closing himself off from the world. It hadn't taken much to discern from her conversation with Cindy and Bob that Simon had become an entity unto himself. He needed no one and had made that plain to the citizens of Groves Point.

"What do you think's wrong with my car?" she asked after a long moment, disliking the silence.

"I'm not sure."

Angie's shoes kicked up the gravel as they walked. Her usual pace was somewhat slower, but she wanted to keep even with Simon. Undoubtedly, he wanted to be rid of her as quickly as possible. But this unexpected reprieve was a welcome respite. Prince marched at his master's side, content to be with Simon rather than run ahead.

Angie's gaze roamed over the trees and flowers that grew in abundance there. Once, years ago, she had been as young and fresh as the wildflowers, pushing through the fertile ground and seeking out the sun. Now she felt as old as the earth and not nearly as wise.

Glancing at Simon, she witnessed the proud defiance

in the tilt of his head. Even the beauty of this land had been tarnished by his hate.

"I've always loved it here," she said quietly.

The subdued tone of her voice drew his gaze. "Then why did you leave?"

"Oh Simon, if I could change our past, rectify all my mistakes, don't you think I would? I left Groves Point because I felt I was doing what was right for us. Don't you realize that it hurt me, too?"

His jaw was clenched and tight, but he said nothing as he stared unfalteringly at her.

A strained silence followed.

"Then why did you come back?"

Angie didn't know how to put into words the emotion that had driven her to Groves Point. "I wanted to return the money." An uncomplicated answer seemed best.

"You could have mailed it."

Her hand burrowed deeper into her jeans pockets. "Yes, I could have."

They approached the back of the property, giving Angie a moment to study the house. Briefly, she wondered if the interior was anything like the plans Simon had drawn for her. Excitement flashed through her and died as quickly as it sprang. Feeling the way he did about her, Simon would have gone to great lengths to avoid a house that would even faintly resemble their dream one.

"This way," Simon spoke, holding a door for her that opened into the three-car garage. The gloomy interior was filled with shadows, the open door dispersing slivers of light into the dark.

Angie's gaze fell beyond the Mercedes to the red convertible.

"Simon," she whispered unsteadily, as she moved into the room. "You still have the car." Reverently her hand brushed the polished fender. Some of the best times of her life had been in this old convertible. Their first kiss had taken place in this '51 Chevy. Simon had come to her house so she could help him study for a science test. Afterward he'd taken her to the A&W for a root beer. And later still, he'd nervously leaned over and lightly brushed her mouth with his. Their first kiss hadn't been much more than that, but with time their technique had greatly improved.

On countless summer evenings they'd driven up to Three Tree Point and gazed at the stars. Some evenings the heavens loomed so close that it seemed all they had to do was reach out and pluck the stars from the sky. Simon had cradled her in his arms and whispered that if it were in his power, he'd weave moonbeams as a crown for her hair.

"I've been meaning to sell that old thing for years," he said flatly. "It doesn't run and hasn't in years. All it does is take up space in the garage."

Angie dropped her hand to her side. "It brings back a lot of memories." She smiled sadly.

He didn't speak for a minute. "Yes, I suppose it does," he said, as though the thought hadn't occurred to him.

Simon would like her to think the old Chevy convertible was a useless piece of junk, but Angie wasn't easily fooled. There had been too many hot summer days when she'd helped him smear the car wax over a spotless surface, her reflection shining like glass from the polished hood. Simon loved this old car. The fact that it was in his garage said as much.

"I'm ready to go." His eyes had narrowed into silver slits as he paused at the door, toolbox in hand. "Are you coming or not?"

Reluctantly, Angie left the car. She would have liked to look inside the glove compartment, to see what secrets it held.

They were several yards down the road before Simon spoke again. "How's Clay?"

The question surprised her. Clay and Simon had never been close. They had tolerated each other. Clay's dislike of the Canfields had been as strong as Simon's distrust of her now. "He's doing well," she said, and didn't elaborate.

Simon breathed in deeply. "What about you, Angie. Are you happy?"

Her throat went dry and a bubble of hysterical laughter choked off a reply. For twelve years her life had been in limbo. Could anyone be content there? She hadn't thought about being happy, not really, not in years. Happiness was relative to her circumstances. "I suppose."

"You must enjoy Charleston. It's a beautiful city."

Each question was a gentle prod. He cared enough to be curious, and that pleased her. "I own a flower shop."

Simon nodded, seemingly unsurprised. "You always did love flowers. Business must be good." He was referring to the envelope she'd given him.

She lifted one shoulder in a delicate shrug. "I can't complain."

Idly she picked up a stick and threw it for Prince. Playing catch had been Blake's favorite game, and his son was sure to appreciate it, too. Immediately the Labrador kicked up his feet and shot into the woods. Angie's musical laughter followed him.

Simon stopped and studied her, their gazes clashing. "Your laugh is the same."

Angie dropped her eyes first. "I wouldn't like to think much about me was different."

"Why not? We all change in twelve years."

"That's not what I meant." She wasn't quite sure what she was trying to explain. Simon was right, there were several things different about her. She was a mature woman now, not a naïve teenager.

Proudly, Prince returned with the stick, and bending over to retrieve it gave Angie a moment to compose her thoughts. "In some ways, I'm looking to recapture that enchanted summer of my life. That summer with you."

"You can't." Simon's words cut at her as painfully as a slashing knife. "That time is gone forever."

Angie paused and felt a compelling urge to reach out and touch him. Tightening her hand around the stick, Angie threw it again. "I know."

"Why did you come back?" Simon demanded harshly. "Why now, after all this time?"

Slowly, she turned toward him. "I had to come. I've wasted too many years as it is."

Panting, Prince returned with the stick, but when Angie bent over to take it from his mouth, Simon stopped her. Gripping her left hand, he raised his eyes to hers.

His dark brows furrowed together. "You've never married?"

Angie swallowed, but her voice wavered emotionally. "I couldn't. I married at seventeen."

# Three

—❦—

Simon went pale, his hand dropping hers. "Are you saying that you never married because of what we did?"

Her head drooped. Angie couldn't find the words to explain. "No. I realized when your mother gave me the check that whatever commitment you felt toward me was over."

"Haven't you got that turned around?"

"How do you mean?" Angie asked, missing the gist of his question. She remembered vividly how Georgia Canfield had come to her and explained that Simon had found another girl at college.

"I wasn't the one who asked to be free." His mouth tightened grimly.

"Not technically," she argued. "You sent your mother to do it for you."

"What?" he exploded. He opened his mouth, then closed it again as if to cut off what he was about to say. "I think we'd better talk." Pivoting sharply, he headed toward the house, leaving a confused Angie to follow in his wake.

He was so far ahead of her that by the time she reached the back of the house, he was already inside and the door was left open, waiting for her.

The back door led to a porch with a matching washer and dryer. Angie wiped the mud from her shoes on the braided rug just inside. Rounding the corner, she paused in the doorway of the kitchen. The room was huge, with bright countertops and shining appliances.

His hip was leaning against the long counter, his arms crossed over his chest. "Now say that again."

"What? That your mother asked for your freedom?"

"Yes." His eyes were measuring her. "How could you have believed such a thing?" He looked as if he wanted to strangle her.

"I didn't!" she shouted, in her defense. "Don't you remember I took the Greyhound bus to the university? I asked you myself."

"You couldn't have." He straightened and began pacing the polished tile floor like a tormented beast trapped in the close confines of a cage. Suddenly, as if he needed to sit down, he pulled out a chair. "I think we had better start at the beginning."

Angie joined him at the round oak table, her hands clasped in her lap. The confrontation with his mother might have taken place twelve years ago, but she vividly remembered it as if it had happened yesterday. And now Simon was acting as if none of this were true.

"Don't lie to me, Simon. Not now, after all these years."

"I swear before everything I hold dear that I never

asked to be free from you, Angie." Every facet of his face was intent, imploring.

Slowly, Angie shook her head, not knowing what to believe.

"Start from the beginning," he urged, his gray eyes wide and rapt.

"You'd left for the university that September."

He nodded. "I wrote to you practically every day and phoned almost that often. How could you have possibly believed there was someone else?"

Her nails cut painfully into her palms. She couldn't deny that in the beginning he'd contacted her daily. Being separated like that had been miserable for them both. But Simon seemed to have adjusted more quickly than she. "At first you did."

"What does that mean?" His eyes narrowed defensively.

"I . . . noticed that around November your letters became less frequent." She lowered her eyes to the quilted placemat on the tabletop. "You didn't phone nearly as often, either."

"I was saving money so I could buy you a Christmas present. The phone bill for October had taken nearly all my trust fund allowance."

She had known that, too. But at the time, she'd been so unhappy without him that every day apart had seemed like an eternity. "I knew you were involved with basketball, so I didn't say anything. But whenever we talked, you were always in such a hurry, and even your letters were getting shorter and shorter."

"Angie, I was about to flunk out of two classes because I spent so much time writing and talking to you."

It all sounded so petty now. She wanted to tear her eyes away from him but found she couldn't. His smoldering gaze held her captive, demanding that she continue.

"The second week in February your mother came into the pharmacy and said she needed to talk to me." Nervously, her fingers toyed with the fringe around an orange-and-brown plaid placemat. "She . . . she said that she'd noticed over the holidays that you were unhappy." This was hard, so much harder than she had ever imagined it could possibly be. Each word was wrenched from her until her voice wavered. "She said you'd found another girl at school, but you felt guilty about me. She didn't want me to be hurt and offered me the . . . money to leave town."

Simon's hand reached for hers, gripping it so tightly that it felt as though he had cut off the flow of blood to her fingers. "Angie, I hadn't."

Tears shimmered in her eyes. "I didn't want to believe her. That's why I took the bus to see you. If you were going to be rid of me, then you'd have to tell me yourself."

Leaning his elbow on the table, Simon wiped a hand over his face and pinched the bridge of his nose. "You were walking in front of the fraternity." Simon's own memory of that last meeting was strikingly clear. Her long, shining dark hair had been tied back and her mournful, troubled eyes had searched his. He had known she needed him at that moment, but he couldn't stand the pressure of another demand.

"I'd been waiting outside your fraternity for an hour, pacing," Angie inserted, caught in her own reminiscence. "I wanted so badly to believe it wasn't true. But you took one look at me and said you hoped to God I wasn't pregnant. A pregnancy would ruin everything."

Simon turned his head and stared out the kitchen window with unseeing eyes. That day had to have been the worst of his life. His grades had been so poor that he was kicked off the basketball team. He'd found Angie after leaving the coach's office, where he'd gotten the lecture of his life. His father had been to the university earlier that week, berating him. The last thing he needed was to have Angie show up and tell him she was pregnant.

"And you assumed from what my mother said that everything was true."

"It made sense at the time," she murmured, the tremble in her voice barely noticeable any longer. "It had been weeks since you'd seen me, and when you did, you acted like—"

"I know how I acted." Rising to his feet, Simon crossed the room. "So you returned to Groves Point, took the money, and moved out of town."

She hadn't wanted that ten thousand dollars. Clay was the one who'd insisted they take it. Simon owed her that much, he had argued. All Angie had cared about was the desperate need to escape Groves Point, and the Canfields. "Yes, I took the money and left." She offered no excuses. None were needed.

"So much for trust and vows spoken before God."

This wasn't a time for accusations, but for understanding and forgiving. In her anger she lashed back at him with a vengeance. "I notice it didn't take you long to seek solace." Her nerves felt threadbare. "How many women warmed your blood before you married Carol?"

Simon raked his fingers through his dark hair. "Three years, Angie. For three years I waited for you to come back." His mouth was pinched; tight.

He'd waited for her to return. Shock waves rippled over her as her eyes widened. "Even when I'd taken the money, you waited?" She stared up at him. "Oh Simon . . ."

He came toward her and paused uncertainly. If he touched her, he wasn't sure he'd ever be able to let her go again. Myriad emotions raged through him like a wildfire on a sun-scorched field. Anger. Surprise. Regret. But paramount was a burning sense of betrayal by the ones he loved and trusted most.

Impulsively, Angie raised her hand and reached out, lightly touching his forearm. Moisture shimmered in her eyes as she raised her gaze to him.

He caught her hand and gripped it as though it were a lifeline to sanity. "Angie, how could we have let this happen to us?"

"I don't know," she whispered, her voice wavering and unsteady. "It was all so long ago."

"I could kill them."

"No, no, don't even think such a thing." Vaulting to her feet, she forcefully shook her head. "There's been enough hate and misunderstanding. Your parents did what they thought was best for you."

The pinched look about his mouth didn't relax. "They had no right—"

"No, they didn't," she agreed. "But who's to say what the future held for us? We were both incredibly young—"

"And stupid," Simon inserted. "But it doesn't change what they did."

The cold ruthlessness was back in Simon. At seventeen she'd never seen that side of him. Their world had been filled with high ideals and warm promises. Who could have said that their love would last less than a year?

"I'm leaving in the morning," she said softly, her hand reaching for his and clasping it tightly. "And when I do I want to look back on these past few days as a time of healing. I came back to Groves Point to make my peace, not to stir up grief. I bear no one malice, least of all your family. We need to forgive your parents and my dad. But most of all, we need to forgive each other."

Simon expelled an angry breath as his gaze narrowed on her upturned face. "I don't know that I can," he ground out. Without warning, he brought her into the tight circle of his arms.

Having Simon hold her like this was like returning safely home after fighting a twelve-year battle. With her ear pressed against his chest, she heard the steady drumbeat of his heart. He released a sigh of contentment and she felt him rub his unshaved chin across the crown of her head. They had shared the most beautiful part of their youth together. Simon would always be someone special in her life, but the love they shared was over. She was free now. Free to return to Charleston and Glenn. Free to love.

A surge of happiness brought an excited bubble of laughter from her throat. "I'm so relieved."

"I don't know what I feel," he confessed, in a strained voice. All the emotions remained, most of which he would need to deal with privately. But Angie was here, in his arms, and he had to find a way to keep her there. "Angie." He murmured her name as he loosened his grip.

A hand on each of her shoulders pushed her gently back so he could study her. She was beautiful. Even the tears that streaked her face couldn't mar the natural beauty of her perfect features. The lovely mouth drew his attention, and he struggled to align his thoughts. "I don't want you to leave tomorrow." Not when he'd just found her again. Not when he'd been offered a second chance. Holding Angie was like stepping into the freshness of a newborn spring after suffering through the bitter cold of winter.

Angie was stunned. Simon's asking her to remain in Groves Point was the last thing she'd expected. "I have to go. My home, my business . . . everything's in Charleston." Suddenly it was vitally important that she get back to Glenn. There was so much she was burning to tell him.

"Stay longer—only a few more days," he pleaded, his fingers tightening their grip. "Just until we have things worked out."

"I can't." Her eyes implored him to understand. She was afraid of what would develop if she did. Simon and Groves Point were a part of her life that belonged in the past. Glenn and Charleston were her future. "In fact," she murmured, glancing at her wristwatch, "I need to be leaving right away. Cindy's expecting me." It was on the tip of her tongue to mention that she'd be at the country club dance that evening. But it wasn't an event she was looking forward to attending.

"Your car." Simon straightened as his gaze shifted to the tools lying on the top of the counter. A near-smile touched his mouth. "Since we're speaking honestly here, I guess I should own up. I disconnected a few wires."

"You did what?" Angie stared up at him blankly.

"I disabled your car. That's why it wouldn't start."

She was flabbergasted. "But why?" She'd have thought he would have gone to any lengths to be rid of her.

"I didn't know the car was yours when I did it. If someone was trespassing on my property, I didn't want them running off until I knew the reason."

"Oh." The logic in that was irrefutable.

"And later, when I discovered it was you"—he paused and smiled wryly—"I was happy to have an excuse for you to stay."

"I'm so glad you did," she admitted, keeping her voice low.

By unspoken agreement they left the kitchen, walking into the sunlight that shone down on them like a healing balm.

His hand rested lightly at the base of her neck as if he needed to touch her. How different their steps on this same bit of road had been only a short time ago.

Simon repaired her car within minutes by simply reconnecting the wires. When he lowered the hood, an awkward silence hung between them.

After wiping his fingers clean on a white handkerchief, Simon stuffed it into his back pocket. "I want to see you again."

Her heart was going crazy, its beat accelerating to an alarming rate. Part of her was crying out to explore the unbelievable tenderness they had once shared. Maybe if so much time hadn't elapsed, she would have been more willing. But the worlds that separated them twelve years ago had widened even more. She couldn't come back.

Her eyes were sad when they met his. She was angry

because he asked and angry because she knew what her answer must be. "I'm sorry, so sorry, but no."

He looked for a moment as if he didn't believe her. "Why not?"

"Because what we shared was a long time ago. We can't recapture our youth. Nor can we alter the past. The time has come to go on."

His brow furrowed in a thick frown, Simon shook his head and captured her hand with his. "Angie, listen to me. I love you. I can live a hundred years and never feel this strongly about another woman."

"Simon, don't," she pleaded, feeling guilty and increasingly miserable. "What you love is a memory."

"No," he argued with a warm gentleness that nearly undid her. "I love *you.*"

"You don't know me," she said desperately in a half-sob, reaching inside the car for her purse. Her fingers fumbled with the clasp as she struggled to remove her car keys.

"I'm not going to push this." His fingertips brushed a stray tear from her cheek. A dry grin twisted his mouth. "But I think it's a sad commentary on our lives if, after twelve years, you suggest we need more time."

Angie's laugh escaped on the swell of a broken sob. "You're going to start me crying all over again. Oh Simon. I've cried more these past few days than I have in years."

"Good," he murmured, taking a step closer. "Let those tears be an absolution." He placed his hand on the curve of her neck, his long fingers sliding into the length of her hair. His other hand wiped the moisture from her cheek. Unhurried, his mouth made a slow descent to hers.

As the distance lessened, Angie closed her eyes. She should break away, she thought guiltily, but the curiosity to discover his kiss again was overpowering. They weren't teenagers anymore, but adults, curious after a long absence.

His lips warmly covered hers, his touch firm and experienced. The tension eased from Angie as she slid her hands over his rib cage, feeling his hard muscles through the material of his shirt.

The pulse point in her neck throbbed against his fingers, betraying his effect on her. Her hold tightened as her mouth clung to his.

"Oh Simon," she whispered, as his mouth released her.

Slowly he lifted his head, awed by the power an uncomplicated kiss held over him. Angie's eyes were wide and faintly puzzled. She resembled a frightened doe, unsure of her footing. His first reaction was to reach out and hold her secure. But he couldn't. As difficult as it was at this moment, he had to let her go. In some ways, it had been easier the first time. He dropped his hands to his sides and took a step in retreat.

"Goodbye, Simon," she said in a choked, unhappy voice.

He couldn't answer her. For him the kiss wasn't a farewell, but a welcoming. He opened the car door for her and closed it once she'd climbed inside.

The car engine roared to life without a problem. Her eyes glistened with tears as Angie shifted the gears, backed the car around, and drove away. Not once did she glance in her rearview mirror, although everything within her was demanding that she take one last look at Simon.

A blazing orange sun was greeting the horizon when the two couples pulled into the country club parking lot.

"I'm as nervous as a virgin on her wedding night," Cindy confessed, as Bob gave her his hand and helped her out of the backseat of Charlie's Lexus.

"How do I look?" Cindy nervously asked Angie, as her fingers brushed at a small crease in the front of her dove-gray silk dress.

"Gorgeous," Angie said, and winked. "We both do." After spending the morning and most of the afternoon shopping, she wouldn't admit to anything else. Cindy did look lovely. Even Bob's jaw had dropped in surprise when his wife had appeared.

Bob inserted a finger under the starched white collar of his shirt. "Are you sure there isn't going to be a problem?" His question was directed at Charlie.

"I'm sure," Charlie returned confidently. "Everyone's entitled to bring guests."

As he'd promised, there wasn't so much as a raised eyebrow as they entered the foyer. Charlie signed in for them, and with a hand cupping Angie's elbow, he led the way into the dining room.

The round tables were covered with pure-white linen tablecloths. An expertly folded red napkin was standing at attention at each place setting. The lights had been lowered, and flickering candles cast a festive glow across the room. The hardwood dance floor was toward the front, and the band instruments were set up and waiting.

Cindy was whispering excitedly to Bob, who was walking behind Angie, but she couldn't hear her friend. Perhaps she would have been more in awe of the fancy club if Simon hadn't brought her here all those years ago. Once for a birthday dinner, and again for a dance. But his parents had objected strenuously to Simon taking Angie to the club. They had fought, and Angie, not wishing to be a source of problems for Simon at home, had refused to come again.

Charlie pulled out the high-backed chair for Angie, and Bob followed suit. The two women exchanged happy smiles.

"I guess I have to come to the country club for Bob to pull out my chair," Cindy teased her husband affectionately.

Within minutes they were studying an oblong menu, a gold tassel hanging from the top.

The women ordered veal piccata and the men chose steak au poivre. Charlie insisted on paying for their meal, but Bob picked up the tab for the domestic wine, a delicious chardonnay.

Nostalgia flowed as freely as the wine, and an hour later while they lingered over freshly brewed coffee, the five-piece band started up.

Only a few couples took to the floor.

"Do you dance, Angie?" Charlie leaned toward her and asked.

"It's been awhile," she admitted. Her lifestyle didn't include many evenings like this. She and Glenn shared many quiet evenings alone, but he was a lumberjack of a man and had never suggested they go dancing.

"My feet are itching already," Cindy confessed, and pointedly batted her curved lashes at her husband.

As Angie recalled, Bob and Cindy made quite a couple on the dance floor. They proved her memory correct as they took to the floor with an ease that produced a sigh of admiration from Angie.

"Shall we?" Charlie held out his hand to her.

"Why not?" Angie answered with a warm smile. "But forgive me if I step on your toes. It's been a long time."

"I'll come up with some penance," Charlie teased, drawing her into his arms when they reached the outskirts of the floor.

Angie felt stiff and a little awkward as Charlie tightened his hold. "You're still as beautiful as ever," he whispered. "I always thought you were the prettiest girl in class."

Angie managed to hide a soft smile. Charlie had dated a long succession of cheerleaders. In four years of high school, she doubted that he'd ever given her more than a second glance.

"You were dating Canfield, and he let it be known in no uncertain terms that you were his."

A part of her would always be Simon's, Angie mused, a thoughtful frown creasing her brow. She didn't want to have to think about Simon.

"You've done well for yourself, Charlie." Early in the evening, Angie had realized that Charlie enjoyed talking about his success. It was easier to listen to self-proclaimed accolades than discuss her relationship with Simon.

The music was slow, and as they turned, Angie caught

sight of a silver-haired woman with delicate features sitting at a table against the window. Georgia Canfield, Simon's mother. Angie's heart stopped cold. The older woman had changed dramatically. In twelve years, she'd aged thirty. One look confirmed that life hadn't been easy for Simon's mother, and a rush of unexpected compassion filled her. She had often wondered what she'd feel if she saw Mrs. Canfield again. The bitterness had been with her a lot of years, just as it had been with Simon.

"Excuse me a minute," she said, as she broke loose from Charlie. "There's someone I'd like to see."

Charlie dropped his arms, surprised. "Sure."

Making her way across the crowded dance floor, Angie formulated her thoughts. This was possibly the worst thing she could do, but the opportunity was here and she wouldn't allow it to escape.

"Hello, Mrs. Canfield." She spoke softly as she stood before the older woman, who was sitting alone at a small table.

A network of wrinkles broke out across her face as she turned, unable to disguise her shock. "Angela."

"I hope you'll forgive me for being so brash as to intrude."

"All young people are brash," Mrs. Canfield said, recovering quickly. "What are you doing here? As I recall, my husband and I paid a steep price to keep you out of this town."

Angie's fingers laced in front of her, tightened. "I realize that. I've only come for a visit."

"I didn't know you had relatives in the area," Mrs. Canfield said stiffly.

"I don't." Angie eyed the empty chair across from Simon's mother. "Would you mind if I sat down? I'd like to talk for a moment."

Georgia Canfield answered with a polite nod, but Angie noted that her shoulders were arched and her back was uncomfortably straight.

"I won't stay long," Angie promised, as she took the seat. Her insides were tied in a double knot, but she knew she appeared outwardly calm, as did Mrs. Canfield. "First, I want to ask your forgiveness for taking that money. There hasn't been a day since that I haven't regretted it."

Gray eyes, so like Simon's, widened perceptively.

"By accepting your offer," Angie continued relentlessly, "I confirmed every bad thing you wanted to believe about me."

"I realized at the time that it was more your father's doing than yours."

"That's no excuse." Both were aware that Clay Robinson was a weak man, but Angie refused to lessen the blame on herself.

"Have you seen Simon?" Georgia Canfield gave no indication that she was concerned, and Angie marveled at her composure.

"Yes, I talked to him at the bank yesterday when I returned the money."

"Returned the money . . ." The piercing eyes held Angie's for a long moment. "Are you planning to move back?"

An intense sadness settled over Angie. Simon's mother was more concerned that she was going to intrude on their lives. The fact they might discover her subterfuge didn't appear to concern her.

"No," she answered simply. "I'll be leaving town in the morning."

The older woman looked relieved. "It was good to see you again, Angela. Although you may think differently, I do wish you well."

Their eyes met and held over the top of the table. "I bear you no ill will," Angie said, and, placing her hand against the edge of the table, stood. "Goodbye, Mrs. Canfield."

The silver-haired woman lowered her gaze first. "Goodbye, Angela."


Angie inserted the key into her apartment door, turned the latch to open it, and reached inside for the switch. A flood of light filled the room. She blinked and lowered her suitcase to the floor. Charleston seemed a different world from Groves Point. Here there was an elegance and grace that had all but vanished from the rest of the South, or at least what she'd seen of it.

Reaching for her cell, she called Glenn.

"Glenn," she said, barely giving him time to answer. "Listen to me."

His husky laugh met her. "Angie, of course I'll listen to you. Are you back?"

"Yes, yes, I just walked in the door and I'm dying to see you."

"I'm on my way, babe."

The phone clicked in her ear, and with a sigh, Angie carried her suitcase into her bedroom. The drive would take Glenn a good twenty minutes; she would have time to shower and look her best.

The doorbell chimed exactly eighteen minutes later, and she crossed the floor quickly, flinging open the door. "Glenn," she whispered. "Oh Glenn." She reached for him, faintly aware that he was taller and more muscular than Simon. Her arms slid around his neck as she met his mouth in a fierce kiss.

With his arms wrapped around her waist, Glenn lifted her from the carpet and swung her around, closing the door with the heel of his shoe.

"If that's the kind of warm welcome I get, I just may send you away more often."

"And I'd go." Angie smiled up into dark eyes. Glenn was a dear, dear man. There were few in all the world whom she trusted more. He wasn't handsome, not in the way Simon was. His brow was wide and intelligent, his mouth a little too full and his nose a trifle too pronounced. But at this moment, Angie couldn't recall a man more wonderful.

"Glenn, dear, sweet Glenn." Leaning back, she held both his hands with her own. "You've asked me this question a hundred times and finally I can answer you."

The teasing, happy glint left his eyes and Angie watched as they grew dark and intense.

"Yes, Glenn, I'll marry you."

# Four

With Prince trotting at his side, Simon rounded the last curve in the road that led him back to the house. The sun was rising, bathing the earth in the golden light of early morning. Sweat rolled off Simon's face as a surge of energy carried him the last quarter-mile.

Just inside the driveway Simon paused, his hands on his knees as he leaned forward and dragged deep gulps of oxygen into his heaving lungs. He hated these early-morning runs and did them only as a means of self-discipline. But this morning had been different. With every foot that pounded the pavement, he filled his mind with thoughts of Angie. For the first time in more years than he cared to remember, his thoughts of her weren't tainted with bitterness. Unbridled, his mind roamed freely over their early days and the little things that had attracted him to her. His heart hammered, and with every beat it repeated her name: Angie, Angie, Angie. He remembered the first time he'd ever really noticed her. She'd been standing by her locker in their high school, laughing with a friend. Her long, straight hair had reached her waist and shone as if blessed by a benevolent sun god. The musical sound of her laughter had caught him by surprise, and he paused to see what was so amusing. His gaze had found hers, and the feelings he had experienced when he viewed this slim, dark-haired girl had enthralled him. He knew she was a girl from Oak Street. Simon hadn't even been sure he remembered her name.

From that moment on, he began to notice little things about Angela Robinson. His classmates often sought her out, pausing to say a few words to her on their way to class. Her smile had a way of lighting up her entire face. Her eyes were the darkest shade of brown he'd ever seen, a mysterious deep color. The girls came to her with their problems, knowing Angie was never too busy to listen. Even the guys set her aside in their minds. Subtly Simon had tried to find out what he could about her and discovered that where the guys were usually loose-tongued about girls, they weren't about Angie. Even his best friend, Cal Spencer, seemed reluctant to talk about her.

"What do you want to know for?" Cal had insisted.

"I hadn't noticed her before, that's all. Is she new?" Simon knew she wasn't. Faintly he could recall seeing her there sophomore year.

"No. She's been around awhile."

"Who's she dating?" Simon pressed.

"Hey, man, she's a nice kid, leave her alone. Okay?"

Cal's words had irritated Simon. *Why does Cal care, anyway?* he had thought. This girl had captured his attention. The truth was, she wasn't even that pretty. Not in the way Shirley Radcliff was, and he'd been dating her for weeks. The way things were going, he'd be sleeping with Shirley by summer. Most of the guys were already sexually active and took pride in recounting their experiences. Simon was seventeen, and he felt it was high time to share his own conquests.

"If you must know," Cal cut in abruptly, "Angie looked over my term paper before I handed it in to that old biddy Carson."

"You mean she wrote it for you, don't you?" Simon teased, nudging his friend with an elbow.

"No. I offered to pay her, but she refused. She said that she'd be happy to help, but she wouldn't do it for me."

"Did she?"

"Yeah, and she's helped me and a lot of the others having trouble, too."

"What do you mean?" Simon didn't like the sound of that.

"She's got brains and isn't a snob about it."

From then on, Simon had found that he watched her even more. Angie wasn't the cheerleader type, nor was she outgoing and vivacious. But she was the heart of their junior class. She was admired and respected, and there wasn't a person in all of Groves Point High who had a bad thing to say about her. It wasn't that Simon was attracted to her. He had Shirley. But he was captivated by this long-haired girl with the shy smile and the warm heart. The longer he studied her, the more he realized that people were comfortable around her. Nothing about her was manufactured.

It had taken Simon a week to gather up enough courage to approach Angie. He had started by passing her in the hall and talking to her as if he'd been doing it for years. "Hello, Angie."

The first time, she had looked shocked. "Hi . . ." It hadn't occurred to him that she might not know his name. Everyone knew the Canfields.

Other meetings, supposedly by accident, followed. He just happened to be driving by one day when she was walking home from school alone.

"Hi." He pulled his shining red convertible to the curb and looped an arm over the seat. "I'm going your way. Can I give you a lift?"

Angie had tucked a piece of hair around her ear and shaken her head. "No, thanks, it's only a few blocks."

Her refusal vexed him. This was Simon Canfield she had just turned down. The boy who scored the most points on the basketball team, the son of a banker, and the richest kid in town. Who did she think she was, anyway?

Another week passed before Simon approached her again. This time they both were in the city library. Simon played it cool and didn't say a word. He did, however, nod in her direction once when he caught her eye. She smiled in return and glanced down at her books.

Simon picked up a book on archaeology and sat at the table across from her. For a full twenty minutes, neither said a word. Simon pretended to be reading, but his gaze was drawn unwillingly to her several times. The feeling of being this close to her was euphoric. But for all the attention she gave him, he thought, he might as well have been a pillar of salt.

Even now he couldn't remember who spoke first. What he did recall was that they sat and talked until the library closed. Simon discovered that he loved to hear Angie speak. Her voice was low and melodic. It wasn't her voice so much as what she said; her insights were refreshing. She made him feel intelligent and awakened a sense of humor in him he'd never known he possessed. He liked Shirley and had even thought he might be in love with her, but after an hour with Angie he found Shirley utterly boring.

Although it was dark when they left the library, Angie again insisted on walking home. Simon remembered that he tried to sound casual about meeting her again sometime and had even made an excuse about needing help with one of his subjects. Undoubtedly, she saw through that. He was an honor student himself.

After that they met nightly at the public library. With each meeting, Simon tasted a little more of the secret beauty that attracted Angie to his friends. She was lovely without being beautiful. Intelligent without being shrewd. And shy without being docile.

At school she smiled at him in the halls, but never sought him out. Since they didn't share any classes, Simon had to go out of his way to see her. He did so willingly, not caring who saw him or what they said.

Two weeks after he first started meeting Angie at the library, Shirley announced that she'd decided to start seeing another guy. If she'd expected Simon to argue, she was disappointed. Actually, Simon was grateful. He wanted to ask Angie to the dance after the game Friday night and would have felt obligated to ask Shirley.

Angie turned him down flat.

For two nights he didn't show up at the library. Nor

did he make a point of passing her in the halls. He wasn't stupid; he'd gotten the message.

The Wednesday before the game, Simon stayed after school, shooting baskets at the basketball hoop beside the tennis courts. Almost everyone had gone home. He didn't know how long he had continued to drive to the hoop . . . long after his muscles had protested the exercise . . . long after his throat felt dry and his stomach ached . . . long after Angie had walked over to watch him. Even when he did notice her, he pretended he hadn't.

"Simon."

"Yeah." He continued to bounce the ball, took aim, and shot from the free-throw line. The ball swished through the net.

"About the dance . . ."

Bouncing the ball, Simon drowned out her words, shot, missed, made a rebound, and slam-dunked the basketball.

"Simon . . . I . . ." She hesitated, and her voice became small.

He tucked the ball under his arm and wiped the sweat from his face with the back of his hand. "Listen, I got the picture. You don't want to go to the dance with me. Fine, there are plenty of other girls who would jump at the chance." His throat felt as dry as sandpaper. Without a backward glance, he walked to the water fountain and drank enough to ease the parched feeling.

Angie followed him. "Would you consider taking me if"—she swallowed—"if I met you there?"

"Met you there?" Simon repeated, astonished. "Listen, Angie, I know you live on Oak Street. I do drive in that part of town. It isn't any crime to live where you do."

"I know, it's just that my dad, well . . . Would it be all right if I met you at the gym?"

"No," he said calmly, "it wouldn't be all right. If I ask a girl out, then I expect to pick her up and take her home. Understand?"

Slowly Angie nodded. Her arms tightened around her books, crushing them to her chest. "That's the kind of thing you should do."

"Are you coming with me or not?" Simon shifted his weight to his left foot, the basketball still tucked under his arm. He tried to give the appearance that it didn't matter to him either way. If she went with him, fine. If not, he'd ask another girl. The choice was hers.

"Thank you for asking me, Simon. I'll always remember that you did." With that, she turned and walked away.

A long minute passed before Simon ran after her. "Angie."

She hesitated before turning around. Her face was so drawn that her dark eyes were in sharp contrast to her bloodless features. "Yes?"

She looked so miserable that he immediately wanted to comfort her. "I could pick you up at the library."

"Would you?" Her voice grew even softer.

"I don't want to go to the dance with anyone but you."

She looked for a moment as if she wanted to cry. Biting her lower lip, she gnawed on it before forcing a smile. "There's no one else I'd want to take me."

"Can I carry your books?"

She nodded, and when he reached for her hand she gave him that, too.

That night they'd shared a tentative kiss. For the first time, Angie let Simon drive her home from the library. They stopped at the local drive-in for something to drink, and sat and talked until Angie glanced at her watch and looked startled. She had Simon drop her off a block before Oak Street. Her fingers were on the doorknob when Simon stopped her by placing a hand on her shoulder. Surprised, she looked back. Simon said nothing as he leaned forward and gently brushed his mouth over hers. He'd experienced far more passionate kisses, but none so sweet.

By the time he arrived home, Simon was whistling.

"You've got it bad," Cal had commented a month later.

"What do you mean?" Simon decided to play dumb.

"You and Angela Robinson."

"Yeah, so what's the big deal? She's terrific; I like her."

"I like Angie, too. Everyone does, but you know what kind of problem you'll face if you ask her to the prom."

Simon did know. It'd been in his mind all week. Angie hadn't mentioned it, but the biggest dance of the year loomed before them like D Day. For all his parents knew, he was still dating Shirley. Neither his mother nor his father would appreciate him asking a girl from Oak Street to the country club dinner scheduled after the prom. For that matter, Angie had never mentioned her home or family, either.

They'd continued to see each other nightly, with Simon dropping her off a block from Oak Street and sitting in the car until she was safely inside her house. A couple times he'd driven down her street without her knowing it and had been surprised at how meticulous the yard and flowerbeds were. As far as he could see, there was nothing to be ashamed of. He worried about Angie and wondered if her father was abusive or an alcoholic. She had given him no clues, but he couldn't press the subject, since he hadn't taken her to meet his parents, either.

A week before the dance, Simon had made his decision. "We're going," he announced that night. They were parked at Three Tree Point, sitting in the convertible with the top down. Angie sat close by his side, her head resting on his chest. Simon's arm was looped around her shoulder, and he pressed her close.

Angie hadn't made the pretense of not knowing what he was talking about. "There'll be trouble."

"We'll face it together." Slowly, reassuringly, his hand stroked the length of her arm. "And this time I won't pick you up at the library or anyplace else. I'm coming to your front door with the biggest corsage this town has ever seen."

"Oh Simon," she had whispered, uncertainty in her voice, "I don't know."

"And with you on my arm, I'm going to introduce you proudly to my parents."

Simon felt the tension building in her. "You're sure?"

"I've never been more positive of anything in my life."

The evening had been a disaster from beginning to end. As he said he would, Simon picked Angie up at her house. He had barely knocked when the door was opened. Simon wasn't sure what he expected, but it wasn't the tall, gray-haired man who stood before him. Simon introduced himself and shook hands with Angie's father, Clay Robinson. Clay was dressed in a suit, his hair slicked down. From listening around school, Simon knew that Angie's father worked at the mill. On weekends he played banjo at a local tavern.

"You've come to take my Angie to the prom?"

"Yes, sir."

"You're that rich kid from on the hill, ain't you?"

"Yes, sir."

"I don't suppose you and your daddy like good bluegrass?"

"Daddy, please," Angie pleaded, her face red with embarrassment.

"We enjoy music." All Simon wanted to do was get Angie out of that house.

"Me and my band play good; you say something to your daddy, you hear, boy?"

"Yes, sir."

Angie didn't say a word until Simon had parked the car in the parking lot. The music drifted from the open door of the school gymnasium. "I'm sorry, Simon," she mumbled, her chin tucked against her collarbone.

"What for?"

"Dad. He shouldn't have asked you to do that."

"Angie, it doesn't matter. Okay?" A finger under her chin lifted her eyes to his. They were so dark and intense that he leaned forward and kissed her. "Have I told you how beautiful you are tonight?" She was, incredibly so. Her hair was piled high upon her head, and small flowers were woven into the design. The dress was new, a light blue thing with an illusion yoke of sheer lace. Angie had designed it herself, and he was astonished at her skill.

For the first time that evening, she smiled. "No."

"Then let me correct the oversight." He chuckled. "You are incredibly beautiful tonight, Angie." He said it with all the emotion he was experiencing and gazed deep into her fathomless eyes.

Her smile revealed the happiness his words produced. "Thank you, Simon."

They should have been able to enjoy the dance, but they didn't. Instead they both were anticipating the confrontation that awaited them at the country club. Simon's mother hadn't surprised him.

"Mom," he said, tucking his arm around Angie's waist. "This is Angela Robinson."

"Hello, Angela." Politely Mrs. Canfield shook Angie's hand, but her eyes had turned questioningly to her son. His mother was far too refined to say anything at the moment, but Simon knew he'd hear about his choice of a date later.

Simon escorted Angie to a dinner table in the front of the room, where they were joined by Cal Spencer and his date. No sooner were they seated when Simon's father approached the table, expecting an introduction. He asked the group to excuse Simon and took him across the room, where he proceeded to demand to know exactly what kind of game his son was playing.

"Trouble?" Cal asked, when Simon returned.

"No." Simon reached for Angie's hand under the table. "Everything's fine." Only it hadn't been, and they both knew it.

Some time later, when Simon was away from the

table, exchanging polite inanities with a friend of the family, Cal came for him.

"Angie's left."

Simon looked around him in disbelief. "What happened?"

"Someone came up and said her kind wasn't welcome here."

Anger filled every fiber of his being. "Who?" He was ready to swing on the bastard.

"It doesn't matter, does it?" Cal murmured. "Shouldn't you be more concerned about Angie?"

It amazed him how far she'd gotten in so short a time. "Angie," Simon called, running after her. A hand on her shoulder stopped her progress down the hill. Her dark lashes were wet and he knew she'd been crying.

"Oh Angie." He pulled her into his embrace and wrapped his arms around her. She sniffled once and broke free, pausing to wipe her cheek, but kept her face lowered, refusing to meet his gaze.

"I'm sorry, running away was a childish thing to do, but I couldn't stay there another minute with everyone looking at me and whispering." Her voice was so muted he could hardly hear her.

"Angie, it was my fault." He brought her back into his arms and breathed against her hair, taking in the fresh fragrance. "I should be the one to apologize."

"No." She kept her head down. "I don't think we should see each other again."

Simon was utterly stunned. "You don't mean that."

She shook her head. "We'll talk about it later."

"No, we won't." He held her at arm's length. "We'll

talk about it now. I love you, Angie Robinson. Do you understand me?"

"Oh Simon, please don't say that."

"I love you," he repeated.

"Don't, Simon. This isn't funny."

"I tell a girl how I feel and she accuses me of joking? You have a lot to learn about me."

She sniffled and wiped the tears from her face. "Stop it right now, you hear?"

"I love Angie," he shouted, tossing back his head. He wanted the world to know. Loving Angie wasn't an embarrassment; she was the best thing that had ever happened in his life.

"Simon."

"I love you," he whispered, drawing her into his arms.

"I won't go back there," she whispered defiantly.

"Don't worry, I wouldn't put you through that." With their fingers entwined, they walked to the parking lot. From there they drove to their favorite drive-in and ate thick hamburgers.

That summer Angie had gotten a part-time job working at Garland Pharmacy. Simon picked her up in the morning and dropped her back home when she was finished. He sometimes worked at the bank, but he didn't recall that he did much of anything worthwhile.

"Are you going to be working there after college?" Angie asked one night. They were parked in their favorite spot at Three Tree Point.

"I'll probably take over for my dad someday," Simon answered, more interested in kissing Angie's earlobe than talking.

"Is that what you want to do?"

Simon grinned and straightened. Angie had a way of doing this whenever their kissing became too hot and heavy. With any other girl he would have pressed her, but not Angie. He didn't want to do anything she wasn't ready to try. It wasn't easy not to touch her. Some nights he was afraid the frustration would kill him.

"I've never thought about doing anything else but working in the bank. Why?"

"No reason."

She was quiet after that and didn't resist when he turned her lips to his and kissed her long and hard, pulling her lower lip between his teeth and sucking on it. Angie had a beautiful mouth: wide, soft, passionate. Simon loved the feel of it under his own. But then he loved everything about her.

As usual, he dropped her off a block before Oak. She sat for a moment, staring at her hands. "Lloyd Sipe was in Garland's today."

"And?"

"He asked me to a movie this weekend."

Simon felt a lead balloon sink in his stomach. "You're not going, are you?"

"I told him I wouldn't."

Simon relaxed.

"But I think it might be a good idea if we didn't see so much of each other for a while."

"Why?" he exploded.

"I'm afraid," she whispered. "Afraid because I love you so much. I . . . I want us both to start seeing others. Just until school starts. We can talk about things in September."

Simon's immediate reaction had been to argue, but

eventually she had worn him down. They stopped dating. The separation nearly drove Simon crazy. He loved her; it was only natural that he wanted to be with Angie. But in the months that they'd been seeing each other, something else, something more far-reaching, had happened. Angie had become his best friend. Nothing seemed right without her. His life had been ripped open, leaving a gaping hole exposed. Even Cal, who had been Simon's friend since grade school, couldn't fill the gap. For a long time Simon didn't date. He couldn't see that it would do any good. When Angie realized he wasn't seeing other girls, she started dating Lloyd Sipe. Simon got the message and asked out Kate Holston. He found her even more boring than Shirley. Later that summer his mother arranged a date for him with the visiting niece of one of her Garden Club friends. Jill Something-or-other had hidden a pint of vodka in her purse and proceeded to get smashed. By the end of the evening, Simon couldn't drive her back to Auntie fast enough. Laughing, her hair in a wild disarray, Jill had placed her hand high on his thigh and claimed she wasn't in any hurry to get home. If he knew "someplace private," there were lots of things she could think of to do to kill time.

The first day of their senior year, Simon had stopped Angie in the hall. "You said we'd talk. Are you ready?"

She smiled and nodded.

They met outside the library and drove to Three Tree Point. Simon parked the car, turned off the engine, and reached for Angie. He held her so hard that for a moment he feared he might have hurt her. "It's not the same," he whispered into her hair. "It'll never be right unless it's you in my arms."

Her own words were muffled as she buried her face in his shoulder, but the strength of her hold told him everything he needed to know.

With Angie, Simon was on the same intellectual and spiritual plane. By early the next spring they were a hairbreadth from exploring the sexual plane.

"Angie, I love you; I want to marry you."

"Don't ask me," she pleaded, spreading eager kisses across his face. "Please, don't ask."

Simon was so inflamed that controlling himself took a superhuman effort. "We've got to stop, Angie. Right now. Do you understand?"

"Yes," she said, her voice soft and willing. "I understand."

He leaned his head against the back of the car seat and took in deep, agonizing breaths.

"Can . . . can you hold me, Simon?" she pleaded. "Just for a few minutes."

"Oh Angie. This does it," he muttered. "I'm talking to my dad tomorrow."

Angie turned stricken eyes to him. "About what?"

"Us."

"Simon, they're not going to let us get married."

"They can't stop us. I love you. After last summer, I know I don't ever want to be without you again."

The confrontation with his parents had been the worst thing Simon had ever faced. Angie had wanted to go with him. Later he thanked God that he hadn't let her. The first thing his mother asked him after he announced that he wanted to marry Angie was if she was pregnant.

Simon couldn't believe that his mother would even

suggest such a thing. It only proved that Georgia Canfield didn't know Angie.

"Of course she isn't. We haven't even made love. Angie doesn't want to until we're married."

"Can't you see what she's after?" his father had demanded. "This little girl from Oak Street isn't stupid. Naturally she doesn't want to do it until after you're married. Men don't like to pay for what they can get free."

It took all of Simon's restraint not to shout at his parents that it wasn't like that with him and Angie. The taste of gall filled his mouth at the thought that the two people who supposedly loved him so much would try to take the beautiful relationship he shared with Angie and make it into a sordid, ugly thing.

"You're only seventeen," his mother pleaded.

"And in this state you need our permission to marry," Simon Senior interjected. "And as far as I'm concerned, you don't have it."

His father had come to Simon's bedroom later and sat on the mattress beside him. He draped a fatherly arm over Simon's shoulder and assured him that Angie was the type of girl for Simon to sow his wild oats with. No need to marry her kind. Later, he suggested, another girl would come along from the right kind of people, and Simon would feel just as strongly about her. At seventeen, Simon wasn't ready for the responsibilities a wife and possible family would entail. He should have fun with Angie, but be careful that she didn't get pregnant. Simon's jaw had been clenched so tight that his teeth ached for hours afterward.

"You don't need to tell me what they said," Angie murmured, when they met later.

"Listen," Simon argued, "I've got everything worked out. We'll get married after my birthday."

"But you'll have left for college and . . ."

"I'm not going to the U."

"Simon, you've got to. Your father went there, and his father before him."

"Marrying you is more important than some stupid tradition."

Angie's shoulders had drooped as she slowly, sadly, shook her head. "I won't let you do that."

"We don't have any choice."

"Your schooling is important."

"You're the most important thing in my life, Angie."

It had seemed crazy that the only serious rift in their relationship had been over getting married. Angie was adamant that Simon continue with his schooling in the fall. She wouldn't marry him otherwise. What she didn't know was that his father had already anticipated his son's defiance and had threatened to cut off Simon's trust fund money. Simon could never manage school while making a home for himself and Angie at the same time. As for college, he didn't care. Even being approached about a possible basketball scholarship didn't faze Simon. All he cared about was Angie.

Not finding a happy solution to their dilemma, Simon had come up with a compromise. It wasn't the perfect answer. But when he said his vows in the church that night, he had meant every word.

———

Sweat poured off Simon from his long run just as effortlessly as the memories of Angie had filled his mind. He moved from the long driveway into the house and headed for the bathroom to shower. Stripping, he turned on the pulsating power spray and turned his face into the jet stream, letting water wash down on him. Even the pounding water whispered Angie's name. He felt like singing. The realization produced a smile. It had been years since he'd sung in the shower.

Stepping onto the bathmat, Simon reached for a thick towel. A frown drove his dark brows together. His wet hair glistened as he eased his long arms into a starched dress shirt and fastened the top button. At seventeen he'd been more in love than he had at any other time in his life, he mused. A love that pure and good wasn't supposed to happen to a rosy-cheeked kid. Most people search a lifetime and never experience what he had in that time with Angie. With a vengeance, he jammed a gold cuff link into place.

Dressed now, and ready for the office, Simon went to the kitchen and poured a cup of hot coffee. He glanced at his gold wristwatch. A thousand times he had questioned what a seventeen-year-old boy could know of love. Little, he admitted freely now, but enough to realize that if it wasn't Angie in his arms, it wasn't love. He emptied the coffee cup in the sink and moved to the garage. The red convertible seemed to smile at him. This weekend he'd see about starting her up again. For now he had to hurry or he would be late to the bank.

He parked in his usual spot and jingled the car keys before putting them in his pocket.

Once inside the bank, he began whistling as he walked

across the large marble floor, drawing his assistant's blank stare.

"Good morning, Mr. Canfield."

"Morning, Mrs. Wilson," he repeated cheerfully. Five people in the bank gaped in surprise.

His secretary located Angie's business number in Charleston. Simon had lost her once; he wasn't going to make that mistake again. He loved Angie as much now as he had twelve years ago.

His heart was pounding as he punched in the telephone number. She answered on the third ring.

# Five

—⁓—

The sharp corners of Angie's mind were crowded with a thousand niggling thoughts. She should be thinking of Glenn, not Simon. She was home now and engaged to a wonderful man who loved her. And she loved Glenn in return, only . . . only things in Groves Point hadn't turned out as she'd expected. She had hoped to find Simon married and happy, with a house full of rambunctious children. Instead she'd found a bitter, disillusioned man trapped in the same limbo that had held her prisoner all these years. She had traveled to Groves Point seeking release from the past. The trip had given her that and washed away the guilt that had plagued her from the moment she had accepted the money from Georgia Canfield. But with the release came another set of regrets. Simon.

Determinedly she pushed thoughts of him to the back of her mind and zipped up the soft pink smock that hung from a hook in the back of her shop, Clay Pots. It had been named for her father, and he was proud of her small business venture. She hadn't told Clay about her week-end trip. It was better that he never know. Her father had yet to learn that she had accepted Glenn's proposal. The three of them were having dinner together Thursday night. Glenn and Angie planned to tell Clay then. Not that he'd be surprised.

"Morning, Donna."

"Morning." Donna was busy placing the cut flowers in the refrigerated compartment in the front of the shop and didn't glance up.

Angie's one full-time employee worked the early shift and stopped on her way in to the shop to buy cut flowers direct from the wholesaler.

"Angie." Donna stuck her blond head around the glass case. "There was a phone call for you earlier. I left the name on your desk."

"Thanks." Absently, Angie leafed through the orders for the day, dividing them between Donna and herself. Donna manned the counter in the morning and Angie took over in the afternoon.

Her heartbeat came to an abrupt halt when she glanced at the pink slip on her desk. The note was brief: *Simon Canfield phoned, will try again later.*

Every time the phone rang for the next four hours, Angie stiffened and prayed it wasn't Simon. Everything had already been said. All Angie wanted to do was bury the hurts of the past and build a new life from the ashes of Groves Point. She couldn't think of what to say to Simon or how to explain her feelings to him. It would sound ridiculous to shout at him that it wasn't supposed to have happened this way. Erroneously, she had assumed him to be married and happy. She wanted to tuck him neatly into a private corner of her life, like a favorite book once treasured but now outgrown.

"You're as jumpy as a bullfrog today," Donna complained early in the afternoon. "What's the matter with you?"

"Nothing," she lied. As she spoke the phone pealed. Something inside her, an innate alarm system, warned her even before she picked up the receiver that it was Simon.

"Clay Pots."

Simon chuckled. "Now, where did you ever come up with a name like that?"

"Hello, Simon." She knew she sounded stiff and unnatural, but she couldn't help it. She realized that turning her back to Donna would only arouse her employee's suspicions. Her hand tightened around the receiver until the pressure pinched her ear.

"Hello, Angie. Is this a busy time? Should I phone back later?"

Briefly, she toyed with the idea of delaying this conversation. Even a few hours would help her compose her thoughts.

"Angie?"

"No . . . no, this is as good a time as any."

"I want to see you. I haven't stopped thinking about you since you left. There's so much we left unsaid, and more that needs to be made right."

Angie closed her eyes and measured her words carefully. "Simon, listen to me. What happened is in the past. We can't resurrect that now."

"Why not?" he argued. "I love you."

"You love a memory. I'm not a sweet, naïve teenager anymore. I can't go back to being seventeen."

"Me neither, but I'm anxious to meet the woman you've become." His voice went low and seductive, as if he'd put his hand over the mouthpiece so as not to be overheard. "I'm eager to show you the man I am now."

Angie's heart slammed to her knees. Her throat went dry and she discovered she couldn't speak.

The bell over the door chimed, indicating that someone had entered the shop. Angie was so grateful she could have cried. "I've got to go, a customer just came in."

"Angie, listen, I'll phone you later."

"Simon, don't. Please, don't." Angry with herself for being so weak, she didn't wait for his farewell, and replaced the receiver. With a forced smile, she turned toward the deliveryman who was approaching the counter.

Simon stared at the auditor's report on his desk, knowing he couldn't concentrate on it when thoughts of Angie dominated his mind. His phone conversation with her earlier had been awkward. He should be in Charleston, not Groves Point. He needed to talk to her face-to-face and not try to carry on a serious conversation with customers walking in and out of her shop every few minutes. But with his father away from the bank so much of the time now, Simon couldn't pick up and leave. He rubbed a hand across his eyes to ease the growing pain that throbbed at his temple. The walls seemed to close in around him and he stood, jerking his suit coat from the back of his chair.

"Mrs. Wilson, I'll be back in an hour," he announced to his assistant on his way out the door.

"But Mr. C-Canfield . . ." she stuttered. "What should I do about your two-o'clock appointment?"

Irritation furrowed his brows. "Reschedule it," he snapped, then stalked from the room before she could comment further.

Georgia Canfield was in the backyard, pruning her rosebushes. A straw hat graced her silver head and was secured under her chin by a brightly colored scarf. Spotless white gloves hid her veined hands. At a glance, his mother looked like an aged southern belle of the era of the War Between the States.

"Hello, Mother."

"Simon." She spoke without turning. "I wondered how long it would take you to come."

"Then you know why."

Turning, she set the wicker basket filled with blossoms on the wrought-iron table. "Sit down and I'll ring for coffee."

Without question, Simon did as requested. The urge to hurl accusations at his mother seared his mind, and he clenched his fists.

The maid quietly delivered a tray with two cups of coffee. Resolutely, Simon glanced away, counting the interminable seconds before he could speak. At the sound of the retreating steps, he returned his attention to his mother. She sat across from him at the round ornate table.

"I understand that Angela returned the money,"

Georgia Canfield began, without preamble. She offered no excuse or explanation, but added two lumps of sugar to her coffee and stirred it briskly. From her outward appearance they could have been discussing the unusually mild weather instead of the gross interference in his life.

Not for the first time, Simon marveled at his mother's aplomb. Sometimes the sheer bravado of her actions astonished him. From his youth, Simon had been taught to look upon his mother as fragile and delicate. At all costs, she was to be protected from the cruelties of life. Now he felt as if he needed protection from her.

"Is that all you have to say?" he demanded.

"I did what I thought was best."

"You interfered in my life."

A nerve near Georgia's eye twitched, and she set the china cup in the saucer. "Don't raise your voice to me, Simon."

It took everything in him not to cry out at the injustice of her actions. The hurt and betrayal must have shone in his eyes.

"I don't expect you to understand why I acted as I did, nor do I expect your approval," Georgia continued calmly.

Unable to sit politely in the chair, Simon vaulted to his feet. "If you think I've come to applaud your wisdom, Mother, you're wrong."

"No," she replied evenly, "I don't imagine you did."

"And what did Dad have to say about this?" Simon doubted his father's involvement. Not that he was incapable of this deception, only that ten thousand dollars sounded like far more than Simon Senior would have parted with freely.

Her slim hand shook perceptively as she sipped from the edge of the dainty cup. "He was in full agreement. Something had to be done. You were barely eighteen and on the brink of your college career. Angela Robinson was ruining that."

"I was in love."

"You were too young to know about love."

"And when I married Carol I was mature enough to know that kind of thing. Is that what you're saying?"

"At twenty-one, I would say so. Yes, you were."

"Do you want the real reason my marriage failed, Mother? The honest-to-God reason?"

"Simon, please, that was all a long time ago. Let's not drag up this unpleasantness."

"You handpicked Carol yourself, but you made one basic mistake, Mother dear. I was still in love with Angie. I married another woman because I'd given up the hope that Angie would ever come back. I didn't love Carol then, and, God forgive me, I didn't love her the whole miserable year we were together."

Georgia Canfield went as pale as alabaster. No longer did she make the pretense of sipping her afternoon coffee. Her eyes became dull and lifeless. Simon's divorce had devastated his mother. Carol had become the daughter Georgia had never had, the one woman Georgia could mold into a replica of herself. The two had taken delight in the pointless avocations that filled his mother's life: bridge, the Garden Club, and numerous charities. For months following Carol and Simon's separation and divorce, his mother had held the hope that they would get back together. Not until Carol remarried did Georgia abandon the possibility of a reconciliation.

For Simon it had been only when Carol remarried that he was released from the guilt of having married a woman he didn't love.

Pulling the long white envelope from inside his jacket, Simon placed it on the table in front of his mother. "Unfortunately, the cost of sending Angie away was higher than you assumed."

"Simon?" A faint pleading quality entered her voice.

"Angie's repaid that now, but I doubt that you'll ever regain my respect."

Painfully, Georgia Canfield lowered her gaze to the envelope, knowing its contents without being told. "I'll ask only one thing of you, Simon. Your father's health isn't good. Don't mention this to him." She hesitated and added softly, "Please."


The air conditioner kicked on, and soothing cool air drifted into Angie's small apartment, relieving the intense afternoon heat. Barefoot, her hair swept up on her head, she filled the claw-footed cast-iron tub with water. Now that the money had been repaid, she could think about moving to a more modern apartment. The thought caused her to pause. *No.* Soon she'd be married to Glenn and they'd find a nice place to live. It bothered Angie the way Glenn escaped her mind. She did love him, she rationalized. She was confused, that was all.

The tub was filled, and still Angie stood with her cotton robe loosely tied at her waist. The urge to locate her high school yearbook from her senior year drove her to the bedroom. She crouched down on her knees and dragged out the narrow, flat box from under her bed. Sitting cross-legged on the polished hardwood floor, she lifted off the lid. Memories sprang out and danced around her on all sides. On the top, in a sealed bag, was the crushed corsage that Simon had given her for the junior-senior prom. Those were the first flowers any boy had ever given her, and Angie had treasured them more than riches. Even when Georgia Canfield had sent Angie away, she hadn't been able to part with these memories. Reverently she set the corsage aside and pulled out the yearbook she sought. With a sense of unreality she turned the pages and stared at the picture of herself as valedictorian of the graduating class. Had she really ever been that young and innocent? A sad smile touched her eyes. For someone so intelligent, she had been incredibly stupid.

She turned the pages one by one and a slow smile grew until it hovered on the verge of laughter. She wasn't the only one who looked young and innocent. Bob and Cindy were barely recognizable. And Simon—the gray eyes that stared back at her were so serious; his dark hair was several inches longer than the way it was currently styled. They'd changed, all of them. Without conscious effort, Angie realized that her index finger was brushing over the black-and-white photo of Simon.

The doorbell chimed and shook her from the deep retrospection. A moment passed before she realized what was causing the noise. Stumbling to her feet, she tightened the sash of the thin robe and hurried into the living room. A glance through the peephole confirmed her visitor was Glenn.

Angie unlocked the dead bolt and pulled open the

door. "Glenn, I apologize, I'm running a little behind schedule tonight."

His loving smile was filled with a warmth women dream of seeing in a man. "I don't mind," he said, taking her in his arms. His mouth claimed hers, parting her lips in a deep, languorous kiss. Angie linked her arms around his neck and tried to kiss him back and found she couldn't. *You'll learn,* her mind assured her, and Angie didn't doubt that she would.

Glenn's grip relaxed and his hand continued to hold her loosely. "I've had quite a day," he announced, and kissed the tip of her nose. "I'm finding that I like being engaged, but I have a feeling I'm going to like marriage a whole lot more."

Tipping her head back, Angie smiled into his shining eyes. "I'm sure I will, too." This man loved her, and she wasn't going to let anything ruin that. "Pour yourself a glass of wine while I hop in the tub."

"Are you sure you don't want company?"

Angie's laugh was light and breezy. "I don't know. That sounds interesting."

She'd been teasing and was surprised when Glenn followed her into the bedroom. He stopped short at the papers, books, and pressed flowers scattered about the floor.

"What's this?"

Angie hesitated. She'd rather not explain, but Glenn had a right to know. "I was looking through some things I saved from high school."

"In Groves Point?" His eyes met hers in a sober exchange.

Angie nodded, sitting on the edge of the mattress. "I can't believe I was ever that young."

Glenn bent down and retrieved the yearbook that lay open on the floor. Sitting on the bed beside her, he turned the pages to the senior pictures and grinned when he found hers.

"You go ahead and look while I take a bath," she suggested, with feigned disinterest. Her back was to him as she took a sleeveless summer dress from the closet.

"Is there anyone else's picture I should look for?" Glenn asked, in a bland voice that revealed all.

A tingling sensation ran up her spine, and Angie's fingers groped and bit into the wire hanger. Removing the dress gave her vital seconds to collect her thoughts. She was marrying Glenn; he had a right to know. "Simon Canfield's."

"And he is?"

"Was," Angie corrected. "Simon was the first man I loved."

"Heart and soul?"

"And body." Angie didn't leave room for any misunderstanding.

A heavy silence fell over the room. When Glenn made no response, Angie turned, her gaze seeking his. For months Glenn had lovingly wooed her. He had courted her in word and deed in the most romantic of ways. Eventually his persistence had won her over enough to encourage her to face the past head-on.

Sending her back to Groves Point had been a measure of how much he did love her. The hurt in his eyes revealed the pain her words caused him. Angie could offer

no vindications or apologies. Nor could she alter the circumstances of years long past.

The last person she ever wanted to hurt was Glenn.
He was the only man patient enough to peel down the
barriers she had erected around herself.

Closing the book, he set it aside. "He was the one you
went to see in Groves Point."

"Yes."

Their eyes were level now, unflinching. A minute
passed before he spoke. "Go ahead and take your bath
and I'll get myself that glass of wine."

The questions in Glenn's eyes were shouting at her,
demanding some kind of explanation. But he asked for
none. The tension flowed from Angie until her knees felt
weak with relief.

The bathwater was lukewarm by the time she had
settled in the bubbles and washed. Her mind was
crowded, uneasy. She had agreed to be Glenn's wife.
Maintaining secrets, even the most painful ones, was not
the way to start their lives together. Before her resolve
could weaken, Angie stood and roughly dried herself
with a bath towel, rubbing her sensitive skin with unnecessary force. Hurriedly she dressed and moved into the
living room.

Glenn was standing with his back to her, staring out
the window to the parking lot below.

"Glenn."

"Angie."

They both spoke at once, then laughed nervously.

"You go first." He took a sip of wine as if to brace
himself, his dark eyes uncertain. Glenn was such a positive, forthright man that it was a shock to read the doubts

in him. He loved her, and by all that was right didn't deserve to be hurt.

"You should know . . ." she began, then paused and gestured weakly with her hands. "The thing is, I don't know where to start."

"You need something stronger than wine," he said.

"I think I do."

Glenn brought down a bottle of bourbon and poured her a glass, adding ice.

Angie so rarely drank anything stronger than wine that when she took a sip, the burning feeling sank to the pit of her stomach and stayed there like a red-hot coal. Grimacing, she handed the glass back to Glenn. "I'll do better without this."

"From the look about you, I think I may need one of those myself." He sat across from her, resting his elbows on bent knees. White lines of tension bracketed his mouth. "Go on."

Angie knew what it had cost him to make light of this situation and appreciated him all the more. "I don't deserve you, Glenn."

"Just don't tell me you're married and have five kids waiting for you in Groves Point."

Her pain-shadowed eyes dropped to her hands. "There were no children," she whispered brokenly.

"But you were married?"

"Yes . . . no." This was the worst part. How could she possibly explain that through all these years she *felt* married?

"Which is it?"

"I was married to Simon, but the marriage wasn't legal."

"You'd better start at the beginning," he murmured after a lengthy pause, his voice aching and confused.

They talked nonstop for an hour until there was nothing Glenn didn't understand or know. When Angie was only a few minutes into the painful details, Glenn crossed the room and sat beside her, holding her close, lending her his strength. Angie was amazed that she could recount the events with such a lack of emotion. It was almost as if she was relating another person's story. Angie started the story when Simon and she were in high school, and ended with the bitter man she had found in Groves Point Citizens Federal and her confrontation with his mother the following evening. Sparing no particulars, accusing no one, she completed her narration and paused to study the grave look on Glenn's face.

"If you have any questions, ask them now," she requested softly. "After tonight, I want us to make a pact to never speak of Simon or Groves Point again."

Glenn was motionless beside her. "I don't think that will work," he said finally.

"Why not?"

"Because if I were Simon I'd be here right now. From everything you've said about him, I'm surprised he hasn't arrived already."

Angie wanted to bury the past, not resurrect it. "No, he won't," she returned, sounding more confident than she felt. "I told him it's over and that he's dredging up a memory. I asked him not to phone again."

Angie felt the room temperature drop ten degrees. "He phoned?"

"Today . . . I told him it's over. We can't go back to being seventeen again."

"Is it really over, Angie?"

"Yes," she cried, her mind in turmoil. "Would I have agreed to be your wife otherwise?"

Naked uncertainty flashed across his handsome face as he clasped her hands tightly within his own. "I want to believe that."

"Oh Glenn. My first instinct is to suggest that we go away and get married tonight. That would settle everything. But I can't. And I won't."

"I wouldn't do that." Glenn drew in a long, labored breath. "Everything will be right for us and between us when I make you my wife." His voice was soft with tenderness.

Angie turned brilliant eyes to him and smiled her gratitude. He was telling her that he understood her need to do everything properly this time. Her marriage to him wasn't going to be a hushed affair, with their vows whispered behind closed doors in the dead of night. She wanted to stand before God and friends and proclaim their love. With Glenn she would have a maid of honor and bridesmaids and her picture in the paper. This marriage was for a lifetime, and there would be nothing to make it sordid. In the years to come she would look back and remember the joy in Glenn's eyes when he slipped the wedding band on her finger. This marriage would be a good one, and with it would come the years of happiness that had been so elusive. The pain in her heart that had spread like cancer into every facet of her life would forever be healed.

Threading his fingers through her hair, he framed her oval face between his hands and gazed into her eyes. "I love you, Angie."

With a sublime effort, Angie forced herself to smile and echo his words.

"The same man as yesterday called," Donna announced, when Angie entered the back door of the flower shop the next morning.

Angie dragged her gaze from her friend to the desk and the offending telephone. "Did he leave a message?"

"No. Only that he'd phone back later."

Angie panicked, then became ice-cold as resentment filled every pore of her body. "If he phones again, tell him I'm not here. Better yet, inform him I've taken a six-month cruise to Antarctica."

Donna stared at her with wide-eyed astonishment. Angie instantly regretted her outburst, ashamed that she was crumbling because Simon Canfield had tried to contact her for the second time in two days.

The worst part, she thought, was that she couldn't chastise and berate him for interfering in her life. They shared a special bond of friendship, love, marriage, and betrayal. Simon could never be just an old "boyfriend" in her life, and finding the proper place in which to fit him could be impossible.

Angie's eyes strayed back to the phone. She hardly believed the surge of emotion she was experiencing. Vividly she recalled the look in Simon's eyes as she had pulled out of the driveway on his property. His gray eyes had grown soft with confusion as if he wasn't sure if he should let her go or plead with her to stay.

The phone rang again ten minutes later. Donna's eyes sought hers. "Do you want me to get it?"

"No." She shook her head as she spoke. "I will."

She drew in her breath and squared her shoulders as she walked to her desk in the rear of the shop. The area was small but granted her more privacy than if she were standing at the front counter.

"Clay Pots."

"Angie, it's Simon."

His voice was a gentle caress filled with the tenderness she had known from him in her youth. A surge of unexpected compassion spread over her, warming her. "Simon, before you say anything, there's something you should know. Something important."

"Nothing could be more important than the fact that I love you, Angie Robinson. Listen, I'm doing everything I can to make arrangements to—"

"Simon, please, will you listen to me?"

"Good. We need to talk. There are a few too many skeletons in our closets."

"I can't talk now," she insisted. "Not in the middle of the day."

"It's not even nine."

"That's the middle of the day to a florist. Please don't argue with me long distance?" She nearly choked at how ridiculous that must have sounded. Simon Canfield drove a ninety-thousand-dollar car, lived on choice South Carolina soil, and dressed in two-thousand-dollar suits. A phone call wasn't even worthy of a mention.

"I want to see you."

"No." It took all her restraint not to cry at him to stop pressuring her like this.

"Why not?"

*Tell him you're engaged,* her mind screamed. *He's got*

*to know. It's the only thing that will get through to him now.* "I won't see you, it's too painful."

"Angie, I swear to you, I'll never hurt you again."

"Oh Simon." Her voice became a throbbing whisper. "There's something you've got to know."

"Angie, please—"

"No," she cried shakily. Her hand pressed against her forehead and lifted the hair from her brow. "There's someone else who loves me now. He's a good man—" Her voice cracked, and she sucked in a calming breath.

A stunned silence echoed over the line.

"Please, Simon, don't phone me again," she begged. "I don't want to hurt you. Just leave me alone." Blind determination gave her the courage to sever the connection. Her hand remained on the phone, half expecting Simon to immediately call again. Hundreds of miles might be separating them, but it didn't take much to imagine the cold displeasure hardening Simon's face. Simon was a man who was accustomed to getting what he wanted. A full five minutes passed before she gave up the vigil. And it was another couple minutes more before she realized that Donna was studying her with a worried frown.

In a flower shop the phone and Internet were essential to run a profitable business. Angie learned that day to hate the phone. With every ring she cringed, fearing it was Simon. No day had ever lasted so long. She was out the door at ten minutes after five, relieved to have escaped partially unscathed.

This was the night she and Glenn were having dinner with her father. An evening to celebrate. Glenn was bringing his grandmother's ring to her, and they were going to announce their engagement.

"This should be the happiest day of your life," Angie muttered out loud, as she slipped her feet into delicate high-heeled sandals. "At least try to look the part." She checked her appearance in the mirror and groaned. Clay would take one look at her and demand to know who died.

She pinched her cheeks, hoping that at least would add color to her ashen features.

As usual, Glenn was on time. His mouth caressed hers in a slow, undemanding kiss. "Are you feeling okay?"

Nodding took a monumental effort. "I'm fine."

The doorbell chimed in short, impatient bursts, and Angie tossed a stricken glance across the room. Panic filled her, and her gaze flew to Glenn.

"Do you want me to get it?" he asked, almost tenderly.

"Please." Apprehension rooted her to the floor.

Glenn walked across the room and pulled open the door. "Hello, Simon," he said firmly. "I've been expecting you. I'm Angie's fiancé."

# Six

—⁓—

Charleston had often been called the Holy City. Her sky-line was punctuated with the graceful spires of churches, the symbols of man's faith in a merciful God. Angie's faith was at its lowest ebb as she sat beside Glenn in his Lexus. Silently, he drove to an elegant French restaurant, where her father was meeting them for dinner.

Angie's thoughts drifted to the scene that had recently happened. Simon and Glenn had faced each other like warlords defending their titles. At Glenn's announcement that he and Angie were engaged, Simon had turned his shocked gaze to her, demanding that she tell him it wasn't true. Instead Angie had inched closer to Glenn's side. To her surprise, Glenn didn't place a proprietary arm around her.

"Does he know about us?" Simon directed his question to Angie, ignoring Glenn.

"Everything," Angie told him.

Simon continued to concentrate his fierce gaze on her. "We need to talk."

"As you can see, Angie and I are going out tonight," Glenn intervened.

Her thoughts drifted to the present as Glenn pulled to a stop at a red light and turned to her, laying his hand over hers. "Are you angry?" He looked as if he could stand fearless against the strongest enemy but crumble under her distrust.

"Angry?" she echoed, and scowled. "How can I be? Why, oh, why, do you have to be so noble? I don't want to see Simon again. I want him out of my life."

Glenn's face tightened as he returned his attention to the road. "As much as I love you, as much as I want you to be my wife, I can't see us ever truly happy with the shadow of Simon looming between us."

"I went back to Groves Point," she argued. Already she had done everything he'd asked of her. More. The future stretched before her like an eagerly awaited journey, and for the first time this heavy load of guilt and unhappiness had been lifted. She was free. It wasn't right that Glenn was forcing her to turn around and go back.

A weary smile relaxed the tight lines about his eyes. "Yes, my love, but you didn't bury the past, you simply stirred it up."

Smoothing an imaginary wrinkle from her favorite blue skirt, Angie said, "But I don't want to see Simon." If Glenn harbored small doubts, then hers were giant mountains.

Glenn's hand reached for hers and squeezed it lightly, lending her his conviction. "He's only here for a few days. If you don't spend time with him, then you'll always wonder. We both will."

Again Angie marveled at this man beside her. He

loved her enough to risk losing her. And although he presented a façade of unwavering confidence, Angie realized that he wasn't entirely convinced things would work out as he desired. "I don't want anything more than to be your wife," she said.

"Good."

The restaurant came into view, presenting another complication. "Glenn," she breathed, "what are we going to tell Clay?"

"Nothing."

"But . . ."

"My grandmother's diamond is in my pocket, but as much as I want to slip that ring on your finger, I won't. The time isn't right for you to wear it yet. Spend this weekend with Simon. A few days will make all the difference in the world."

That was exactly what Angie feared most. Another concern bobbed to the surface of her mind: her father. "Clay mustn't know I was in Groves Point."

They exchanged meaningful glances. "Is it the money?"

"Yes."

"Whatever happened to it?"

She lifted one delicate shoulder, not wanting to say the words.

"Clay spent it?"

"It gave him the chance to follow his dreams. He's a wonderful musician," she said, a trifle too defiantly. "He went to Nashville looking for a chance to sell his songs."

"And blew it." Glenn completed the sad tale in three simple words.

"I don't think he's ever forgiven himself. Although he

never mentions the Canfields, he hates them almost as much as he detests Groves Point."

Clay had followed his dreams, and in doing so had shattered Angie's. With the money in his hands, he had become a stranger. He left Angie staggering with shock and grief in Charleston and bought a secondhand car to drive to Nashville. The way to impress the powers-that-be was with money, Clay had claimed. He'd return, he promised, as rich as Rockefeller. Wealthier than the Canfields, at least. Within a month he was back, broke and broken. For a time he tried to convince Angie that she had sold herself cheap, and that the thing to do was to return to Groves Point and get more money. For the first time in her life, Angie refused her father something. Now he hated Groves Point and the entire population. His music would never be sung, and it was easier to blame the Canfields than to accept fault with his own actions.

"But he's going to wonder why we're celebrating. In all the time we've been going out, we've never taken Dad to a fancy restaurant. He's expecting us to announce our engagement. What are we going to tell him?"

Glenn grinned suddenly. "We'll simply have to make up something. Should I tell him you're pregnant?"

"Glenn!"

"All right, you come up with something."

In the end, they called it a belated Father's Day gift, until a sober, disappointed Clay reminded Angie that she had already given him a shirt and tie.

———

Friday morning, Angie must have glanced at her wristwatch fifteen times between eleven and eleven-thirty.

"You're doing your bullfrog routine again," Donna
mentioned casually. "You sure have been jumpy this
week."

Arguing with Donna would be useless, especially
since she was right. In spite of herself, Angie glanced at
her watch again. Simon had said he'd be by to pick her
up for lunch between eleven and noon.

The door opened and Angie looked up. Her breath
froze in her throat, nearly choking her. Simon's smile
was filled with a wealth of love. A slow, admiring grin
crept across his face. He was dressed casually in an open-
collared sport shirt and cotton slacks. Angie couldn't
recall him looking more devastatingly handsome. Her
eyes were glued to him, and for the life of her she couldn't
speak or move.

Donna's gaze swung from the immobile Angie to
Simon and then back to Angie.

"Can I help you?" Donna intervened, obviously confused.

"I've come to take your employer to lunch."

Angie's fingers worked furiously with the satin ribbon she was forming into a huge bow. With a dexterity
that came with years of practice, she wove the ribbon in
and out of her fingers, twisted it with a thin wire, and set
it aside for Donna to insert into a floral centerpiece.

"Are you ready?" Simon directed the question to her.

"Yes. Give me a minute."

Donna's face scrunched up with a frown. "You're the
man who called earlier this week."

Simon's gaze didn't waver from Angie's. "Yes."

Flustered and eager to make her escape before Donna asked any more questions, Angie moved around to the front of the counter. "I'll be back at two."

"Make it three." Simon's gaze traveled to Donna as he flashed her a quick smile.

Once outside, Angie squinted in the sunlight. Simon strolled at a leisurely pace through the historic section of Charleston. Actually, Simon strolled and Angie followed, her arms crossed in front of her to convey her feelings about this arrangement. They drifted in and out of quaint shops along the way, browsing. Simon didn't seem to be in a hurry, but Angie wanted this afternoon over with.

"Are you hungry?" he asked, after an hour.

Her stomach was in tight knots. "Not particularly."

"You know, if you don't loosen up, someone might mistake you for a wooden Indian."

"Very funny."

Reaching out, Simon pressed a forefinger to the curve of her cheek. "None of this is the least bit amusing. Let's find someplace to sit and talk."

Simon chose the restaurant. Angie was too wrapped up in her feelings to notice the name. The hostess directed them to a table in the sun and handed them large menus. Angie couldn't have choked down soup, let alone an entire meal. This meeting was awkward and unpleasant. Yet Simon appeared oblivious to it all. With the least amount of encouragement, he looked as though he would pull her into his arms and kiss her senseless. Angie was determined that he wouldn't get that opportunity.

Simon studied the menu without reading a word. This wasn't going well. He had spent the morning finding out everything he could about Glenn Lambert. The man had a good reputation as a stockbroker and investor, and was coming up in the largest brokerage firm in Charleston. More important was the fact that Glenn loved Angie. They both did. Under different circumstances, Simon would have liked the man. Lambert was an experienced gambler, but he was a fool to risk losing Angie. Now it was up to Simon to press that to his advantage. Too much was at stake to lose her again.

The waitress arrived, and Simon ordered the special of the day, not knowing what it was. Angie ordered the same. Maybe they would both be surprised, he thought.

"When did you cut your hair?" Simon didn't know why he asked that, but anything was better than the tense silence between them.

Angie spread the starched linen napkin across her lap. It gave her something to do with her fingers as she composed her thoughts. She then lifted her gaze, looking directly into Simon's eyes. "A long time ago. I don't remember when."

He acknowledged her answer with a brief nod.

"When did you cut down the tree?" She had neither the time nor the patience to skirt around the issues.

His fingers tightened around the water glass. "Two years ago, June seventh."

Their anniversary. In a flash, Angie knew. She knew! Her breath jammed in her lungs as the knowledge seared her mind. He'd chopped down the tree because he couldn't endure the agony of having it in the clearing as mute witness to her betrayal.

She dropped her gaze, trying to find the words to

comfort him, afraid that if she stated her true feelings it would complicate an already uncomfortable situation.

"I don't think we need worry," she murmured, drawing in a long, quavering breath. "Our divorce wasn't any more legal than our marriage."

A shadow of pain crossed his features. "It's not that simple. I married you with my heart and discovered it was impossible to divorce you."

They each grew silent then, trapped in the muddy undertow of pain-filled memories.

By the time their lunch arrived, Angie's linen napkin was a mass of wrinkles from all the nervous twisting she had done. Simon had depleted his water glass twice.

Simon was annoyed with himself at being so unnerved by this encounter. Angie hadn't left his mind from the moment he had found her in the clearing last weekend. All week he had carried a clear picture of her in his mind. Now they sat like strangers, not knowing what to say. It was obvious that she was uncomfortable. For that matter, so was he. Silently he prayed; he didn't want to lose her. She was everything he had always known she would be: sweet, fresh, vital. He adored her frankness, her spirit, her capacity to love.

"How long have you known Glenn?"

The question came at her from out of the blue, causing the tight line of her mouth to crack with the beginnings of a smile. They had come to bury the past, and Simon was already challenging the present.

"We met two years ago when I invested the capital from the Petal Pusher."

"The what?"

Deliberately, she set the fork down beside the plate.

"For three years I had two businesses. Clay Pots and another I called the Petal Pusher."

"Petal Pusher? What was that?"

"I made weekly visits to restaurants, doctors' offices, or anyplace else that needed someone to come in and make sure their plants were healthy. It seems surveys prove that patients who wait in a doctor's office with dead and dying plants sitting in the corner lose confidence in their physicians."

Simon was enthralled. The idea was a marvelous one. "What happened to the business?"

Angie didn't hesitate. "I sold it for a tidy profit. I invested most of it and put aside the ten I owed you."

"And that's how you met Glenn."

"Right."

"You always were clever," Simon said, and a thread of pride laced his words.

For the first time that afternoon, Angie lowered her defenses. "I prefer to be thought of as intelligent. I simply found a need and filled it."

"Do you still play tennis?"

Simon had taught her the strenuous game and lived to regret it. Less than six months after he demonstrated the proper method of holding the racket, she was beating him at his own game. "Twice a week. What about you?"

"I've switched to racquetball. If you like, I'll teach you that, too."

Glenn already had, but Angie preferred tennis. "No, thanks." She made a show of looking at her watch. "I should be getting back. A teenager comes in part-time on Friday afternoons, and Donna likes to leave early."

"It's barely two." He studied Angie and made a conscious effort not to argue. "Will you have dinner with me tonight?"

"Simon," Angie said, and groaned. "It isn't going to do any good to continue to see me. We're different people now, with nothing in common except a lot of pain. I'd rather we buried it and went on with our lives."

"Fine. I want that, too, but I also want you in my life. Now and forever."

Clenching her fist, Angie deposited her napkin on the table and pushed back her chair to stand.

"Tonight?"

Glenn's words echoed in the chambers of her mind. Neither of them wanted the shadow of Simon looming between them. "All right," she agreed reluctantly.


That evening, dressed in a Caribbean-blue linen suit, Angie nervously paced the living-room floor. She regretted having succumbed so easily to Simon's wishes. Tonight was it, she argued silently with herself. She wouldn't see him again. Every meeting was a strain-filled confrontation that left her facing nagging doubts she preferred to ignore. Yes, she agreed, Glenn was right to force her into doing this, but she hated it.

Nervously she glanced at the wall clock. Clay had a habit of sometimes dropping by unannounced on Friday nights. The last thing she needed was to have him find her with Simon Canfield.

She stood by the window of the second-story apartment and gazed to the lot below. From her position, she viewed Simon's Mercedes pull into the parking lot. The vehicle looked incongruous with the cheaper models that filled the spaces. Unfolding his long, powerful legs, he climbed from behind the steering wheel, paused, and leaned over to retrieve a small box. Even from this distance, Angie recognized what it was. She should—she had seen others like it often enough. Simon—dear, wonderful, Simon—was bringing her a corsage. No one but him would think to do that for someone who owned a flower shop.

Opening the apartment door, she stared at him, hardly able to believe what she saw and felt. Simon, who could afford to give her the most expensive orchids, had brought her a corsage of white roses and blue carnations, made in the very shape and color of the one he had given her for the junior-senior prom.

Their eyes met in silent communication as he walked into the apartment.

"Hello again," he said, handing her the plastic container.

Unshed tears glistened in her eyes. "Thank you."

"You're welcome." His look was full of warmth. "A boy remembers things, too."

Her fingers fumbled with the opening as she struggled to avoid his gaze.

"There are a lot of other things I remember, including this." He reached for her and slowly bent his head toward hers. She knew he was going to kiss her, but instead of pushing away, she lifted her face and met him halfway, seeking the proof that she needed. She loved Glenn, and what she had shared with Simon was over. His kiss would confirm that.

Simon's mouth caressed hers in a long, tender exploration, and Angie's theory went soaring into space.

Deepening the kiss, Simon shaped and molded her lips to his own. Angie realized that with the least resistance he would let her pull away at any time. Part of her was demanding that she do exactly that. Instead, she dropped the corsage and slipped her arms up and over his shoulders, her fingers seeking the patch of hair that grew at his nape.

"Angie." He groaned, weaving his fingers into the thick length of her hair. Then his hands cupped her face as he studied the doubtful, almost accusing light in her eyes. His slow smile was followed with equally unhurried, lingering kisses that caused her world to orbit crazily. Alternately, he tormented and teased her until she was only too happy to oblige him. His kisses became a sensuous attack that left her trembling uncontrollably and clinging to him with an unaccustomed helplessness. Sensation shot through her as he repeated the assault. His hands roamed her back while he intimately explored her mouth. Her mouth broke from his. "No more," she pleaded.

In response he crushed her tightly to the hard length of his body. At the same moment his mouth came down on hers, silencing the forming protest.

Simon groaned again, louder, his lips leaving hers to explore her earlobe before blazing a path across her cheek, then covering her lips again. His hands released her and moved to the front of her, searing her flesh with every intimate brushing against the scented hollow of her throat. This newest intrusion penetrated Angie's senses, and drugged with passion, she battled desperately for reality by jerking free. Immediately Simon relaxed his hold and Angie went stumbling backward.

Expertly, Simon caught her in his arms and hauled her back into his embrace. "Okay, love, we'll stop." His voice was little more than a throbbing whisper as he rubbed his chin across the top of her head until their labored breathing had returned to normal. Color invaded her face.

Simon took in a deep breath. "Do you have anything to drink here?"

She answered him with a slow nod. His gaze followed hers into the minuscule kitchen.

"Sit down, I'll bring us both something." She brought down the bourbon, and he poured them each a drink.

Angie marveled at his control.

"What does all this tell you, Angie?" he asked, as he sat beside her and handed her a drink. She stared at the ice cubes floating in the amber liquid. Bourbon. Oh no, bourbon reminded her of Glenn. She was engaged to Glenn and had allowed Simon to kiss her like that. She could have wept with shame.

"Angie?"

"It tells me," she answered forcefully, "that I was a fool to let Glenn talk me into seeing you. I don't want this." Surging to her feet, she stormed across the room to the kitchen and dumped the contents of the drink in the sink. More than at any other time in her life she needed her wits. Being with Simon was enough to cloud her perception without adding alcohol. She thought she saw Simon's mouth twitch, but when she narrowed her eyes and searched his face, he willingly met her gaze.

"Something is funny?" she challenged.

"I find it amusing that your attitude toward alcohol remains the same. As I recall, you were never angrier with me than the night Cal and I got drunk on moon-shine."

"You nearly killed yourself."

"I didn't know which was worse," Simon said, chuck-ling, "your outrage or the headache I had the following morning."

"As it happens, I do have an occasional drink. Mostly wine." Her smile was involuntary.

"Good, I'll order a bottle with our meal. Are you ready?"

She hesitated and then said, "In a minute. I'd like to freshen up." Whole lifetimes could pass and she'd never be ready for Simon, not the way he intended.

It took far longer than a minute to repair the damage to her makeup. By the time she reappeared, Simon was standing, his drink empty.

He drove to an elegant restaurant situated on a cliff overlooking the Charleston Peninsula. The specialty of the house was lobster, Angie's all-time favorite food. It astonished her that he remembered these minor details about her.

"You remember how much I love lobster."

"There isn't a thing about you that I've forgotten," he answered, as he closed the menu.

"Not everything," she said, and lowered her gaze. He couldn't. It was impossible.

"I remember that you wanted to name our first daughter after your mother, and we decided on Carolyn Angela Canfield. And we both liked the name Jeffrey, so if it was a boy we'd decided on Jeffrey Simon Canfield. A second boy was to be named Clay. We had it all planned, remember? Two boys and a girl." His voice became low and thick, as if it hurt him to recall the intimate details of their early marriage.

They sat across from each other at the narrow table, lost in each other's eyes. Angie didn't want to be sucked into the past and gestured irritably with her hand. "What about you and Carol? Why didn't you have children with her?"

Simon lowered his gaze. "Marrying Carol was not my most shining hour. There was never any thought of children. We weren't in love."

"Never?" The thought of Simon making love with another woman produced a surge of jealousy that threatened to choke her.

"Never. What about you and Glenn?"

Angie knew instantly what he was asking, but decided to play dumb. "Yes, we're planning to have children. A house full, if Glenn has his say."

Simon blanched. "That's not what I meant."

"It's the only question I'm answering."

The wine steward arrived and began removing the cork from an expensive bottle of chardonnay. Simon's attention remained riveted on Angie. He spoke at last: "Fair enough. We won't mention Glenn again."

The meal was the best that Angie could remember. When Simon decided to be charming no one could resist him. Least of all Angie, who had dreamed of shared moments like this.

From the restaurant they drove to a beach. Angie removed her shoes and they walked along the shore as dusk settled over the land. Fresh breezes blowing in off the peninsula cooled the evening. Simon attempted to take her hand, but she wouldn't let him. Neither spoke. Angie felt content and melancholy, pensive and troubled, desolate and revived, as contrasting emotions swarmed at her from all sides. She had to think, to plan. There had to be some way to sort through these emotions. But not now. Not when Simon was at her side and it seemed as if twelve years had fallen away and she was seventeen again and so much in love that all was right in the universe.

"My father has taken a turn for the worse," Simon murmured, and looped an arm over her shoulder. She wanted to shrug it free, but discovered she enjoyed the warm, protected feeling it gave her.

Pleased that she let him, Simon paused to drink in the fresh fragrance of her hair and press his cheek to the crown of her head.

"I'm sorry about your father," Angie whispered. Clay, for all his faults, was her only family. If anything happened to him, it would devastate her. Angie was uncertain how close Simon was to his father.

"He's been ill for several years now. I don't imagine he'll live another year. I've got to go back, Angie." The appeal in his voice pierced her heart.

"I know."

"Come with me."

"Simon, I can't . . . My life is here now."

"I love you."

Dread weighed her heart. "I love you, too." Her voice throbbed with the admission. "I don't think I could ever not love you. But that doesn't make things right."

Turning, Simon gripped her shoulders. "Angie, of course it does."

She was close to tears. "We can't go back."

"Why not?" he argued. "I love you, you love me, and baby makes three."

"What?" she exploded.

Simon laughed and kissed her brow. "For the first time since I was eighteen, I'm aware of life. This afternoon I took a walk through the park near your shop. Children were laughing and playing and I stood watching their antics, thinking how much I want a child. Our child."

"Simon . . ."

"No." He pressed his forefinger to her lips, silencing her protests. "Hear me out. Two weeks ago if someone had suggested that I'd be talking about a family, I would have laughed in their face. I'd given up that dream and a thousand others that we'd planned. I need you. My life is an empty shell without you there to share it with me."

Angie's smile was rueful. "What can I do? My home is here. Clay Pots is here."

"Glenn is here." Steel threads laced his words.

"Yes. You may dislike him, but it was Glenn who forced me to go back to Groves Point."

"You were planning to come anyway, or else you wouldn't have wanted to return the money."

"I was going to mail it. Never, at any time, did I intend on going back."

"You went to see my mother, didn't you?" That was one thing that had troubled Simon. Georgia Canfield had known from the minute he'd stepped onto the garden patio the reason for his visit.

"No. She saw me."

"What did she say?"

"Nothing—she just wanted to be sure I wasn't planning on intruding on your life."

Resentment seared through Simon and he squared his shoulders. His jaw was set with implacable determination. "Is she the reason you—"

"No," she assured him quickly. "It's all of it. We accepted it twelve years ago even better than we do now. I'm from Oak Street and you live on Country Club Lane."

"Used to."

"It doesn't make any difference; you understand my point." She broke from his grip and crossed her arms, staring bleakly over the water. Her voice was flat and emotionless when she spoke. "It's time I went home."

Simon was silent on the drive to her apartment, and with each passing second Angie felt her confidence drain out of her. Simon was leaving, and she wasn't sure she wanted him to go. And at the same time, with the same heartbeat, with the same breath, she wasn't sure she wanted him to stay.

Simon pulled into the parking lot and turned off the engine. His hands tightened on the steering wheel before he turned and draped an arm over the back of her seat. "I'm not going to pressure you into something you don't want. All I ask is for you to promise me you won't make any decision while I'm away."

They were saying goodbye, at least for now. She was astonished at the wave of bittersweet nostalgia that bordered on sadness.

Simon watched her intently. His face contained an uncharacteristic appeal that relaxed his jawline and faintly curved his mouth. She released a sigh of regret. He was, she mused, all the things a man should be.

Slowly his mouth moved closer to hers. "Promise me, Angie," he said softly. "Promise me you won't make any decision about us when I'm not here."

Instinctively her arms reached for him, her lips parted to receive his kiss. Simon didn't disappoint her. His kiss sent a jarring jolt through her.

"Promise," he whispered.

"Simon."

His hand cupped the undersides of her breasts.

"I promise," she whispered, and the shock waves of his touch racked her.

# Seven

—◆—

Angie's dreams were filled with Simon. He satiated her senses until she woke feeling warm, secure, and loved beyond measure. It was as though twelve years had been wiped out and she lay content in her bed, knowing Simon would come to her soon and take her to the clearing in the woods. Moisture formed tiny teardrops in the corners of her eyes and slowly spilled onto the pillowcase. When Simon had made love to her, it never failed to move Angie to tears. The experience had been so beautiful that she had cried with joy. Even the first time, when they'd both been innocent, it had been the most poignant experience of her life. Man hadn't created the words to describe the tenderness of that first time. Angie had thought it would be awkward and painful. Instead they had shared a love so ideal, so exquisite, that tears had flowed freely down her cheeks. She had gazed up at Simon in the moonlight and discovered that his face was as moist as her own. They had cried from happiness, their hearts swelling with joy, knowing the love they shared was perfect. It didn't matter what followed in her life, Angie would always treasure that first night in the woods with Simon. The thought of sharing that kind of experience with another man seemed foreign and wrong. No man could ever reach so deep inside her that he touched her soul. No man could ever love her the way Simon had.

Wrapped in tranquility, Angie pulled the sheet over her shoulder and snuggled into the warmth of her mattress. Simon loved her still, and together that love would overcome all the barriers that stretched between them like an impassable mountain range. Together they would forge a pass.

Drop by drop, the dream drained from her consciousness, and reality intruded. Angie rolled onto her back and stared sightlessly at the ceiling. Moisture pooled in her eyes and slid haphazardly down her face. Only these tears weren't ones of joy. They had been born of heart-wrenching sadness. A love such as theirs was doomed to face more difficulties. But Angie had learned long ago that love didn't make everything right. She stood to lose Glenn, and only heaven knew how her father would react. They'd talk soon and she'd find out. He hated the Canfields, his judgment tainted with the bitterness of his own weakness.

The cost to Simon for loving her would be just as great. His family would never accept her.

Tossing aside the covers, Angie climbed out of bed and reached for the phone. Glenn would want to talk.

A half hour later he was at her door with a white bag in tow. "Warm croissants," he said, kissing her on the cheek.

"Coffee?" She rubbed her hands together to chase off a sudden chill.

"Please."

Glenn followed her into the kitchen and pulled out a chair. The look he gave her was long and penetrating, as if he could surmise her feelings with an exaggerated glance. Angie tried to ignore the questions in his eyes. He would wait until she volunteered the information, preferring not to pressure her. Angie didn't know how she could ever hurt a man as good as this one. And she was about to do exactly that.

She set out two plates and delivered steaming mugs of coffee to the table, then took a seat. The white lines of strain about his eyes revealed how tense he was. Waiting for her to tell him what had happened was killing him by inches. Her heart lurched with sadness. He cared for her, and she was about to repay that devotion and patience by crushing him. With a concentrated effort, Angie carefully composed her words.

"Simon and I had a chance to talk last night," she began haltingly.

"Good. I was hoping you would." He blew into the mug before taking a sip.

Angie stared into the black depths of her coffee. "We didn't settle anything. Apparently his father is ill and he couldn't stay."

"So he's gone?"

Angie nodded.

"But not forgotten," Glenn added.

"I don't know if I'd ever be able to forget Simon."

Glenn's hand reached for hers and squeezed it reassuringly. "Angie, I've known that all along. I wouldn't have insisted you see him otherwise."

Angie felt as if the weight of the world had come crashing down on her. "Why are you so good to me?" she pleaded in a low voice.

Glenn chuckled and shook his head. "Do you honestly need to ask?"

Angie swallowed, profoundly touched. "I don't want to hurt you."

His hand continued to squeeze hers. "Loving someone is a strange phenomenon. At least the way I feel about you has taken me by surprise. Your happiness is more important than my own. I'd be lying if I said I wanted to see you and Simon together again. The thought does funny things to my heart, if you want the truth. But I'd never stand in your way if you decided that you love him and want to share his life."

"Oh Glenn," she murmured miserably, on the verge of tears. "I don't deserve you."

"But I'm yours," he whispered, lifting her fingertips to his lips and kissing them gently. "No matter what you decide, I'll always be here for you."

A hundred and fifty miles down the road, Simon stretched out his arms as he tightened his grip on the steering wheel. Within three hours he would be back in Groves Point. The six-hour drive would eat up most of the day, but he'd still have time to phone Angie once he arrived home. He felt seventeen all over again, happy and carefree. He had the world by the tail, and this time he wouldn't let anyone destroy that happiness. Never again.

Not after he'd realized just how much he loved her and always would.

The road felt good beneath him. Everything felt good. The sun was shining and the birds chirped from their lofty perches. For the first time in a lot of years, Simon thought, he was ready to look at life head-on. There was time to appreciate the beauty of the world around him. He had Angie.

When Simon pulled into the driveway, Prince was sleeping on the back steps, grateful to see him after spending the night with the housekeeper. Simon's wheels spit up gravel, and he eased his foot onto the brake, coming to a stop. The sleek, black dog was eagerly wagging his tail in greeting. Simon paused only long enough to affectionately scratch the dog's ears before rushing inside the house, taking the back steps two at a time.

The phone number was in his pocket, and he dug it out with anxious fingers. Humming, he hit the number with his index finger, thinking that even the rhythm of her phone number had a musical appeal. He closed his eyes and waited for the soft sound of her voice. Even after all these years it didn't fail to affect him. Heavenly angels couldn't sound more beautiful than Angie.

After several rings Simon hung up, disappointed. He had to hear her voice again, just to know this inexplicable feeling was real and he hadn't imagined it.

Pulling a chair from the kitchen table, Simon straddled it and smiled. Bringing her the corsage the other night wasn't a brilliant idea. Good grief, the woman owned a flower shop. But that wasn't the point. He'd wanted to take them back to the days when she had been his and life had been about as perfect as anyone could expect. The minute she'd seen the flowers, those brilliant eyes of hers had softened and he'd known the time was right to take her in his arms. At first he'd tasted her resistance, but he hadn't been persuaded by it. She had probably felt disloyal to Lambert, but she hadn't held back from him for long. Simon's spirits had soared, and he had realized that without much difficulty he could have taken her right then. Only the time was wrong and he had known it. No need to rush. She'd felt so soft in his arms, so right. Her body had responded to him as freely as if the years apart had never happened. Simon didn't try to fool himself; he knew Angie hadn't been pleased about that. Just as he had tasted her resistance, he had also been aware of her surprise. She hadn't wanted to feel those things with him. She might even have been testing herself, thinking she would feel nothing when he held her. Instead it had been like throwing gasoline on a small fire. The years apart hadn't dulled their bodies' instinctive message to each other.

Simon walked back down to his car and lifted the leather suitcase from the trunk. He deposited it in the bedroom, returned to the kitchen, and opened the cupboard. He should be famished, he realized, but a meal without Angie sitting across from him would always make him feel lonely now.

On impulse, he tried her line again, holding the cell to his shoulder as he checked out the contents of the refrigerator.

"Hello."

Angie's soft voice caught him off guard. "Hello yourself," he said, straightening. The refrigerator door made a clicking sound as it closed.

"Simon?"

"The one and only."

"Where are you?"

"Home." She had the most beautiful voice. She was relaxed, and none of the apprehension he'd heard in their previous phone conversations was evident.

"You must have driven like a madman."

"I got an early start."

She hesitated, and he could feel the tension crackle over the wire, as if she were freezing up again.

"How was the drive?" she asked.

"Fabulous. Thinking of you helped pass the time. I told myself I'd play it cool and call you sometime this week. Then I walked right into the house and reached for my cell. I've gone without you for twelve years and suddenly eight hours is more than I can take."

Now she did freeze up. Simon prayed that the day would come when he could speak freely to Angie. But for now he had to be patient.

"Simon, please don't. It's difficult enough keeping everything straight in my head without you saying things like that."

"But it's true."

"I . . . know, I thought about you, too."

"See," he declared triumphantly. "You love me, Angie. When we're apart, nothing is right. We were meant to be together."

She didn't say anything for what seemed like an eternity. "Maybe."

This was wrong. He shouldn't press her. He knew Lambert wouldn't. The stockbroker would play his hand carefully and press his advantage when the time was right. Simon had too much at stake to bungle this now.

"I'll make the arrangements to come back next weekend. But this time I'll fly in. That way we can have more time together."

"Okay. By then I should know what I'm going to do. It's not fair to keep you dangling this way."

"I'd wait a lifetime for you, Angie, but don't make me. We've wasted enough time as it is."

Simon hung up, feeling frustrated and irritated with himself. He had to be more patient. Their conversation had started out well, but as soon as he started relaying his feelings, she had become uncomfortable. In the future, he vowed, he'd be more careful about what he said.


The late-afternoon sun burst through the window as Angie replaced the telephone receiver. Her heart had soared when she recognized Simon's voice. Even when she'd spent most of the day with Glenn, her thoughts had been on Simon. The stupid dream that morning was the source of her discontent. Even now the memory had the power to disturb her.

Angie clasped her clammy hands together in her lap and stared at the light fixture on the ceiling, taking in several long, even breaths while she tried to clear her thoughts. Her simple life had taken on major complications, and there seemed to be no one who could understand her dilemma.

When her doorbell chimed, Angie didn't need to guess who was on the other side. Clay almost always stopped in sometime on Sunday, usually around dinner-time.

His look was sheepish as he smiled at his daughter. "Hello, Angelcake." He was a tall man, thin and ungainly. His hair was mostly silver now and receded at the forehead to a sharp W at his hairline. The square jaw dominated his face.

Angie stood on the tips of her toes to lightly kiss his cheek. "I wondered if you'd be coming today."

"Been busy."

"I know." Clay was playing with a new band. For a while he had given up on his music, but his life seemed empty without it, and with Angie's encouragement he had gone back to playing weekend gigs. Although he was involved with music again, Clay had lost his dreams, having long ago abandoned the idea of making it big. He was content to play in taverns and for an occasional wedding. Fewer of those these days.

"I don't suppose you got supper cooking. It's been a powerful long time since I ate a home-cooked meal, you being gone last weekend and all."

Here it was. The perfect opportunity to tell Clay where she had been and whom she had seen, she thought. Her tongue swelled, and her throat went dry. The words refused to come.

"I'll check out the kitchen and see what I can come up with," she said finally. Emotions were warring so fiercely inside of her that for a moment Angie felt like blurting out the truth. Instead she turned toward the kitchen and took the leftover ham from the refrigerator. She cut off thick slices and placed them in the frying pan.

Chancing a look from the corner of her eye, Angie

noticed that Clay was engrossed in the Sunday paper. Misery washed over her and she squeezed her eyes closed.

"Dad."

"Yes?" He lowered the paper.

"I . . . I saw . . ." She paused. "I'm not sure where to start."

"Just spit it out, girl."

Angie braced herself for the backlash. "Simon Canfield was in Charleston this weekend."

Clay gave no outward appearance of having heard her. Angie knew by his look that he was struggling to control his response. "And?"

"And what?"

"Did you see him?"

Angie would have thought that much was obvious. "Yes, we had dinner."

With deceptive calmness, Clay laid the newspaper aside and stood. "You had dinner with that bastard after what he did to you?" A muscle leaped in his tightly clenched jaw.

Angie's fingers squeezed around the handle of the spatula, cutting off the blood supply to her fingers. She forced herself to relax and give the appearance of being calm. "Simon recently learned . . . we . . . we learned that the whole thing was a lie. Simon's mother made up the part about Simon finding someone else. He—"

"Of course he'd tell you that now."

"I believe him."

"Then you're a fool."

Angie blanched and turned back to the stove, making a pretense of turning the meat and rearranging it in the pan. A brittle smile cracked her mouth. She hadn't even turned on the burner yet.

There had been only a handful of times in her life that Clay had raised his voice to her. In some ways it was as if their roles had been switched. Oftentimes it was Angie who did the parenting. Clay was the one who needed protecting. Angie forgave him for his weaknesses and loved him for his strengths. He was a rogue who had claimed her mother's heart thirty years ago. Carolyn Robinson had died when Angie was eleven, and Clay's world had shattered. For months he had drifted from job to job like a lost soul seeking his place in eternity. It had been Angie who had held them together, finding excuses for the creditors, smiling calmly at the landlady with the promise that the rent money would be there on Friday. Angie was the one who had insisted they move to Groves Point and settle down. Clay was running, chasing rainbows with his music. They couldn't eat dreams or pay the rent with good intentions. Clay had hated the job at the mill, but it had given them the stability they needed. Soon he had found other musicians and formed a small band. Within six months of settling on Oak Street, he was a semi-happy man. At least as happy as he would ever be without his beloved Carolyn.

Clay's attention was riveted on Angie. "What other foolish lies did he feed you?"

"Dad, they weren't lies."

"I thought I raised a smarter girl than this."

"Dad," she protested. "I'll be thirty years old this year. That's old enough to know when someone's telling the truth."

Clay snorted loudly and crossed his arms. "Darn fool, that's what you are—a darn fool."

"Dad." Angie couldn't believe that this was her father talking to her like this. In many ways they were alike. All his life Clay Robinson had loved only one woman. As far as Angie knew, he'd lived the past eighteen years celibate.

"I just hope to God that Glenn didn't hear anything about you and that Canfield boy."

"He was the one who encouraged me to meet Simon. In fact, he insisted upon it."

"I can't believe that." Clay continued to pace the confined area of the kitchen in giant, power-filled strides that ate up the distance in two steps.

"Glenn feels that we can't make a future together until we clear away the past."

Clay splayed his finger through his hair in a jerking movement. "Just how much does Glenn know?"

"Everything."

"Everything!" he exploded. "Only an idiot would have told him how you gave yourself to that rich boy."

"I don't have any secrets from Glenn."

"Well, you should have. You gave yourself to him like a shameless hussy."

Angie's head jerked back as if he had physically slapped her with the words. Her fingers tightened around the oven door as she fought to maintain her composure and hold back the tears.

"I'll just pray that you didn't tell Glenn about your so-called marriage."

"He knows that, too."

Clay turned on her with mocking disbelief. "He

knows that you behaved like a common tramp and still has anything to do with you?"

"Dad." Angie reeled under the vicious attack of words. "Don't say that."

"Why not? It's true, isn't it?"

The words sliced into her heart like the serrated edge of a knife. This was Clay speaking to her, she reminded herself. But not the lovable roguish father she loved. This Clay was a stranger filled with rage and bitterness. One Angie didn't know or recognize.

"Glenn loves me."

"He must."

Angie's vision blurred until the tall stranger before her became a haze. Somehow she managed to hold back the tears.

"I suppose Canfield claimed undying devotion. That sounds like something those greedy rich folks would do. He couldn't stand the thought of you loving another man." He rammed his hands deep within his pants pockets as he turned toward Angie. "I bet he's kept tabs on you all these years, just waiting for you to find another man. Then the minute you did he popped back into your life, claiming he's always loved you. Ha! The only things those Canfields love is greenbacks."

"I don't believe that." Angie's voice was little more than a hoarse whisper.

"I hope you told him a thing or two."

"No. In fact, I'm seeing him next weekend."

Clay looked stunned. "You won't. I forbid it."

Angie's short laugh lacked humor. "It's a bit late for placing restrictions on me, Clay Robinson. I'm a woman now, not a child that you can order about."

Clay's hand gripped the back of the chair as anger contorted his features. "I can't believe my ears. This isn't my Angie talking. You'll do as I say or live to regret it."

"Just what do you plan to do? Lock me in my room or send me to bed without supper?" Angie didn't budge, but boldly met his gaze. "You're talking to a woman now. Threats aren't going to intimidate me."

Clay was quiet for an exaggerated moment. "If you so much as speak to that rich boy, then you can forget you've got a father. You hear me, girl? I was fool enough to stand back and let you get involved with him the first time. No more. From now on you're on your own. Understand?"

The thoughts that swam through Angie's mind were ludicrous enough to bring a trembling smile to her lips. She recalled the last time she'd argued with her father. She had been twelve and afraid they were going to be kicked out of the small boardinghouse in which they were living. Clay hadn't paid the rent in two weeks, and no amount of sweet talk was going to persuade the landlady to extend their welcome without payment. At the time Clay was playing the fiddle on street corners, collecting change. Angie had been the one to sit her father down and tell him the time had come to look for a job that paid real money. In his usual jovial way, Clay had sung her a song and claimed that a band would come along needing a fiddler and they'd be in Fat City. Angie had shook her head and calmly explained to him that there wasn't any band. They needed money for the rent. She needed new shoes. Clay argued that all he needed was a little time. And twelve-year-old Angie, mature beyond her years, had told him time had run out. Clay had wept bitter tears, wetting her patched dress with his emotion.

"You hear me, girl?" Clay repeated.

"I'm seeing Simon." Composed now, Angie met his gaze without flinching.

"Then you've made your decision. You won't be seeing me again." He stalked from the apartment, slamming the door as he left.

Crossing her arms to ward off the cold of Clay's departure, Angie slowly shook her head. This had been far worse than anything she would have believed. Clay hated Simon with a bitterness rooted so deep that it had choked off even the most basic reasoning. Given time, Angie was convinced that Clay would come around. She was his daughter, his only child. By tomorrow he'd be back to apologize, she reasoned. When he'd had time to think things through, they would have a reasonable discussion and everything would be made right.

Monday afternoon Angie called Clay before she left the flower shop. Her day had been miserable. The argument had hung over her like a storm cloud from the minute she had climbed out of bed. Even Donna had commented on how unusually quiet Angie was. Clay didn't answer.

Ten tries and five hours later, Angie broke down and drove to Clay's apartment. It was just like him to be stubborn enough not to answer the phone. Fine, she'd face him head-on. This whole affair had gone on long enough. All the family they had in this world was each other. She wouldn't be blackmailed by his demands, but the least they could do was talk things out reasonably.

No light shone through the window of Clay's residence and, after knocking for several minutes, Angie gave up. Reluctantly she returned home, weighted with despair.

Simon phoned her Tuesday evening, sounding happy and carefree.

"Angie, you won't believe what I did today."

Despite her mood, Angie felt herself drawn into his happiness. "Tell me."

"Are you sitting down?"

"Should I be?"

"That depends. No, on second thought, you wouldn't completely understand this."

"Then tell me."

"I phoned the Y and volunteered to coach basketball next season."

He was right, Angie didn't know why this was such a monumental decision. Simon had always been a talented athlete. It seemed natural that he would share his gift. Maybe, she thought, she was supposed to be surprised that he chose something as common as the Y. "Congratulations."

"I didn't think you'd understand," he said with a chuckle. "Angie, I've holed myself up in my own little world since my marriage ended. I've been little more than a recluse. Yes, I played tennis and racquetball and occasionally attended a social function, but it was only the motions of living."

"Simon—"

"Angie," he interrupted, "it's taken me all this time to

realize that when you left, something vital in my life went with you: the reason for living."

"Oh Simon." She felt the thickness building in her throat. When she left, all Simon knew was that she'd taken the money. All he knew was that she'd sold out. It was little wonder that animosity had dominated his life.

"Do you remember that I mentioned watching children play?"

"Yes." Her voice grew soft. Children were her weakness. Clay Pots kept her busy enough to make her forget about the family she'd planned with Simon. Glenn had talked about marriage long before Angie had ever considered it. Only when he mentioned children did he sway her.

"Angie, you have to understand that was the first time I stopped and noticed children. I couldn't bear to, knowing you and I would never have any."

She closed her eyes and placed a hand over her mouth.

"Angie?"

"I'm here," she answered, in tortured misery.

The line went silent. "Angie, what's wrong?"

"I'm afraid."

"Oh love, I am, too." For twelve years their lives had been in limbo. Now she knew if she chose to marry Lambert, Simon would be condemned to a life alone.

Her throat felt hoarse, but she forced herself to go on. "With the past cleared, you'd be able to find another woman to love. I did. Glenn and I were thinking of marriage. In time, you'd do the same."

"Yes," he agreed, seeming not to want to coerce her into a relationship. "I believe that in time I could. But I'm hoping I won't have to."

Hours later, Angie lay in bed, sleepless. Charleston was hot and humid, and the night seemed the loneliest of her life. She tried not to think about Simon or Clay or the consequences if she turned away from either of them.

Unwillingly, she remembered Cindy's words about Simon: an entity unto himself. Simon was independent; he needed no one. And yet he had built a house on the very property that they had once claimed as their own. A house that was little more than an empty monument to a marriage destroyed in its infancy. The house had become testimony to the stark loneliness of Simon's existence. The house had looked huge from the outside, and although she'd only been in the kitchen, it had obviously been built with a family in mind. Briefly she wondered if he'd built it when he was married to Carol. Pain shot through her. No, she reasoned, from everything she knew of his ex-wife, the woman was a social butterfly handpicked by Georgia Canfield. Carol wouldn't have wanted to live outside the social circle of Country Club Lane. The realization eased her mind, but it quickly grew troubled again. The thought of Simon living in the huge house alone distressed her. A part of Simon had never abandoned the hope that she would come back. Knowing that made her decision all the more difficult. How could she ever turn away from this man?

By Wednesday Angie was frantic to know Clay's whereabouts. Every day she phoned the apartment. No one was there to answer, she discovered. Finally Glenn went with her to the tavern where Clay played to patrons who cared little for him or his music. The proprietor claimed that Clay hadn't showed up since Saturday night and that if Angie saw him first, she should tell him there wouldn't be a job waiting for him when he got back.

As he had always done when life became uncomfortable, Clay had run. The rascal, he'd done that to worry her, Angie knew. And succeeded!

"I wouldn't be too concerned. Clay will show up." Glenn placed an arm around her shoulder as they walked back to the car. This was a run-down section of town, poorly maintained. The streetlight had burned out, and without Glenn at her side Angie would have been anxious. Yet Clay came here night after night.

"He's only doing this to punish me."

Glenn unlocked the car door and held it open for her. "From the look in your eye, he's doing a good job."

"He's my father."

"Honey, I know." He took her hand and squeezed it.

"We were both angry and said things we didn't mean." Angie waited for Glenn to comment about the argument. She'd given him a few details. Just enough for him to surmise what had taken place. Another man would have pressed his advantage, reminding her that if they married, Clay would bless that union. But Glenn remained silent, allowing her to form her own opinions.

They rode silently through the streets back to Angie's place. Glenn stayed only long enough for a cup of coffee. If Clay didn't show up by the weekend, they would look more seriously, he assured her. Glenn had connections. He kissed her lightly and left soon afterward.

Angie was anxiously watching the eleven-o'clock news for reports of unidentified bodies, and hating herself for being so dramatic, when someone rang the door-bell.

Clay stood on the other side, dirty and ragged. He didn't look as if he'd had a decent night's sleep since Sunday. For that matter, she hadn't, either. Only Clay looked far worse.

"Dad." Angie was so relieved to see him that she threw her arms around him and hugged him close. "I'm so glad you're all right."

He simply nodded and patted her back. "Can I come inside?"

"Of course."

He didn't take a seat, but clasped his hands in front of him like an errant child. "I guess I've come to apologize for the things I said to you."

"Dad, it's forgotten."

"I'll always love you, Angelcake. But if you decide to have anything to do with the Canfields, it'll ruin what we share. Glenn loves you. He's good to you, better than that rich boy ever was."

"It's not that easy." Her voice was low and pleading. She didn't want to rehash Sunday's argument.

"I can't decide for you. But I think you should thank the good Lord for someone like Glenn Lambert. Don't ruin your life a second time."

Angie hugged her father.

"Now that I've said my piece, I'll be on my way. The decision is yours. I just wanted you to know I was sorry for the things I said."

"Thank you, Dad." Angie recognized what it had cost him to come to her like this. The argument was the first serious rift in their relationship. Long after he had left,

Angie marveled at the depth of this man who was her father.

She tossed restlessly most of the night and waited until nine to phone Simon.

"Angie." He sounded both pleased and surprised that she'd called. "I tried to catch you last night."

"I was busy."

"I know. It was nearly eleven when I quit trying."

"Was there something you wanted to tell me?" *Coward,* her mind screamed. *Tell him now. Get it over with.*

"Nothing in particular. I was going to tell you I chartered a plane and what time I hoped to arrive—"

"Simon," she interrupted, her eyes closed and her back ramrod straight. "It would be better if you didn't come."

# Eight

—⁓—

The force of Simon's shock could be felt through the telephone. "Not come?" His tone demanded an explanation.

"Dad and I had a long talk and—"

"What has your father got to do with you and me?"

Angie pulled out the chair at her desk and sat down, propping up her head with the palm of one hand. "Everything. He's been hurt. He doesn't trust the Canfields, and when I told him that I'd seen you—"

"What's the matter, Angie?" Simon cut in sarcastically. "Did he think I could fix him up with a gig at the country club? Maybe he wanted more money. My mother took delight in telling me how he came back looking for another handout."

Angie gasped, utterly shocked. She sucked in the oxygen so fast her lungs hurt. "That's not true," she cried. "Clay wouldn't do that." Yet in her heart she knew he had. He'd begged her to go back and demand more money, and she had refused. So he'd done it himself. Angie's face burned with humiliation. "He didn't mean any harm," she said, her voice cracking. "I'm sorry . . . so sorry," she managed, struggling to keep her voice even. "It should never have happened . . . It won't again." Before she lost her self-control, Angie disconnected the call. For a full minute afterward, she sat frozen, as misery washed over her.

Love wasn't supposed to be like this. Love should tear down barriers, build bridges, and make everything rosy and wonderful. But in Angie's life, it had erected barriers. Walls so high that even the purest forms of love couldn't conquer the granite fortress.

Tilting her chin proudly, she sat, unmoving, until a reassuring calm came over her. She wasn't going to resort to tears. When she turned around and faced Donna, there would be a bright smile on her face.

Somehow Angie managed exactly that, but she didn't fool her astute employee.

"Things sure have been different around here lately," Donna commented, as her fingers busily assembled a funeral wreath.

"Oh?" Angie did her best to disguise her feelings. "I can't say that I've noticed."

"Since most of the goings-on involve you, I don't suppose you have," she mocked.

"You're imagining things." Angie, too, found something to keep her hands busy.

"Hmph! Is it my imagination that you jump every time the phone rings, then run to the back of the shop if it's a certain low voice calling? Half the time you come into work looking like you're ready to burst into tears."

"You're exaggerating."

"Could be," Donna asserted, shaking her blond head, "but I see what I see. I figure that I'm going to be making a wreath for you one of these days, but whether it's for a wedding or a funeral I can't rightly say."

Angie's light laugh was decidedly forced.

Later that morning, when she had a free moment, Angie called Glenn at his office to tell him she'd talked to Clay. When Glenn suggested tennis at his club and dinner afterward, Angie agreed readily. The thought of spending another humid night cooped up in the apartment was intolerable.


Simon closed his eyes, cursing himself for having blurted out the fact that Clay had returned to Groves Point wanting more money. His mother had taken delight in informing him of the event. She hadn't needed to elaborate; Simon could well picture the scene. Simon Senior had handled Angie's father and had made certain the man would never care to return again. It was little wonder Clay Robinson hated the Canfields. His father could be scathing when the situation called for it, and undoubtedly that one had.

He took another long swallow of his whiskey sour and rubbed a pensive thumb across his furrowed brow. He was going to lose Angie; he could feel it in the pit of his stomach. She didn't want him to come this weekend, and he knew why. That was the worst part. She loved him. But she was going to marry Lambert. After all these years, she was unwilling to overcome the differences that separated them. Love wasn't enough for Angie. It didn't conquer the fear.

Another sip of his drink dulled the ache that came with thoughts of her. He remembered holding her in his arms and the way she had melted against him. Her lips had been filled with a sweet passion, and although she'd refused to answer his questions about sleeping with Lambert, Simon doubted that she had. Angie was warmth and fire and sweetness and love all rolled into one. And he was going to lose her.

He slammed down his drink and called Prince to his side. Getting out of the house was paramount. Running, walking, anything was better than sitting here tormenting himself. He stood on the top step and looked into the woods. Their woods. A low-lying mist was coming in with dusk, covering the grounds until they resembled a graveyard. Without Angie this place would become little more than that.

The plane he'd chartered was scheduled to leave for Charleston tomorrow evening. He was going to be on it. If Angie was going to choose Lambert, then he wasn't going to make it easy for her. Too much was at stake.

Glenn worked out almost every night at the fitness center. Periodically, Angie joined him as his guest. After they were married, he told her, he would add her to the membership. Angie wasn't looking forward to pumping iron and pretending she enjoyed it.

She'd gone inside to change clothes before meeting Glenn at the outside tennis courts. Glancing around the room at the Nautilus equipment and the trim, muscular bodies of the men and women working out, Angie was reminded that Glenn did indeed love her. If he could spend time each night in the company of these sleek, fine-tuned bodies and then come to her, with all her weak muscles, it had to be love. A set of tennis every week or so was all the exercise she wanted. Working in Clay Pots tired her out enough as it was. The past two weeks had been the worst. Angie felt she was at her lowest ebb emotionally and physically. Her tennis game showed it.

"Are you sure you're feeling up to this?" Glenn asked her, after she had lost the second match with nary a return.

Angie wiped the sweat from her forehead with a white hand towel. "I have played better tennis."

"My grandmother plays better tennis," Glenn teased. "Why don't we call it quits and get something to eat?"

Angie agreed with a short nod, although her appetite was practically nil.

Because of the early hour, the restaurant was nearly deserted. No sooner were they seated when a tall blonde waved from across the room and sauntered to their table. Angie self-consciously crossed her legs and ignored the glossily oiled body that claimed the chair next to her. The long-haired beauty had stopped off to say hello to Glenn and proceeded to drape her lithe build over him, making sure he was given the opportunity to admire her ample cleavage. Angie took delight in thinking catty thoughts. The blonde was at least ten pounds underweight. What did it matter if she looked fantastic?

Glenn's glance was apprehensive when the blonde left. "Sorry," he muttered under his breath.

"For what?" Angie's lips twitched with suppressed

laughter. "You couldn't possibly believe I'd be concerned that Miss World would turn your head?"

A slow, appreciative smile worked its way across his face as he reached for her hand. "Her beauty pales when she sits next to you." He took her hands and clasped them firmly in his warm ones, his eyes smiling into hers.

"Then the saying that love is blind must really be true."

"Not in this instance. I'm a man who knows what he wants, and I want you, Angela Robinson."

The words caught in her throat as she opened her mouth to reassure him that she was his. Instead she looked at him imploringly and miserably lowered her gaze.

"I would have introduced you as my fiancée, but . . ." He let the rest of the sentence fade.

"It doesn't matter," Angie murmured, picking up the menu and focusing her concentration on that. *Good grief, did people honestly eat this stuff and live to tell about it?* she wondered. A spinach salad was the safest item listed. Angie decided on that and set the menu aside. When she glanced up she discovered that Glenn was continuing to study her.

"You say your dad stopped by last night?"

"Shortly after you left." She reached for her water glass and took a long swallow. Even that tasted as if minerals had been added. Determinedly, she set the glass aside.

"Is something else bothering you, Angie? You don't look relieved."

"I am. It's just that Clay didn't look well."

"The argument probably had him as upset as you've been the past few days."

"I suppose," Angie drawled, toying with the napkin.

"Have you heard from Simon?" Glenn's voice deepened and his eyes grew dark as their gazes locked.

The question caught Angie off guard. Glenn never brought up the subject of Simon. She knew it took great restraint and self-discipline for him to ignore her feelings for the other man.

"I phoned him this morning."

"You called him?"

Angie decided to ignore the implication in his voice. "I asked him not to come this weekend."

Glenn's eyes rounded with surprise, and when he spoke there was a quiet tenderness to his voice that touched her heart. "Does this mean that you're ready to accept my ring, Angie?"

Niggling doubts assaulted her, and she lowered her head as she wondered what madness had overtaken her even to hesitate. Yes, she was ready, as ready as she would ever be where Glenn was concerned. He represented love, security, and all the things she'd lacked in her life.

"Glenn . . . I . . ."

"No." His hold on her fingers tightened. "That was unfair. Forgive me."

"Forgive you?" Angie felt a breath away from insanity. The most wonderful man in the world sat across from her and loved her enough to risk everything, placing her happiness above his own.

"I shouldn't have asked about Simon."

"You have a right."

"No." Slowly, he shook his head, his look thoughtful. "The only rights I have are the ones you give me."

Their conversation was interrupted by the waiter, who came for their order. The moment the man left, Glenn took pains to unfold his napkin and place it in his lap. "You realize he'll come anyway, don't you?"

Angie didn't need to ask whom Glenn was referring to; they both knew. "Yes, I think I do."

Almost immediately Glenn changed the subject, and to Angie's delight he began telling her about his misspent youth in San Francisco. During Glenn's first year of college, his father had been transferred to Charleston, but through the years Glenn had maintained the childhood friendships he'd made in California. With glee, he relayed several hilarious stories about his high school days and the crowd of young people who were his constant companions. Instantly Angie's mood lightened. When he told her about his eccentric next-door neighbor, Muffie, she laughed outright.

"Her honest-to-goodness name was Muffie?"

"We called her Muffie because we wanted to muffle her mouth."

"She sounds wonderful. I'd love to meet her someday."

"You will. Some mutual friends of ours are getting married sometime in October. Muffie's the maid of honor and I've been asked to serve as the best man."

Angie liked the way he naturally assumed that she would be with him months into the future. He lent her the confidence she wasn't feeling. "I'll look forward to that."

By the time they left the club, the sun was descending

into a cloudless blue horizon. Since they had met at the fitness club, Glenn followed her back to her apartment in his car and accepted her offer to come in for coffee.

Angie made the pretense of fixing it for him, knowing it wasn't the coffee that had brought him inside. She filled the brightly colored red kettle with water from the kitchen faucet. A hand at her shoulder stopped her.

"I didn't come here for something to drink," he murmured, turning her into his arms.

Willingly, Angie yielded. Glenn had held her and touched her often over the past several months. Faintly, she recalled that he was taller than Simon and more muscular. Her heart pounded painfully. Why, oh, why was it when Glenn held her that her thoughts automatically went to Simon? Angry with herself, she looped her arms around Glenn's neck and fit her body intimately to his.

Apparently sensing her need, Glenn kissed her so long and so thoroughly that Angie could almost forget there ever had been a Simon in her life. Almost forget, but not quite.

Angie was struggling over the accounting books Friday afternoon when Donna came to the back of the shop.

"He's here again."

Angie's pencil froze as she glanced at the smiling round face of the yellow clock above her desk. Simon was earlier than she had expected. He must have left Groves Point early in the afternoon, she thought distractedly. Mentally she had prepared herself for this.

"He asked me to give you this." Donna set a small

white box on top of the desk and returned to the front counter.

Angie's heart pounded so loudly her ears hurt with the hammering vibrations. Sluggishly and with extreme caution, as if she were handling something radioactive, Angie picked up the box. He wouldn't. No, please, no, he wouldn't. Her fingers were trembling so badly she paused before removing the lid, biting her lip as she did so. The ring. Fleetingly she had wondered how long it would take Simon to play his trump card. The simple gold band with the tiny diamond had cost him far more than the money involved. He had saved for it out of the monthly allotment from his trust fund. Simon had sacrificed to buy her the ring, going without the little things that would have made his life away from home more comfortable. The wedding band had been his Christmas present to her, and he'd made small monthly payments on it long after she had left Groves Point. The day Georgia Canfield had given Angie the money, she had handed his mother the small white box and asked that she return it to Simon. During all these years, Simon had kept the ring.

"Do you remember the night I gave you the ring?" His low, enticing voice came from behind her.

"No," she lied. It was unfair that he do this to her. No woman would forget a night like that. They couldn't be together Christmas Day because of Simon's family, so he had come to her late Christmas Eve with the box wrapped and hidden in his jacket pocket.

Angie had been so delighted that the lump in her throat had prevented her from speaking. Only that lump had been one of intense happiness.

"Don't you think it's time I gave my wife a wedding ring?" Simon had whispered in her ear. His gray eyes had filled with love and adoration as he slipped his class ring from her finger and replaced it with the small diamond. Later they had made love with an aching tenderness that stole her breath away. After so many weeks apart, Angie had assumed their lovemaking would be hot and urgent. Instead, Simon had loved her with a reverence, holding her so close Angie had been convinced that nothing could ever come between them. Not parents, not a whole town, not even God Himself. The beauty of their love-making was so profound that tears had shone in her eyes. With his arms wrapped securely around her, Simon had whispered the most beautiful words, his voice hoarse with tenderness. He murmured all the words a woman longs to hear, telling her of the unchanging love repre-sented in that ring. He asked her to wear it proudly as a symbol of his devotion to her.

Clay had noticed the ring soon after Christmas, glee-fully assuming that Angie and Simon were engaged. In her innocent happiness, Angie had told her father about what she and Simon had done that summer in the church. Clay wasn't pleased, and Angie regretted having said anything.

"Angie," Simon spoke again. "You remember, just as I remember that Christmas."

"Why did you keep it?" She was amazed that the squeaky, high voice was her own.

"You forget that for three years I waited for you to come back."

"But I didn't." She held herself rigid.

"Yes, you did, only it took longer than three years. You returned to Groves Point, Angie."

"You're forgetting something," Angie said tightly. Her fingers were clenched fast to the box, and she mentally ordered them to relax before she set it aside. "You're forgetting Glenn."

"I haven't forgotten anything." He placed his hand on her shoulder and his touch was like a slow fire that moved toward her heart. "Angie, look at me," he requested, on a husky murmur.

Slowly she turned the desk chair around, keeping her eyes focused on the tiled shop floor. Tenderly, Simon lifted her head to look at him and drew her to her feet, taking both her hands in his.

"I've been away for five long days." He wrapped his arms around her waist and brought her close. "Welcome me back, love. Tell me you missed me as desperately as I missed you."

Angie felt like a rag doll, powerless to resist Simon. She didn't want to kiss him, and yet she knew that nothing on this earth would prevent what was about to happen. Very slowly she slid her hands over his chest and pressed her mouth to his. Immediately Simon deepened the kiss. Simon groaned and leaned against her. Gently, Angie laid her slender fingers over his cheek and her mouth clung to his, moving back and forth in passionate surrender, aroused fully by the wildly erotic kiss.

Simon stroked her hair, weaving his fingers in and out of its length as his mouth slanted over hers in a lingering kiss that left them both breathless.

"Oh love." He half laughed and half groaned on a long, unsteady breath. "That kiss was worth the wait."

Angie buried her face in the open throat of his shirt and shivered with delight when he pressed her so close to his hard length that it felt as if their bodies were fused together. "Oh my sweet Angie," he said, and groaned into her hair. "I've gone twelve years without you, and a minute more demands all the restraint I can muster." There was an unmistakable quaver in his voice.

Angie was experiencing many of the same sentiments. Knowing that Simon had saved the wedding ring had pushed her over the brink.

"Please, Simon, this shouldn't have happened." It took a great effort to keep her voice steady. "Not here."

He lifted her chin and kissed her lightly on the lips. "All right. Your place or mine?" His eyes sparked with mischief.

She broke from his embrace, fighting the urge to laugh.

He took her hands in his and leaned back to study her, as if seeing her for the first time. Several electrifying moments passed before either of them spoke.

"Have dinner with me tonight?"

"No." Angie shook her head and lowered her gaze. "I can't."

"'Can't.'" His grip on her fingers tightened painfully. "Is it Lambert?"

"I asked you not to come this weekend."

"You honestly didn't expect that would keep me away, did you?" He was upset now and struggling not to reveal how much.

"Glenn knew it wouldn't . . . I guess I'd hoped."

"What exactly were you hoping?"

Angie had edged up against the desk so that the sharp

rim cut into the back of her thighs. "I wish you hadn't come."

"You couldn't have proved it by me just now."

"We have . . . a physical thing." She tried desperately to play down the attraction between them.

"Is that a fact?" He gave a sad laugh as he said it. "And do you share this attraction with Lambert as well?"

"Yes," she lied, her heart throbbing painfully with the deceit.

Simon stiffened and held his body so tense that Angie was convinced he couldn't breathe. The battle waging within showed plainly on his face. His eyes narrowed, and one side of his mouth twitched. He didn't want to believe her, and at the same moment didn't know if he dared not.

"I see," he spoke at last.

Angie's legs felt as if they were water, and she leaned her weight against the desk, praying it would keep her upright until she'd finished. "You asked me to make my decision," she began, in a voice that trembled so hard she wondered if Simon could understand her.

"You promised not to until I was here."

"You're here now." She gestured weakly with her hand. "You will always be someone special in my life. You were my first love, and for a lot of years I didn't think I could ever love again. Glenn taught me that I could."

"Angie—"

"No," she cried desperately. "Let me say what I have to, otherwise I may not have the courage to do it and the whole thing will drag out the agony."

Simon's eyes were hard. His jaw was clenched so tight

that his face went white. Slowly, as if he couldn't bear to look at her for another minute, Simon closed his eyes.

"Things would never work for us, Simon. I've thought it all out. That you could still love me is the greatest honor of my life. In the years to come I will always remember you with a fondness—"

"Fondness." His control snapped. "Save that weak, insipid emotion for your precious Glenn."

Her heart slammed against her chest at the pain she was inflicting upon them both. Her eyes ached with unshed tears, and she bowed her head, unable to look at him. "Simon, I'm so sorry . . ." she whispered, and nearly choked. "So sorry."

Angie wasn't sure what she'd expected. Her thought was that he would try to inflict the same kind of pain on her with bitter words or cruel accusations. The last thing she had thought he would do was laugh. Admittedly, the chuckle was mirthless and devoid of amusement, but it caught her by surprise, and she raised her eyes to his.

"I let you walk out of my life once and I'm not about to make that mistake again," he taunted.

"Simon—"

"You've had your say, now listen to me. More than anything that's happened in the past couple of weeks, you just proved how much you do love me."

"That kiss was—"

"Not the kiss, Angie, but your reaction to it. It scared you. You couldn't possibly love another man as much as you do me. I don't believe it's in you to marry a man you love less."

"I'll learn," she cried.

Simon was gambling and knew it. He struggled not to

reveal his fear. "I know you. In some ways better than you know yourself. You wouldn't cheat Glenn by marrying him when you feel this strongly for me. And you do love me, Angie, so much it's nearly killing you."

"It won't work with us. Can't you accept that?"

"We'll make it work," he argued. "Go on—run away, marry Glenn if you think you can, salvage your father's pride, but my love will haunt you. There won't be a minute of any day that I won't be on your mind and in your heart. I'll be waiting for you, Angie, in Groves Point, where you belong, where we belong."

"Simon . . ."

His mouth silenced Angie. Her mind screamed a warning as her emotions rocked and waves of longing racked her. She tried to push herself free, but he wouldn't let her, holding her fast. His mouth softened, stroking hers with a gentleness until she mentally acknowledged that she had lost. Her mouth parted helplessly beneath his. The very hands that had pushed against his chest seeking freedom now slid convulsively around his neck, clinging to him. Wildly she returned his kiss, on fire for him, loving the feel of his body rasping against her. Abruptly she was free. Reeling under the shock, Angie swayed until a hand at her shoulder righted her and she gained her balance.

"You think of me, Angie, waiting," he murmured, his voice raw with emotion. For interminable seconds he stood, staring at her, as if studying every line of her face, drinking his fill before the self-imposed thirst.

Angie didn't move, didn't breathe. The four walls closed threateningly in around her, blocking her vision.

Before she could utter a word to bid him stay or leave, Simon was gone.

Angie didn't know for how long she stood, rooted and unable to move. Simon was right. She couldn't marry Glenn. To do so would be cheating him of the kind of wife he expected and needed.

With confused, sorrowful brown eyes, Angie stared ahead at the road that stretched before her. All she could see was a life of loneliness.

# Nine

—⁓—

"You haven't seen that Canfield boy again, have you?" Clay asked a week after Simon had left Charleston. They sat around Angie's small kitchen table on a lazy Sunday evening, eating lemon meringue pie. Clay's favorite.

"No." Angie cast a pleading glance in Glenn's direction. His hand reached for hers under the table and held it firmly in a warm clasp.

"Angie won't be seeing anyone but me from now on," Glenn said, and his eyes glowed with a triumphant happiness.

Angie had spent long and difficult hours sorting through Simon's parting words. He was right, she did love him. Nothing could change that. The years hadn't diminished the intensity of her feelings, and she realized she shouldn't expect time to ever gloss them over. But that didn't have to ruin her life. Glenn loved her, really loved her. Enough to accept the fact that her feelings might never be as strong as his.

Clay pushed his half-eaten pie aside and dabbed the edges of his mouth with the paper napkin.

Not for the first time, Angie examined her father's tired face. "Are you feeling okay, Dad?"

He looked surprised that she would notice. "I've been having these funny pains lately. Nothing serious, but I been thinking about seeing a doctor."

In twenty-nine years Angie had never known her father to admit he wasn't feeling up to par. Not once could she ever remember him visiting a physician. For years Clay had blamed the medical profession for her mother's death and claimed that all doctors were crooks.

"Would you like me to make an appointment for you?" She broached the subject carefully, not wanting to appear overly concerned.

"Maybe you should."

"I'll do that tomorrow, then." Worried, Angie looked to Glenn for support and found his eyes studying Clay. Glenn's features were uneasy.

"I think I'll be headin' home," Clay announced, pushing against the table and scooting out his chair. "I'm feeling a mite under the weather."

"I'll go with you," Glenn offered, dumping his napkin on the table beside his plate.

"No reason for that," Clay scoffed. "What I'm really doing is giving you two young'uns time alone. A boy like you should be smart enough to see that."

"In that case," Glenn said with a chuckle, delivering his plate to the sink, "I'll put the time to good use."

Angie walked her father to the door and felt his forehead. Annoyed, Clay brushed her hand aside. "I ain't that sick. Now you get back in the kitchen with Glenn and give me a call tomorrow, you hear."

But behind his words, Angie sensed an underlying fear. There was something wrong, and Clay was both worried and confused. Agreeing to a doctor appointment proved as much. "Yes, Daddy dearest," Angie murmured solicitously, and kissed him lightly on the cheek.

"Have you two set the date yet?" Clay whispered, glancing into the kitchen. "I've been doing a lot of thinking lately. It seems time I was bouncing a grandbaby on my knee. I might even compose a lullaby or two."

Angie stiffened. The pressure was on her from both Glenn and Clay to set a wedding date. As it was, Angie had yet to accept Glenn's grandmother's ring. Her emotions were too unsettled to leap into a rushed engagement and marriage. She needed time, and both Glenn and Clay were growing impatient. "Not yet."

"You aren't still hankering after that rich boy?"

Angie had been "hankering" after Simon Canfield since she was a high school junior. She shook her head. "No, Clay," she lied. "I'm over Simon Canfield."

"Good." His low hiss was filled with relief. "You won't be seeing him again?"

"No."

"He's not coming to Charleston?"

Angie felt like screaming. Why did Clay insist on dragging this inquisition out? "No."

Clay wiped a hand across his wide brow. "For all our sakes, I hope so," he said. Angie stood in the hallway watching the dejected figure as he waited for the elevator.

Glenn had cleared the remaining dinner dishes from

the table by the time Angie returned. She paused, deep in thought, and gripped the back of a chair.

Glenn spoke first. "I'm concerned about Clay. I'd bet you anything those little pains of his are a lot more than little."

Angie agreed with an abrupt nod, worried herself. "I'll make an appointment for him in the morning."

"I'd suggest he see an internist."

"What do you think it is?" Angie turned imploring eyes to Glenn, fear playing havoc with her composure.

"I don't know, honey. I'm not a doctor."

Angie nodded, fighting down a sense of panic. For all his weaknesses, Clay was still her father and her only living relative.

"I've got the coffee poured," Glenn announced. "Let's sit in the living room."

Angie followed him into the other room. They sat so close on the blue sofa that their thighs touched. Relaxed, Glenn stretched his long legs out in front of him and crossed his ankles. He draped an arm over the back of the sofa. "Is there anything interesting on TV tonight?"

Angie flipped through the pages of the *TV Guide* and shook her head. "The usual."

His hand cupped her shoulder and moved slowly down the length of her arm. Angie closed her eyes, wanting desperately to feel the comfort of his touch.

"Dinner was wonderful," Glenn whispered, and gently kissed her temple.

"Thank you, but I hardly think of fried chicken as wonderful. Wait until you taste my Shrimp Diane."

"I'll look forward to that."

Involuntarily, Angie stiffened. It was coming; she

could feel it in every breath Glenn drew. He wanted to talk about getting married and her mind was devoid of arguments.

"Sitting here watching television after a big Sunday dinner seems natural," Glenn said, setting his coffee aside.

"Yes, it does," Angie agreed.

"Like folks who've been married for years and years."

"Yes." The word barely made it through the growing thickness in Angie's throat.

"You know how I feel about you, Angie. I've waited a long time for you. I don't want to lose you now."

"You're not going to lose me," she argued, straightening. Turning, she looped her arms around his neck and pressed her cheek against his throat. "Be patient with me just a while longer." She paused to lightly kiss his Adam's apple.

Glenn's arms tightened around her. "How much longer?" Disappointment coated his voice.

"I . . . I don't know."

"Two weeks, a month, six months?" he pressed.

"I don't know." She squeezed her eyes closed, hating herself for doing this to someone as wonderful as Glenn.

"When will you know?"

"Soon," she promised. "Soon."

A finger under her chin lifted her face to his. For a long moment, Glenn gazed into the dark depths of her troubled eyes. His voice was deep and velvety as he spoke. "I want you, Angie." Slowly, enticingly, his mouth inched closer to hers and stopped just when she felt he could go no nearer without touching. "Don't hold back from me, love."

Angie saw the look in his eyes and a warning screamed along the ends of her nerves. Glenn wanted to love her completely. He was finished with having her so close and being denied what he craved most. For her own part, she could see no reason to hold back from Glenn. She had shoved Simon from her life—oh no, it was happening again; she groaned inwardly. Glenn took her into his arms and her thoughts flew to Simon.

Filled with self-loathing, Angie twined her arms around Glenn's neck and eagerly parted her mouth to his.

"Oh love." Glenn groaned and hungrily devoured her waiting lips. Urgently, his hands moved down her shoulders and back, molding her to his upper torso. His kisses were insistent, thorough, and seemingly endless.

Angie's resolve to finally give in to Glenn splintered with every kiss, every caress. She longed to be warm and yielding, gifting him with the love he deserved. He had been patient with her, and soon she was going to be his wife. Yet she felt paralyzed with alarm, bewilderment, and even shame, as if she were contemplating something as appalling as adultery.

"Glenn," she whispered, not knowing how to deal with these reservations.

He didn't seem to hear her, kissing her with flaming demand. Angie squirmed and jerked Glenn's arms free. Undeterred, he continued kissing her while fiddling with the buttons of her blouse.

Weakly, Angie submitted, not knowing how to stop him as he slipped the polished cotton cloth from her shoulders. Instantly his fingers sought to release her lacy bra.

"Glenn," she pleaded with him, but her voice was little more than a strangled whisper. "Don't, please."

When he finally drew back, Angie's forehead fell against his chest. Her hands were flattened against his crisp shirt. She felt disoriented, frustrated, and so confused and guilty. Tears filled her eyes and crept down her face.

"Angie," he pleaded, "did I hurt you?"

He loved her, urgently wanted her to be his wife, and she'd turned him away from the very things he should expect. Yet he wanted to know if he had hurt her. She buried her face in her hands and wept.

"Oh Angie, I'm sorry." He wrapped his arms around her, holding her as if she were a child. He pressed a brief kiss on the crown of her head and rocked her in a gentle swaying motion. "I wouldn't hurt you for anything in the world."

"Glenn," she cried. "I'm the one . . ."

"Shhh." He kissed her again. "No, it was my fault, I shouldn't have pressed you."

"But I don't think I'll ever feel differently."

"Yes, you will," he whispered confidently. "In time, love. In time."

Angie couldn't get Clay an appointment for the internist until the middle of the week. She picked him up at his place and was shocked at his drawn, ashen features. For half a minute she toyed with the idea of taking him directly to the hospital emergency room, but the receptionist had gone to a lot of trouble to squeeze Clay in for the last appointment of the day. Wordlessly, she drove to the doctor's office, chatting to keep her mind off how worried she was.

The time in the waiting room while Clay was with the doctor seemed interminable. Angie leafed through the magazines with unseeing eyes and checked her watch every few minutes. After an hour, she began pacing the deserted room. What could possibly be taking so long?

The receptionist appeared moments later. "The doctor would like to see you in his office."

"Of course." Angie's stomach had coiled into a hard knot by the time she shook hands with the doctor and sat in his compact office.

"I'd like you to take your father directly to the hospital."

Angie scooted to the edge of the woven beige cushion. "What's wrong?"

"Don't alarm yourself. There are a few tests I'd like to run. Unfortunately, he seems averse to the idea."

"My . . . my mother died in a hospital." Angie knew how inane that sounded, but it was the only thing she could think to say. "Don't worry, Doctor, I'll get him there."

Saying she'd deliver Clay to Charleston General and doing so proved to be a formidable task.

"I'm not going to any hospital," Clay announced stubbornly.

"Dad."

"I mean it."

"Okay, Dad."

Angie started the engine of the car and eased into the evening traffic.

"This isn't the way to my house."

"I know."

"You're taking me to that hospital, aren't you?"

"Yup. You can shout, scream, and do anything else you want, but you're going to that hospital."

"Angie, don't. I'm begging you, girl. You take me there and I won't ever walk out. Mark my words. If I'm going to die, I want to be in my own bed with my own things around me."

"You're not going to die, you understand," she cried, pressing back the growing fear. "I won't let you. Now quit your arguing."

"You're killing me as surely as if you'd stuck a knife in my heart. You're sentencing me to death."

"Stop it right now, Clay Robinson. The doctor said that he was only sending you there for a few tests. You'll be there a couple of hours. Then I'll take you home."

"You promise me?"

The doctor had mentioned the possibility of admitting Clay, depending on the test results. "I promise that you're going for tests."

"But you won't let them keep me, will you?"

"We'll see."

"Angie." Clay doubled over in the front seat, gripping his stomach. "Oh God, the pain. I can't take it."

Angie's hand tightened around the steering wheel. "I'm hurrying, Dad. We'll be there in a minute." Pressing on her horn, Angie wove in and out of traffic, driving at breakneck speed. She pulled up to the emergency entrance and rushed inside for help. Two men with a stretcher raced to her car and jerked open the passenger door. By the time they arrived, Clay was writhing with agony. He tossed his head to and fro and flung his arms out like a madman.

"Angie," he cried pitifully. "Don't let them take me."

"Daddy." She gripped his hand. "You're sick; they only want to help you."

He squeezed his eyes shut. "They're taking me to my death."

The two attendants stopped her from going inside the emergency room cubicle. Angie came to a halt outside the room and leaned against the wall, needing its support to remain upright. Clay was right. He was going to die and there wasn't anything she could do about it. She wiped the tears from her face and smiled gratefully to the nurse who led her to a seat in the waiting room. What seemed like hours later, but could have been only a few minutes, a doctor approached her.

"I'm afraid your father will require emergency surgery."

"Why?"

"He has diverticulitis."

The word meant nothing to Angie. "Will he be all right?"

The doctor hesitated. "We'll let you know as soon as we do. If you'd like, you can see him for a few minutes before we take him upstairs."

"Yes, please." Angie followed the doctor into the cubicle. Clay lay with his eyes closed on the stretcher bed, his face as ashen as the sheets and marked with intense pain.

"Oh Dad," she whispered, reaching for his hand and kissing his fingers.

He rolled his head to the side and tried to smile. "I

want you to remember that I always loved you, Angelcake. You were the light of your mother's and my world."

"Daddy, don't talk like this."

"Shhh . . . a man knows when he's going to die." He was so calm, so sure. "I'm ready to meet my Maker . . ." His voice faded. "Lots of regrets . . . loved you."

As the hours passed, Angie grew as certain as Clay that this day would be his last. And with the certainty came the realization that there was nothing she could do. She prayed, pleaded, bargained with God to spare her father. Forcing happy thoughts into her troubled mind, she recalled the times as a little girl that he'd sung her to sleep and made up jingles just for her. He'd tugged her pigtails and called her his Angelcake. She remembered how desolate Clay became after her mother's death and knew she would feel the same without this roguish old man to love. He was a rascal, a scoundrel, a joy, and a love, all in one. Life wouldn't be the same without him. He was her link to the past and her guide to the future. And he was dying.

Sweat outlined the greenish-blue surgical gown the doctor wore when he approached Angie several hours later. She could see from the disturbed frown that marred his face that his news wasn't good.

Linking her hands together, Angie slowly rose to her feet, bracing herself for the worst.

"I'm sorry," he said softly. "We don't expect him to last the night."

Angie's head jerked back as if the man had physically struck her. "Can I see him?"

"In a few minutes."

"Is there someone you'd like to call?" he asked her gently.

Blankly Angie stared at the exhausted man. Clay hadn't been to church in years. There was no one in all the world she wanted now, save one.

"Yes, please," she murmured, her voice barely audible. The card he'd given her was in her purse. The phone number was inked across the printed surface of the business card. For several exaggerated seconds she stared at the telephone dial, knowing what it would mean if she called.

He answered on the sixth ring. "Yes?"

"Simon," she whispered, trying to gain control of her voice. "Clay is dying. I need you."

# Ten

The early light of dawn had washed away the dark, lonely night. Angie sat beside her father's hospital bed, pressing her forehead against the cold metal railing, fighting off the enfolding edges of exhaustion. Clay remained unmoving, his head lolled to one side as he battled for each breath. Nurses moved in and out of the room with silent steps as they checked Clay's vital signs and marked their findings on the metal clipboards they carried.

Sunlight crept through the slits in the blinds, and the nurse quietly turned them completely closed. Angie yearned to tell her that she wanted Clay to die with the sun in his eyes. But it took more energy than she could muster just to speak. Instead she waited until the woman had left the room, and then she stood, intent on opening the blinds and flooding the room with glorious light.

"Angie." Simon's husky voice stopped her.

An overpowering surge of relief washed over her as she turned to him. They met halfway into the private room, reaching out to each other like lost souls released from a hellish trap. Simon's arms surrounded her, and he lifted her feet from the floor as he buried his face in her hair.

"Thank you," she whispered chokingly, over and over. Her body shook violently as she clung to him with the desperation of a drowning woman.

"Angie," he answered. "Tell me what happened." Simon's gaze drifted to the face of the man on the bed. For all his differences with Clay Robinson over the years, Simon felt a stirring sense of loss. Angie and her father had always been close, and her grief affected him now more than he would have believed. Her softly murmured phrases were unintelligible and he could do little more than smooth the hair from her brow and hold her close to his warmth.

The doctor arrived, and Angie and Simon stepped outside the room while the middle-aged man with the serious, dark eyes examined Clay.

Angie's hand held Simon's in a tight grip as if she were afraid that he would leave her. If it were up to Simon they would spend the rest of their lives together, starting at this moment.

"Dad had diverticulitis."

Simon blinked and repeated the words. "What does it mean?"

"I'm not sure I know exactly, but from what the doctor explained, the intestines have tiny sacs along the outside edges. When the diet doesn't include enough roughage, these sacs can fill and become infected. That's what happened to Clay. His infection was so advanced that the sacs were filled and ready to burst. If they had, he'd be dead now. As it is . . . his chances aren't good." She paused and ran her fingertips along the hard, sculptured line of his jaw. "How did you get here?"

"Drove." He hadn't stayed under the speed limit the entire way. The desperation in Angie's voice had affected him like nothing he had ever known. Angie had always been the strong one in any crisis. People leaned on her. From the time they were in their teens, Simon had marveled at the way others sought her out with their problems. Now in her own grief, Angie had turned to him. Simon's heart pounded with the comfort he found in that. She hadn't called on Glenn, who was so close and who would have been so willing. She had reached out to him.

"Oh Simon, I'm so sorry to put you through this."

"Don't be." He took her in his arms again, unable to keep from holding her. "I tried to book a charter but couldn't last-minute like this, so I drove." He didn't mention the fruitless time spent trying to locate a private plane and pilot. "I'm here now and I'm staying. That's all that matters."

"The doctor didn't think Clay would last the night, but he has. That's a good sign, don't you think?"

She was pleading with him like a small child, as if it were in his power to change the course of fate. Gently he kissed her temple. "Yes, I think it must be." The sight of the old man shook Simon. The Clay Robinson on the bed was barely recognizable as the man Simon had known. Clay had aged drastically in the past twelve years. His hair was completely gray now, and the widow's peak was more pronounced. His skin color was beyond pale, the grayish hue of a man just on the other side of death. Simon ached with compassion for Angie; his heart surged with the need to protect her from this.

When the doctor reappeared, Simon slipped his arm around her shoulders and held her protectively to his side.

"He made it through the night," Angie said eagerly, the grip on her emotions fragile.

The doctor's returning smile was tight. "Yes, he's surprised us all."

"How much longer will it be before we know?"

"It could be days. I suggest you two go home and get some rest. The hospital will contact you if there's any change in your father's condition."

Angie turned stricken eyes to Simon, communicating her need to remain at Clay's bedside. "Would it be all right if we stayed awhile longer?" Simon asked.

"If you wish. Only I don't think it's necessary to continue a twenty-four-hour vigil. Mr. Robinson is resting comfortably now. I doubt that his condition will change over the next several hours. At this point I'd say we are optimistic for his recovery."

"Thank you, Doctor," Angie whispered fervently, her trusting, dark eyes filling with tears of gratitude.

"No need to thank me. I can do only so much; the rest remains with God and your father."

Together the couple returned to Clay's room. With Simon on the other side of the bed, Angie sat across from him, her hand gripping the railing as if needing to hold on to something tangible in a sea of uncertainty.

Simon coaxed her once to get something to eat, but she refused with a hard shake of her head. Her hand clasped Clay's and she whispered soothingly, as if her words would give him comfort. Gradually her head began to droop, and eventually she propped it up against the back of her hand as it gripped the metal barrier.

"Come on, Angie." Simon spoke softly, taking her by the shoulders. "Let me drive you home. You need your rest. We'll come back later."

Rubbing the sleep from her face, Angie yawned and slowly shook her head. She'd been awake for more than thirty-six hours and was so rummy that she would have agreed to anything. Simon was here. She trusted him. Simon would take care of everything.

He helped her stand, and she leaned her cheek against his chest as he looped an arm around her shoulders, leading her to the parking lot and into the bright light of day.

The sun was shining and reflected off the hood of his sports car as Simon drove down the busy Charleston streets. Most of the traffic was heading for the downtown area, and since they were traveling in the opposite direction, toward Angie's apartment, they weren't hampered by rush hour.

Once inside the apartment, Angie flipped the switch to the air conditioner. Immediately a shaft of cooling air weaved its way through the apartment.

"You go ahead and get ready for bed; I've a few phone calls to make," Simon said softly. He wanted to contact the flower shop so they wouldn't worry about Angie not showing up and to call his bank.

His words barely registered as Angie moved into her bedroom and began stripping off her blouse and slacks. She glanced longingly into the bathroom and decided to shower.

Simon heard the running water and paused to rub the exhaustion from his eyes. While waiting for Angie he discovered that the hall cupboard held an extra set of bedding. He'd get whatever sleep he could on the sofa when the opportunity presented itself.

Spreading the sheets for his makeshift bed, Simon felt a great weight ease from his heart. These past days without Angie had driven him to the brink of insanity. The agony of walking away from her with nothing more than a few parting words had filled him with regrets. His mind had ached like a throbbing bruise that didn't lessen with time, taunting him. Like Lambert, Simon had gambled. Clay's illness had hastened Angie's ultimate decision, but Simon had realized the minute he picked up the phone and heard her voice that she would never leave him again. She was his and would always be his.

The sound of running water stopped and Angie reappeared, standing just inside the living room. Her thin satin gown was lilac-colored. Simon's breath stopped short. She was so exquisitely beautiful that he slowly straightened, unable to tear his gaze from her. Her loveliness reminded Simon of the way she'd come to him in the clearing in the woods. The neckline of the gown formed a deep V to reveal the valley between her breasts, and she stood there waiting for him, as innocent as spring.

"Simon," she whispered, and held out her hand. "Don't sleep on the sofa."

Briefly he closed his eyes to the gnawing ache in his loins. She couldn't possibly expect him to go to bed with her and not touch her. As desperately as he wanted to, he realized he couldn't take her now. Not with Clay on his deathbed and Angie distraught and confused. Yet he didn't know if there was anything he could refuse her.

"Here, let me tuck you in." He struggled to keep his voice cool and impersonal, and crossed the room, not daring to look at her.

Her bedroom was small and dominated by the bed and dresser. Her slacks and blouse were neatly folded across the foot of the mattress. Simon turned back the covers and fluffed up the pillow. "There," he said. "Your bed awaits you, my lady." Again he avoided looking directly into those soulful, dark eyes as she slipped between the crisp sheets. Wordlessly he pulled the covers over her shoulders and tucked them under the lip of the mattress as if he were putting a small child to bed.

Angie cast him a look of mild surprise. "Simon," she said in a low, husky voice. "Could you . . . would you mind lying down with me? I don't want to be alone."

Simon felt like gnashing his teeth. She had no conception of what she was asking of him. "Sure." He removed his shirt and trousers and slid between the sheets beside her. The narrow bed that forced her to scoot her thinly clad body close to him was an additional torture. He gathered her in his embrace and closed his eyes to the agony of being so near her. Breathing in the fresh scent of her hair, Simon held himself completely still. He tried not to think of the satin feel of her ivory skin and forced himself to concentrate on anything but the warm, vital woman in his arms.

Angie sighed contentedly, not completely unaware of what she was doing to Simon. Maybe it was selfish to use him this way, she thought sleepily, but she couldn't help herself. Today, more than any time in her life, she needed him. Dreamily, she smiled up at him and nestled in his embrace, pressing her face to the hardness of his chest. Her arm was draped over his lean ribs, and she paused to murmur. "Thank you," she whispered, grateful for his sacrifice. Already she felt groggy, as if she were floating away on a thick cloud. Her eyes felt heavy, and Simon was warm and smooth and wonderfully masculine. Gradually she could feel the tension drain out of him. After an exaggerated moment, he released a long, slow breath and curved an arm over her.

"I love you," Simon whispered sleepily, as his hand roamed down her back in long, soothing strokes.

His voice sounded far away. "I know," she murmured back, and shifted her head so she could lightly kiss his jaw. "I love you, too."

"Be good, understand?"

"Yes."

Neither spoke again, and Angie drifted into a deep slumber, content to be in his arms.

Sometime during the morning, Angie's sleep became filled with resplendent, color-filled dreams that were vivid with detail. Pleasant dreams of when she was young and her mother was alive. Clay was handsome and happy, singing his songs and loving her mother with everything that was in him to love. Their trio was on a picnic by a clear blue lake. The sun was shining and the birds sang merrily from the flowering trees. Clay and her mother and Angie were in a long wooden canoe on the crystal-clear water. Clay had brought along his guitar and was serenading them with the silly jingles he loved to create.

Angie clapped her hands with delight and doubled over with laughter. When she straightened, her mother was gone and Clay sat across from her, old and gray-haired and in terrible pain. His hand was clenching his stomach and he looked at her in such agony that Angie cried out with shock. Clay begged her to get him to the hospital and Angie reached for the paddle—only it was missing. If she didn't hurry, Clay would die.

Frantic, Angie cried out, her voice piercing the still room. Weeping and thrashing about, she knocked aside the blankets and bolted upright.

"Angie." The voice was low and frenzied, and Angie opened her eyes to find Simon standing above her.

"Oh Simon." Her breath came in deep, uneven gasps. "I had a horrible nightmare." Blindly she reached for him, seeking his comfort. Simon was her closest friend, her most trusted love. Vaguely she recalled that he had been in bed with her, but now it was obvious that he had come from the living room.

"It was a dream." He bent over her, his hands folding around her back.

Angie's arms tightened as she clung to him. "Hold me, please, hold me." She whispered the words against his throat as her hands clenched at him with fear and anguish.

Simon braced a knee on the edge of the mattress and pulled aside the blankets as he came onto the bed and lay beside her. Angie's arms remained locked around his neck as the full length of his hard body joined her.

"Hold me, hold me," she repeated again and again.

Simon did as she asked with a tenderness and love she had known from no other. His hands stroked her hair, her shoulders, and her back. Angie buried her face in the hollow of his throat and drew in deep, shaking breaths as she closed her eyes. He didn't try to soothe her with words but simply held her, his hands caressing her.

Gradually the fear subsided and in its place came another emotion so strong, so powerful, that her senses clamored with the intensity. Her grip relaxed and the muscles under her exploring fingers flexed powerfully. This was Simon holding her so tenderly. Her husband of twelve years.

As if aware of what was happening to her thoughts, Simon's hands stilled and he tossed back his head. "Angie?" His voice was filled with question.

She answered by kissing the salty-tasting skin at his throat, darting her tongue in and out in a provocative action.

"Angie," he pleaded hoarsely, "are you sure?"

In response, she kissed his Adam's apple, her tongue teasing and challenging him as it explored the throbbing pulse point on his neck.

"Angie . . . It isn't in me to refuse you . . . I don't have the strength to turn you down."

"Love me, Simon. Please, oh please, love me."

Angie heard the sharply indrawn breath and opened her eyes to stare into the stormy, doubt-filled gray ones looking down on her.

Her hands slid over his shoulders and back again as their eyes continued to drink in each other. One palm slid down over his chest, and then lower, to his muscle-hard belly. "I want you," she whispered.

Simon groaned and positioned his hard body over hers. His breath was heavy, coming in deep pants as if he'd recently finished working out. He continued to hold her as he gradually lowered his mouth to hers, feasting on the sweetness of her lips with unhurried ease. He kissed her again and again until her mind was lost, incapable of any function beyond feeling the incredible sensations Simon awoke within her.

Simon's hands were unsteady as he pulled the satin gown over her head in an urgent movement, tossing it carelessly aside. "Simon," she moaned, her fingers digging into his hair as she arched her back to the exquisite sensations burning through her.

His lips found hers and she kissed him back greedily. Simon's fingers worked at removing the last barrier of his clothing that separated them. Free of the restricting material, he laid her back against the pillow.

Mindless of anything but the taste and feel of Simon, Angie dug long nails into his shoulder blades. The pleasure that had been denied her for twelve years burst forth gloriously within her and sent her swirling to the heights of heaven. She gave a small whimper and clenched his neck, kissing him again and again as the tears slid down her cheeks.

"Angie, my sweet Angie, I'll love you on my dying day."

Her hands framed his face and she kissed him, her mouth slanting over his. "Simon," she whispered, poignantly moved by his lovemaking. "It's even better than I remember." She sniffled, smiling up at him. Lazily, his thumb wiped the moisture from her face.

"Yes," he agreed. He didn't move, kissing her again and again. "Am I too heavy for you?"

"Never." She closed her eyes, drinking in the warmth of his body sprawled over hers. "Don't leave me again."

"I won't," he murmured, close to her ear. "Never again."

Angie didn't know how or when it happened, but she fell into a deep slumber. She stirred once and felt the dead weight of Simon's arm over her waist. He was cuddling her, spoon fashion, in the narrow bed. The sound and feel of his even breathing assured her he was asleep. She nestled closer within his arms and returned to a contented, blissful sleep.

When she woke again it was to the warm sensation of someone kissing her earlobe.

Caught in the delicious sensations that shot through her, Angie rolled onto her back. "What time is it?" she asked, not bothering to open her eyes.

"Almost dinnertime."

Her eyes flew open. "That late?" She sat up, pulling the sheet with her. "I've got to . . ."

"I've already called the hospital. Your father is showing definite signs of improvement. He's not out of the woods yet, but he's in better shape than last night at this time," he told her, sitting beside her, fully dressed. His hands were positioned on the delicate slope of her shoulders and his gaze was filled with fierce tenderness.

It didn't seem possible that it was less than twenty-four hours ago that she had been sitting in a doctor's office with Clay.

"Are you hungry?" Simon questioned.

She smiled at him with all the love stored in her heart these past years. "Starved."

"Good. I took the liberty of snooping through your kitchen and fixing us something to eat."

Angie leaned against the headboard and stretched her arms out in a long yawn. "I feel wonderful."

Simon leaned forward and kissed her lightly. "You cried."

Self-conscious, Angie lowered her gaze. "I always did."

"I know," he said in a husky, low voice. "Angie . . ." He paused. "There hasn't been anyone else, has there." It was more a statement than a question.

"No. I couldn't."

He gathered her in his arms and buried his face in her throat. "I don't deserve you."

"I love you."

"I'm going to spend the rest of my life letting you know how much."

"Do you honestly think that'll be long enough?" she teased.

Clay's eyes were closed when Angie went into the hospital room an hour and a half later. The nurse standing at his bedside glanced up as Angie entered the room.

"He's been comfortable," the woman whispered, answering Angie's question before she could ask it. "He's showing signs of improvement."

Angie felt a rush of intense gratitude flow through her. "Good."

The nurse left a few minutes later after charting her findings. Angie pulled out a chair and sat, taking Clay's hand between hers.

"Hi, Dad," she said softly. "Simon and I are back."

Simon stepped forward and placed a hand on Angie's shoulder. "I don't think he can hear you."

She turned around and smiled up at him warmly. "Maybe not, but I feel better talking to him."

Simon located a chair and scooted it beside Angie's. "How is Clay going to feel about us?"

"I . . . I don't know." Some of her happiness dimmed. "Once I talk to him and explain how much I love you, then he'll come around."

"He's hated me for a lot of years."

"Simon, Clay doesn't hate you."

His hand squeezed her shoulder. "That's something we'll find out soon enough."

"Yes, I guess we will."

They sat, both caught in their doubts for a long half hour.

"Clay never says your name," Angie said. "He calls you 'that rich boy' or 'the Canfield boy.' He'll be surprised when he sees you to note that you're far from a lad."

Simon's soft chuckle was interrupted by a low strangling sound. At first Angie didn't hear it. Only when the amusement drained from Simon's eyes did Angie pick up on the soft sound. Standing, she stood over her father. "Daddy?"

"Angelcake." His voice was incredibly weak.

"How do you feel?"

"Like hell . . . should be dead."

"No," she protested.

Quietly, Simon stood and moved to the back of the room, out of Clay's line of vision.

"You did wonderfully well," she continued.

Clay scoffed at her with a small mocking sound. "Do the doctors expect me to kick the bucket?"

"No one's given up on you yet," Angie told him softly, and brushed the hair from his temple. "Least of all me."

"I may prove you right yet."

"Good."

Clay closed his eyes. The effort of keeping them open this short length of time had apparently drained him of all strength.

"Go back to sleep."

"I dreamed—"

"Shhh." She placed a finger over his lips. "We'll talk later."

Within minutes, Clay returned to a peaceful slumber. Angie tossed a triumphant glance to Simon, her heart soaring. Her greatest fear had been that Clay would never wake up.

A jubilant sensation filled her breast. "He's going to be all right," she announced confidently, holding her hand out to Simon. "I can feel it in my bones."

Simon's arms slipped around her waist and he held her close. "I don't doubt that Clay Robinson will be seeing his grandchildren."

Angie and Simon left the hospital after visiting hours. Night was settling like a restless cloud over the land. The sky was dark and threatening, promising an imminent rainfall.

Simon followed Angie into her apartment.

"Angie." His voice was a husky caress. "Come here, love."

Obediently she walked into his embrace, sliding her

arms around his waist and tilting her head back to smile at him. "You wanted something?" she teased.

"If only you knew."

"I think I do." She undid the first button of his shirt.

"Just what do you have in mind?" he asked with mock surprise.

"Let me show you, Mr. Canfield." The second button followed. She smiled a little and arched a suggestive brow. When the shirt was unfastened, she eased it from his shoulders and let it drop to the floor.

Hesitant at first, she reached out a hand and touched him, trailing her fingertips over the hard muscles of his naked torso. Simon closed his eyes and grinned. Angie's exploring hands paused at his belt buckle.

"You aren't going to stop now, are you?" he challenged.

"No." Her voice was shallow and low. Her hands resumed their task, and she ceased breathing completely. "Simon," she whispered, a little afraid. In their lovemaking he had always been the initiator.

Apparently understanding her hesitancy, he opened his eyes and kissed her lightly. "It's my turn now." He captured her hand and kissed her fingertips.

Seconds later her cotton blouse slid soundlessly to the floor and was soon followed by her slacks, so that she stood before him in only her bra and bikini panties.

"Oh Angie," he moaned. "You are so beautiful."

She bowed her head and her dark hair fell forward, wreathing her face.

"What's wrong?" He raised her eyes to his. "You don't believe me?"

She couldn't answer him with words. Instead she

stood on her tiptoes and kissed him. "Thank you," she whispered reverently. "Thank you for loving me."

"Oh Angie." He picked her up and carried her into the bedroom, stopping every few steps to press a thick, seductive kiss to her eager mouth.

He laid her on the unmade bed, his mouth feasting on hers while his hands fumbled with the tiny hooks of her bra. Once it was free, he tugged it from her arms.

"Oh love," he breathed. "I want you so much."

Long afterward, Angie lay in his embrace, her head cradled in the crook of his arm. Lazily her fingers toyed with the short, dark hair that grew at his navel. Words weren't necessary. They were completely and utterly content. The living-room light dispersed its golden shadow into the bedroom, and when Angie lifted her head she was surprised to note that Simon was asleep.

Easing herself from his embrace, she kissed him lightly on the forehead and reached for her robe, wrapping it around her nakedness. As ideal as their few moments together had been, there were still many roads they had yet to traverse. Gazing down at him, Angie's heart swelled with love. Together, she knew they would cross any bridge that was necessary. As long as they were together, nothing else mattered.

Angie was in the kitchen, putting on coffee, when the doorbell rang. Her hand froze and she looked frantically toward the bedroom. There was only one person who would visit this late. Dread settled over her as she toyed with the idea of ignoring the bell. But Glenn would only ring again and wake Simon. That thought caused her to hurry across the room and open the door.

"Angie." Glenn stepped past her into the room. "Where the hell have you been? I've been trying to get you for the past two days." He paused, as if taking in her appearance for the first time. "I didn't get you out of bed, did I?" He checked his watch. "It's barely ten."

"Clay's in the hospital."

Glenn raked his hand through his hair. "I feared as much. What was wrong, and why didn't you call me?"

"I . . ." She struggled for the right words. She didn't want to hurt Glenn.

"Angie?" Simon staggered into the room, his hair in disarray. His hastily donned pants left little conjecture as to his whereabouts. He stopped cold and straightened when he caught sight of Glenn. The two men eyed each other with shocked disbelief.

# Eleven

—⟋m⟍—

Glenn's mouth twisted up at one corner as he regarded Angie with shock and embarrassment. "How long has this been going on?"

"Glenn, please, I'm so sorry . . ." Angie's eyes pleaded with him.

"Angie's been under a lot of stress," Simon intervened, as he stepped into the room.

Angie glanced at Simon and asked, "Let me have a few minutes alone with Glenn."

His nod was filled with understanding. He returned to the bedroom and was back a minute later fully dressed. He paused by the door, his eyes warming her as he murmured that he'd return in fifteen minutes. The door made a clicking sound as it closed.

She smiled her appreciation and turned back to Glenn. His thick brows were bunched together to form a single intense line. His eyes were cold and angry; they looked as if they had frosted over. Angie had never seen Glenn like this.

"Glenn," she began haltingly, "I can't tell you how sorry I am that you found out about Simon and me this way."

"Tell me one thing," he ground out savagely. "How long have you been sleeping with him?"

Angie struggled to keep her voice calm, but her eyes pleaded with him for understanding. "Today was the first time . . . I would have let you know, only . . ."

"Only what, Angie? Only you thought you might be able to hold on to me awhile longer, is that it?"

"No," she insisted.

"I've always been honest with you. But I was a fool to expect that same kind of integrity from you."

"Glenn," she begged, "it's not like that."

"Then what was it like? You made a fool out of me. Couldn't you have had the common decency to let me know about Clay? At least then I wouldn't have worried and shown up here like an idiot."

She struggled to find the words. "You have been the most wonderful, patient man in the world."

"I'm not Saint Thomas Aquinas," he barked. "Don't try to pin those saintly virtues on me. I loved you. I wanted you to be my wife. But most of all, I respected and trusted you."

"I know what this must look like—"

"It looks like exactly what it is: a sordid affair with an old lover."

"No." Angie recognized that Glenn was lashing out at her with his pain, but she couldn't allow him to distort the love she shared with Simon. "I won't have you talk to me like that. I've loved Simon all my life. You knew as well as I did that . . . that if I'd married you I could never have given you the love you deserved."

Glenn's reply was a low, mocking snort. "Do you want me to give you a medal because you gave Simon the love *he* deserved?"

"Oh Glenn, you've twisted everything."

"I don't know," he argued, "it seems that for the first time in six months, I'm finally seeing everything clearly. You used me to get Simon back. That's what you really wanted—your old lover."

Angie could see that arguing was useless. "You have been extremely patient and dear. I'm so sorry everything's turned out like this, but when . . . when Clay became deathly ill I knew I couldn't face losing him without Simon. He was the one I reached out to."

Glenn grimaced and his clenched jaw tightened all the more.

"I wouldn't want to hurt you for the world. I can't tell you how sorry I am."

"Sorry. You're sorry?" He glared at her explosively.

"I owe you so much. It pains me to do this to you."

"I was the fool," Glenn barked. "A hundred times I could have had you. We should have been married weeks ago and you wouldn't have any choice but to stay with me."

His words were cruel and mocking, and with every minute he looked more enraged.

"I don't think there's any way to make this up to you. But I want you to know there will always be a special place in my heart for you."

"You used me."

Angie couldn't deny it. "Please try to forget me,

Glenn, and forgive me if you can. A thousand women would count themselves lucky to be loved by you."

"But you're not one of them."

Her gaze dropped to the floor. "I'm sorry . . . so sorry."

"Don't waste that emotion on me." The air between them was as tight as a hunter's bow stretched to its limits, ready to spring. "I can see there's no need to waste my time. Enjoy your lover, Angie."

She kept her eyes shut until after the door was viciously closed. The harsh sound reverberated in the room.

A few minutes later, Simon knocked lightly against the door. Angie hurried across the room to let him in. Instinctively she reached for him. He folded her into his embrace, his hands running soothingly down her back.

Gratefully she accepted his comfort, pleased that he had given her this time alone with Glenn. It hadn't been easy for him; she'd known that by the troubled look in his eye.

"What did he say?" Simon asked.

She shook her head hard. "It isn't important."

"He was angry."

"I wish I could have spared him the pain of finding us like this. I blame myself for that. I should have called him."

"He'll recover," Simon said confidently.

"I hope so," she whispered, tightening her grip.

They slept in each other's arms, content just to cuddle close. It surprised Angie that after all the years of sleeping alone her body would adjust so easily to sharing a bed. Somehow she knew it wouldn't have been that way with another man. Only Simon.

She woke to find him grinning at her beguilingly. "Morning," he whispered, and kissed her warmly.

Angie looped her arms around his neck and smiled into his eyes. "I could get used to waking up next to you."

"You'd better. I don't plan to sleep without you."

"Good." Her index finger wove around his curly chest hairs. "Have I told you lately how much I love you?"

"No." Simon's voice was deep and resonant.

"Yes, I have." She giggled. "You simply weren't listening."

"Hmm, I was listening," he said, and buried his face in the rounding slope of her shoulder to tease her unmercifully with small, biting kisses. "But I'm a man of action. Shall I demonstrate just how much I love you?"

"Oh yes," she whispered, her leg sliding provocatively up and down his. "But I feel I should warn you, it may take a lifetime to prove it to me properly."

"You drive a hard bargain, Angie Canfield," he growled, before hungrily lowering his mouth to claim hers.

The morning was half spent before they ever left the bedroom.

After a leisurely brunch, Angie dressed and prepared herself for a visit to the hospital.

"You've gotten quiet all of a sudden." Simon stood behind her, his hands cupping her shoulders as she rinsed off the breakfast dishes. "Are you worried about your father?"

Angie had phoned the hospital twice and each time received an encouraging report. "No," she whispered unconvincingly.

"You're frightened of what he's going to say about us, aren't you, love?"

"I'm afraid it's all going to happen again." She turned around and gripped his waist, pressing her cheek to his chest. She was comforted by the even, reassuring sound of his heartbeat. "Dad hates Groves Point . . ."

"And the Canfields," Simon added.

"Yes."

"But he's forgetting something important. Something that we'll need to remind him of today, if necessary. You, Angie, are a Canfield. You have been for twelve years."

"But, Simon . . ." she argued, and lifted her head to meet his gaze.

He pressed a finger to her lips, silencing her. "Today we'll make it clear that we have no intention of ever being separated again."

"But he's ill."

"Good," Simon argued. "There won't be much fight in him. He'll simply have to accept what we say."

Angie didn't feel any of the confidence Simon apparently did when they drove to the hospital. She hesitated outside Clay's room. "Maybe it would be better if I talked to him first," she suggested, her eyes seeking his approval.

Simon paused. "You're sure you don't want me with you?"

She answered him with a short nod, laid her open

palms on his hard chest, and kissed him briefly on the lips.

Clay was awake when Angie entered the room. He didn't make an effort to greet her. From the disapproving look in his eyes, Angie wondered if Glenn had come to Clay. As quickly as the thought came, Angie rejected it. Glenn would never do anything so petty. Clay looked so incredibly ill that her steps faltered. The hospital had assured her that her father was out of immediate danger, but she knew that the road to a complete recovery would be long and difficult.

"Hi, Dad." She leaned over and brushed her lips to his forehead.

"What took you so long? I've been waiting for you all morning. The least you could do is visit a dying man who happens to be your only living relative."

Feelings of guilt immediately assailed her. "I . . . woke late. When I called the hospital they said you were resting comfortably."

"Ha! That just goes to show you what they know."

"I'm here now." She clenched his hand in hers and held it close to her heart. "How are you feeling?"

"How do you expect me to feel? The pain would have killed most men. I nearly died. Do you think those doctors were gentle with that knife?"

"No . . . you suffered terribly."

"It ain't much better now."

Angie sighed miserably. This wasn't going well. Clay was like a demanding, unreasonable child. She lowered her gaze to the hospital bed and the white sheets. "I have something to tell you." Her voice nearly failed her, and her resolve wasn't much better. If Simon hadn't been standing on the other side of the door, Angie wouldn't have had the courage to continue. "When you were so deathly ill and I didn't know if you were going to live or die, I was so afraid. I was terrified of losing you."

Clay patted her hand impatiently. "You nearly did lose me. That's why I can't understand the reason it took you so long to get to the hospital." He looked at her empty hands. "And the least you could do is bring me the newspaper."

Angie felt like gritting her teeth. "Dad, let me finish. I . . . I thought you were going to die and I reached out to someone I've loved forever . . . someone I knew would comfort me." She swallowed against the tightness forming in her throat. "I called Simon Canfield." Not waiting for a reaction, she quickly moved to the door and stepped outside the room and took Simon's hand. He smiled encouragingly at her and squeezed her fingers.

By the time they entered the room, Clay had half risen from the bed, lifting himself up on one elbow. His face was contorted with rage and fury. "Get out," he hissed. "I won't have Canfield scum in my room."

"*Dad,*" Angie cried.

"And you get with him. If you don't know any better than to bring him here when I'm dying, then you ain't no daughter to me."

The color drained from Angie's face. "Don't say that."

"I'll say that and more." He fumbled with the button to summon the nurse and fell limply against the pillow, his face twisted with pain. "Get out."

"Maybe you have reason to hate me," Simon said, clearly fighting to control his temper. "But I love Angie and I won't allow you to come between us, old man. So understand that here and now."

The nurse with the crisp white uniform entered the room. "Get them out of here." Clay pointed a finger accusingly at Simon and Angie. "Leave me to die in peace." His voice shook, he was so weak. His face filled with angry color as he glared accusingly at Simon.

The nurse's face was grim as she turned to Angie. "Maybe it would be best if you came back another time."

Angie regretfully nodded.

"Just get one thing clear," Simon said in a low, hard voice. "I'm marrying your daughter and nothing on God's good earth is going to prevent that."

Clay lay on his back and stared at the ceiling, his features void of expression. "I ain't got a daughter."

"Daddy," Angie cried.

"Leave him to sulk," Simon whispered, gripping her elbow.

The nurse followed them out of the room, closing the door behind her. She hesitated and cleared her throat. "I don't want to become involved in family squabbles, but I feel you should understand that at this point your father's condition is extremely delicate. It would be best if you didn't do or say anything to upset him. If coming here is going to provoke him, then I suggest you stay away."

"But . . ." Angie couldn't bear the thought of having Clay step back from the brink of death only to lose him to stubborn pride.

"Any one of the staff would be happy to report his condition to you," the older woman continued.

"You don't think I should come at all?" Angie was aghast at the thought.

"Not if it's going to drain his strength. Your father is going to need all the fight he can muster just to recover properly."

"Come on, Angie." The pressure of Simon's hand at Angie's elbow increased. "Let's get out of here."

She nodded and smiled her appreciation to the nurse who had spoken so freely. On the ride back to her apartment, Angie didn't say a word, her thoughts dragging her spirits lower and lower with every mile.

Simon pulled in to her parking lot and turned off the engine. For a long minute, they didn't move. "What are you going to do?" he asked finally.

"What can I do?" She choked and covered her face with her hands. "Simon, he's my father."

"I'm your husband."

Angie felt as if the two men were waging a battle over her. Each was pulling on an arm, driving a wedge between Angie the daughter and Angie the woman, placing her in an impossible position.

Simon looped an arm around her shoulders and breathed into her hair. His voice was a gentle whisper close to her ear. "Let's go inside. We can talk there."

They made two cups of strong coffee and sat next to each other on the sofa. Simon's shoulder supported Angie's head as they became lost in the tangled web of their disturbed thoughts.

"With my own father so ill, I can appreciate your position," Simon began hesitantly. "The best solution would be for us to separate ourselves from family altogether. I could leave Groves Point and you could leave Charleston and we'd start a new life."

"We can't do that," Angie protested.

"I know, love." Wearily, he leaned his head back and let his eyes slip closed. "With my father sick, it'd be impossible for me to leave Groves Point."

"And Clay needs me in the same way."

"If you think I'm going to suggest the noble thing, you're wrong," he said quietly. His hand gripped hers. He'd endured too many miserable years without Angie. A hot anger surged through him at the thought of facing more of the same. He couldn't part with her when he'd come this close.

"What are we going to do?" Angie whispered, close to tears.

"About the only thing we can do for now. Wait. When Clay has recovered, we'll face him again. Only next time we won't back down. Agreed?"

Angie didn't hesitate. "Agreed."


Simon returned to Groves Point three days later when he could no longer ignore the commitments awaiting him. Clay Robinson was released from the hospital sixteen days after being admitted. Angie had visited him daily. At first he refused to speak to her. That was fine; she did most of the talking, chatting with him about little things that went on at the flower shop. She brought him the afternoon edition of the newspaper, his mail, and a daily supply of fresh-cut flowers. After a day or two Clay started asking her about Simon. Angie ignored his questions.

"You aren't seeing him, are you?" Clay had demanded.

Angie opened the blinds and stared into the sun. "I can't ever remember a more glorious afternoon. The sun is brilliant."

After two or three days of that type of response, Clay quit asking.

Because his condition remained weak and he would need someone to care for him, Angie drove her father to her apartment when he was released from the hospital. "You're to stay here until you're completely well, understand?" She didn't expect much of an argument. Clay knew a good thing when he saw it.

The situation wasn't ideal, but it soothed Angie's conscience.

With Clay at the apartment, Simon, who phoned daily, was forced to contact Angie while she was at Clay Pots. Their conversations were often short, as she was interrupted by customers and the usual hectic activity of running a flower shop.

"Simon." She drank in the sound of his voice after one particularly bad morning. "I'm so glad to hear your voice."

"How's Clay?"

"Demanding."

"In other words, he's running you ragged."

"Nothing seems to satisfy him," came her trembling reply. "Yesterday he called me three times with different requests. He wanted me to pick up his mail, which I do every night anyway. Then he didn't like what I'd planned to cook for his dinner and wanted me to shop at the grocery store and pick up something that wasn't on his diet.

I don't know why he bothered to ask. He knew I wouldn't."

"Angie, this can't go on much longer."

"I know," she agreed with an exaggerated sigh. "He's playing the deathbed recovery to the hilt. He makes it sound as if each request is his last."

"If I got hold of him it would be."

A slow smile touched her tired eyes. "Simon, just let me complain. I need someone to sympathize with me."

"I'm willing to comfort you as well." His voice went low and suggestive.

"Are you, now?"

"Eager, even."

Angie giggled. "I bet you're not half as eager as me."

"Angie," he groaned, "don't say things like that. Three hundred miles never seemed so far. I'm dying for you."

"It shouldn't be much longer," she promised. "Clay's going to the doctor tomorrow afternoon. I'll ask about having him move back to his own place. As much as I love my father, he's driving me crazy."

"Another minute without you is too long," Simon argued. "I'm coming this weekend."

"Simon." She breathed his name, pushing the hair back from her forehead with one hand. "Do you think you should?"

"I'll go crazy if I don't."

"Me, too," she admitted.

"You are going to marry me, aren't you?"

Her smile was filled with contentment. "I've been your wife in my heart for twelve years. I'd say it's time we made it legal."

"More than time."

Donna glanced to the back of the shop, and Angie straightened. "I've got to go."

"Me, too."

But neither hung up. "Bye, love."

"I love you, Simon Canfield."

"You better. I'm counting on collecting on that promise this weekend."


Saturday morning, after being assured by the doctor that Clay would be with her for another two weeks and perhaps longer, Angie was as nervous as a teenager about Simon's visit. Simon's flight was due to arrive shortly after noon. From the airport he was checking into a hotel, where she was meeting him for lunch.

"What's the matter with you this morning?" Clay snapped. "You're as jumpy as water on a hot griddle."

"Sorry."

"You should be sorry to leave a sick man on a Saturday."

"That can't be helped," she said, and swallowed down the guilt.

"Where did you say you was going?"

"To a meeting."

"You're dressed up mighty pretty for a simple meetin'."

"This one is with someone important."

Clay snorted. "You just remember what that fancy doctor said. I ain't out of the woods yet. I could have a relapse any day."

"You're getting stronger by the minute," she countered. Checking her watch, Angie brought Clay the television guide and kissed him briefly on the cheek. Dutifully, she tucked the blanket around his waist.

"What time will you be back?"

"I . . . don't know."

"The least you can do is give me my cell so I can reach you in case something terrible happens while you leave me."

Angie froze, making a pretense of checking the insides of her purse. "I'll have to call you."

"The person you should be calling is Glenn."

Glenn's name had been mentioned at least five times every day. "How come he ain't been around lately? I would have thought Glenn would stop by to see me. It's the least my future son-in-law could do." He paused, and Angie could feel the heat of his gaze as he studied her.

Angie decided the best thing to do was ignore him. "Bye, Clay." The minute the door was closed, Angie released a pent-up breath and relaxed. This was worse than anything she'd endured in her secret meetings with Simon the summer they were seventeen.

The drive seemed to take forever. Angie was anxious to get to him. She was afraid of wasting a single minute, afraid Clay would demand an accounting of her afternoon.

Simon was waiting for her in the hotel lobby. Their eyes met from across the width of the room. At the intense emotion shining from his deep, gray ones, Angie paused. He seemed to be digesting everything about her as if he couldn't determine if she was illusion or reality.

The tension eased from Angie and she offered him a

trembling smile of happiness. They met halfway into the room.

"Hi," she whispered, as their eyes drank in the sight of each other.

"You are so beautiful." He stopped himself from taking her in his arms and kissing her in front of a lobby full of people. Impatiently he glanced around. "Are you hungry?"

Shyly, Angie lowered her lashes. "Only for you."

"Room service?" he asked with a chuckle, tucking her hand in the crook of his arm.

"I think we'd better."

The minute they were inside Simon's suite, he took her in his arms and kissed her with a hunger that had been building inside of him for three interminable weeks. They undressed each other with trembling, eager hands, pausing only long enough to kiss. Their bodies were on fire for each other, their mouths clinging, twisting, yearning. Their hands paused to explore with awe and promise. When they were both completely nude, Simon's head drew back to look into her dark eyes. His thumbs lovingly brushed the high arch of her cheekbones.

"Oh my sweet love." He dropped his forehead against hers. "I love you so much I think I'd die without you now."

"I'll always be yours," she whispered emotionally, then surrendered to the exquisite agony he inflicted upon her with his hands and mouth. Angie thought she would die from the sweet torture before he carried her to the bed. He took her then, with a tenderness that was unlike anything she had ever known.

When they had finished, Simon drew her into his

arms and kissed the trail of tears that ran down her cheek. Nestled in his embrace, she laid her cheek upon his chest and breathed in even, contented breaths, thinking that nothing this side of heaven could be more wonderful than being loved by Simon.

"Are you asleep?" he whispered, after a long moment.

"I don't want to waste a moment of our time together by sleeping." Each second was precious. Angie didn't know how long it would be before she could see him again.

"In some ways I think I'm going crazy. I'm still warm and content from loving you, and already I'm worried about how soon it'll be before I can have you again."

She smiled and kissed his neck, letting her tongue tease his Adam's apple. "Any time, Mr. Bank President."

His arms tightened around her. "Angie, I've thought of a way to bridge the gap between our parents."

He sounded so serious that she lifted her head and turned onto her side, supporting her head with the palm of her hand. "You must be more of a genius than I give you credit for."

"A baby," he whispered reverently, placing a hand on her trim stomach. "The best thing that could happen to us is to get you pregnant as soon as possible."

Angie closed her eyes to the tenderness in his voice.

"My mother would give anything for a grandchild. I can think of nothing better to make us acceptable to the other's parents."

Angie recalled Clay's words about wanting to bounce a grandbaby on his knee. "Jeffrey Simon Canfield," she responded dreamily.

"Or Carolyn Angela Canfield." His hand traveled

from her smooth stomach to capture her breast. "Only I think we should make this marriage legal, and the sooner the better."

Happiness beamed from Angie. "Yes," she said, and gave him a watery smile. "I think we should."

"Next weekend?"

Angie shook her head. "I don't ever expect Clay to give me his wholehearted approval, but I'd rather wait until he's at least well enough to be on his own."

Simon's hand caressed her shoulders. "As soon as possible, though."

"Yes," she agreed.

Long after Angie had left, Simon lay staring at the tiled hotel ceiling. A feeling of dread he couldn't shake settled over him. He didn't usually have premonitions, but the fear continued to grow in his chest until he couldn't bear to stay still. Jerking to a sitting position, he sat on the edge of the mattress and buried his face in his hands. Angie was close to being his. He could think of no reason that this fear should assail him now. She loved him more than he dared hope, more than he deserved. They had talked of making their marriage legal and starting a family. There were twelve years of wasted time to make up. Years of love and laughter.

He glanced at the phone, more than half tempted to call her. These past few weeks, he had lived for those few minutes each day when they spoke. It was never enough time.

The irony of their situation caused a frown to mar his brow. Twelve years ago, his family had stood in their way.

They'd been forced to meet secretly then. They had been married twelve years and the first time he'd spent the night with Angie had been when Clay was in the hospital. Now they were compelled into that same kind of clandestine meeting, only it was her father who was keeping them apart. Their relationship, he thought pensively, was only a sad reflection of yesterday.


Angie let herself into the apartment and painted a smile on her face. Her heart was heavy. In some ways it would have been easier not to have seen Simon. It hurt so much to say goodbye.

"How are you feeling, Dad?"

"I thought you were going to call?" He didn't take his eyes from the television.

"I'm sorry, I forgot." Angie knew immediately that she'd said the wrong thing.

Angrily, Clay tossed the television guide to the floor. "Your own father is near death and you run off to some all-important meeting and completely forget about him."

"I didn't mean it that way." She flushed guiltily.

"It'd serve you right if I was to up and die."

"Good grief, I was only gone three hours."

"And ten minutes. I'm bored. Did you bring me my mail? I wasn't hungry at lunchtime, but I could eat something now. You can bring it in to me."

Gritting her teeth, Angie stepped into the kitchen and took the lunch she'd made for him earlier out of the refrigerator. She carried it out to him on a tray. "Do you want anything else?"

He ignored the question. "The way you snuck off like that, one would think you were hurrying to meet a lover."

Angie's step faltered, causing her to nearly drop the lunch tray. "Stop being so dramatic," she chastised in her sternest voice. She set the lunch on the coffee table and straightened.

"That's exactly what you was doing, wasn't it?"

Angie returned to the kitchen, her composure rapidly disintegrating. "The subject isn't open for discussion."

"You're a fool, girl."

"And you're interfering in my life."

Clay pushed the tray aside, disinterested. "Tell me somethin'. What makes you think that those highfalutin Canfield folks is going to want you any more the second time than they did the first? Can you see Mrs. Canfield inviting you to the Garden Club? Not hardly."

"I'm not talking to you about it."

"Sure you're not, 'cause you can't answer me. Nothin's changed in twelve years that will make you more acceptable to those rich folks."

"Dad, you heard me. I refuse to discuss this with you."

"All these years I thought I was raising me a decent girl," he mumbled, as he crossed his arms and leaned back against the pillows supporting his shoulders. "You ain't no better than a common . . ." He hesitated, apparently thinking better of his choice of words. "You're making a big mistake, girl. I'm begging you to reconsider having anything to do with the Canfields."

"Dad. Why do you have to do this to me? I love him. If Mom had come from a rich Atlanta family, would you have loved her less? Would you have decided not to marry her?"

Clay's cheeks expanded until he looked as if he were about to explode. "I won't have you dragging the good name of your mother into this. You hear me, girl?"

"I hear you," Angie said, her voice coated with defeat.

# Twelve

—⧟—

At five-thirty Angie closed up Clay Pots for the night. She had finished counting the money from the till when there was a knock at the bolted glass door. Glancing up from behind the counter, she was shocked to see Glenn standing on the other side.

"Glenn," she murmured, turning the dead-bolt lock.

"Hello, Angie." He regarded her sheepishly. "I apologize for stopping by unexpectedly."

"Please come in." She re-secured the lock. "Is something wrong?" He didn't look right. He was darker, tanner, as if he'd spent lots of time in the intervening weeks working outside. As always, he was meticulously dressed in a three-piece business suit and silk tie. Glenn had always been a stickler for neatness.

"I've come to ask you to forgive me for the things I said the last time I saw you."

"My forgiveness," she gasped. "Oh Glenn, don't make me cry." He was such a wonderful, dear man, and she had hurt him immeasurably, and then *he* came to apologize.

"What I said that night was unforgivable."

"You were only reacting to your anger. I don't hold any of it against you. We've been good friends for a long time. I knew you didn't mean it."

"I've felt bad about it for weeks. In thinking it over, I realized that the only thing to do was to come back and tell you that I wish you and Simon every happiness. I'll always love you, Angie, but I know that you belong with Simon. The only thing I want is to be certain that my anger didn't hurt you in any way."

"It didn't. I understood."

"I thought you might, but I wanted to be sure." An uncomfortable silence followed. It was so good to see Glenn again; she had missed his friendship, especially now that Clay was recovering and being so difficult.

As if reading her mind, Glenn asked. "How's Clay?"

"On the mend. Why don't you stop by and visit him sometime? He's at my apartment and I know he'd love to see you. He's bored and out of sorts and would welcome the company."

"Would you?"

Angie lowered her gaze, ill at ease. She didn't want to give Glenn any reason to hope there was a chance they could get back together again.

"I didn't mean it that way," he amended. "I only wanted to make sure that you didn't mind if I came by."

"I wouldn't have asked you otherwise." Briefly her hand touched his in an assuring action.

"You don't look happy, Angie. What's wrong?"

How like Glenn to look past his own troubles to recognize hers and comfort her. "Clay has strong feelings about Simon and me. He doesn't want me to have anything to do with the Canfields, let alone marry Simon. There's a continual cold war waging between us that is wearing me down." It felt so good to talk to someone about Clay. Someone who would understand. Any mention of her difficulties with her father would have only added to Simon's problems. And he'd been having plenty of those lately.

"In other words, he's constantly nipping at your heels."

Glenn had a way of describing it perfectly. "Yes."

The worst part was that Simon's father had died suddenly, and Simon had been tied up in Groves Point for the past two weeks. Angie's heart had gone out to him in his grief, recalling her own overwhelming emotion when Clay had been close to death. Simon had explained that he'd known for several months that his father was extremely ill. The two had never been close, and although he gave no outward sign of oppressive sadness, Angie knew that the death had affected him greatly. Many times in the past weeks she had wanted to be with him, to offer what comfort she could. Simon had assured her that he understood the reason she couldn't. He was fine. Just knowing that she loved him and wanted to be with him was enough for now. The demands on his time from his mother, settling his father's affairs, and those of the bank had prevented him from coming to Charleston. But he would be there as soon as circumstances would allow. Angie lived for their daily telephone conversations.

For the funeral, Angie had sent an elaborate floral arrangement, but Georgia Canfield hadn't acknowledged the gift. Angie comforted herself with the knowledge that it was too soon to expect a note of appreciation.

Only when Clay continued to harp on the differences between the two families, the Robinsons and "those rich folks in Groves Point," was it difficult to dismiss the doubts. Simon was sure that their love would construct all the bridges necessary. If not, fine. They didn't need anyone else, they had each other. Angie's confirming echo grew weaker every day. She needed Clay, and as much as she resented his intrusion into her life, he was her father. Clay had been her staunch supporter when she'd started in the flower business, and now it was her turn to stand by him. Clay's unfailing belief in her had helped Angie at a time in her life that she'd needed it most. As far as he was concerned, there wasn't a thing in this world that she couldn't do. Even though she'd bragged to Simon about Petal Pushers, Clay had often helped her. Some days he had spent more hours than she had, taking her assignments until Angie found her feet with Clay Pots. Unwittingly, Clay had worked to repay the Canfields all those thousands. Although Simon might not readily agree, he relied on his mother, too. Especially now. In death Simon's father had healed the gap between mother and son. They shared an emotional bond, and as the days passed it became all the more evident that Georgia Canfield needed Simon for moral and mental support during the difficult days.

"Maybe you'd like to come tonight," Angie suggested to Glenn. "Make it a surprise for Clay."

The handsome male features broke into a smile. "I'd like that. I'll follow you."

A couple times Angie checked her rearview mirror on

the way home. Glenn had been stopped at a yellow light at a major intersection so she was about three minutes ahead of him when she came through the door.

She greeted Clay with a warm smile and kissed his cheek. "How was your day?"

He grunted and threw back the blanket that covered his legs. "About as good as you can expect a man to feel who's been cooped up in a stuffy apartment for the last month of his life."

"But Dad!" Her voice rose indignantly. "I've begged and pleaded with you to get some fresh air. It's not good for you to sit around all day and do nothing."

"You're just looking for a way to kill me off so you can marry that rich Canfield boy."

Angie's fingers curled around the leather strap of her purse as she battled down the rising irritation. Clay had been living with her for almost a month now, and every day the atmosphere grew more strained.

"I've got a surprise for you."

"Don't want no surprises."

"I think you'll like this one," she said confidently.

The doorbell chimed and Clay's eyes flew to the door. "Why don't you get that? The exercise will do you good." Not waiting for an argument, Angie disappeared into her bedroom, where she changed into a cool pair of shorts and a sleeveless knit pullover. She paused and smiled when she heard Clay's happy exclamation of surprise.

Slipping her feet into sandals, she returned to the living room to discover Clay sitting on the sofa, his shoulders shaking with huge sobs. "She's going to marry him.

I know it in my heart, and he'll ruin her for decent men just the way he did twelve years ago."

"Clay!" Angie gasped. She couldn't believe that her own father would talk about her this way.

"See what I mean," Clay said, and leaned closer to Glenn. Tears ran unrestrained down his face. "Already he's turned her against me. You've got to do something." Clay's hands gripped Glenn's forearm as he regarded the younger man with pleading, sad eyes.

"If anyone's turned against anybody, it's you against me."

"Angie." Glenn stood and crossed the room, taking her by the shoulders. "Listen, it's easy to see that you've worn yourself to a frazzle taking care of your father. Let me stay with him tonight. Go do some shopping or take in a movie. Anything. Just leave for a while and relax."

"But I've got to fix his dinner."

His finger lazily wiped a lone tear from her cheek. "I've cooked before."

"He's on a special diet."

"Clay knows what he can and can't eat. Now, don't you worry. Just go and enjoy yourself."

She placed her hand in his and squeezed it with all the appreciation in her heart. "Thank you."

She left without saying a word to Clay, who sat regarding her mutinously. His eyes were slightly red as he glared at her.

In the mood for a peaceful ride, Angie drove to Sullivan's Island and walked along the sandy beach for what seemed like hours. A gentle breeze ruffled her hair, and the tangy scent of saltwater followed her as the waves crashed against the peaceful shore. Her thoughts weren't profound. She was too run-down, mentally and physically, to deal with any of the problems that plagued her. She didn't want to think about Clay or Simon or anyone. The beach had often offered her solace she couldn't find elsewhere. As if not to disappoint her, the sky turned a vibrant shade of pink and the warm sand welcomed her bare feet. Granules of the wet beach squished between her toes as she sat and stared out over the swelling rolling waters, at peace at last with her world.

It seemed ironic that the one to rescue her from another night of bickering with Clay would be Glenn, the man she had rejected. Intuitively, it seemed, Glenn had known when she was at her weakest point, struggling to maintain some semblance of sanity. Glenn Lambert was a rare man, she realized anew.

After a peace-filled hour, Angie called Groves Point.

"Yes." Simon's answer was abrupt and impatient, as if he, too, was stretched to his limits with the demands and pressures made on him.

"Hello, Simon." It was so good to hear him that the effort to keep her voice steady was monumental.

"Angie." Her name was issued on a rush of air that sounded like a warm caress. "Is anything wrong?"

Nothing was right, but Simon didn't need to hear that. He was under enough stress as it was. "No," she answered softly. "I just needed to hear the sound of your voice." She could almost feel the tension drain out of him as he began to speak.

"Where are you? I can hear a strange noise in the background."

"Landlubber," she teased affectionately. "Don't you know the sound of the ocean when you hear it?"

"The ocean?"

"You won't believe this."

"Knowing you, I'd believe anything," he said, chuckling.

"I'm on Sullivan's Island. Here, listen." She held up her cell toward the beach. "What do you think?"

"I think I'm going to go crazy if I don't see you soon."

"This weekend?" she asked, trying to disguise how anxious she was.

Simon hesitated, his voice filled with angry frustration when he spoke. "Honey, I can't. There are a thousand things I have to do with Dad's estate."

"Don't worry, we've got the rest of our lives. Another week or two isn't going to matter." She tried desperately to hide her disappointment.

A long moment of silence stretched between them.

"How's Clay?" Simon asked finally.

Angie forced a light laugh. "Cantankerous as ever. He seems to be recovering, but he refuses to do any exercise." Angie had come to believe that he was purposely making himself an invalid to prevent her from marrying Simon. Only she wasn't going to allow him to do that. The next appointment with Clay's doctor was the following week. Once Clay was given a clean bill of health, she would move him back to his own place so fast it'd make his head swim.

"How are you?" Simon asked next.

"Cantankerous as ever," she said with a light laugh. "I miss you, and I wish I was pregnant so Clay would insist that you make an honest woman of me and fall right into our plans."

Simon chuckled. "My thoughts toward you at the

moment are completely dishonest. Angie, I love you. I can hardly wait to show you how much."

"Believe me, I'm just as eager to prove my love." Where Angie had felt cold and tense before, she now felt warm, loved, and utterly secure.

They talked for an hour of silly inanities and ones not so silly. It was the most time they'd had together since Simon's one-day visit to Charleston two weeks before.

Even when she hung up the phone, Angie felt the warm glow of contentment that covered her with its serenity. Times were difficult for them now, but they would be better and soon. It was vital that she didn't look down at the mire she was standing in, but raised her line of vision to the long and happy life that stretched ahead of her with Simon.

After talking to Angie, Simon twined his fingers behind his head, balancing his chair on two legs as he leaned against the kitchen wall. Without Angie these past two weeks, he would have been driven to the edge of insanity. He had known and accepted that his father was gravely ill, but his death had still caught Simon unprepared. He had heard that from others but hadn't recognized the truth until his own father had gone. Maybe if he hadn't been so involved with Angie he would have seen to his father's business affairs sooner and they wouldn't be in this mess now. What did he know about all these legal matters? Darn little. His father had known he was close to death, Simon was convinced of that, and yet he had done practically nothing to get his affairs in order, leaving Simon with the distasteful task.

His mother was little help. She appeared totally ignorant of their financial affairs and was content to have Simon sort through the legal hassles.

A frown drew his thick brows together as Angie filled his mind. By all that was holy, he loved her. It seemed a miracle that their love had endured all these years and they were back together. He'd lost her once. Heaven and hell would pass away before he'd let that happen a second time. The pressures on her had been difficult these past several weeks, with her father underfoot night and day, making constant demands. The phone call tonight had come as a surprise, a pleasant one. They'd needed that, both of them.

Somehow, some way, he'd get to Charleston this weekend, even if it was for only a few hours. Angie needed him. Snickering softly, he shook his head. Who was he trying to kid? He needed to see her. Not since his early college days had he felt like this. He was supposed to be a serious businessman, yet every spare thought revolved around a wisp of a woman who had claimed his heart so completely that he would never be the same without her. He didn't just want to sleep with her, although that was a part of it. He wanted to care for her, ease her burden with her father, and protect her from Clay's angry words. He wanted to laugh with her and hear her laugh in return. And if she needed to cry, then he wanted her to do it in his arms so that he could comfort her as well.

His resolve tightened. He was going to Charleston. Nothing would keep him away from Angie. Not ever again.

———

Glenn was sitting on the sofa waiting for her when Angie returned to the apartment. "Hello." At her anxious look around, he quirked his head toward the bedroom. "Clay's asleep." He smiled then, his mouth rueful. "I can see why you're so worn down. Clay has a way about him."

"I suppose he talked your ear off," she said with mock seriousness.

"And then some." He paused and chuckled. "There's coffee on if you'd like a cup."

Angie moved into the kitchen and automatically poured two mugs, carrying both into the living room and handing Glenn one. "I don't even know how to thank you for tonight." She felt better than she had in days.

"By having dinner with me tomorrow."

Angie hesitated before sinking into the thick sofa cushion. Seeing Glenn again would serve no useful purpose. He was kind and good, but she wouldn't take advantage of that.

"As friends," he inserted quickly. "I realize that you're involved with Simon now, but I've missed your friendship. There's nothing that says we can't be friends, is there?"

"Nothing," she agreed. If anything, she needed a friend now more than she had at any other time in her life. Only she didn't want to hurt Glenn, and a prolonged relationship, even a friendly one, could do exactly that. "As long as we understand each other." She paused to wipe a weary hand over her tired eyes. "I have a feeling I'm going to end up feeling guilty about this. I don't want to use you as an escape from my troubles."

Glenn ran his index finger along the rim of the coffee cup several times, seemingly unconscious of the action. "I told you this once, but perhaps now it bears repeating. Loving someone means accepting them as they are. I know you love Simon. I'm not saying that doesn't hurt and that I don't regret the fact you can't love me in the same way. I should have known from the minute you returned from Groves Point that I'd already lost you. Blindly I chose to believe otherwise."

"Glenn . . . stop, please. I feel guilty enough already."

"No, let me finish. I want you to be happy, Angie. I wish I could say all the bitterness is out of me, but I can't. That will come with time. The two of us having dinner is as much for me as you. Say you'll come as a gesture toward the friendship we once shared."

Angie studied him for a long time before speaking. "All right," she agreed reluctantly.

"As friends," Glenn reiterated.

"As friends," she echoed softly.


The following morning Clay was much more himself. When Angie woke she found her father dominating the lone bathroom, humming to himself as he shaved. The round mirror above the sink was fogged up with steam from his recent shower.

"Better wipe that mirror off or you'll cut yourself," she quipped.

"I been shavin' a lot more years than you been livin'. I know what I'm doing."

Angie laughed and tightened the cinch of her robe. "Yes, Daddy dearest." She was halfway into the kitchen before she realized that this was the first morning in weeks that they'd had a testing, loving conversation. Usually Clay lingered in bed, claiming that he was in terrible pain and accusing Angie of being no better than those uncaring nurses who didn't give a hoot if he lived or died as long as his medical bills were paid. Angie had given up arguing with him for being so wrong and unreasonable.

She dressed in a simple two-piece skirt-and-blouse outfit of pale pink colors and returned to the kitchen to cook Clay breakfast.

"You're looking might pretty today," Clay commented. "Are you doing anything special tonight?" The intonation of his voice told her instantly that Glenn had discussed with Clay the fact that he was going to ask her to dinner.

"I might."

"Might?"

"Glenn offered to take me to dinner tonight." She decided to play Clay's game and busily cracked two eggs against the side of a dish.

"Always did like that young man. A smart girl would know what she was turning down. All my days I thought I was raising me a smart girl, but—" Abruptly he stopped. "You goin' to dinner with Glenn or not?"

"How could I possibly leave you? A loving daughter would never leave her father alone when he's been so sick and near death."

"Bah, I can take care of myself." He dismissed her concern and sliced the air with a heavy hand for emphasis.

Holding back a laugh was nearly impossible. "You've

been telling me for weeks that you've got one foot in the grave."

Clay looked flustered, his impatience growing. "I feel better today."

Angie studied him skeptically. His doctor's appointment wasn't until Monday, and at that not a minute too soon. Until Clay moved in, Angie hadn't realized how much she treasured her privacy. This togetherness was slowly driving her crazy.

"I'm glad to hear that you're more chipper today. Why don't you take a nice walk this morning before it gets too hot and muggy?"

"I might," Clay answered noncommittally.

"And I *might* go to dinner with Glenn."

Clay's fiery gaze clashed with hers. "Then I'll go on that walk you've been pestering me about for the last few weeks."

"Which means I'll probably be late tonight."

"Good." Clay's boyish smile went from ear to ear.


As it turned out, dinner with Glenn was the most relaxing night she'd spent in weeks, maybe even months. He could have taken her to an elegant restaurant and impressed her with wine and song. Instead he chose a Mexican place that was close to her apartment, where the food was fabulous and the atmosphere didn't cost a dime.

"I'll have you know that my agreeing to this dinner has gotten Dad out of the house for the first time since he left the hospital."

One side of Glenn's mouth lifted with a dry smile. "I thought it might. Your father's quite a character."

"I can imagine the things he told you about me last night."

"He's frightened, Angie. Frightened of losing you to Simon. Once you're married, you'll move to Groves Point and he'll be left in Charleston alone. Losing you is his greatest fear. I don't think he can bear the thought of being separated."

"He can move back to Groves Point with me."

"I know that," Glenn replied calmly.

Warming to the subject, Angie clenched her fists. "Dad's got some twisted emotions that need to be sorted through," she declared hotly. Clay's attitude on the subject of the Canfields was relentless. They never openly discussed Simon anymore. Yet the subject loomed between them like a concrete wall they each stepped around and couldn't ignore. "Dad seems to think everyone in Groves Point knows what went on between Simon's family and us. I'm confident that simply isn't so."

"I'm sure you're right."

"Honestly, Glenn," she returned angrily, "quit being such a yes-man. It isn't like you, and I don't like it."

Glenn burst into laughter as he placed his napkin beside his plate, his eyes avoiding hers.

Recognizing that he was simply letting her blow off a little steam, Angie felt sheepish. "I'm sorry. I didn't mean that."

"Don't worry about it."

"Quit being so nice," she snapped playfully.

Shaking his head, Glenn rolled his dark eyes at the

revolving ceiling fan. "It's little wonder Clay complains. There's no satisfying you, is there?"

It felt so good to laugh again that Angie's heart swelled with appreciation for this man who was more friend than she had ever known or deserved. She wasn't completely sure of Glenn's motives. In that respect, he worried her. No one was that wonderful. There had to be something that he expected in return for this. Quickly, Angie discarded the thought, disliking the cynical meanderings her mind had taken lately, and concentrated on having a good time for the rest of the evening.

The following day she sent Glenn a basket of fruit and a brief note as a thank-you for their evening together.

Glenn stopped by the apartment Thursday after work and took Clay out for a walk. Clay didn't look pleased when Angie declined the invitation to join them. Instead she took a leisurely bath, painted her nails, and phoned Simon. The evening was young, and she wasn't surprised that she didn't catch him.

When he phoned her at the shop at their regular time the next morning, she mentioned her call.

"Believe me, I could have used a sweet voice to clear away the insanity," Simon murmured. "Has Clay moved out? You seem to have some free time in the evenings of late."

"Monday," she whispered, purposely avoiding his question. "His appointment with the doctor is the twenty-fifth."

"Believe me, love, the minute he's given a clean bill of health I'm coming to get you. We're going to get married as fast as I can make the arrangements."

"My head is swimming just thinking about it."

"Honey, listen, I'm not making any concrete promises, but I'm doing everything I can to clear Saturday."

Angie felt ridiculously close to tears. Even a few hours in his arms would be enough to wipe out several days of bickering with Clay. "I'll ask Glenn to keep Clay occupied so we can spend more than an hour or so together."

A heavy, stone silence stretched over the line.

"Glenn?"

How stupid she'd been to mention him. She didn't want to hide the fact she was seeing him, but she would rather not have discussed it with Simon over the telephone. "Yes, he's the one who's responsible for—"

"You've been seeing Glenn?"

The ice in his voice sent chills up Angie's spine. "Not the way you're implying."

"What's going on?"

Slowly, Angie mentally counted to ten before answering. "He's been helping me with Clay."

"I'll just bet."

Angie's temples began to throb and she pressed two fingers to them to ease the pounding ache. "A customer just came in . . . I've got to go."

"Angie," Simon breathed impatiently. "I didn't mean anything. I think we're both going a little crazy."

"You might be able to come Saturday?"

"I'm coming." He didn't leave any room for speculation. He was going to be there, and her heart throbbed with anticipation.

"You'll phone me when you get into town, then? I'll be in the shop until noon."

Simon hesitated. "I'll phone."

If Angie felt guilty about going out to dinner with Glenn, it was nothing compared to what she felt when she asked him if he'd mind keeping her father occupied while she met Simon Saturday afternoon.

Simon hadn't contacted her by the time she left the shop Saturday, which meant he'd probably catch her at the apartment. Normally this would have been a cause for concern, but Glenn and Clay were going for a long drive and would be leaving shortly after Angie arrived back at the apartment.

Their mood was light and teasing when she sauntered in a little after one o'clock.

"Beautiful day, Angie girl. Are you going to join us this time?" Clay asked her on a cheerful note. "Can't see you wasting away in a stuffy apartment when two handsome men are eager for your company."

She was pleased at the color in Clay's cheeks. "Another time, Dad." She shared a conspiratorial smile with Glenn.

"We'll catch her another day," Glenn interjected.

"But I thought she'd want to come along today." Clay pursed his lips like a discontented child who had been outwitted by his parents.

"I'll join you another day," Angie promised.

"But what are you going to do that's so all-fired important that you can't come with us?" Clay insisted.

Angie looked imploringly to Glenn, but was saved from answering by the doorbell.

Clay stood closest, and swung open the door. Angie couldn't see who it was since Clay was blocking her view.

But her father's body language gave her all the clues she needed.

"Hello, Angie." Simon stepped around her father and gave her a phony smile. His gaze went from Clay to Glenn. "I hope I'm not intruding on anything important," he said.

# Thirteen

Simon recognized immediately that by arriving unannounced to the apartment he'd done the wrong thing. The hurt and confused look in Angie's eyes sliced into him. His gaze clashed with Glenn's as he avoided looking toward Angie. Earlier, he'd tried her cell, but it had gone directly to voicemail. He was dying for the sight of her. For weeks he'd dreamed of taking her in his arms and loving her until they were both sated and exhausted. Every minute apart these past weeks had been torture. Yet Angie had gone back to the apartment without waiting to talk to him and that rankled.

"Simon," Angie said, her dark eyes round and imploring. "What are you doing here? I thought . . ."

"Sneaking behind my back." Clay's pale face turned to his daughter with a hurt look that went far deeper than words. "You two were going to sneak behind my back."

Glenn took the old man's hand and lowered him into

the cushioned chair. "Maybe this is the time for the three of you to sit down and talk things out."

Angie's bewildered gaze went from her father's ashen features to the intent look marking Simon's features. She stood defenseless between the two of them, knowing that she was about to be forced into taking sides. To one she was a puppet, pulled by the strings of guilt and duty. To the other, impatient in his way, she was a love long lost.

Clay crossed his arms over his chest and looked straight ahead with stony eyes. Anger and bitterness emanated from every pore. "There's nothing left to say."

"Dad, stop acting like a two-year-old," Angie said, looking desperately to Simon. "Why did you come here now, like this? Couldn't you have waited until Clay was well?"

"I believe I'll leave this to the three of you to settle," Glenn murmured, heading toward the door. "Good luck."

Simon watched the other man's departure with a sinking feeling. Glenn did indeed love Angie. Far beyond what Simon had suspected. He would like to hate the man, but discovered that he couldn't. Instead, a grudging respect came, and he wondered if he could have been half as decent over this situation as Glenn. With that realization came another. Glenn wasn't coming around Clay and Angie for his health. Obviously the man thought there was still a chance he could win Angie. Glenn wasn't a masochist, nor stupid. He was standing ready to pick up the pieces. And now, in his impatience, Simon had fallen directly into the other man's hands.

"Simon, maybe it would be best if we sat down. We

should be able to reach some kind of understanding."
Angie's words helped clear the fog in his mind.

"All right." He moved into the room and took a seat
on the sofa. For the first time he studied Angie and was
mildly shocked to see how tired and run-down she
looked. The faint purple smudges under her eyes were
artfully camouflaged with makeup. Her mouth drooped
just enough for him to recognize that she was struggling
with her composure. By forcing the issue today, he'd
done nothing but increase the pressure on her. Silently, he
cursed himself.

"I owe you an apology for showing up like this."
Simon directed his words to the stiff, motionless man
who sat across from him.

Again Angie turned questioning, hurt eyes to Clay
and Simon. She could see talking would do no good.
"Then why did you?"

"I want to marry you, Angie. I'm tired of meeting in
hotel rooms. We're consenting adults. There shouldn't
be any reason in this world to keep us apart any longer,
and if that means forcing Clay to accept certain truths,
so be it."

Clay gasped and his eyes narrowed into thin, accusing
slits as they centered on his daughter. "So you've been
giving yourself to him. Again."

Angie dropped her face to her hands, and again
Simon realized that every time he opened his mouth, he
was only making things worse for Angie.

"Is this the way I raised you, Daughter?" Clay asked
in a choked voice that was barely above a whisper. "Your
mama, God rest her soul, was a lady. I tried my hardest

to raise you to be just like her. Until now, I didn't realize how miserably I've failed."

"It isn't like that." Angie moved from the sofa and took her father's hands in her own. "I don't know why Simon is doing this, but—"

"I'm doing this because we shouldn't need to hide the fact we're in love. From the time we were kids we belonged together. As long as I breathe, nothing's going to stand in the way of our happiness."

"Simon . . ." Angie ground out his name. "Don't say anything more. You're only making matters worse." Could he be so blind as not to see what he was doing to her? She was Clay's daughter, and although he was playing on his recent illness to keep her apart from Simon, that wasn't any reason to drive a wedge between her and her only relative.

Frustrated, Simon rolled to his feet and buried his hands in his pockets. "Listen, maybe it wasn't such a great idea to show up like this. Maybe I should have been patient and played it cool. But for how much longer?"

"Only a few days. A week at the most," Angie cried, not bothering to disguise her hurt.

"Just who are you trying to kid?" Simon asked, watching her closely. He hated to see her on her knees, groveling at her father's feet. "Do you honestly believe that Clay's going to let us find any happiness together? I can guarantee that there'll always be another reason to prevent our marriage."

"You don't know that."

"Angie, look at him. He's never going to give his approval."

Angie shook her head as if to clear her thoughts. "Yes, he will," she cried. "In time."

"I'm through waiting," Simon said on a cold, sober note. "I want us to get married now."

"It'll only be a little while," she pleaded.

Simon released a low moan of frustration. Angie was living in a dream world. "The doctor will give Clay a clean bill of health soon, and immediately after that something else will magically appear to delay our marriage."

"That's pure conjecture."

"That's fact," he shouted in return. "We're adults. I'm through with living my life to satisfy parents. I want us to be married and I want it now. Are you with me or not?"

Angie hesitated, slid her eyes closed, and inhaled deeply. Here it was. She'd known from the minute Simon stepped in the doorway that it was coming. With everything that they'd shared, she would have thought he'd know not to do this. The impatient, frustrated man standing over her wasn't the Simon she loved. This was a man driven to the limits of his patience, irrational and demanding.

"You can't ask me to do this. Not now."

Simon paused. "When?"

"I . . . I don't know."

In a blinding flash he knew that he was right. Angie was tied to her father and the bonds were far stronger than he'd realized. In pitting himself against the old man, Simon would lose the very thing he treasured most in life. He had to reach Clay.

Simon took a seat across from Angie's father and

swallowed down his pride. "Can we lay aside the hurts of the past? I love Angie, and I'll spend every second of my life proving just how much. We want your blessing. We need it. Can you overlook everything that's happened and give us your blessing?"

A full minute passed before Clay spoke. "No words could ever undo the embarrassment and pain your family caused mine."

Simon realized that he should have known the old man would demand blood. "What is it you want, then?" He fought back the building anger, clenching his hands so tight that his fingers ached with the effort.

Clay didn't respond.

"What do you want from me?" Simon repeated.

Silence.

"More money, is that it?"

"Simon," Angie cried. "Don't do this."

"If you don't want money, maybe I could—"

"All I want from you is to leave my Angie alone. You hear me, boy, leave my daughter alone."

Simon expelled a ragged breath. "That's the one thing I won't do."

"Dad." Angie's voice was so weak that Simon could barely hear her. "Simon and I need to talk."

Clay grunted and crossed his arms. "I suppose you're going to do your talking in that hotel room."

Knowing it was useless, Simon stood and took Angie's cold, limp hand in his. "Let's get out of here. We don't have to listen to that kind of garbage."

Angie stared up at him, undecided, her look rotating from Simon to her father. "I . . . don't think I should leave Dad like this. Not now."

"Yes, you can," he argued fiercely, shouting.

Angie pulled her fingers free of his grasp and shook her head, placing her hands over her ears to blot out any protest. "No."

"All right," Simon murmured. He had brought this on himself by coming to the apartment, forcing the issue. He was pressuring her to choose between a lifetime of love and loyalty to her father and the reclaimed love she and Simon shared. She couldn't choose one and not betray the other. The crazy part was that all he had ever wanted to do was love Angie and cherish her, protect her, give her his children, and love them with the same intensity with which he loved their mother. Instead he had set her up for more anguish. Very gently he placed his hands on her shoulders, cupping them. He leaned forward and kissed her lightly on her cheek, shocked at the chilled feel of her skin.

"You know where I'll be," he whispered. It could have been his imagination, but Simon thought he felt her stiffen as if to pull away. His heart plummeted to the very depths of hell. He was so close to losing her, and powerless to reach out to her now. Angie Robinson was the only woman he'd ever truly loved, and he had somehow managed to louse up their relationship . . . a second time.

"I'll talk to you later," she whispered in return.


For two hours Angie wrestled with her emotions. The more she thought about what Simon had done by coming to the apartment, the more upset she became. Maybe he was right. Maybe Clay would always find an excuse to keep them apart. But now wasn't the time to catapult her

into making a decision. For days she had eagerly anticipated being with Simon, looking upon his visit as a time
for renewal and rejuvenation, mentally and physically.
Their time together was to be a brief oasis in a life whose
route had taken her deep into the arid, lifeless desert. In
the past weeks, they'd both been taxed to the limit of
their endurance with family pressures. They'd needed
this time for their sanity.

Clay sat so motionless that for an instant Angie wondered if he'd stopped breathing. When Simon had gone
she'd half expected her father to blast her with a fiery
tirade of insults. In the past he'd done exactly that,
knowing how much it hurt her. Instead his eyes revealed
a deep, bitter pain that words wouldn't easily erase. So
they didn't speak, but sat like strangers, yearning to
reach out to each other and not knowing how.

When she could endure the agony no longer, Angie
stood and reached for her purse.

"I . . . need to think," she whispered. "I don't know
when I'll be back."

"You're going to him," Clay said with cruel certainty.

Angie's jaw sagged as she prepared to argue. Dejected, she closed her mouth. She hadn't given thought to
where she was going, only that she couldn't tolerate another minute in the tension-filled apartment.

"Don't lie to me, girl. You're going to him."

Clay was right, that's exactly where she was going.
"I'll be back" was all she said.

The ride across town took her through heavy traffic,
giving her plenty of time to think. She loved Simon, had
loved him nearly all her life. When she'd taken the money
and left Groves Point, something keen and vital had died

within her. For a long time she couldn't look at men without experiencing a deep, harrowing pain. After a while, more for Clay's sake than her own, she'd started dating again. If her date was tall, Angie decided she preferred someone shorter. If her date was quiet and introspective, she found him boring. If he was intelligent and opinionated, she wished for someone dull. After a while, Angie gave up dating completely. Until Glenn . . .

The front desk at the Hilton connected her with Simon, who gave her his room number. She marched across the lobby, her indignation building. She loved him, but she couldn't allow him to pressure her this way.

She'd hardly had time to knock when the door was opened. "Thank goodness you came," he whispered.

"Why?" The word barely made it through the tightness in her throat. "Why did you come to the apartment? Didn't you stop to think what would happen?"

"Angie, listen—"

"No," she cried, "you listen. I want to marry you. All I'm asking for is a little patience. My dad is lucky to be alive. I'm not prepared to do *anything* to endanger his health, and that includes upsetting him the way you did this afternoon. You . . . you may have blown everything. I can't understand you."

Simon pushed the hair off his brow. "I think I went a little crazy when I learned Glenn was coming around."

She couldn't believe that he could possibly be jealous of Glenn. "He's been wonderful." She said this to imply that Simon hadn't been.

A grimness tightened his face. "Of course he has. Glenn loves you. Why else do you think he's been hanging around?"

Angie struggled for a response. "Glenn came to apologize for that last scene . . . He saw the toll that nursing Dad was having on me and offered to give me a break."

Simon heard this with a frown of distaste. "You don't really believe that, do you?"

Angie raised stricken eyes to him. "I do believe that. It's exactly what happened."

Simon's snort was filled with disgust as he stalked to the far side of the room. "Are you so naïve as to believe that your father didn't have a hand in that? I don't doubt for a minute that Clay was responsible for Glenn's sudden appearance."

Angie stared at him in shocked disbelief. She thought she knew Simon so well, but discovered that she didn't know him at all. Together they owed a great unpayable debt to Glenn Lambert. Glenn's love and patience had given her the courage to face the past and go back to Groves Point. Even after she'd returned to Charleston, he had loved her enough to step aside until she'd sorted through her feelings for Simon. Angie didn't try to kid herself. None of this had been easy for Glenn, but he had acted with a patience, love, and understanding that was, at times, almost superhuman.

A frozen, deadly silence iced the room.

"You may be right." Angie's words shattered the cold quiet. "But we both should thank God for Glenn."

Simon lifted one dark brow at her, assimilating her words. "I didn't realize your feelings were so intense."

"Stop trying to make something sordid out of Glenn's affection for Clay and me. He at least had the common decency not to pressure me into—"

"Choosing between your father and me."

"Yes," she finished, her voice quavering.

"That's the beauty of the situation," Simon returned with heavy sarcasm. "With Glenn there would be no decision to make. Clay would love to see you married to him."

"I've already agreed to be your wife. What else do you want?" Swallowing down her irritation, Angie sank onto the side of the queen-size mattress, struggling against the rising hysteria. She had so looked forward to this weekend with Simon. She couldn't believe that they would waste this valuable time together fighting.

"Where's the ring I gave you, Angie?" His slicing gaze fell to her bare fingers.

One hand curled over the top of the other. "With Clay feeling the way he did, I couldn't wear it. Surely you can understand that."

"No." Simon's voice was deadly calm. "I'm afraid I can't."

"All right, I should have worn it," she cried, knowing he was hurt and hating herself for being so weak. The ring, the most precious piece of jewelry she owned, was locked in a desk drawer at Clay Pots. A hundred times she'd thought to slip it on her finger and decided against it, knowing the sight of it would cause an argument. She'd been so tired lately and hadn't wanted to battle Clay at every turn.

"What's in a ring? Right?"

Her head snapped up, positive she hadn't heard him correctly.

His eyes narrowed on the soft rise and fall of her breast.

"Simon," she whispered pleadingly. "Your ring is a symbol of your love. I'm sorry I haven't worn it."

"Not sorry enough." He sat beside her impatiently and tugged at the buttons of her blouse, jerking it open and off her shoulders. Shocked and appalled, Angie was stunned.

"If you love me so much," he taunted, "I'll let you prove it."

"Simon, what are you doing?" she cried, attempting to cover herself.

In answer he stripped off his shirt and slacks, his eyes avoiding hers.

"I love you," she murmured in a choked voice, "only don't do this to me. This isn't making love."

He was a stranger whom she didn't recognize.

Tears swam in her eyes as she slumped onto the mattress. "Simon, what's come over you?"

"You keep saying that you love me so much." He leaned toward her. "I want you to show me how much."

Angie was numb with disbelief. This couldn't be happening to her. Not with Simon. He'd always been such a gentle, kind lover. He had given of himself, never taken. Their lovemaking was special, a sharing of their intense joy of each other.

"Why are you doing this?" she begged, her hand stopping his.

"Why?" he echoed cruelly. "Because it's clear to me now that you don't love me enough," he said. Harshly, he took her mouth, grinding his lips over hers until Angie pushed herself free.

"You think I should have been more diplomatic with your father."

"Yes," she cried. "He's ill."

"The time for diplomacy is past. Either you want to be my wife or you don't."

"Oh Simon," she whispered, needing his tenderness. "I do love you." She turned her face to him and hesitantly laid her fingers over his rigid jaw. He was angry and hurt and lashing out at her in a way she'd never expected.

Momentarily, his steely eyes softened. "Then marry me. Today. Now." Again, his mouth claimed hers, parting her lips with a deep, languorous kiss. Angie locked her arms around his neck and kissed him hungrily in return. He burned a hot trail of kisses down the scented hollow of her throat to just above her bra line. "Simon," she whispered, "please."

"Do you want me?" he taunted in a low voice.

"Yes," she pleaded.

"Enough to come away with me today for the rest of our lives?"

Angie's eyes flew open and she went limp against the mattress. Simon raised his head, his eyes boring into hers. "Today," he repeated starkly.

"I . . . can't. Don't ask that of me."

"I just did."

"All I want is your love." She raised her head and tried to kiss him, but he held himself stiff and unyielding, avoiding her touch.

"I won't settle for what's left over when Clay takes advantage of you," he said harshly.

"But I'm offering you everything," she said desperately. "Everything. If you'll only be patient. I love you so much."

A long moment of tormenting silence passed as his expression clouded over with bitterness. "Words no longer satisfy me."

She tore herself from his grasp when he tried to reach for her and bring her back into the comfort of his arms. Grabbing her purse, she rushed to the door. Her throat was burning with the effort to suppress the tears. She hesitated as she turned to look back and found Simon was sitting at the end of the bed. His face was buried in his hands, his shoulders hunched over, giving a profile of abject misery. As she reached the door Simon raised his head, his eyes pale and haunted.

"Angie, wait."

She didn't hesitate, but turned the doorknob.

"Please."

Her hand tightened around the doorknob and she paused. "Clay always said you were a spoiled rich boy," she whispered through her pain. "I never believed him until today."

Dejected and utterly defeated, Simon didn't try to stop her as she pulled open the door and walked out of his life.

In the long days that followed, Angie had plenty of time to think over their last meeting. In many ways she understood why Simon had behaved the way he had. That didn't excuse his actions, but granted her the time to be more forgiving. In the beginning, she decided that when he phoned she'd treat him aloofly, with mild contempt. A miserable week passed and she realized she would have given her soul to hear from him. Another week and she recognized that Simon never planned to contact her. He'd given her the option either to marry him then or it was over. She had made that choice.

Not knowing what had transpired, Clay watched her guardedly for several days. The afternoon following the doctor's appointment, he moved back to his own place and showed up only at periodic intervals. They never mentioned Simon.

Glenn called once a week to chat and ask how she was doing. Their conversations were brief and one-sided. He didn't ask her out, intuitively recognizing, she supposed, that she'd turn him down. In many ways Angie would always be grateful to Glenn. He had been a good friend when she needed one most, but she had abused that friendship and was paying dearly for it now. She didn't know if Clay had asked Glenn to visit her or if he'd come of his own initiative. It didn't seem to matter, and she didn't inquire.

When she realized that she wouldn't be hearing from Simon, Angie prayed fervently that she would become pregnant, and wept the morning she learned she wasn't. For a time she thought he might contact her if only to ask if that last time together had given life to his seed. Angie didn't know if her tears were from bitter disappointment that she wasn't going to have his child or that Simon didn't seem to care enough to find out.

Slowly, each day a test, Angie began to gain her perspective again. She had a good life, a meaningful one. Her business was profitable, and she made casual inquiries into opening a second shop on Calhoun Street near Marion Square. At the end of the third week, Angie discovered that she could smile again and occasionally even laugh.

The hottest days of summer came in late August and the muggy afternoon heat was unbearable. Angie took long walks along the beaches, watching the children play in the sand. The world seemed full of children and young mothers. In a month they would both be thirty. Friday afternoon, a half hour before closing time, Angie was working in the back of the shop when she heard the small bell ring, indicating that someone had entered. She set aside the centerpiece she was constructing from dried wildflowers and approached the counter. Her eyes met the elegant ones of Georgia Canfield and she faltered slightly. Quickly regaining her composure, Angie braced her hands on the counter.

"Hello, Mrs. Canfield."

"Hello, Angela."

She looked calm but out of place in something as common as a flower shop. "It's a lovely place you have here."

"Thank you."

"I understand you named it after your father."

"Yes." Angie didn't feel all that comfortable with this woman. She couldn't understand what Simon's mother would be doing here unless something had happened to Simon. An instant of panic filled her mind, but she dismissed it quickly. Knowing Georgia Canfield, she was sure the woman would tell her soon enough the reason for her unexpected visit.

"I never wrote to thank you for the arrangement you sent for Simon's funeral."

"I understand that you were very busy."

"Yes." She hesitated. "My husband's death was a shock."

"I'm sure it must have been."

The phone rang and Angie excused herself to take an FTD order from Boston. As she wrote it out, she noticed that Georgia sauntered around the shop as if she hadn't a care in the world. The woman was amazing.

Replacing the receiver, Angie cleared her throat softly. "Was there something I could do for you, Mrs. Canfield? I'm sure this isn't a social call." Angie wanted to fill this order before closing time and there were only a few minutes left. She didn't know what kind of game the woman was playing, but she wasn't in the mood to go along.

Georgia Canfield sighed appreciatively. "Charleston is such a lovely city."

"Yes," Angie agreed, letting her eyes drop to the FTD order. "Mrs. Canfield," she said, breathing heavily, "I don't mean to be rude, but if you have something to say, I wish you'd say it. I don't have time to play cat and mouse with you."

The older woman paled slightly. "If you insist on being direct, then I shall. I'd like to know what happened between you and my son."

Angie's smile was bittersweet. "You'll have to ask Simon that."

"My dear girl, I would hardly come three hundred miles to quiz you if I wasn't forced into doing so." Her voice was calm and even. The only outward sign that she was angry was the drumming pulse in her neck.

In spite of herself, Angie smiled anew. "No, I don't suppose you would."

"My son is deeply in love with you."

Angie walked briskly past the woman to the flower case. Opening the refrigerated cabinet, she withdrew several long-stemmed roses and a variety of other flowers she would need for the arrangement.

"Doesn't that mean anything to you?" she demanded.

"Yes," Angie admitted with an uncomfortable feeling of guilt. "It means a great deal."

"Do you love him?"

"I don't believe that's any of your business."

A small, admiring smile twitched at the corner of the older woman's mouth. "I strongly suspect that you do."

Angie's fingers tightened around the unstripped stems in her hands. The thorns cut unmercifully into her palms. "If you'll excuse me."

"No," the woman barked.

Angie turned, surprised at the uncharacteristic rise in the older woman's voice. "Twelve years ago, I paid you ten thousand dollars to leave Groves Point," she said in a low, controlled voice. "Today I would offer you everything I own if you'd agree to come back."

# Fourteen

—m—

"I promised myself I wouldn't intrude on Simon's life a second time," Georgia Canfield continued, more subdued now. "But my son needs you." Her gloved hands were folded primly in front of her creaseless linen suit. "I thought at first it was my husband's death that had affected him so greatly. But now I believe it's you."

"Mrs. Canfield, if Simon loves me as much as you say, then he would have come back for me."

"And if you love him as much as you say," she fired back, "you'd make the effort to go to him. Listen, Angela, you're not the woman I would have chosen for Simon, but I've already had my chance at handpicking one wife. All I want is my son's happiness, and if that means you, then I'm willing to accept you as a daughter-in-law."

"Maybe we should understand each other, Mrs. Canfield," Angie shot directly back. "I don't play bridge and have no intention of learning. I don't want to have anything to do with the country club and I plan to be far too busy to join all the charities that interest you. Furthermore, if I come back to Groves Point I plan to bring my flower shop with me and work in it until the babies come."

The frown that drew the delicately lined eyebrows into one stiff curve relaxed at the mention of children. "You do want children?"

"A house full."

"And you wouldn't restrict me from seeing them?"

"Mrs. Canfield, we've all made mistakes. I don't hate you. I couldn't. You're Simon's mother, and the very things I love about Simon are the best parts of you. You would be the only grandmother our children would have. They would need your love just as much as Simon and I would."

The older woman's tight mouth relaxed and trembled at the corners. "My dear," she whispered, so softly that Angie had to strain to hear, "perhaps you would consider being a guest speaker at the Garden Club someday."

Angie's own voice was soft and quivering. "I'd enjoy that very much."

Mrs. Canfield opened the clasp of her purse, took out a dainty lace handkerchief, and dabbed the corners of her eyes. "Believe me, I didn't expect to resort to tears, but I've been terribly distressed about Simon."

"What's happened?" A niggling fear invaded her happiness.

"I think it would be best if you saw for yourself. Do come soon, Angela."

"I'll be there within a week."

"Thank you."

"No, Mrs. Canfield," Angie whispered through the emotion blocking her throat. "Thank you."

Saturday morning, after furiously making arrangements with Donna regarding the flower shop, Angie packed her bags. Her first stop on the way out of town was Clay's. Apprehensive, she sat in her car an extra minute to compose her thoughts. This was the moment she dreaded. She was going home to Simon, to where she'd always belonged, but in doing so she was pulling away from the loving, protective arms of her father. Long ago Angie had recognized that Clay's actions had been motivated by love. Fear and pride had played a large part in his actions, too, but mostly there was love. He had used his health as a means of emotional blackmail so that she stood torn between the two men she loved the most in the world. Clay thought he'd won.

He opened the door and gave her a look of mild surprise.

"Angie." He glanced at his wristwatch. "It's barely eight. What are you doing up so early?"

She gave him a kiss on the cheek and raised her eyes to his. "I'm leaving, Dad."

The smile drained out of Clay's face inch by inch, leaving him pale and deadly sober. "You're going to him."

Angie nodded. "It's where I belong."

He smiled a little sadly and hunched forward as he slumped onto the sofa. "I guess I've always known you would."

"Thank you for not trying to stop me."

"I wouldn't," he said, and his low voice was edged with pain. "You go to him, Angie girl, and tell him for me that he's the luckiest man in South Carolina."

Sitting beside her father, Angie took him by the shoulders and gently laid her soft cheek to his jaw. "I'll be moving Clay Pots with me."

Clay nodded and closed his eyes. "You've done well for yourself. I've been proud of you from the minute your mama laid you in my arms for the first time. No matter what I've said to you, I've always been proud you are my daughter."

"Dad . . . do you remember how Groves Point gave us a second chance after Mom died? It'll do that again. I want you to move back . . ."

"That's impossible, Angie." He lowered his head and studied his clasped hands for a heart-wrenching minute. "I've never told you how deeply I regret taking that Canfield money."

Angie laid her hand over his. "I was the one who took it."

"No," he argued. "Not only did I convince you to accept that money, but I took the chance of giving you the college education you deserved. I wasted all those thousands on a pipe dream."

"Dad—"

"No, I want you to listen. I've got some money saved, not much, a few thousand. When you go to Simon I want you to give him that with the promise that I'll repay him the rest of the ten thousand when I can. I realize it's a little old-fashioned, but I want you to think of this as your dowry."

"Oh Dad," she whispered hoarsely, fighting back tears. "I should have told you."

"Told me?"

"Remember when I sold Petal Pushers?" She gave him a moment to absorb the meaning of what she was saying.

He looked puzzled, a deep frown narrowing his brow into three thick lines as he studied her.

"That was our business, yours and mine. You worked as many hours as me. Often more. I sold it, invested the profit, and returned the ten thousand dollars to the Canfields with twelve years of compound interest."

Clay's puzzled frown turned to one of amazed stupefaction.

"We don't owe the Canfields a penny."

"Why didn't you tell me?"

She shrugged one shoulder. "I wish now I had."

Clay hugged her close, squeezing her head with his long arms. "Go to him, Angie. With my blessing and with my love."

"Thank you, Dad," she whispered through a heart pounding with happiness.

The drive took the better part of seven hours. Angie stopped twice. Once for gas and another time to grab a sandwich and something cool to drink. As her car ate up the miles, Angie grew more content. She felt as if she was going home, really going home, after a long time away.

She didn't stop in town, but drove directly to Simon's house. Their house, her mind corrected, with its four spacious bedrooms, office, and family room.

Prince barked when she pulled into the long driveway, but stopped when she climbed out of the car and gave him her hand to smell. The short-haired black dog seemed to recognize her and wagged his tail in greeting. Laughing, she found a stick, threw it into the woods, and watched him scramble after it.

The back door was jerked open, and Angie turned to see an angry scowl on Simon's face disappear into one of shocked disbelief.

"Angie," he whispered, as if seeing an illusion. He rubbed his hand over his eyes. "Is it really you?"

Unexpectedly, she felt shy. It took everything within her just to meet his gaze. "Hello. The real estate man said I might want to look at this place as a possible home for a family."

Slowly he came down the concrete steps, measuring her words as though he couldn't believe that she had come back to him a second time. Every instinct in him urged him to pull her into his arms and thank God for giving him another chance with this woman. A crippling thought paralyzed him on the bottom step. No woman would return to him after the way he'd abused her body and spirit. Not unless there was a good reason. Angie had every right to hate him.

Immediately he wondered if Angie could be pregnant. She just said she was looking for a family home. After all the weeks that he had prayed she would conceive his child.

A gnawing fear froze the smile on Angie's face as she watched Simon. The happiness that had filled her heart left as quickly as it came. He didn't want her. "Simon," she whispered achingly, "please say something."

"Why did you come?" He wanted to hear her say the words, telling him what he already knew. From the way she spoke, he'd know her feelings on the matter. He studied her face, praying he'd find some clue that she didn't hate him, though she had every right.

"Why?" she repeated, dropping her gaze, her mind discounting his mother's visit. So this was to be Georgia Canfield's ultimate revenge. She'd persuaded Angie to return to Groves Point when Simon no longer loved or wanted her. "If you need to ask, then you don't know." She felt sick with defeat and failure. Her stomach heaved and she placed a calming hand on her abdomen.

He stiffened, his body tensing into a rigid line as her hand moved to her stomach. He closed his eyes and groaned inwardly. The hurt, betrayed look told him everything. His eyes flickered open. No matter what her feelings were, Simon realized, he wanted their child enough to fight her in every court in the land for the right to raise him. It didn't matter that his son had been conceived in anger and pain. The child was a part of Angie he had never dreamed he'd have. His gaze narrowed menacingly, and, frightened, Angie took a step in retreat.

"I shouldn't have come," she whispered miserably.

Her fear sobered him, and he drew back slightly. She would be a wonderful mother, gentle and caring. Tender and nurturing. No man in his right mind would tear a child from her arms. She'd die before she would let it happen. If she wouldn't have him, then, by God, he'd give the child his name. Some way, somehow, he'd make her marry him.

"I'll make the arrangements for the wedding as soon as possible."

She swallowed and stared at him. "Don't you think we should discuss things first?"

"No," he barked, taking her by the elbow and escorting her into the house. He pulled out a kitchen chair and sat her down. Pacing the area in front of her, he threaded his fingers through his hair angrily. "Maybe I should get you to the doctor first. Who have you seen?"

"Seen?" Simon wasn't making any sense whatsoever. "The only person I've talked to was your mother."

"My mother," he raged furiously. "You went to her and didn't have the common decency to tell me? I wondered, God knows I wondered, but I thought you'd contact me first. I never dreamed you'd go to her."

"I didn't go to your mother," she shouted back, on the verge of tears, her voice shaking. "She came to me."

"How did she know?"

Angie blinked twice. "She must have guessed . . . Simon . . ." She paused, drew in a deep breath, and shook her head. "What are we talking about?"

"The baby," he told her evenly. He knelt beside her and took her hands in his. Shocked eyes met tender ones and Simon smiled at her with a fierce gentleness that robbed her lungs of oxygen. "After everything I've done and said to hurt you, can you find it in your heart to forgive me and marry me?" He drank deeply from her eyes and continued. "I love you more than life itself. These past weeks have been a living hell."

He thought she was pregnant! She laid her hand on his smoothly shaved cheek and smiled. When she spoke her voice was filled with tears. "You may not want to marry me when I tell you something."

"I've wanted you from the time I was a teenager. Not once in all those years has that changed."

She dropped her forehead to his and closed her eyes. "Simon," she whispered brokenly. "I'm not pregnant."

The words went through him like a bolt of lightning. "You're not?"

"No. I wanted to be so badly. Every day I prayed that I was." Shyly, she closed her eyes. "If I was pregnant, then I'd have an excuse to come to you."

"Come to me? Oh my sweet, darling Angie." He couldn't believe that this incredible woman loved him after all he'd put her through. He'd suffered the agonies of the damned these weeks without her, knowing that after what he'd done he couldn't go back to her. Pleading for her forgiveness wasn't enough to take away the pain of their last meeting. "Oh love, I don't deserve you. You're far too good for me."

Through joy and tears and an immense relief, her arms sneaked around his neck and she smiled at him through the watery haze. "Simon, dear Simon, I love you so much."

His arms came around her, crushing her. His eyes were dark with emotion as his mouth found hers with all the aching longing of this last separation. "I hope you're sure," he whispered against her lips, "because I'll never have the strength to let you go again."

"I'm sure. Very sure." She kissed him in all the ways he'd taught her, until she was faint with joy and longing.

Simon's mouth and hands moved over her with a fierce tenderness until their breaths became mingled gasps of pleasure. They strained against each other, wanting to give more and more.

When Simon stood, lifting her in his arms, Angie tossed back her head until her radiant gaze met his. "Where are you taking me?" she teased, finding his earlobe and sucking it until she felt the shivers race through him.

"Who said you weren't pregnant?" he asked, and traced the delicate line of her chin with his forefinger. "After today I can guarantee you that will change."

And it did.

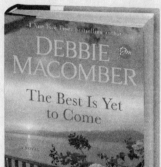